AND THE WAR GOES ON . . .

"Zulei, Grace, Nimshi and the Damnyankees"
by Anne McCaffrey—with her father and brothers
gone off to war, Grace would need a spell of
extraordinary luck to keep the family plantation
from becoming another spoil of battle. . . .

"Death Fiend Guerillas" by William S.
Burroughs—there were those who fought for
glory and those possessed by the madness of
slaughter. . . .

"Hell Creek" by Karl Edward Wagner—it had
seemed as though the dying would never stop,
but now the dead could rest at last—or could they?

These are just a few of the compelling, all original
tales you'll find in this volume, the stories of
those who fought, and those who died—and those
who wouldn't—

CONFEDERACY OF THE DEAD

CONFEDERACY
OF
THE DEAD

edited by
Richard Gilliam,
Martin H. Greenberg,
and Edward E. Kramer

A ROC BOOK

ROC
Published by the Penguin Group
Penguin Books USA Inc., 375 Hudson Street, New York, New York 10014, U.S.A.
Penguin Books Ltd, 27 Wrights Lane, London W8 5TZ, England
Penguin Books Australia Ltd, Ringwood, Victoria, Australia
Penguin Books Canada Ltd, 10 Alcorn Avenue, Toronto, Ontario, Canada M4V 3B2
Penguin Books (N.Z.) Ltd, 182–190 Wairau Road, Auckland 10, New Zealand

Penguin Books Ltd, Registered Offices: Harmondsworth, Middlesex, England

First published by Roc, an imprint of New American Library,
a division of Penguin Books USA Inc.

First Printing, June, 1993
10 9 8 7 6 5 4 3 2 1

LIBRARY OF CONGRESS CATALOGING-IN-PUBLICATION DATA
A Confederacy of the dead / edited by Richard Gilliam, Martin H. Greenberg,
  and Edward E. Kramer.
      p.   cm.
  ISBN 0-451-45249-6
  1. United States—History—Civil War, 1861-1865—Fiction.
2. Fantastic fiction, American. 3. Horror tales, American. 4. War stories, American.
I. Gilliam, Richard. II. Greenberg, Martin Harry. III. Kramer, Edward E.
PS648.C54C64—1993
813'.0873808358—dc20   92-44821
                                                                              CIP

 REGISTERED TRADEMARK—MARCA REGISTRADA

Printed in the United States of America

Contents

Preface: A Confederacy of the Dead

Michael Bishop

In your hands, an unusual and often powerful book of original stories about the American Civil War. Its co-editors have titled it *Confederacy of the Dead*. What credentials recommended me to them as a suitable introducer? Frankly, having found in several of the tales they've chosen an enviable historical expertise and some fine storytelling, I *doubt* the legitimacy of my credentials.

The unforgivable truth is that despite having lived in Georgia for a major part of my adult life, I've never methodically studied the American Civil War. That the editors of *Confederacy of the Dead* have turned to me for an introduction is thus highly ironic, and the fact that I've acceded to their request bespeaks either my unbalanced mental state or my hubristic folly.

You see, until I was an adult, I purposely avoided every formal history book, celluloid production, or fictional narrative about the Civil War (or, as some unregenerate Confederates still call it, the War Between the States). It was as if I were afraid that even fleeting contact with a Bruce Catton volume, or a Hickman brothers TV series, or a macabre story by Ambrose Bierce would contaminate my soul and my optimistic Middle American outlook forever. I would grow sere, I would wither, I would die.

In short, nothing about the Civil War held any fascination for me. I undoubtedly disguised my uneasiness about the whole topic by dismissing it as "boring." Because I had a fifth-grade teacher who demanded that we memorize and recite the Gettysburg Address, I knew Lincoln's eloquent words by heart. I can also recall thumbing with interest through a sheaf of Confederate bills that a classmate had brought in both as a curiosity and as a launching pad for wild-hair speculations. But the names of such historic Civil War battles as Bull Run, Antietam, Fredericksburg, Chancellorsville, Chickamauga, among dozens of others, had no power to stir me: I was deliberately ignorant of the poignant human details that would have lifted them off the printed page and branded them on my heart.

As a teenager, I weakened a little and read Stephen Crane's *The Red Badge of Courage,* Ambrose Bierce's "An Occurrence at Owl Creek Bridge," and Mark Twain's pre-Civil War picaresque about the moral bankruptcy of societally authorized racial oppression, *Huckleberry Finn.* (Twain's masterpiece, which Hemingway in *The Green Hills of Africa* calls the fountainhead of all American literature, seems to me the spiritual godfather of several fine stories included here, notably Nancy A. Collins's "The Sunday-Go-to-Meeting Jaw," S. P. Somtow's "Darker Angels," Anne McCaffrey's "Zulei, Grace, Nimshi and the Damnyankees," and possibly even Lee Hoffman's "The Third Nation.") But I got into the Crane, the Bierce, and the Twain not because they touched on the crucial conflicts that precipitated or defined the Civil War, but because, by the age of thirteen, I had decided to become a writer and these works looked as if they would be entertaining and instructive.

I liked the Crane because it had such striking symbolism and imagery ("The red sun was pasted in the sky like a fierce wafer"), not because it was a Civil War novel. I admired Bierce's story (a dreamlike French-made dramatization of which once showed up as an episode of "The Twilight Zone") for its gloomy romanticism and its stunning twist ending, not because it highlighted an incident from our bloody fratricidal war. And I liked *Huckleberry Finn* because the dialogue was knee-slappingly vivid, and because Huck and Jim's adventures on the raft were an exciting summons to adventures of my own. That Twain had pointed things to say about the mindset that instituted and successfully rationalized slavery meant very little, if anything, to me.

I still didn't want to study the Civil War, even if I could occasionally tolerate—as anyone born into our culture must—incidental exposure to the fact that the Union, a philosophic if not always a pragmatic whole, had split asunder and warred against itself for four brutal years. Why this weird personal aversion to shining a cold spotlight on the Civil War?

I have two theories.

First, like many other Baby Boom kids in the 1940s/50s, I had already experienced an intramural family conflict leading to—in Tammy Wynette's syllables of one word—D-I-V-O-R-C-E. After a tour of duty in Japan, my father was sent to Francis E. Warren Air Force Base in Cheyenne, Wyoming, while my mother returned stateside to a civil service job at McConnell Air Force Base outside Wichita, Kansas. In the 1950s and '60s, I lived from September through May with my mother, who had legal custody, but every summer, with her blessing, I took a Greyhound or flew to Dad's latest duty station, to spend those three months swimming, playing baseball, and getting reacquainted with Dad's Labrador retriever, Mike, and the trio of mixed-breed cats belonging to my stepmother, the often justifiably jealous Scottie. Things could have been worse, a *lot* worse, but any sort of flap between family members made me queasy. I tried to play peacemaker, or I ran for cover when the shooting turned loud and spiteful. Why *read* about the Civil War when there was a civil war playing for real on the doorstoop?

Second, the Cold War raging every evening on NBC's "Huntley-Brinkley Report" (the mushroom-cloud menace of nuclear conflict, the fearful challenge of Sputnik, the mad spread of basement bomb shelters) had robbed me of any hope of dispassionately surveying the historical spectacle of a house divided, of brother bayonetting brother, of a family squabble grown to the apocalyptic dimensions of Armageddon. It was hard enough being the crewcut son of a man who carried me into bars, sat me down with a Coke, and, drinking a beer or three, discussed with utter strangers the likelihood that the United States and the Soviet Union would obliterate each other with H-bombs, undoubtedly before the next election. Why complicate matters, or further scare myself, by looking into the nation's past for a terrible mayhemic precedent?

Once out of high school (I spent my senior year in Seville, Spain, with my father, attending a school for military dependents in the American housing area), I found myself at the University of Georgia in Athens, Georgia. The Dean of Men, William Tate, told amusing anecdotes about the War Between the States. At football games, the band played Dixie. Good Old Boys rode around in pickups with novelty license tags proclaiming, *"Forget, Hell!"* The Stars and Bars of the Confederate flag manifested almost everywhere, and the favorite movie of the young woman who eventually became my wife was *Gone with the Wind*.

Not surprisingly, I had never read Margaret Mitchell's novel, which Jeri loved. (May Jefferson Davis forgive me, I *still* haven't read it.) When we went to see a refurbished print of the film at Atlanta's Fox Theater in 1966 or '67, I didn't much endear myself to Jeri by nodding off at a crucial point about two-thirds of the way through the War Between Scarlett and Rhett.

Even so, I may have started to believe that if the living heirs of the defeated could live with, even take a perverse sort of pride in, daily reminders of that terrible war, that bitter defeat, then *I* could make an effort to learn something about our nation-defining struggle—something a bit more esoteric and searching than, say, the firing on Fort Sumter on April 12, 1861, and the heartbreaking, anticlimactic assassination of President Lincoln at Ford's Theater on April 14, 1865, almost exactly four years later.

Actually, if I really did believe that I owed my new region an obligation to learn its history, I still pretty much failed to act on my noble intentions. Maybe I resisted going wholeheartedly into the war's history precisely because I was surrounded by folks whose ancestors had fought in it, died for the South's doomed cause, and still felt unfairly diminished by the naked condescension and the often hypocritical assumption of moral superiority of many of those outside the region. I had never identified with the South's cause, if that cause was preserving slavery, but I could easily identify with the lingering feelings of both loss and pride that defeat had impressed upon many white Southerners.

So I continued to read and to write about subjects *other than* the Civil War.

When Jeri read McKinley Kantor's *Andersonville* and spoke to me of the power and tragedy of that fictionalized look at an infamous Southern prison camp, I agreed that I must read it too, but I never did. When a friend recommended *The Killer Angels,* Michael Shaara's Pulitzer prize–winning novel about the Battle of Gettysburg, I went out of my way to find a copy in a secondhand bookstore, but I read only forty pages before growing restless and setting it aside. In the late 1970s, I did read, in its entirety, Edmund Wilson's great survey of the literature of the American Civil War, *Patriotic Gore,* in which Wilson asks the rhetorical question, "Has there ever been another historical crisis of the magnitude of 1861–65 in which so many people were so articulate?" But *Patriotic Gore* sneaked onto my reading list because I admire Wilson and because his emphasis is the literature of the war, not—at least not directly—the battles and the suffering occasioned by the war. For when it came to no-holds-barred accounts of engagements, subterfuge, and consequences, I remained as gun-shy as ever.

That pattern holds today. For several years, I've belonged to a book club specializing in history. During my entire membership, I've bought from it only two books dealing primarily with the Civil War: *Mary Chesnut's Civil War,* a voluminous diary richly commended in *Patriotic Gore,* and Joseph Stanley Pennell's novel, *Rome Hanks,* first published in 1944, to which the club's portrayal of Pennell as an unjustly neglected literary figure drew me. (You guessed it: I still haven't read either of these books.) The oddness of my inability to buy Civil War books grows clearer if I note that every issue of the club's monthly bulletin contains more listings of Civil War titles than it does of any other topic. Ancient Civilizations, the Middle Ages, the British Empire, even World War II—none of these headings comes close.

In fact, an essay in Vol. 4 of the Macropedia of my *Encyclopedia Britannica* points out that "[the] Civil War has been written about as has no other war in history. More than 60,000 books and articles give eloquent testimony to the accuracy of Walt

Whitman's prediction that 'a great literature will . . . arise out of the era of those four years.' " Considering the age of my encyclopedia, I'd bet that the number of books and articles has almost doubled since that essay was written.

More recently, director/compiler Ken Burns' documentary series *The Civil War,* shown at least twice already on most of our nation's PBS stations, has either sparked or rekindled interest in the topic for many Americans. As an habitual refugee from most matters Civil War-related, I guess you'd have to file me with those in the former category—but the elegance and the accuracy of what Burns has put on film have converted me; and, not too long ago, I even rented a videocassette of the film *Glory,* a fine account of the organization and deployment of a black Union regiment, and of its harrowing, and painfully moving, fate.

So I now believe that I decided to accept Messieurs Gilliam, Greenberg, and Kramer's invitation to write the introduction to *Confederacy of the Dead* not out of craziness or egotism, but out of regret for not having written a story for them and out of shame for having consistently declined to face up to the central and defining event of American history, the Civil War. By requiring myself to acknowledge this failure, I hope to lay to rest forever my recurrent Civil War cowardice.

If, come next spring, I still haven't read Shelby Foote, or Bruce Catton, or McKinley Cantor, or Margaret Mitchell, or Michael Shaara, or Joseph Stanley Pennell, or at least one of the dozens of meticulously researched volumes offered every month by my history book club, well, I may be hopeless. . . .

Let me conclude by quoting two passages, the first from Algis Budrys's "Grabow and Collicker and I," included here; the second the last sentence of Edmund Wilson's introduction to *Patriotic Gore*:

War . . . war is stupid, and often utterly without point, and young men die so that old men can make what point there is. But we go to war so often. So often. And we die.

The unanimity of men at war is like that of a school of fish, which will swerve, simultaneously and apparently without leadership, when the shadow of an enemy appears, or like a sky-darkening flight of grasshoppers, which, also all compelled by one impulse, will descend to consume the crops.

Books and stories about war are written, I believe, not only to allow us to experience vicariously the quickened pulse of conflict, but also to warn us against becoming addicted to the deadly rush of "patriotism." It's a warning that we've yet to heed, but we still repeatedly issue it—as we must. I like the title *Confederacy of the Dead* because it emphasizes the truths that people inevitably die in wars and that the dead are helplessly united in the ultimate democracy, that of wracked flesh and fled spirit. (I should therefore point out that the editors might have called their book, with equal justification, *A Union of the Dead*.)

Until we grasp that every war is a civil war, it will probably always be so.

Pine Mountain, Georgia

CONFEDERACY
OF
THE DEAD

Introduction

Richard Gilliam

No conflict in world history has had more words thrown at it than the United States Civil War.

On the modern side, you had new, improved killing machines—better guns, better artillery, battleships with sides of iron, lighter-than-air observation balloons, and a not so successful attempt at submarine warfare. A young Ferdinand von Zeppelin visited the U.S. to try to interest the Union in a rigid airship. He was unsuccessful, but would live to see his creation used in combat in World War I. The American Civil War was the first technology war, fought by a nascent industrialized nation with a never before seen efficiency for creating death. Six hundred and twenty thousand died in the conflict, nearly as many as in all the rest of the country's wars combined.

On the medieval side, you had the last vestiges of the feudal system, complete with romanticized plantations and their notions of honor, duty, and chivalry. The Southern generals were brilliant in fighting for a lost cause. Both sides could claim many acts of heroism.

On the barbaric side was slavery. By 1860, the United States stood alone among Western nations in continuing this malignant practice.

The much venerated U.S. President Abraham Lincoln had his moments of barbarism, too. He suspended the constitutional right of habeas corpus and issued orders that resulted in the arrest of nearly 14,000 persons who were imprisoned without trial. When Roger Taney, the Chief Justice of the Supreme

Court, told Lincoln his acts were illegal, Lincoln threatened to have Taney arrested. At Lincoln's assassination, just before the war's end in 1865, slavery remained legal in the United States, and most of the 14,000 detainees were still in jail and still without trials. Hardly the image by which "The Great Emancipator" is remembered in schoolbooks.

The literacy of the participants was an important factor in the recording of the war. In prior wars, the writings of the individual combatants almost always came from officers. The Civil War was the first war in which a significant portion of the enlisted men could read and write. It is the first war for which we have a substantial record of the thoughts and observations of all levels of those involved. Photography evolved during the war, the works of Mathew Brady possessing the enduring success Brady himself was unable to find during his life.

Separating the history from the mythology is tough, especially if you were raised Southern. There is a distinction between being raised in the South and being raised Southern. I was raised Southern.

Like most Southerners, I was brought up to believe in Thomas Jefferson, Robert E. Lee, and college football. Those were a few of the positive things about being raised Southern—Jefferson's individualism, Lee's honor, and Bear Bryant whooping up on Yankees. Even Auburn fans liked it when The Bear beat one of those snotty northern schools. The South didn't have much else that it could claim was better than the rest of country—the traditions of honor, the rights of the individual, and sports as a substitute for the field of combat. All too often these principles were applied in contradictory and inappropriate ways.

Among the first things a Southern child learns is that the Civil War was fought over states rights and not over slavery. There is a distorted truth to this. Only a small percentage of white Southerners owned slaves. The states rights issue was a manipulation by which wealthy Southerners rallied non-slave owning whites to the cause, not so coincidentally protecting the economic interests of the slave owning gentry.

Concomitant to this lesson is the learning of the proper name for the conflict. "The War Between the States" is the preferred title, although acceptable alternatives include "The War of Northern Aggression" and "The Late Unpleasantness." The term "Civil War" is a Yankee appellation, one which good Southern children avoid speaking. Just because we lost the war doesn't mean they can make us use their term for it.

A great deal of my Southern upbringing wasn't positive. The class prejudice, for example, which included racial prejudice, but also transcended the various layers of white society. Southerners take great pride in being able to trace their families back to the earliest settlers in the Virginia and Carolina colonies. While attempting to imply aristocratic forbearers, these scions of the South overlook that to a great extent their ancestors were the first ones to be run out of Europe.

Certainly that's true in my case. One of my ancestors was burned at the stake in Germany for his religious beliefs. His ashes rest today in an urn in the Tennessee state museum, carried across the Atlantic by his widow. For the most part, my ancestors were common farmers. Most came from England. They settled in Virginia beginning in the early 1600s. Time and missing records have obscured the exact events. There is a well-documented account of an Indian assault in 1644 that killed more than 300 Virginia colonists, including one of my forefathers. All of the various parts of my family had emigrated to the South by the Revolutionary War. Like I said, we were the first ones run out of Europe.

We have family legends. Some of them are provably true. Several are not.

There are two legends which are universally told to Southern children who have an antebellum home somewhere in the family. The first is the legend of how the house avoided destruction in the war. The second is the missing wealth that was never dug up after it was hidden from approaching Yankees.

I'm from north central Alabama. Both sides of my family were farmers. The antebellum home comes from the Kellys, my mother's family, who left Tennessee, settling west of Huntsville in 1819, the year Alabama became a state.

The Kellys have the Sherman variant of the save-the-house legend. You know, the one where General Sherman and his army are about to torch the mansion when they are stopped by the heartfelt plea of the family matriarch, asking only that the children be spared. It didn't raise my status in the family any when I checked out Sherman's march and discovered he hadn't come within one hundred miles of the family farm. "Must have been his scouts," my grandfather told me upon hearing the news.

Alongside this is the legend of the buried silverware, which is usually trotted out soon after the kids have wised up to the snipe hunt. With Sherman rapidly approaching, it only made sense to hide the valuables—unfortunately cousin so-and-so who did the hiding was killed defending Atlanta—and to this day no one has been able to find them. They're probably near the irrigation creek, which could use a little digging out anyway. You won't find any jewels. The family gave all its jewelry to the cause, right down to your great-great-grandmother's wedding ring.

Some of the Kelly family lore is documentable. The Kelly family sent twelve soldiers to the Confederacy, all of them either brothers and/or first cousins. One Kelly was lost at the battle of Franklin, Tennessee, missing in action and presumed dead. Another died in a Union prisoner of war camp in Delaware. Against the odds, ten returned.

My favorite family legend is that of my great-grandfather, David E. Kelly, age seven as the war came to an end. David was so incensed at an enemy patrol camping on the family farm, he snuck out and stole the feedbox used for the Union horses. The family still has the feedbox.

The Gilliams have fewer legends, and most of them center on one man.

We're not much for creating new names for the boys in our family. I'm named Richard Holland Gilliam, a name shared with my father, grandfather, and great-great-grandfather. Even great-great was named after an earlier Richard Gilliam, though without the middle name. This led to some substantial confusion growing up. Great-great-grandad had died in 1892, so that wasn't a problem, but there were three of us Richard Holland Gilliams as I grew up in the late fifties. My grandfather used our middle name, and my father used our first. I was given a choice of Rick or Ricky and chose the former, despite no particular enthusiasm for either. Fortunately at the time, there was a flamboyantly gay black rock 'n' roller attending the Seventh Day Adventist divinity school in Huntsville, so there was never any chance I'd be known as Little Richard. Some of my Kelly cousins were not so lucky and had "Little" tagged onto their first name, something which seems to me to border on child abuse. Pet names for children are part of the risk of growing up Southern.

Great-great-grandfather Gilliam had been known as "The Colonel," a name derived from his service in the Virginia state militia. In May 1864, he was captured at Spotsylvania, Virginia, and sent to the same POW camp in Delaware where my Kelly ancestor died. He was one of the lucky ones, obtaining release in a prisoner exchange five months later. He resumed his command and was with Lee until the war's end at Appomattox, Virginia, in April 1865.

The surrender records at Appomattox list his formal rank as captain, and it is noted he was a company commander. He's listed as his own commanding officer, so it is plausible that his battlefield rank may have been colonel. Then again, the name may simply have been an exaggeration.

The Colonel's adventures continued after the war's end. Upon returning home, he found a Yankee deserter stealing from the family smokehouse. He disarmed the thief, killing the intruder with the captured gun. The Colonel took his eight-year-old son, Floyd, and lived as a fugitive from the law, hiding out in the homes of various persons all too eager to shelter a Southerner from Yankee justice. Eventually, the family raised sufficient gold to buy his freedom. Before long he remarried, Floyd's mother having died before the war.

Floyd was a teenager when he moved to Brownsboro, just east of Huntsville, joining his half-brother Richard Lee Gilliam. (We really weren't much for new names.) Floyd married Bobbie Lee Lawler, who was forever thankful that if she had to be named after a Confederate general, it was Robert E. Lee and not Stonewall Jackson. Bobbie Lee's brother Thomas became probate judge. His murder, in 1916, by corrupt politicians and police officials, made nationwide news, and required three companies of the National Guard to maintain control in the area.

Bobbie Lee and Floyd's youngest son was my grandfather. During the Depression, he acquired the farm onto which my parents would settle. I was raised on that farm, with all the traditions, both good and bad, of the South.

I note with some irony that I now live in Clearwater, Florida. My co-editors Marty Greenberg and Ed Kramer both have far more substantial Florida ties than I.

Although Ed was born in New York, he was raised in South Florida and currently resides in Atlanta. Ed is a health care consultant by profession and an organizer of science fiction conventions by avocation. That's how Ed and I got to know each other, through various convention projects, at first separately and later working together.

Ed and I had the idea of publishing a special book for one of our conventions. We'd solicit stories with a Southern gothic setting from various guest authors we had gotten to know. When a mutual friend suggested we call Marty Greenberg for advice, we jumped at the chance for a favorable referral. Marty has published more than five hundred anthologies during his distinguished career. Ed and I were delighted to have Marty as senior collaborator. Marty is maybe the busiest person in publishing, with interests ranging from books he has authored on international terrorism to his activities as a principal advisor to the Sci-Fi Cable network. In his "spare" time, Dr. Greenberg is a professor of political science at the University of Wisconsin-Green Bay. Marty was born in Miami, making him easily the most Southern born of the editors.

Marty made two important suggestions. First, he narrowed the focus of the book to the Civil War. Second, he suggested we not limit the idea to a convention book, but expand the size and offer it to a major publisher. Marty would handle the business end. Ed and I would handle story acquisition. It took nearly a year longer than we anticipated. Ed and I thank Marty and NAL for their patience in allowing this project to come to its proper fruition. Not everyone has such tolerant partners.

To Ed and me, obtaining the stories was much fun. When planning a science fiction convention, you get to invite those authors whose works you most admire and whose personalities are most conducive to the enjoyment of your attendees. We took the same approach to inviting people to participate in this anthology.

In his speculation as to why we asked him to write our preface, Michael Bishop lists every reason but the real one. Ed and I are big fans of Michael's work. I prefer short fiction, so I'm partial to Michael's collections *Blooded on Arachine* and *One Winter in Eden*. Ed prefers novels, so he recommends *No Enemy But Time* and *The Secret Ascension*. You'd do well to select any Michael Bishop effort.

We really thought the project was about completed when we asked Michael to do the preface. Projects have a way of growing, and when we had the opportunity to obtain additional stories from some top-notch people, we extended things a little further. Asking Michael to revise his preface around these additions was unnecessary. Michael's insightful comments on his longtime lack of interest in the Civil War demonstrate a degree of wisdom on the subject most learned scholars fail to possess. It is what makes him a great writer, his ability to understand the motivations of people—his speculations on the motivations of your editors notwithstanding.

In planning the project, we decided to give our contributors the widest possible latitude in creating historical settings. Even with scrupulous research, it is still within the province of the storyteller to take license where needed. I add this comment because I know readers who zealously guard the historical accuracy of fictional stories, both book and film. The most diehard of these are aficionados of the Civil War. All works of fiction are to one degree or another set in an alternate reality. Our goal is storytelling, not history. And even so, I feel safe in recommending the veracity of the stories, alternate realities and all. There's some good, solid historical extrapolation here.

No one wrote this type of story better than Manly Wade Wellman. Manly's knack was to make the reader feel a part of the setting, especially when the story was set in the rural south. From his first professional sale in 1927 to his death in 1986, Manly wrote more good stories about the South than any other author. His most acclaimed work, *Who Fears the Devil?*, is a collection

of interwoven short stories about John the Minstrel, who, armed
with a silver-stringed guitar, wandered the Appalachian Mountains fighting all manner of evil. I have a special reason for liking
Manly's Newbery award–winning historical novel, *Settlement on
Shocco*—it is a fictional account of my Jones ancestors who lived
in North Carolina.

Much of Manly's work appeared in critically ignored popular
fiction magazines. Even so, he received many honors, including
a Pulitzer prize nomination. His work continues to influence a
new generation of authors, especially those who write fantasy or
set their stories in the South. Your editors dedicate this book to
Manly Wade Wellman.

Clearwater, Florida

Death Fiend Guerillas

William S. Burroughs

William S. Burroughs is among the very few authors whose influence can be said to have had a great effect upon contemporary society at large.

From victories in landmark First Amendment cases to the hippie and punk movements of the 1960s and '70s, and from motion pictures to the performing arts, the life and the works of William S. Burroughs have changed American society.

Born in 1914, Burroughs graduated from Harvard and later studied at the University of Vienna and at Mexico City College. After a brief stint in the army, he tried a variety of jobs before finding success as a writer.

His first novel, the autobiographical *Junky: Confessions of an Unredeemed Drug Addict,* was published in 1953 under the pseudonym "William Lee." Even after a considerable toning down by the book's publisher, the material was sufficiently controversial that *Junky* was bound with a reprint of Maurice Helbrant's similarly autobiographical 1941 true-crime novel, *Narcotics Agent,* as if to give "both sides" an equal say.

Much has been written about Burroughs' position as a forerunner of the counterculture, or the various musical groups, such as Steely Dan, who have drawn from his work. Those influenced by his writings include several new filmmakers, with such motion pictures as *Naked Lunch* (David Cronenberg) and *Drugstore Cowboy* (Gus Van Sant) helping to introduce Burroughs to yet a newer generation.

So, why is Burroughs in this book? What's his connection to the Civil War?

As I explained earlier, one of the fun parts of editing an original anthology comes when you receive a story from someone whose work you greatly admire. For many of us who attended college in the counterculture era, William S. Burroughs is very much a hero. But also, really interestingly also, there's a Burroughs' family legend which has often seen print and which, despite the best efforts of researchers, can neither be confirmed or denied.

Very possibly the story is apocryphal. Certainly Burroughs himself doubts it. The story concerns the William Lee pseudonym which was taken from his mother's maiden name. Her family came from the South, the deep South, where many families claim relationship to Confederate heroes, none more grand than Robert E. Lee. . . .

When we make camp, we split into groups of twenty or so, several hundred yards apart. On this occasion we are lolling around, using our saddles as pillows and swapping stories. Others are cleaning their guns.

There is a pot of hot soapy water, into which the cylinder and frames go to soak and then are wiped dry and finally oiled, inside and out. You have to be sure the nipples are open and the caps fit tight, and be real sure to put a gob of grease on the end of each bullet. Otherwise all six cylinders can go up at once. Don't neglect to grease your balls, or you will be missing fingers.

We are on our way to join General Price of the Confederate Army. Bill Anderson is stalking around, he can't sit down, muttering:

"By God, we can still raid through Boone and Howard Counties, tear up telegraph lines, blow bridges and join Price in time."

George Tod is laid back with a big smile on his face, and he says:

"We'll just raise hell in general. We have to keep in practice, you know."

Everyone laughs at that, except Anderson. He just doesn't hear laughter. Bill doesn't hear any laughing but his own, and when he laughs, no one else does, 'cause Bill has laughed it all up.

Next morning at about six, a scout rides into camp.

"Union troops heading this way."

The guerillas are on their horses in minutes. They catch the Union column in the open, and give the rebel yell and charge.

As always, Tod feels the battle high, the pure killing purpose. In a charge, he flows into his horse and out of his guns, his eyes blazing like a raccoon's. Two empty guns in a saddlebag . . . he pulls out two more, wheels, and charges again.

Twelve Federals is dead on the spot. The others ride into Lafayette, where they get off their horses and take up positions in a barn of stone and heavy logs. They are armed with short-barrelled long-range rifles.

Anderson leads a charge into deadly fire from the concealed soldiers.

"By God, if the bastards could shoot, we'd all be dead."

Anderson snarls and charges again.

Well, the Feds can still shoot well enough to kill six of our men on the spot and wound three more.

Tod decides to pull back, and Anderson has to go along. We take time to stampede the Union horses, and then head for the woods, doubling back and forth and up and down across streams. Finally we make camp.

I am George Tod. *Tod* means "death" in German, so I dropped the extra D. I know that we will be described in history books as men consumed by fanatical hatred. And some of us are, like Bloody Bill. Well, hate can carry a man just so far in a deadly direction. If Anderson wants to get himself killed, that's his decision. But he shouldn't be allowed to take the men under his leadership with him on a one-way trip to Hell. People who go around looking for death often seem invulnerable . . . until their time runs out.

No, it isn't exactly hate that motivates me. It's the sheer joy of battle, the pure death purpose that burns all the fear out of a man. I read somewhere that when a man faces death directly, for that time he is immortal, and there is no exaltation like it. But you get to need it and feel like nothing when you don't have it, just like a dope fiend needs morphine.

I guess I'm a death fiend. We all are. But you have to be able to laugh and take it easy now and then. Anderson can't do that.

He has just lost six good men in a foolhardy charge against a fortified position. We all knew it was time to take a vote and select a leader. And they selected me.

Anderson took it better than I had expected. He didn't say anything. He was cleaning his guns and loading cylinders. He didn't even look up. But then, Bill never was one to do much talking.

But when he does talk, people jump. His voice cracks like a whip. It must be a terrible job, being God and being responsible for all the misery and death in the world. Who would want a job like that? Anderson, maybe. And what a disaster *that* would be for everyone on earth.

I reckon old Bill set the stage when he outbloodied hisself at Centralia, dragging twenty-five Union soldiers, some of them wounded, off the train and blasting their brains out, one after the other, on the station platform. When the gun was empty, he'd hold out his hand and that nasty little weasel, Archie Clement, would slap a fresh gun into Bloody Bill's hand. . . .

When Major Johnson learns of this atrocity, he is hot to trot hisself up to full colonel. He rides out of Centralia with a hundred Union troops. My decoy team of twenty men, led by Dave Thrailkill, engages the column out of town, swaps a few shots, and falls back.

Whereupon Major Johnson does exactly what I was hoping he will do. He orders his men to dismount, leaving every fourth man to guard the horses, and rides out ahead of his foot-soldiers.

I am on the hill, out of sight of the Union troops. And Major Johnson is screaming.

"Why don't you stop and fight, you women-killing bastards, instead of running like rabbits!"

Wait, Major, just wait.

When he is far enough ahead of the horses and near enough to our men, I raise my hat and put it back on my head three times, which is the signal for a charge that catches them all bunched up, off-guard.

I am gambling they won't have the savvy to spread out, take cover and call their shots. They could have cut us to pieces before we got into pistol range—they don't. They get off just one volley at eighty yards, killing three of our men. Then we are on top of them, screaming like banshees.

Seems like my horse don't touch the ground, and like I can't miss. But I always pick one target. . . . Years ago, I went out quail shooting. First time twenty quail zoom up right in front of you, you fire into the middle of them. You can't miss, but you do. After that, I always picked out one quail, and then another, and usually nail two in a flush. Same way here. Pick one target and then another.

Many of them drafted Union troops have never fired a gun in their lives—city boys, never had to kill game or go hungry. They run like rabbits, those who is still in a condition to run.

The major tries to rally his men, even shooting after them, but his aim is bad—what with his horse shot out from under him. He is dead before he hits the ground. There are fifty-seven Federals dead on the spot, and the others don't get far. The men left to guard the horses get on them and take off. Only fifteen escape.

After that, there was no doubt who is the leader. But I don't push Bill too hard, and he retains the lead over his eighty-six hand-picked murdering bastards.

I know that some of the men and boys who are riding or did ride with us will go on to become ranchers and farmers and legislators and businessmen or bankers, and live on to a ripe old age. But not me. It's not in the cards. I am an actor, designed for one role only. And what's the point of staying around after your act is over?

I wasn't brought up a Catholic, but the Catholics are the only ones who have an inside track. So I'll cover my bets and call for a priest if there is time for that. What is a priest? He is a mediator in a patently unjust and arbitrary system. I don't want any folksy Methodist talking about the Pearly Gates and the love of God. I figure God has about as much love as Bloody Bill. Otherwise, the job would have killed Him a million years ago.

Look out in the night sky. Millions of worlds out there. All the Christian God amounts to is a little tribal chief on a speck of dust. And what are we, but helpless pieces in the game He plays . . . on this checkerboard of nights and days . . . hither and thither moves and checks and slays . . . and one by one back in the closet lays.

If He cared about the players, he would have to pack it in. And who would take His job? Lots of folks would jump at it like a hungry pike. Sure, kill all your enemies. And then what? After a few years, they'd be screaming to get out from under and look for another fool to take their place.

Not me. I don't have the qualifications. God's in His heaven and all is wrong with the world. Let Him keep the power and the glory for ever and ever, amen. Me, I'm just a player in an old game, from here to eternity. It's known as War.

Win and lose, round and round.

Wind it up, it's running down.

Zulei, Grace, Nimshi and the Damnyankees

Anne McCaffrey

Although Anne McCaffrey began her career in 1953 with the story "Freedom for the Race" in Hugo Gernsback's magazine *SF Plus,* it was not until the publication of "Weyr Search" in the October, 1967 issue of *Analog* that she began her phenomenally popular series of stories set on the planet Pern.

Anne has won eleven major awards in the science fiction field, including the Hugo and the Nebula. While the latter is voted on by the Science Fiction Writers of America, it is the fans who are members of each annual World Science Fiction Convention who issue the former. In winning the Hugo for "Weyr Search," Anne joined a very select group of authors who were published by the father of the science fiction magazine and have received the award named after him. Her Nebula came for "Dragonrider," which along with "Weyr Search" formed *Dragonflight,* the first of Anne's Pern novels.

Anne seldom travels from her home in Wicklow, Ireland, to the U.S., and when she does it is a major event for her fans. In 1989, when she attended Ed's annual Atlanta convention, DragonCon, her autographing sessions were huge, causing gridlock for the 3500-person gathering. I've seen other writers cringe at much smaller crowds, but Anne smiled and signed until every fan had had a trip through the line. She did three such sessions, one each day of the event. Then, on Sunday night after the convention concluded, she came by Ed's staff party and signed for another hundred or so fans whose work duties at the convention had kept them from meeting her earlier. No wonder the loyalty of her fans is perhaps the strongest in the SF community.

Along the way, Anne's done much good writing outside her Pern saga, in particular some much deserving short fiction, but the rarity her fans most prize is her 1973 recipe book *Cooking Out of This World,* where she collected the culinary specialties of various SF writers. With the success of her novels, new Anne McCaffrey short stories have regrettably become a different sort of rarity.

I remember very clearly the day Zulei and her son, Nimshi, arrived at Majpoor Plantation. Papa had just finished giving me a sidesaddle jumping lesson on Dido when Mr. James, our overseer, arrived with the new slaves. Despite Mama's best efforts, there had been some deaths among the field hands from an outbreak of measles. So, when Papa heard of the auction of prime bucks being sold off in Greensboro, he'd sent the overseer, Mr. James.

"And if you should chance to find a likely lad to exercise the 'chasers . . ." I'd also heard Papa say, when Mr. James stopped by the office on his way out of the place. Petey, a wizened little black who looked more like the monkey Mrs. LaTouche owned, had been broken up by a bad fall at the Greensboro 'Chase, and no other black boy could measure up to Papa's high standards to ride our 'chasers.

I wasn't supposed to know that, but I did. Being the youngest of six, and the only daughter, I knew a lot more of what went on than Mama would have thought proper for a girl. She had been plain scandalized when I had informed Papa that I was perfectly willing to ride our entry in the next 'Chase. Hadn't he said I had the lightest hands and the best seat on Majpoor? My brothers had howled with laughter, and I'm sure that even Papa smiled a bit behind his full beard, but Mama had made me leave the table for such pertness.

"I declare, Captain Langhorn, I just don't know how I'm going to raise Grace properly if you, and your sons, encourage her improper behavior."

Mama was a Womack of Virginia and had standards of behavior from her strict upbringing that sometimes clashed with Papa's. Most of the time she laid that to his being English and having lived so long in India, fighting for Queen Victoria among pagan heathens. He even treated our slaves as if they had minds of their own and opinions to be heard.

"He never has understood how to treat darkies and I don't think he ever will," she would often complain, usually when someone had made allusions to the comforts and latitude Papa allowed our people.

"Why, lands, Euphemia," Mrs. Fairclough said to Mama once during a visit I'd had to attend, though of course I said nothing at the time (that much I had learned from Mama), "I do declare that her father treats your nigras like they was human."

"Captain Langhorn believes that it's only good husbandry to keep stock in healthy surroundings," Mama had inclined towards Mrs. Fairclough in sweet reproof. I knew she agreed completely with Mrs. Fairclough, but she wouldn't be disloyal to Papa. "I do believe, Samantha, that his methods have genuine results. Majpoor certainly gets more cotton and cane per acre than most anyone else in Orange County."

But that day, as the farm wagon brought the new purchases into the yard, I saw Zulei and Nimshi arrive.

"Ah found ya that rider, Captain," were Mr. James' first words. "Stannup thar, you Nimshi boy."

As Nimshi rose to his feet, he was facing in my direction and caught my astonished look. I knew all about high yallers, quadroons, and those sorts of distinctions among the blacks, but I'd never before seen a boy with coloring like Nimshi. His hair was red, curled close to his scalp but not kinky curls: his eyes were blue and his skin a light coffee color. He was slender, with fine bones and a face that I thought far too beautiful for any boy to have. More than that, he held himself with a casual dignity that no slave should display.

"D'you ride, Nimshi?" Papa asked, looking him straight in the eye and not as if he were a piece of merchandise. (Nimshi told me much later that that was the first reason he had to be grateful to Papa.)

"Yessir."

"Who'd you ride for?"

"Most lately, Mr. Bainbridge of Haw River."

"Why'd he sell you down?"

"He died and Mrs. Bainbridge sold up all the racers."

Nimshi did not speak in the pidgin speech most blacks used. He spoke as well as one of my brothers and much better than most house slaves. I'd heard Papa say once at a race meet that Mr. Bainbridge had some very unorthodox notions, coming as he did from Massachusetts. Mr. Bainbridge also had curly red hair, but I wasn't supposed to notice such things.

"What sort of a character was Nimshi given?" Papa asked Mr. James.

"Good 'un, Captain, or you kin bet yore bottom dollar I wouldn't've bought him. A well-grown fifteen years and not liable to grow too much taller. Not a mark on his back nor a word agin 'im."

Even then I was sensitive to what wasn't said, and so I looked at the others in the wagon, to see which one did have marks on their backs or words against them. That's when I noticed Zulei. And realized that she had to be Nimshi's mammy for, despite the terrible gauntness of her face, her features were unusually fine, like Nimshi's. Her nose was particularly aquiline, unusually so for a Negress. Her hair was brown and straight, showing a few reddish glints, not blue black ones; her eyes were gray, and she wore an expression of strange detachment that reminded me of the English porcelain doll Papa had given me for my birthday. She sat, hands limp and palm up in her lap, unaware of her surroundings. Her wrists were badly bruised and bloody.

I don't remember what else Papa and Mr. James discussed, but on such occasions it was their habit to learn the names of every new slave and what he or she had done for their previous owner. I kept trying to catch Zulei's gaze and reassure her that she would never wear fetters at Majpoor, for Papa did not believe in such measures.

Then our head man, Big Josie, a gentle man for all he was twice the size of most field hands and very black, gestured for the new slaves to get down out of the wagon. I saw Nimshi go to her assistance, his expression full of concern. Papa saw the deference, too, and saw the telltale marks on her slender wrists.

"You, there," Papa said, gruff because he couldn't abide what he called sadistic treatment. He frowned, too, because he couldn't help noticing, as I did, that the bones of her shoulders poked through the flimsy fabric of a dress that seemed too ample for the slight figure it covered. "What's your name?"

"Zuleika," Nimshi replied.

Papa frowned at the boy, for he didn't tolerate impudence even if he was lenient. Then he gave Zulei an intent scrutiny.

"She can speak for herself, can't she? Your name, woman?" and Papa spoke gently. Even though Nimshi was tenderly assisting her, she also had to hang onto the wagon side to descend.

"I am called Zulei, Captain Langhorn," she said in a firm, low voice.

"James, she's no field hand," he said to the overseer in a testy voice. He stared long and hard at her, puzzled. Abruptly, but still kindly, he asked, "Zulei, why were you chained? You run away from Mr. Bainbridge?"

She lifted her head, the gesture denying that suspicion. Nimshi said a single phrase to her, but it didn't sound like geechee to me, much less English. She gave her head a tiny shake.

"No, Captain Langhorn, I did not run away." Her voice was still low and even, but the way she said "run" struck me as odd, for the "r" was guttural, the way Mrs. La Touche said her "r's."

Mr. James cleared his throat. "Now, Cap'n, Ah did deal on this female 'cos I figgered you an' Mrs. Langhorn might find a place for her now Miss Grace is growing up, like. She was trained as a lady's maid and she's well spoken, like. Then, too, Cap'n, seeing as how you never like to split up families, she's Nimshi's mammy. I didn't get no character for her, no character at all. Seems like she'd been some troublesome."

"Are you troublesome, Zulei?" Papa looked her squarely in the eye at his most military. No one lied to my Papa when he gave them that look.

"I have never studied trouble, Captain Langhorn. Sometimes it comes where it's not wanted."

I remember Papa *hmmmed* deep in his throat as he does when

he won't commit himself. I was then much too young to appreciate what sort of trouble might be meant: much too young to realize that Zulei's "trouble" was generated by her appearance.

"We will contrive to see it doesn't come to you here. Now, Josie," and Papa beckoned to him, "take Zulei up to the big house. Her injuries are to be treated. She looks half starved. Ask Dulcie to fix her something nourishing. You are Nimshi's mother?" When she gave a brief nod, he added to Mr. James, "Then see that she is quartered with him in the mews."

The horseboys lived in quarters right in the stableyard to be close to their charges at all times, in case one got cast or became colicky at night.

"You will not regret this, Captain," Zulei said, and made the oddest curtsy, clasping her hands palms together, their tips touching her forehead as she bowed her head. Papa gave her the strangest look, but when she dropped her hands she shook her head just once in a curious denial. Papa brought his riding crop down hard on his boot, then used it to point at Nimshi.

"Nimshi, you may take the pony from Miss Grace. Down you get, my dear," Papa said, and turned back to hear the rest of Mr. James' report.

I didn't wait for Nimshi to come to Dido's head but unhooked my leg from the sidesaddle horn and slipped to the ground, patting Dido's shoulder in appreciation. Nimshi was not much taller than I in those days, but what recommended him to me was the way he held out his hand to my pony for her to get the smell of him before he so much as put a hand on her bridle. She was a spirited pony and didn't like unfamiliar hands on her.

Nimshi smiled as she blew into his hand, then, taking the reins from me, he ran the stirrup up the leather and loosened the girth expertly. I smiled in approval, for he had done exactly what I was going to tell him to do. Sometimes even Bennie, who was head groom, would forget to loosen the girth of a horse that had been worked hard. Nimshi gave me a look that suggested I should never doubt his competence.

"I hope you'll be happy here at Majpoor, Nimshi. You must ride my Papa's horses to win."

"I always mean to ride winners, Miss Grace." And then he gave me a timid smile.

"That'll suit Papa down to the ground," I said, and then I decided it was time I got back to the house. Mama didn't like me lingering in the stableyard, even if that was the best part of Majpoor in my estimation and especially when new slaves were brought in. She always worried about the diseases they might have on them until they'd all had a lye bath, had their hides scrubbed with good yellow soap and been flea-powdered.

So I had a very clear recollection of the day Zulei and Nimshi came to Majpoor. Mama wasn't as easily reconciled to Zulei's arrival ("That female's going to cause trouble, Captain, you mark my words"—which Papa did not) and somehow there never was any trouble about Zulei. Nimshi proved to be every bit as good a rider as he'd been touted. He truly loved horses and they responded to him as if they knew they could trust him.

My brothers, Kenneth, David, Lachlan, Evelyn and Robert, might complain that Papa said Nimshi this and Nimshi that, but they didn't object when Nimshi won race after race, and they collected sizeable wagers from everyone in the county.

Mama reluctantly admitted that Zulei was more use than trouble, for the quadroon (that's what Mama said she was with her light skin, straight brown hair and gray eyes) had a knowledge of herbs and remedies that was nothing short of miraculous—Mama's phrase. There were some murmurs about voodoo and obeah and conjure, superstitious twaddle like that which Mama wouldn't abide, not mutters that Zulei was different. My mammy said that Zulei wasn't one of them, not no way no how, but as Zulei was a slave, I didn't know what Mammy meant. A slave was a slave. I asked Mama and she thought I was worried about all the superstitious talk. She made it quite clear to me that Zulei's understanding of simple remedies was quite unexceptional, nothing to do with black magic; only common sense.

Any resistance from the other slaves ended soon after Zulei concocted a potion that cleared up Daisy's rash and a poultice that eased old Remy's arthritis. She had a salve that made burns disappear, even those from splashings of boiling lye soap. She was a dab hand at lying-ins, though I wasn't supposed to know such things. I also heard—from Lachlan—about how Zulei's clever hands had turned the foal inside Joyra, Papa's expensive new thoroughbred mare, when it wasn't lying right to be born. Bennie had given up, but she'd brought the colt live into the world.

Zulei also made creams which the other county ladies begged of Mama, for they reduced freckles like nothing else could. She had all sorts of other female potions that Mama loved to dispense to her friends who didn't have anyone half so clever as Zulei. I do remember that Mrs. Fairclough wondered how Mama could stand to have such a frowsy slave attending her. Even Mama was surprised by that comment. Dulcie's feeding had put weight on Zulei's bones, and Mama had given her one or two of her old gowns to wear so Zulei couldn't be called "frowsy." Mama privately thought that Zulei was a shade too fastidious.

Zulei had a knack for refurbishing Mama's dresses or pinching in a bodice, altering a sleeve so that somehow the gown looked twice as elegant as it had new. She was deft at dressing Mama's lovely blond hair into the most intricate and fetching styles.

And when I was old enough to put my hair up, it was Zulei who curled it so fashionably and flatteringly.

In fact, that was one of the few times she had occasion to dress me for a ball. The year I was sixteen, the Confederacy declared war on the North. All the young men in the county, and some of those old enough to know better—like Papa—decided to teach the damnyankees a thing or two and rode off to war.

I thought it was all very exciting, with six Langhorn men stomping about in their fine gray and gold uniforms: Papa had had so much experience in the British Army, even if that had all been in India, that he was immediately made a colonel in the County Regiment. Kenneth and David became captains and Lachlan, Evelyn, and Robert were lieutenants. And most of our beautiful horses became war steeds.

Our men rode off, handsome in their broad-brimmed hats, gold sashes around their waists and sabers and pistols on their hips. Everyone was on the front steps to wave them to victory. For it wouldn't take long for Southron gentlemen to teach those damnyankees whatfor.

Mr. James was left in charge of Majpoor, but no one minded that for he was a fair man: even Zulei said so. Josie supervised the field hands and Bennie, with Nimshi as his right hand, took care of Brass Sultan, Majpoor's stallion, and his mares and foals. I had let Lachlan, my favorite brother, have my very own Cotton as his remount so I was reduced to Dido again. That is, until Nimshi had backed a promising three-year-old flea-specked gray that Papa had promised me to replace Cotton.

Mama fretted from the moment she lost sight of Papa and the boys until the day she died of typhus three years later, despite all Zulei tried to do to break the fever. We all knew Mama wanted to die anyway once she heard that Papa had been killed in one of Jeb Stuart's cavalry charges against that damnyankee Mead, so it wasn't Zulei's fault. Though, by then, we all knew why she had had no character from the Bainbridges at Haw River.

"I know my medications, Miss Euphemia," Zulei had told Mama one time in my hearing, "I know how to reduce fevers, set broken bones and help a woman in labor, but there was nothing I could do with snake venom. When they finally got Mr. Bainbridge home, the poison was all through him. What could I do then?" She had a very elegant way of shrugging her shoulders.

There was another reason why the Bainbridge overseer had chained Zulei up, but Nimshi told me that later, when I was much older and understood such matters better. It had had nothing to do with her nursing skills but a lot to do with why Zulei looked frowsy to some people.

But when Zulei had confided in Mama, we all trusted her, having seen the near miracles she could work. But there are no miracles, near or true, to mend a heart broken by the deaths of her husband and three of her sons, and weakened by the privations that the war visited on all Southern families. Zulei and I nursed Mama together and made her as comfortable as we could with what limited medicines we could find or Zulei could concoct.

We were luckier than most, I suppose, due to Majpoor's location. We suffered from the lack of supplies and things we had previously taken for granted. While battles raged in Virginia and up and down the coast of both North and South Carolina, we

were not in the path of the combat nor near enough to benefit
from blockade-run goods. We had trouble enough with deserters
or, worse still, the cavalries of both armies that came hunting
horses from Majpoor's acres.

It was Nimshi who devised the means to hide what few good
horses we had reared, including my flea-specked gray gelding,
Jupiter. And especially our precious stallion, Brass Sultan. He
was old, twenty-five years now, brought from England by Papa
to be Majpoor's foundation stud. He neither looked nor acted
his age and, with the Confederacy three years into the war, any
horse that could walk and trot went into the cavalry. Loyal
though we were to the Confederate cause, Brass Sultan was far
too valuable to be wasted as a remount.

Mind you, Sultan, a fine seventeen hands high, was not an
easy horse to manage. Nimshi had an understanding with Sultan
that was almost magical, and the stallion would follow Nimshi
wherever he led. This became tremendously important when we
had to hide Sultan.

Mr. James had pickaninnies stationed on every road and track
to Majpoor to watch for "visitors" and warn us, particularly of
mounted men. When their whistle alarm was relayed across the
fields to the big house, Nimshi would take Sultan and Jupiter
down into the now-empty wine cellar and swing a door covered
by old trunks to cover the entrance.

As the war continued, Mr. James enlarged the hidey-hole to
include whatever young stock we had and any barren mares.
With Nimshi there to calm them, they stayed as quiet as mice
no matter how fractious they'd be at other times.

That ruse worked very well for us until that morning when,
with no warning at all, Yankee raiders came out of the woods
from the mountains behind us. Sultan was actually covering a
mare at the time. Six good strong two-year-olds were grazing in
the front field where they could be rounded up easily. The pregnant mares and those with foals at foot in the far paddocks were
not vulnerable—yet—at least not to the Confederacy. You'd
never know what damnyankees would do, and our mares were
proud, strong ones, with plenty of bone and spirit. Damnyankees

might shoot the foals and take the mares, although Mr. James didn't think that likely.

But this morning, we had no chance to hide Brass Sultan, or Jupiter or the two-year-olds. We could only watch in horror as the troops trotted up from the back fields, their uniforms so dusty that at first we thought they were our soldiers.

"Morning, ma'am," the captain said, saluting me as I stood on the veranda, terrified by his arrival. Zulei was at my side, for we'd just come up from the smokehouse, turning the few hams we had from this year's slaughtering. "Sorry to trouble you," he added, which was as untrue as anything any Yankee ever said. His eyes lingered briefly on Zulei behind me, before they ranged down to the paddock and the young horses.

To my horror, Sultan bugled his success, an unmistakable sound so that, even before he swung off his tired horse, the captain signed several troopers to go investigate.

I prayed for Mr. James to come to my assistance. I felt so vulnerable with just Zulei beside me to confront such unwelcome visitors. I remembered how Mama had acted when she faced down damnyankees and I tried to emulate her calm disdain. But my knees were shaking and I felt sorely inadequate at that moment.

As the captain trudged up the veranda steps, Zulei flashed me one of her piercing looks. Usually I knew what Zulei meant, but this time I couldn't interpret it. So I just stared through the captain, wondering how in God's name we were going to save my precious Jupiter and the young stock this time.

"We're looking for remounts, miss. We need 'em badly," the captain said, slapping the dust from his dark blue trousers with worn leather gauntlets.

"You Yankees have been here before," I said as inhospitably as I could.

He turned his head, squinting at the youngsters in the field. Jupiter was lying down in the shadows of the live oak. Maybe he wasn't visible. There was a queer look on the captain's face as he turned back to me.

"I'll just take a gander at those in the paddock, ma'am," he said, blinking suddenly at me as if I had changed shape. "We might find something we can exchange for our lame ones."

"They're only . . ." Zulei pinched my arm sharply and I faltered. ". . . the only ones we have left," I finished lamely when he shot me another odd glance.

Zulei gave me a shove, so we followed him down to the paddock, a corporal and a private falling in behind us. My heart squeezed with fear. Surely they'd see that these horses were too young to be backed. Usually the young stock would come charging up to me, hopeful of some tidbit from my pocket, but today they stayed where they were, picking at the grass or standing hip shot and half asleep. Jupiter hadn't moved from his shady spot.

Halfway across the field to the nearest two-year-old, a fine bay by Sultan out of one of the best 'chaser mares remaining to us, the captain stopped, pushing his hat back off his brow. He turned to his corporal, shaking his head.

"Those all you got, ma'am?"

"That's all we have left," I said, trying not to hope that they were going to leave us the two-year-olds: that for once a Yankee would leave empty-handed. Surely any horseman worth his salt could see that these youngsters hadn't grown into themselves, hind quarters higher than their withers, knees still open.

"Cap'n, what we got's better'n those crowbaits," the corporal said, giving me a sympathetic glance.

I blinked, astonished, for there was no way you could call the two-year-olds "crowbait." Out of pride, I started to protest when again Zulei nipped the soft part of my arm.

"They're what the last troop left behind for us," Zulei said with bitter dignity, and I contained my surprise. "Took all the chickens and the last cow." Somehow she sounded exactly like Mama just then.

"Sorry, ma'am," the captain said and, gesturing to his men, started back to where the rest of his small troop were watering their horses in the fish pond.

The two troopers who had been sent to the stableyard had returned, shaking their heads, grinning slightly.

"Nothin' there, sir," the sergeant said, "but a rack of bones with big ideas."

While I was relieved beyond measure, for Sultan's loss would
have meant disaster for Majpoor, I was surprised. No one could
call Sultan a rack of bones! He might be a bit stiff, but his coat
gleamed and he held condition.

Another pair of troopers swung into the yard, their tired
mounts at a shambling trot.

"Just mares and foals, Captain, and none of the mares worth
bothering about," was their report.

I didn't protest, quite willing for their opinion to stand, though
none of those mares were poor, either. One shouldn't question
minor miracles. Majpoor might not have much grain to give its
horses, but the grass was lush even with only manure to fertilize
it in the spring, and every animal we owned had fine glossy coats
and good condition on them.

"Captain," and a grizzled sergeant came around the corner,
our hams looped over his neck and draped down his pommel.
He was grinning, all white teeth in a dirty face, "got us some
prime eating for tonight."

"Captain, those are our last hams!" I cried in considerable
anguish. The pigs had not been as fat as in previous years, but
they would add sustenance to hominy and beans and give the
field hands some strength.

"Sorry, ma'am. My men haven't had a decent meal in weeks.
Horsemeat's not so bad if you're real hungry. I know," he said
grimly, and then waved a gloved hand at the paddock. "Not that
there's much meat on that lot, but it's all they'd be good for now
anyhow. My compliments."

And, while I stood there with my mouth hanging open, he
gestured for his troop to move out down the wide avenue to the
main road.

Although the two-year-olds were forever racing up and down
their paddock, especially if any horses were on the avenue, they
stood where they were, like statues.

"Yankees! It's like them to suggest that we eat our horses," I
muttered in outrage when they were far enough away. "Mind
you, I regret those hams like the dickens, Zulei. I'm so tired of
rabbit and pigeon I could scream. That captain can't know much
about horses nor those troopers of his. Strange, though that the

two-year-olds didn't run about like they—" I broke off for, as I swung around to Zulei, I saw how pale she had become. Her eyes went back in her head and she sort of folded up. I just caught her in my arms before she fell to the veranda floor. "Zulei? Zulei?"

I still carried a vinaigrette in my pocket, despite the fact that Mama was no longer alive to need it. So I held it to Zulei's nose. Feebly she batted it away but didn't open her eyes.

"I'll be all right, Miss Grace. It takes so much strength."

I stared down at her for a long moment, trying to absorb the significance of her words. Then Nimshi came racing around the corner of the house and up the steps, dropping to his knees at his mother's side.

"Mother?" He looked at me in alarm.

Her eyelids fluttered, but she managed to lift one hand to his arm, reassuring him. I was anxiously feeling her pulse and her forehead, fearful that she had been stricken down with some fever.

"It's not a fever, Miss Grace. Mother must have done the biggest working ever to save the horses from the Yankees." Nimshi grinned proudly at me. "She's just weak. I'll just put her to bed. She'll be right as rain in the morning."

I stumbled to my feet as he picked up his mother's slender body, all limp in his arms, her lashes long against her cheeks.

"A big working? What do you mean, Nimshi?" I was frightened again. I remembered then the murmur of "voodoo, obeah, conjure" that had flickered through the slave quarters when she and Nimshi first arrived. "What happened in the stableyard? They didn't take a single horse. Said they weren't worth taking."

Nimshi smiled at me. "What *they* saw sure wasn't. Mother made sure of that, Miss Grace. Now, if you'll excuse me. . . ." He carried her off the veranda, leaving me staring after him, trying to make sense of his words.

Just then Mr. James came running around the side of the house, breathless and perspiring. He'd been in the top field and that was a long way for an old man like him to run. The expression on his face told me that he had feared the worst. Now he stared in astonishment at the foals cavorting about in the paddock, Jupiter leading the pack in their racing, and at the Yankee dustcloud barely visible down the Greensboro road. I decided then and there not to tell him what had happened. I didn't *quite* understand it, but I thought I did. But this could not be classed as silly voodoo or obeah or conjure, which always dealt with black magic and death and evil things. What Zulei had done was good. Just as her salves and potions and poultices had been good, helping people. She had just helped us save the only valuable items left to Majpoor, our horses. I wasn't about to question this major miracle.

Considering that the Yankees found Sultan too poor to steal from us, it was gratifying when the colt foal that service produced was one of the best ever born at Majpoor. He was his sire's spit and image, a deep liver-chestnut that was very like the dull brass of Sultan's hide, three white socks, a well-placed white blaze on his forehead and superb conformation. He was up and nursing his dam fifteen minutes after his birth, strong and energetic enough to kick anyone trying to come near and dry off his fuzzy foal coat.

Nimshi called him Wazir and the name was so appropriate that it stuck. It was a splendid homecoming surprise for Lachlan, though he had a sad surprise for us: he lacked half an arm and was deeply embittered by all he had seen of North Carolina as he made his way home. Amazingly enough, Lachlan still had my own dear Cotton who was very much indeed a rack of bones, walking short from a saber slice on his left rear, with hooves split from lack of care and a hole on his once full neck where a Yankee minié ball had plowed through it. Lachlan had only a blanket for a saddle, but their return was a minor miracle for me.

I saved my tears until my exhausted brother had been fed and tucked in his bed. Then I cried my heart out in the stable, while Zulei comforted me and Nimshi handfed old Cotton.

"You've been brave so long, Miss Grace," Zulei said, stroking my hair. "Major Lachlan needs only rest here at Majpoor."

"He needs good nourishing food, beef broth, meat, butter, cream, and we haven't so much as a chicken or an egg for him."

I wept afresh at my inability to care for my dearest and only brother now that he had finally come home.

"Rabbit's good eating," Nimshi said, "and there're deer in the woods if you know where to look. Don't you worry."

I saw the look that passed between mother and son, but they often exchanged speaking glances and I was too woebegone to pay much heed.

The next day, I rode Dido while Lachlan took my Jupiter about the place. He was amazed that we had saved anything, much less the bales of cotton we had hidden in the woods.

"That was Zulei's idea. We couldn't sell it, she said, but we could save it. Wars don't last forever and the English would buy Majpoor cotton."

Lachlan regarded me as if I'd turned green. "Zulei's idea? How could Mr. James allow a slave to . . ."

"Mr. James can't keep two thoughts together in his head, La-chie," I said for I'd have thought my brother would have seen how vague the old overseer was. "Nimshi figured out where to hide Sultan and the others, and he and Big Josie see to what planting we've done. Majpoor would be a ruin if it hadn't been for Zulei and Nimshi."

Lachlan didn't reply to my heated defense, but I knew it gave him much to think about, and I lost no opportunity to point out other ruses, contrived by either Zulei or Nimshi—like the kitchen garden hidden behind used banks of old manure on one side and thorn thickets on the other. Zulei's idea. I've often thought that the sight of the three-year-olds in the paddock was all that saved his sanity. By the time we walked back into the stableyard, Nimshi had finished gutting a big stag.

That night, Lachlan made a fine meal of the venison, washing it down with moonshine, procured by Big Josie from who knew where. After that, Lachlan seemed to drink rather more than I thought a gentleman should. Every morning, Zulei had to force one of her remedies down his throat.

"He feels the phantom pain," Zulei told me, "of the hand they amputated. That happens."

"Can't you make it go away, Zulei?" It was wrong of me, I know, to wish for another miracle from her, but how could I

have known then just how much these years had cost her in
strength; how often she had clouded the avenue so that deserters
didn't find their way to our house or cavalry see the true form
of Majpoor's horses, or even see me young, innocent and
vulnerable.

As I clutched at her arm, Zulei gave me a long piercing look,
the expression in her eyes going from anguish and deep sorrow to
such resolution that I was ashamed of my momentary weakness.

"I'm sorry, Zulei," I said, ashamed of myself. "How could
you have a salve to heel a hand that's not there? And I know
we've no laudanum left, so that corn liquor will have to do to
cut the pain." We used the last of Mama's supply when one of
the field hands had nearly severed the calf of his leg with a cane
knife.

Lachlan tried, though, with white lips and pain-wracked eyes
to take up plantation duties. He told me how brave and resource-
ful I had been to keep everything going as well as I had. I repeated that I'd had help from Zulei and Nimshi, and he gave me
an odd look. But it was so good to have my brother back that I
scarcely noticed anything other than my joy at having one Langhorn spared by the terrible conflict. As a mark of that joy, I
willingly gave him Jupiter to ride, until Cotton was restored, I
told him with a laugh, though we both knew Cotton's working
days were over. But, having a fine horse between his legs did
Lachlan a world of good. Until darkness fell and he had to wres-
tle with the phantom pain again.

Often I would see Nimshi supporting my brother up the stairs
to his room in the small hours of the night. I would see Zulei
ascending them in the morning with the tisane to cure his hang-
over. She looked as worn as Lachlan.

Then, those occasions dwindled and, at my tentative inquiry,
Lachlan muttered something about an itch being an improvement
over an ache. He began to take a real hold of the management,
consulting with Nimshi and Big Josie. Mr. James was relegated
to sitting on his porch and swinging, seeming not to notice the
passing hours. I assigned one of our older women to tend to his
needs and see that he ate.

So many of our people had drifted off once conditions at Majpoor deteriorated and, some months, we could barely feed those who remained. Lachlan organized the loyal ones who had stayed with us, and planted what seed we had. He and Nimshi took two geldings in to Greensboro to sell, and although there were few people able to buy anything, he did get some gold, though most of the sale price was our Confederate legal tender which few of the Greensboro merchants would accept. The gold bought flour, mealy though it was, and machine oil and other things we could not make ourselves.

The next week we found Sultan dead in his box. Three days later the news of Robert's death reached us. The following week we learned of Appomattox. Lachlan sat in Papa's study and drank himself stupid.

He apologized to me the next day—once Zulei had got one of her remedies down his throat. He looked awful, even worse than the day he'd come home.

"I understand, dear Lachlan, really I do," I said, and inadvertently glanced down at his arm.

"No, it's not my arm that made me want to get drunk, Grace, and it's not losing the war. It's what will happen now that the North has won."

"What more could those damnyankees do to us?"

Lachlan eyed me pityingly. "We're the losers. Papa used to fret a lot about what would happen after the war. Spoils are always divided after a war. And taxes raised to pay for it."

"How could we possibly pay taxes, Lachlan?" I cried, fear rising in my throat. I thought of the wads of now worthless Confederacy notes which we had so loyally accepted.

"Thanks to Nimshi, Majpoor's horses will provide us gold . . ." Lachlan said, and then grimaced, "if we can find buyers with any."

Buyers appeared, if not the sort we cared to sell our Majpoor horses to: dreadful encroaching people with smug smiles and loud voices and no manners whatever; carpetbaggers, scalawags, poor white trash pouring down from the North to pick what flesh remained on the defeated Confederate bones. At that we were once again luckier than many of our neighbors. For when horrific taxes were levied on the struggling impoverished South, many of the county families were reduced to penury, having to sell their family homes for a pittance. Majpoor's horses, so cherished during the war years, paid the crippling ones we were charged.

I know it grieved Lachlan to see them led away, tied to Yankee carriages or ridden by sniggering Yankee grooms, but it saved us Majpoor's acres and put chickens in the yard, two cows in the barn, pigs in the pen and new clothes on our backs.

It was then that I realized that Zulei was nearly as thin as she'd been the day she arrived at Majpoor. I picked her out a gown myself, even before I bought material for my own, but when I made her unwrap the tattered shawl from her shoulders, I saw how the war years had eaten into the very fiber of the woman. And when I pinned up the sleeve of Lachlan's new coat, I could have sworn that I'd mistaken how much of his arm had been amputated. No, not arm, for he had forearm to the wrist.

He looked at it, too, surprise on his face. He'd long since got over people staring at his injury, but that didn't mean he, or I, looked at it often.

"Does it still itch?" I asked him, not thinking of anything but surprise at my faulty recollection.

"No, it doesn't itch," he said in such a short tone that I regretted my question and stood back to admire my fine-looking brother. He had lost the haunting in his eyes and filled out much of the flesh the war had burned from him. His hair was glossy and his skin tanned right to the place where his hat covered his brow. "At least we won't disgrace the crowd at the 'Chase tomorrow."

For Wazir was old enough to race and the event had been scheduled—by Yankees, to please all the Yankees who had bought plantations and now lived in our area, though of course they weren't received at Majpoor.

Then Nimshi, slimly splendid in silks Zulei and I had sewn him, rode Wazir to win, against Yankee horses, which made their owners mad. And some offered Lachlan paltry sums for the stallion, thinking we were poor enough to take what gold was offered and be grateful.

I was just coming to see if Nimshi had Wazir ready for the trip home, when I heard one man offering Nimshi a job, telling

him how much better off he'd be in a *grand* big Northern stable
with many fine horses to ride and proper quarters and money in
his pocket. I admit I wanted to hear what Nimshi would say to
such an offer. Loyal though Nimshi was to Majpoor, every man
has his price, or so Lachlan said. We certainly hadn't been able to
put much money in Nimshi's hand, even if he was emancipated.

"I ride for Major Langhorn," I heard Nimshi say with quiet
pride.

"You can go where you want to now, boy," the Yankee said,
his face flushed at the refusal. He clapped Nimshi on the arm,
unaware of how Nimshi moved away from such familiarity.
"You're not a slave anymore. You don't have to take orders
from Southerners anymore."

"I have no wish to leave my employment with Major Langhorn," Nimshi replied.

"If you will excuse us," I said, sweeping in from the aisle
between the stables, brimming with pride and relief over Nimshi's
reply. "Lachlan's waiting for us, Nimshi," I said, and making a
great show of not letting my skirts touch the damnyankee, I put
a hand on Wazir's halter and together we led our winner away.

"Well, I'll be damned! Did you see that? And she looked like
a real Southern belle, too. One of them high yallers, I 'spect."

"See how she looked at him? I heard some of them Southern
ladies got mighty fed up with all their menfolk away in the war."

I nearly choked at such insult, and Nimshi began to trot Wazir
firmly away.

"Don't you take offense, Miss Grace," he said, but there was
something so fierce in his tone and his expression that I feared
what he might do. And I was far more worried about that than
any loose-mouthed talk from an ill-bred damnyankee.

" 'I have no wish to leave my employment with Major
Langhorn,' " I said, mimicking him. "Nimshi, that was priceless.
Wait till I tell Lachlan how you answered that damnyankee."
Then I stopped, appalled at my selfishness. "Oh, Nimshi, maybe
you should take that offer. We certainly can't pay you what
you're really worth. . . ."

Nimshi hauled Wazir to a stop and glared at me. "You will

say nothing about that incident to the major. He has enough to worry about."

"But, Nimshi . . ."

He fixed me with the sort of haughty stare that Zulei used effectively, his eyes glittering dangerously. "My mother and I owe you more than any Yankee could pay us."

"We barely pay you at all," I began, painfully aware of that.

"You paid us in a coin few people in our position ever receive, Miss Grace—respect and appreciation," and I never heard such fervor in Nimshi's voice before. "Your Papa and your brothers left my mother alone. Your Papa let me ride his best horses. Your Mama never belittled us in front of her friends, and you gave us back our pride. And we've been free from the moment Colonel Langhorn went to war. Mr. James gave Mother the papers."

I hadn't known that, and I had to run to catch up to Nimshi as he rushed Wazir onward.

"We've always been proud to work at Majpoor, Miss Grace, and do what we can to repay your parents for all their considerations."

"Oh, Nimshi!"

"Just for the record," and Nimshi smiled around Wazir's head at me, "I'm not high yaller, though I am half-white. The other half of me and all of my mother is Arabian. But mother was sold into slavery. In spite of that, I'm the grandson of an emir, so you can't be insulted for being in my company. I'm better born than any of that Yankee white trash."

By then we had reached the wagon that Lachlan used to transport Wazir to the 'Chase. Once the tired stallion was loaded up, we all climbed to the high seat for the long trip back to Majpoor.

Our affairs began to improve with Wazir's win, for it was not only the purse but also the publicity about his speed and scope that helped us. Mares arrived for him to cover, Southern as well as Northern. Stud fees brought us money to restore the big house, the stables, repair the quarters for those blacks who still lived on Majpoor, and to pay them a wage, and those we needed to hire to get the repair work done.

So I was surprised when Lachlan began to drink again—brandy

this time, and he suffered his hangovers without benefit of Zulei's tisanes. At first I thought that Lachlan was being considerate because she seemed to be wasting away. I had her moved to the room next to me, for she often had bad dreams at night and needed to be roused to sanity. But when I took pity on him and made a potion, he wouldn't take anything Zulei had concocted, despite the fact that they had always done him good. Then he began to avoid Nimshi instead of spending every minute of the day working side by side with him in Majpoor's management and the breeding operation. I thought at first it was because Lachlan was handicapped in helping Nimshi break and school the young-sters. That it was painful for him to watch someone else do what he had been so good at before the war. When I did notice the estrangement, and the hurt it caused Nimshi, I confronted Lachlan.

"I don't know why you're angry with Nimshi, Lachlan, after all he's done for us . . ."

"It's not the all, Grace, but the how," was Lachlan's cryptic response. We were having dinner and Lachlan was drinking brandy with the meal.

"Whatever do you mean?"

Lachlan gave me a blank stare. "I wish they'd both go!" he blurted out, giving me a look that made me shudder.

"Both? Zulei . . ." My protest was simultaneous to his denial.

"No, no, I don't really mean that, Grace. I just . . . don't know . . . I'm afraid, Grace. I don't understand what's been happening. Or how!"

I hadn't really noticed until then that he had been keeping his stump in his coat pocket. Now he brought it out and laid back the cuff.

I gaped at what I saw—a tiny hand, growing out of the re-newed wrist. The regenerated portion of his arm was healthy firm flesh, and the little hand complete despite it being miniature.

"It's growing, too. Noticeably," Lachlan said, frowning at the grotesquerie. "I spotted the fingers coming out of the wrist be-fore the 'Chase. I didn't think about it then because I didn't believe my eyes. I . . . don't know whether I want it or not."

"Not want your hand back? But you could ride and write your

name instead of that scribble, and dance," I heard myself say,
for I wanted nothing now so much as my favorite brother a whole
man.

Lachlan stared at me and made an odd strangled sound. "You
amaze me, Grace. You really do," and he looked down at his
budding hand. Carefully he pulled down the cuff and shoved his
arm back into the pocket.

"Does it hurt?"

"No, and it doesn't itch," he replied, then he went on in a
different tone, pouring more brandy into his glass. "Tell me what
else happened at Majpoor during the war, Grace. Tell me what
else Zulei did with her black magic."

I shook my head. "She doesn't use black magic, Lachlan."

"Then what the hell is that?" he demanded roughly, jerking
his chin at his pocketed limb.

"I don't know what art she uses, but I do know that black
magic is evil. Zulei isn't evil. Whatever"—and I remembered the
word Nimshi had used the day Zulei fooled the Yankees—"working she does is not evil, for with it she protected me, and Majpoor. Restoring what you lost is not evil, either. And she's not
a Negro, so it's not conjure or voodoo or obeah that she's using."

"Not a nigra?" That surprised Lachlan so completely that I
grinned at the effect.

"She's an emir's daughter and was sold into slavery," I said,
willing to startle him into belief of Zulei's goodness. "Nimshi
wouldn't explain why."

Lachlan gave a snort of disbelief. "And don't try to tell me
Nimshi's not get of old man Bainbridge with that hair and those
eyes."

"We're not discussing Nimshi's parentage," I said as primly as
I could, recalling that Mama would have been scandalized to
hear my brother mention such a topic in my presence, "which
shouldn't matter a hill of beans when we owe everything we have
at Majpoor to Zulei's help during the war."

"Exactly what form did this help actually take, Grace?"

I'd never heard my brother use quite that sort of tone before
and, because I remembered the incident with that Yankee cap-

tain and Sultan, I related that and what Nimshi had said—that his mother had made the horses look different. And me.

"When they left, Zulei fainted—" I broke off because at that moment, I realized why Zulei was so ill. I stared at Lachlan, at his pocketed arm, and nearly fainted myself. "Oh, no. . . ." The chair toppled, I sprang from it so abruptly. I picked up my skirts and ran up the stairs, Lachlan calling for me to stop, to explain. "She's working herself to death for you!"

I burst into the room, not surprised to find Nimshi there, he often sat with his mother in the evenings. I fell on my knees at her bedside, staring down at her face, all bones and nearly skull-like in a deterioration that was rapidly seeping her life away.

"Oh, Zulei, you must leave off the working. . . . You must! You and Nimshi have done enough!"

A wan smile curved on her lips, and I remembered how lovely she had been in the days before the war, and wept to see her so wasted now, as wasted as the South was.

"Nimshi, how could you let your mother . . ." I cried, turning on him in my anger.

He shook his head and then I felt Zulei's fingers on my arm.

"It is not this working, Miss Grace, but the other which has drained me, as evil will."

"What other? You're not evil."

"The man who sold me into slavery," she said, and her eyes glittered feverishly, "has taken a long time to die. He could never get far enough away to shake the curse I put on him, though it has taken my lifetime to do it. And my life. Evil takes its toll, and the good I have done has not been enough to balance the vengeance exacted, rightful though it is. War is not the only way to waste the breath of life, Major Langhorn," and she looked beyond me to Lachlan standing in the doorway. "For the kindness of your father and your mother, I used the Great Arts I was taught to heal the sick and injured, and to veil Majpoor's wealth and goodness from its enemies, hoping that that would expiate the other harm I did. Inshallah! May God now have mercy on me!"

Her breath fluttered and ceased. We were all so stunned by her death that we stared at her incredulous for many long moments. Then I closed her eyes and, marvelling at the look of peace on her ravaged face, slowly covered it.

We buried Zuleika bint Nasrullah in the family cemetery with her real name on the headstone. You can see it there—if your heart is pure enough to find Majpoor, for even now, Lachlan says that some folk still can't find the avenue though it is plainly marked.

His hand grew, although it was never quite the same size as his left one. But he could now break and train the horses we bred. I was bridesmaid at his wedding to the daughter of a Northern lawyer who'd been sent South to see about claims of misappropriation of funds and carpetbagger chicanery.

Nimshi did go North but for himself, with a son of Wazir, and enough mares to found his own stable. And I, I went North, too. Where I could marry a red-haired emir's grandson who bred horses that always won their races.

Hell Creek

Karl Edward Wagner

A practicing psychiatrist turned writer, the stories of Karl Edward Wagner are noted for strong characterization set against a dark background and fast-paced action.

Where science fiction has the Hugos and the Nebulas, fantasy literature has the Howards, named after noted horror writer Howard Phillips Lovecraft. Somehow, the name Howard awards has never caught on, and those working within the field usually refer to it by the name of the issuing body, the World Fantasy Convention. Unlike the Hugos and the Nebulas, this is a juried award, selected by a five-member committee who faithfully promise to read each and every eligible work published within the previous year. The voting members of the committee change annually, but Karl's position as a nominee doesn't. He has been nominated frequently, and is the only person to win the award both as a publisher and as a writer of fiction.

The publishing award came in 1976 for his Carcosa imprint, which in addition to the stories of Manly Wade Wellman, has preserved the works of Manly's contemporaries E. Hoffmann Price and Hugh B. Cave. Karl and Manly were close friends, residing near each other in Chapel Hill, North Carolina. Karl has also received four British Fantasy awards, perhaps reflective of the serious time he's spent there researching the pubs.

Karl is very much a traditionalist. His collection of pulp magazines from the first half of this century is one of the finest extant. You'll find very few professional writers as knowledgeable in the roots of modern fantasy. Karl's traditionalism extends to his methods of writing as well. He composes his first drafts on a legal pad, then types the revisions one finger at a time on a manual typewriter. When you read Karl, you are reading unprocessed words.

As editor of *The Year's Best Horror* series, Karl is noted for finding offbeat gems published in obscure places. His taste in clothing is no less esoteric—usually a distinguished tweed jacket worn over an outrageously shocking T-shirt. With his flaming red hair and broad-shouldered build, you'll have no trouble recognizing Karl at a convention.

Like Manly, much of Karl's best work has a Southern regional flavor. He was honored for it by the Deep South Science Fiction Convention in 1978 with their life achievement award, the Phoenix, given exclusively to Southern literary professionals. Karl won the award when only thirty-three, a stunning tribute to the speed with which his writing skills developed.

This story is part of a projected series of alternate history stories involving the protagonist, Adrian Becker. Karl's stories are known for their detailed accuracy. The Harpes mentioned in "Hell Creek" were a notorious predatory family menacing travelers throughout the southern Appalachian Mountains. As to Grant's defeat at Chattanooga . . .

It had been raining for at least three days—he'd lost count—and Adrian Becker wanted nothing more than a warm, dry place to lie down, maybe then a hot meal and a mouthful of whisky. It was the fourth year of the war, and after Grant's crushing defeat at Chattanooga in the winter of 1863 and England's subsequent breaking of the Northern blockade to supply the South with needed matériel, it seemed likely that the war would drag on for another four bloody years. Becker, not yet twenty, had already killed more men than he could remember, and he knew that the time for killing had only begun.

There was light ahead through the darkness and drizzle, and Becker rode wearily toward it. Smoke was on the air, and with it the stench of hog pens. He was somewhere in the mountains between Tennessee and North Carolina—dangerous for a Confederate soldier despite the South's new hold over this embattled territory—but the chinked-log inn on the bluff above the swollen river promised warm shelter for the night, and Becker was not disinclined to kill for far less.

He tethered his bay horse where the porch overhang kept back most of the downpour from the hitching rail. He shook the dampness from his gray cavalry hat and unbuttoned his gray woolen coat. Beneath it he carried two braces of .36 Colt Navy revolvers—two holstered at his belt, two beneath his shoulders—and he hoped the powder would be dry in one of them when needed. If not, there remained his saber—razor-honed and oiled with Yankee blood: Quantrill did not train his raiders for parade drill.

The latch was out and, hearing other voices within, Becker let himself in. There was a large common room, a good fire on the hearth, some rough tables and a bar. A drovers' inn, Becker guessed. A few guests were seated close by the fire; a young girl in homespun eyed him boldly from beside the bar. Becker touched his hat and muttered a general "Good evening." Aware of their scrutiny, he crossed to the bar and asked for whisky.

The barman poured. Becker drank. He sighed and put down his glass. "Are you the innkeeper?" he asked, trying to minimize his German accent.

"This is my place," said the barman, a heavyset man almost as tall as Becker. His eyes were wary above a broken nose and bristling black beard. "My name's Culpepper."

Becker signaled for another whisky. "I seek food and lodging for the night, Mr. Culpepper. Can you accommodate me?"

"How do you intend to pay?" Culpepper had no liking for Confederate paper.

"In silver." There were coins in Becker's hand almost before the innkeeper saw him reach for them.

A gap-toothed smile flashed through Culpepper's beard. "Reckon then we got a room that will suit you. You can stable your horse around back. Kate's got venison stew on the cook stove."

"Excellent," said Becker. "As is this whisky."

"Culpeppers here have been making it in these hills three generations," the innkeeper said with a note of pride. "Here's another on me."

Becker moved to the fire and found a place to hang his sodden

greatcoat. The fire and the whisky warmed him, reminded him
how tired he was. He could smell the stew from the kitchen close
by. A steep flight of stairs invited him toward a room and dry
bed upstairs. But first he must see to his horse.

When he returned, Kate showed him to his room. There was
a fire and a washstand, some rough sticks of furniture and a
posted bed with a corn shuck mattress—far better than Becker
had dared hope for. Kate lingered as he began to wash up. She
was a well-turned woman of about twenty, with rich black hair
piled loosely above a round face with sparkling dark eyes and a
ready smile. Becker smelled her lilac perfume as she watched
him from the doorway.

"I'm Kate."

"Becker. Captain Adrian Becker." He almost clicked his
heels, but four years with Quantrill had delayed some of the
reflexes. Nonetheless, he bent over her hand. Her nails were
dirty.

"You're a Dutchman, ain't you?"

"Prussian."

"I could tell by your accent. We get a Dutchman come through
here time to time. How long you been fighting for the South?"

"I've served under General Quantrill's command for four years
now."

Kate stared at him as he bent over the washstand. "You must
have started killing Yankees mighty young."

"I learn such things quickly."

Adrian Becker was not yet twenty years of age, but the war
had aged him beyond his years. He was tall—just over six feet—
broad-shouldered and hard-muscled, and he carried himself with
a distinct military bearing that Kate found irresistibly dashing.
He had longish blond hair, blond mustache, and a few days'
growth of blond beard. Beneath the stubble and dirt, Kate
thought his face was handsome—aristocratic in its aloofness—
and she envisioned him in dress uniform, escorting her onto the
dance floor: she, exquisite in silken hoopskirt and glittering jewels, the envy of every woman at the ball. His eyes were a sort
of faded blue—almost gray—and there was a certain disturbing

coldness in their gaze. Kate imagined that she could make them flash with passion. Altogether, it was a pity that he would be dead before morning.

"I'll see to getting you your dinner ready." She smiled. "Don't you be too long in coming down."

Becker sopped up the last smear of gravy with a hunk of cornbread, washed it down with strong coffee—now in better supply since the Royal Navy had joined with Confederate ironclads to break the Yankee blockade. The stew was good—venison, probably some pork, with unidentifiable bits of game. The thick spicy gravy made it hard to tell, and Becker had missed too many meals to be an epicure just now.

"Some pie, Captain?" Kate bent low as she cleared away the bowl. "Apple."

"Yes, thank you. And some more coffee. I find myself growing sleepy after your very excellent meal."

Kate rewarded him with a smile, and her father carried over glasses and a jug.

"Join me in a drink, Captain?"

"Yes, thank you. You are very hospitable."

"The war's kind of passed us by here." Culpepper poured. "Not often we have officers as our guests. Kate said you was riding with General Quantrill. Last we heard tell, he and his army was garrisoned near Memphis."

"He is." Becker knew to be on his guard for spies, but this was information to be read in months'-old newspapers. Of the dispatch papers he was carrying to General Lee from Quantrill, he would say nothing.

Becker continued: "The Mississippi River is now a Confederate lake." He smiled, but his host had no appreciation of the allusion. Well, he hadn't really expected him to.

"Likely, this whole valley below here is going to be a lake by morning," commented one of the drovers from beside the fire. "Creek's been at full flood two days now and rising. Ain't no way we can ford our hogs across till the water's down. Mast is scant this year, and I just hope we can keep them fed. Hogs get real mean when they're hungry."

"I saw the rising waters," said Becker. "What is the name of this creek?" He had merely followed the rain-washed drovers' trail for most of the day, assuming that it would eventually lead him across the mountains and into western North Carolina, whence he might board a train to Richmond, assuming Sherman's guerilla raiders hadn't blown the trestles east of the Appalachians as well.

"Why, this is Hill Creek." The drover seemed aghast that a Confederate captain could be so ignorant. "Runs into the Laurel River maybe ten miles from here."

"Only, now they call it Hell Creek," said his companion at the fire—another drover, hunched over with too many years to be following the mountain trails. But there was an insatiable market for hogs, just as the war stole away men young and fit enough to drive them from farmyard to slaughterhouse.

"Hell Creek?" Becker paused with his glass to his lips. "The Hell Creek Massacre?"

"So you boys heard about that out West." The old drover smacked his lips and gazed thirstily at the whisky jug. "I'll bet you don't know the whole story. Not likely you'd have heard it from a man who was there."

Becker was intrigued. "Mr. Culpepper. Glasses, please, for my so informative friends. I enjoy hearing a good tale on such a night as this."

Culpepper flashed a scowl—almost too quick to catch, but Becker was very fast—then smiled and remembered his duties as tavernkeeper. The two drovers pulled their chairs over to Becker. Kate brought dried-apple pie and coffee to his table. Becker applied himself to pie, coffee and corn whisky as he listened.

"My name's Zachariah Warren," said the older man—gray-bearded, skin weathered and callused, face shadowed by slouch hat, well the far side of sixty. "This here's my boy, Ephraim." His boy, probably about fifty, heavyset, slightly less gray in his beard, same worn and dirty work clothes and muddy boots. Becker noted that the old man carried a Bowie knife; the younger man packed a Walker Colt about his thick middle.

The inn's few other guests had by now retired, or were half-listening to Zachariah Warren's tale. Outside the rain hammered at the walls, forced sudden gouts of smoke down the chimney, sucked it back again, greedy for its warmth.

Not far below, Hell Creek's raging flood ripped away at its banks, hurling rocks and chunks of earth into the torrent.

"They was," began Zachariah Warren, "back in April of sixty-three, a Yankee raiding party that rode through here—irregulars commanded by a Colonel Hayes. They was nothing but a pack of thieves—stealing horses, livestock, meal, anything they could make away with. Most of the young men were off to war, on one side or t'other. Colonel Hayes' boys was free to do what they wanted, and it didn't much matter to them whether you was Reb or Yank.

"Now, they was a settlement on Hill Creek—not more than a few houses, a church, a general store and tavern, a mill, and a blacksmith's and stable. Place was also named Hill Creek, and it had been there since white men first come across these mountains, and the town and the creek was both named for a fur trader name of Hill who built a station there.

"Now, I had started into Hill Creek that morning to get the mule's shoe tended to, and I was just about to come down out of the trees when I could see that Hayes and them was there ahead of me. Knowing they'd take my mule, I hung back to watch until they rode on."

Zachariah Warren paused to sip his whisky. He seemed to shrink back within his chair under the weight of remembering.

"Well, sir. They was a shot, and Colonel Hayes tumbled off of his saddle and was dead where he fell. And I never could say where the shot had come from.

"Now, Hayes had a lieutenant name of Hyatt, and he took command, and he had his men fan out through the town, and then they searched the buildings there, and they rounded up all the folks they could find in Hill Creek, and they herded them together in the middle. They was twenty-seven of them, grown men, women, children and babes in arms.

" 'Who killed Colonel Hayes?' Lieutenant Hyatt, he asked of them all. And not a man would own up. 'Then this whole town is guilty of murder and treason,' declares the lieutenant, 'and I sentence this town to death!'

"So then, they commenced to open fire, and afterward they moved through the bodies with their bayonets, and the screaming of them women and the crying of their children is a memory there ain't enough whisky in Tennessee to make me forget. And through it all, and I know he'd been shot a dozen times or more, old Preacher Wells, a bull of a man, kept a-shouting: 'I'll see you all on the road to Hell!' and I could hear him back in the trees, until they pinned him to the dirt with a bayonet through his heart."

Zachariah helped himself to another drink, shaking his head. "They was most all just women and children."

"And then they just rode away?" asked Becker, who had seen as bad along the Kansas–Missouri border.

"Only after they'd looted the town and set everything ablaze. Left the dead just lying there, ashes drifting down like snowflakes to cover them. I crept down there finally, but they was nothing any man could do."

Zachariah shuddered, and his son mumbled some assurances to him. Becker reflected that there were too many such aspects of war never discussed in military training.

"Well, they didn't get far. They was a militia regiment come over from Tennessee under a Colonel McCauley, where they'd had word of the Yankee raiders. Them boys wasn't far enough away not to see the smoke arising from Hill Creek, and Colonel McCauley brought them up fast. Now, Hill Creek was high with the spring rains, so they was just a few places where men and wagons could find safe ford, and when the Yankees started to come across after burning Hill Creek, McCauley and his militia was waiting on both banks, and they pure cut them down. Them as didn't fall in the first volleys tried to surrender, and they just shot them dead with the rest. Them as wasn't washed away in Hill Creek, they dug a shallow trench for along the bottom, and buried them all there without prayer or marker.

"Afterward, they buried the dead of Hill Creek out behind the burned church, and that's the story of the Hell Creek Massacre, told by the only man who seen it all and lived to tell it."

Becker passed around the jug. It emptied, the fire fell to embers, and it was time for bed.

In her room, Kate Culpepper spoke quietly with her father.

"I saw it while he was washing up. It's a thick money belt under his shirt. That's where he's carrying them Yankee silver dollars, and most likely gold as well. You reckon he stole it?"

"Rebel captain riding alone?" surmised Culpepper, fingering his beard. "He'd got shed of that uniform if he'd stole it. Said he come from Quantrill. Most likely carrying dispatch papers, and travel money enough to pay double for room and whisky, and never blink an eye. He finish that pie?"

"Just a bite or two. He was listening to that old drover tell about the massacre on Hell Creek, and that put him off his feed. The drover claimed he had seen it happen."

"He's been walking too many years through too much pig shit. Never you mind. Tired as he is and that much whisky, the captain won't likely be on his guard. You go to him now, and you know what to do."

Kate hiked up her skirts to show the straight razor stuck beneath a beribboned garter. "Won't be no different this time."

Culpepper grinned. "I'll be in the hall with the scattergun, if you need me. Looks like stew again tomorrow."

Hill Creek was in flood, high over its banks. Rain sliced down from the night sky. In the flooded creek bottom, soil rapidly was being ripped away by the torrent.

Rotting flesh saw the night once again.

Cursed flesh began to stir.

Began to walk.

Already it hungered.

For the living.

Kate Culpepper had not removed her corset before throwing a robe about her bare shoulders. A simple "Can you unlace me?" had often been enough distraction to some eager traveler, and when she turned to kiss him, the razor was there in her hand and then across his throat.

Kate's main concerns were for the blood on her camisole or, far worse, on the bedding if the poor fool was asleep. She hated washing up, even with the formula her Harpe ancestors had passed down for removing bloodstains.

She wasn't surprised, after some experience in such things, but neither was she pleased, upon slipping into the death room to find a pistol leveled inches from her face.

Adrian Becker was fully clothed, fully awake, and there was a light of madness dancing in his eyes. Perhaps it was a trick of the candle and the raging storm.

"I . . . I thought you might want something before you turn in." Kate smiled and fell into her practiced routine. "Sure gets lonely up here."

Becker moved away and allowed her to enter. He was amusing himself by tracking her left breast with his revolver barrel; the Colt held left-handed, casually at his waist. When he wanted, Becker would place six leaden balls through her heart, in less than the space she might have lived to draw breath.

"Laudanum has a scent no soldier forgets," Becker said, shaking his head. "And in apple pie without cinnamon. Such scent!"

"You mean, *taste*." Kate had given up on the razor. Now it was to be her wits until her father came in.

"No. Scent is correct, I think. *Odor*. It is from the tincture substance, perhaps. Had the pie been warmer, it might have evaporated."

"I always flavor the pie with some of Father's whisky. It helps the dried apples. And now, Captain, I'll await your apology." Kate pouted prettily and let her robe slide a bit more from her shoulders.

"These mountains are rotten with Yankee sympathizers," muttered Becker. "But I think you do not care whom you rob and kill."

He was peering through the window into the rainswept night. Kate started to slide toward the door, but Becker's gun did not waver in aim, and she sensed that his trigger was quicker than her feet.

"Go sit on the bed, please," Becker said, still not appearing to watch her. "I have not yet decided to kill you."

"You will answer to my father for this!" Kate did as she was told, giving a flounce of her petticoats as she sat. Her hand fell close beside the straight razor.

"I knew such a place as this in Kansas," Becker told her, still watching at the window. "After they took the money and stripped the bodies, they fed them to the hogs. Hogs, don't you know, will eat everything. They even eat the skulls. No white, white bones to wash about and roll down Hill Creek, my lovely Lorelei."

Kate hiked her petticoats toward her knees. "I don't know what you are talking about. You are drunk. I'm going to my room now."

In the stable, horses began to scream.

A burst of lightning flared across the clearing.

Shapes were moving toward the tavern.

"Soldiers!" Becker hissed. "Your Yankee friends are coming!"

"You're mad!" Kate palmed her razor as she leapt up to join him at the window. What she saw outside made her forget Becker.

They were only visible in the long bursts of lightning. They shuffled stiffly toward the inn, rain sluicing away the mud from their sodden blue uniforms, rinsing the maggots from their rotting flesh.

"No weapons," observed Becker. "They carry no weapons."

"They're all of them dead men!" Kate screamed. "It's Colonel Hayes and his raiders, come back for revenge!"

"They look to be very solid for ghosts," Becker scoffed. "I think they were camped near here and were caught in a flashflood."

"Preacher Wells cursed them!" Kate moaned. "Now their graves can't hold them! They're walking down the road to Hell!"

Becker examined his pistols. "Alive or dead, they are nonetheless damn Yankees. I think they're looking for me."

"I tell you, they're walking dead men!"

"Then I'll have to shoot them all the same."

"You can't kill the dead!"

"I can certainly try."

From downstairs resounded heavy blows against the door.

Glass shattered as shutters banged. Hoarse shouts echoed from below. Some drovers had remained by the fire. Someone fired a pistol. Then another.

"Time to kill," said Becker. "You go out the door first. I don't like razors."

The pistol in his left hand was leveled at her head. Kate pushed open the door, moving as if in a dream. A nightmare.

Culpepper was waiting on the balcony outside the door at the head of the stairway. He had a shotgun in his hands, pointed toward Becker, but he was looking in genuine horror at the scene below. As he turned his head, Becker shot him through the heart twice. The shotgun went off. Kate clutched her middle, where her corset used to be, and doubled over. Culpepper tumbled on down the stairs. Kate rolled about, making gobbling sounds. Becker stepped over them both.

The Yankees had broken down the barred door of the inn. A number of drovers had bedded down in the common room. They were on their feet now. Those with guns were firing wildly at the shambling creatures from the grave.

Becker emptied his Colt into the nearest dead thing. The .36 calibre lead balls punched into decaying flesh with no discernible effect. The creature shuffled toward Becker. Becker drew a second revolver and emptied it into the rotting face. Bits of bone and maggot-riddled brain exploded as the hammering barrage burst through the back of its skull. With half of its head blown away, the dead soldier swayed, then continued toward Becker.

At least they were slow. Becker leapt back from the rotting fingers and vaulted up the stairs. The creature sprawled across the corpse of Culpepper, its smashed jaws champing at the inn-keeper's bloody chest. Another dead thing was already stumbling toward the stairway.

Kate's body was still twitching as Becker stepped past her. "Kate, I apologize." He wasn't sure she could hear him. "You were indeed right."

Becker lunged into his room and grabbed his cavalry saber. The razor-honed blade glinted as it came away from its scabbard. Becker drew another Colt with his right hand, then rushed back onto the balcony. He would have liked to reload, but there was little time for that and, apparently, little purpose.

Becker skidded at the doorway, as Ephraim Warren's big Walker Colt fired past him down the balcony. The heavy .44 slug knocked back the dead thing that had buried its face in Kate's ripped-open abdomen. Recovering, the creature crawled forward again and dipped its blood-covered face back into its feast.

Zachariah Warren's Sharps rifle let go with a tremendous boom. The .50 calibre slug obliterated the dead soldier's skull, flinging it back along the balcony. Headless, it again began to crawl for Kate's body.

"Bullets are no good!" yelled Becker. "Hold your fire!"

He leapt upon the headless creature, swinging his saber at its arms. Under his full strength, the heavy blade chopped through decaying flesh and bone. Armless, the dead man still writhed blindly forward toward Kate's body.

Zachariah gaped. He and his son had been asleep in another room when the attack began. "What are they!" he shouted.

"I think they may be Colonel Hayes' soldiers, come back from the dead!" Becker peered over the balcony rail as they joined him. "Perhaps there is another explanation?"

"God Almighty!" Zachariah pointed. "That *is* Colonel Hayes!"

The light below was uncertain, but it revealed a scene of madness by yellow firelight and lantern. Twenty or more blue-clad soldiers had pushed into the inn. More were following. Ten or so drovers had been there in the common room. Most of them were down, writhing beneath the clawing hands and tearing teeth of the undead soldiers. A few still fought to get away. Their guns empty, they fought with knives and clubs—all to no avail. Impervious to wounds, the dead things simply closed over them and began their ghastly feast upon still-living flesh. An overturned lantern began to spread flame across the floor.

The Warrens seemed paralyzed, but this was not Becker's first encounter with the supernatural. He had won out before, and he reacted to the horror about him as if it were a regular military problem.

"We must get through them to the horses!" he said. "Since they cannot be killed, escape is our only hope. Bullets are useless, but they can be dismembered. Blows can knock them back. Is there another way out?"

"Only the windows."

More of the undead were shambling for the stairway. More were filling the doorway below.

"Then it's the windows," Becker decided. "Back into my room. We'll barricade the door and let ourselves down."

Becker closed the latch to his room, knowing it wouldn't hold. As the Warrens pushed the few bits of furniture against the door, Becker smashed out the windowpanes with a chair, then knotted a corner of a blanket to the bedpost. Blows were already pounding against the door.

"Hold onto this!" Becker tossed the blanket through the window. "Brace your boots into the chinking, and it might hold. After that, it's not too long a drop onto the mud. We'll make a rush for the stable!"

The door was pushing open.

Not feeling particularly noble, Becker slid down first. To his surprise, the blanket held, and he had only about six feet to drop. He landed easily enough on the soft ground and drew his saber. In the lightning, he could see shapes stumbling about the clearing, but they were intent upon the inn's doorway. Flame was licking past the shattered windows.

Zachariah clambered down next, his Sharps rifle slung over his shoulder. Becker caught him as he let go of the blanket.

The knot tore free under Ephraim's weight, and he landed heavily. From above came the sounds of crashing furniture as the door burst inward. Ephraim groaned and staggered to his feet, limping badly.

"Let's go!" Becker ordered.

"I can't run!" Ephraim moaned.

"And I can't wait!" Becker said. He started for the stable. The Warrens struggled to keep up.

Already the dead creatures were closing in on them. The stench of their rotting corpses overwhelmed the miasma of the hog pens. Becker's saber slashed, driving through maggot-covered arms that reached for him through the darkness. Behind him, Ephraim's Walker Colt boomed several times, and then Becker heard screams. An instant later, Zachariah was running beside him, swinging his Bowie knife in butchering blows.

"We can't make it!" Zachariah gasped.

Lightning crackled over the clearing, giving view to the encircling army of the dead.

"If we can reach the horses . . ." Becker yelled through the glare.

"Oh, God Almighty! That's Colonel Hayes himself!" Zachariah shouted as the thunder hit.

Another blast of lightning matched the growing blaze of the burning inn.

A huge man, dressed in dirt-matted homespun, black beard flaring with the lightning blast, stood at the gate of the hog pens.

"That's Preacher Wells!" Zachariah screamed.

Worms crawled about his face, but Wells could somehow still cry out: "This is the road to Hell, Colonel Hayes!"

And he opened the gate.

Two hundred or more half-starved, half-wild hogs, ravenous at the stench of rotting meat, burst over and past him in a feeding frenzy. Hungry tusks ripped into rotting flesh; huge, two hundred to three hundred pound barrel-like bodies smashed into staggering legs, bowling over the undead creatures. Eager tusks ripped into decaying bellies; snouts rooted hungrily into maggot-stuffed entrails.

The roof of the inn let go in a geyser of flames, giving hellish illumination to a nightmare from Hell.

"The horses!" Becker shouted, and he pushed Zachariah toward the stable.

They rode until dawn, until the stench of death and the smoke of the burning inn had cleared from their nostrils, moving as fast as they dared along the trail beside the river.

At first light, they paused to rest the horses.

Becker stretched wearily. He eyed Zachariah's Sharps rifle. "They attacked the inn for some reason. And you were witness to the Hell Creek Massacre. I think it was you who shot Colonel Hayes. From the edge of the woods. With that rifle."

Zachariah's eyes narrowed. "So what if I did?"

"So many people died," said Becker. "And you nearly got me killed."

As Zachariah went for his Bowie knife, Becker shot him three or four times.

Then he left his dead ass there by the side of the road.

(For Manly Wade Wellman)

The Sunday-Go-To-Meeting Jaw

Nancy A. Collins

Nancy A. Collins is a writer whose credentials belie the brief period in which she has written professionally. Her first novel, *Sunglasses After Dark,* appeared from NAL/Onyx in 1989 and has since won the Horror Writers of America's Bram Stoker Award for First Novel, and the British Fantasy Society's Icarus Award. Not limited to traditional prose, her scripts for DC Comics *Swamp Thing* have been among the most popular in the history of that venerable title. As a short story writer, she has appeared in several outstanding anthologies, such as *Splatterpunks, Hotter Blood, Under the Fang, The Year's Best Fantasy and Horror,* and *The Ultimate Werewolf.* Impressive for her first two years of professional writing.

Nancy is a native Southerner, born in 1959 in Dermott, Arkansas. This story was suggested by oral history within her family concerning her great-grandfather, who lost his lower jaw during the Civil War. It is one of several stories Nancy has set in a cracked-mirror version of her native Southeast Arkansas. Nancy cautions to reassure us her great-grandfather suffered only some of the problems borne by the story's protagonist and lived a reasonably normal lifespan following the war.

The hungry man squatted in the shadows of the tree-line marking the boundary of the Killigrew land, never once taking his eyes off the back of the house. His hot, bloodshot eyes followed the handful of chickens scratching haphazardly in the dirt.

Although he had not eaten in three days, the chickens had nothing to fear from him. His hunger could no longer be appeased in such a simple fashion.

He hugged his bony knees with broomstick arms and studied the faded lace curtains that hung in the long, narrow windows of the two-story clapboard house. He stiffened as he caught a glimpse of a woman dressed in black. He began to sweat and shiver at the same time. Had the fever come back? Or was it something else this time?

The back door slammed open and an elderly Negro woman, her head wrapped in a worn kerchief, stepped out on the porch, drying her wrinkled hands on a voluminous apron that hung all the way down to her ankles. After studying the coming twilight, the old Negress descended the stairs and hobbled toward a small, neatly kept two-room cabin near the house.

From the looks of the rest of the half-dozen slave quarters, the old mammy was the only remaining servant on the place.

It was getting dark. The family inside the house was no doubt gathered around the dinner table. If he was going to do what he planned, he'd have to move from his hiding place soon. The starving man's stomach tightened even further.

Hester Killigrew pushed the food on her plate with her fork. Collard greens, roast sweet potatoes, and corn pone. Again. White trash food. Nigger food. Least that's what Fanny Walchanski said.

Fanny's father, Mr. Walchanski, owned the dry goods store in Seven Devils. He was one of a handful of merchants who had benefited from the arrival of the railroad in Seven Devils last year. Mr. Walchanski was very well-to-do, Fanny was fond of pointing out to anyone within earshot. Hester could just imagine what Fanny would have to say if she discovered the Killigrews took their meals in the kitchen instead of the dining room.

Hester looked at her mother, seated at the head of the table, then at her little brother. Francis was busy shoveling food into his rosebud mouth. Francis was only two and a half and couldn't remember how it'd been before the war. Back when there'd been more than just Mammy Joella to see to them. Back when they ate in the dining room every day on proper china.

Hester knew better than to complain about their situation. It was sure to make her mother scold her or, worse, break into tears. Hester realized they weren't as bad off as other folks in Choctaw County. They still had a roof over their heads and ate on a regular basis. There wasn't as much red meat as before, and they had a goat for milk instead of a cow, but there were plenty of chickens and eggs.

She remembered how Old Man Stackpole sat in his big old empty mansion until he went crazy and set it on fire before shooting himself in the head. Maybe he got sick of eating greens and corn pone all the time, too.

There was a knock on the back door. Since Mammy Joella had gone back to her cabin for the night, Mama answered it herself.

Hester craned her neck to see around her mother's skirts. A tall, thin raggedy man stood on the stoop, his hair long and grimy. He looked—and smelled—like he hadn't washed in weeks. For some reason Hester was reminded of the nutcracker soldier she'd seen in the window of Walchanski's Dry Goods.

"If you want work, I don't have any to give you—and no money to pay you with, if I did," Penelope Killigrew said tersely. In the year since the war ended, ragged hungry strangers looking for food or temporary work were common. Most were trying to make their way back home the best they could. Others, however, were trouble looking for a place to happen.

The stranger spoke in a slobbering voice that reminded Hester of the washerwoman down the road's idiot son.

"Nell—don't you know me?"

Penelope Killigrew started to cry and shake her head "no." Francis, who'd been happily crumbling corn pone with his pudgy little hands, looked up at the sound of his mother's sobs.

Hester thought the funny-looking stranger had done something. She jumped from her chair and hurried to the door.

"What did you do to my mama?!" she demanded.

Penelope Killigrew turned and grabbed her daughter's shoulders. She was smiling and crying at the same time, like the time she wouldn't put Francis down. Hester started to get scared.

"It's alright, honey! Everything's going to be alright! Daddy's come home!"

Confused, Hester stared at the half-starved stranger dressed in the tatters of a Confederate uniform. He stared back, his rheumy eyes blinking constantly. Now that she had a good look at him, she realized why he'd reminded her of the nutcracker soldier.

He had a wooden jaw.

Hester slammed the door to her room as hard as she could. She didn't care if it shook the whole house. She didn't care if it knocked the house to the ground, for that matter! Mama made her go to her room. Well, that's just fine! She could be just as mad as Mama!

Mama lost her temper because she refused to kiss him. Hester didn't care if she got switched for it later. She wasn't going to kiss him! She didn't care what Mama or anyone else might say!

That man wasn't her daddy!

Everyone kept insisting that Hester was too young to remember things from before the war. That was stupid. If she could remember their ole dog, Cooter, why not Daddy? She certainly could remember the war—leastways the occasions it wandered into their lives. Hester didn't know why Mama kept telling the Nutcracker she didn't know better. Maybe it made her feel better about having a stranger in the house. But why did Mama have to pretend he was Daddy?

Daddy was the handsomest man in Arkansaw. At least Choctaw County, anyway. He was big and strong, with shoulders like a bull. He had dark hair with deep blue eyes. He laughed a lot and had a charming smile. Even other men said so.

Hester remembered how she used to sit on the floor in the parlor, playing with her rag doll, listening for the sound of his boots in the hall. Then he'd sweep her up in his arms, swinging her high in the air. Sometimes the top of her head brushed the chandelier and made the crystal drops shake and dance. It sounded just like angels singing.

She'd squeal and giggle and Daddy would laugh, too—the sound booming out of his chest like thunder. Mama didn't approve of such tomfoolery, though. Hester supposed she was afraid they'd break the chandelier.

Hester was six when Daddy went off to fight for President Davis. Mama cried a lot, but Daddy said it was something he had to do. Hester didn't really understand what was going on at the time, but she thought Daddy looked handsome in his gray uniform.

They all went down to Mr. Potter's daguerreotype palace down near the train depot and Daddy had his picture taken. Mama kept it in the family Bible, pressed between the pages like a dried flower.

Daddy left in 1861 to go help General Lyon fight General McCulloch at Oak Hills, near Missouri. He wrote letters every day, and Mama would read them aloud in the parlor before going to bed. Most of the time he wrote about how much he missed them and how bad the army food was.

In 1862, Daddy's unit joined with General Van Dorn's to keep the Yankees from pushing the Confederacy out of Missouri. That was Pea Ridge. The Confederates lost and the Yankees ended up marching all the way to Helena. Daddy came home for a visit after that. He was skinny and had a beard, but as far as Hester could tell, he was still Daddy. He hugged her so hard Hester thought her ribs would bust. He smelled bad, but she pretended not to notice so he wouldn't get hurt feelings. When Mama saw him, she started to cry, but Daddy shook his head at her.

"Hush, Nell. Not in front of the child."

He left two days later.

Just before Christmas of that year, Daddy fought with General Hindman at Prairie Grove. When they had to retreat to Fort Smith, Daddy was one of the men who didn't desert. He kept writing home, but sometimes they didn't get the letters until a long time after he mailed them. Hester knew sometimes he never got the letters Mama sent him, like the one telling him about Francis being born that winter.

The last letter Daddy wrote said he was going with General Holmes to kick the Yankees out of Helena. That was 1863.

*   *   *

They didn't get news of what happened at Helena until a month or two later. Mama found out first. It was a massacre. That's how Mama said it. A regular massacre. Hester didn't know what that meant at the time, but judging from how everyone was carrying on, she figured it had to be real bad. Mama cried a lot and carried Francis around and wouldn't put him down or let Mammy Joella take him.

Mammy Joella got upset and begged Mama to eat something. If not for herself, then for "the chirren's sake." All that did was make Mama cry even more.

Things changed after that. Mama took to wearing black and made Hester wear it too, even though it was way too hot for that time of year. Mama cut her hair real short and was sad most of the time. Although they never got an official notice from the army, she was convinced Daddy was dead. Or as good as.

Things at home got hard. Most of the niggers ran off when they heard about the proclamation Mr. Lincoln made freeing the slaves. Not that Hester's family had a lot of slaves to begin with, unlike Old Man Stackpole's plantation up the road. The only nigger that stayed behind was Mammy Joella, who claimed she was too old to start someplace new.

Mama sold off several parcels of Killigrew land to keep from being thrown out on the road. After General Lee surrendered, she sold almost all of her fancy dresses, saying she'd never have anything worth celebrating ever again. She also sold off the dining room set and the good china and silverware.

At first Hester thought Mama was joking about the dirty, foul-smelling man being Daddy. Then Mammy Joella came out of her cabin to see what all the fuss was about. She took one look at the Nutcracker and gave a little scream like she'd just seen a ghost.

"It's Mr. Ferris! Mr. Ferris!"

Mammy Joella helped Grandma Killigrew deliver Daddy, long time ago. She'd known Ferris Killigrew longer than anyone outside his own family. But she was old and didn't see or think as well as she used to. Everyone knew that.

*   *   *

Penelope Killigrew sat on a chair in the kitchen, a clean towel folded in her lap, and silently watched Mammy Joella scrub what was left of her husband. She stared at her long-lost husband's back. His vertebrae looked like the beads on a necklace.

The numbness was beginning to fade, like it had years ago, when she'd thought Ferris was dead. Part of her felt guilty for having surrendered hope and resigned herself to widow's weeds so prematurely.

Ferris Killigrew, her husband of fifteen years and father of her two children, was, like Lazarus before him, back from the land of the dead he'd been so hurriedly consigned to.

Wasn't he?

Steam rose from the dented metal tub, wrapping the gaunt figure in a damp haze. Penelope blinked the tears from her eyes and looked away.

Mammy Joella moved purposefully about her former master, scrubbing his grayish skin, occasionally pouring warm water over his tangled hair with a ladle, clucking under her tongue.

Killigrew realized he should have undone the leather straps that held his jaw in place before bathing, but he was not ready to subject Nell to that yet. She'd had a bad enough shock as it was, what with him showing up unannounced on the back stoop.

The smell of Mammy Joella's skin and the touch of her calloused hands on his naked flesh reminded Killigrew of how she used to bathe him as a child. The memory was so sharp, so unexpected, he began to cry.

He was both surprised and disgusted by the hot tears rolling down his cheeks and how his sides shook and shuddered from the force of his sobs. He'd never cried in front of Nell before, not even when his mother died. He squeezed his eyes shut, too ashamed to look at his wife.

Mammy Joella's voice whispered in his ear. "Go 'head an' cry, Mister Ferris. You have yourself a good cry. If anyone deserves one, it's you."

Hester woke up when her mother screamed.

Although it was dark, the moon outside her window cast a

cold, dim light into the room. Hester lay on her bed and held her breath. What was happening? Was the house on fire? Had something happened to Francis?

Then she remembered the Nutcracker, and she leapt from her bed and hurried across the narrow hall to her mother's room. She grabbed the doorknob, but it refused to turn in her hand.

Hester pounded her fists against the door, shrieking at the top of her lungs. "What are you doing to my mother!?! Leave her alone! Get out of our house! Get out! Go away! Leave us alone!"

The door jerked open so quickly Hester nearly fell headfirst into her mother's room. Mrs. Killigrew stood in the doorway, her face white and tense—whether from anger or shock Hester could not tell.

"Hester, what are you doing up at this hour? Return to your room, immediately!"

Hester could make out the rail-thin form of the Nutcracker seated on the edge of her parents' bed, his face hidden by shadows. "I heard you yell, Mama . . ."

"Nonsense, child! You must have been having a bad dream."

"It *wasn't* a dream! I *heard* you." She scowled and pointed at the Nutcracker. "What's *he* doing here, Mama?"

Mrs. Killigrew frowned and glanced over her shoulder. Her grip tightened on the doorknob. "Come along, honey. Be quiet, or you'll wake up Francis! I'll tuck you back in bed," she whispered, pulling the door shut behind her.

"But Mama, you *did* scream! I *heard* you!" Hester protested as her mother herded her back into her room.

"I told you to hush once already, child!" Mrs. Killigrew hissed. "You'll have the whole house up if you're not careful!"

Hester crawled into bed and looked into her mother's face. "Is that man *really* Daddy?"

"Yes, honey. It's really him." Mrs. Killigrew drew a quilt over her daughter and smoothed it with trembling hands.

"But why does he look so—funny?"

Mrs. Killigrew took a deep breath, like a woman preparing to jump into a cold stream. "When your father went with General Holmes to try and chase the Yankees out of Helena, he ended up getting himself captured. They sent him to a camp somewhere up North, where they kept Confederate soldiers. He was in that place over a year.

"A couple of weeks before . . . before General Lee surrendered, your daddy led a protest for more food and decent clothing for the prisoners. He got smashed in the face with a Yankee rifle butt for his trouble. The Yankee doctors ended up cutting off his lower jaw to keep the gangrene from spreading. So they gave him a wooden one to replace it and let him go. He's been working his way back home ever since."

"Is he going to stay here with us?"

"Yes, darling. Forever and ever."

"Do people have to see him?"

The slap came so suddenly Hester was too stunned to react. Mrs. Killigrew spun on her heel without another word and slammed the door behind her, leaving her daughter alone in the dark.

Hester lay in her bed, refusing to cry. She pressed her red, stinging cheek against Grandma Killigrew's patchwork quilt and wondered what was wrong with grownups.

She felt like she was trapped inside a bad dream and that she was the only one who knew she was asleep. It was like everyone was crazy but her. But maybe that was what being an adult was all about: believing things you know aren't so.

Like the Nutcracker being Daddy.

Hester had seen the lie in her mother's eyes when she'd assured her that the Nutcracker was her father. She knew in her heart, just as Hester did, that whoever this gaunt scarecrow might be, he *wasn't* Ferris Killigrew. So why did Mama keep pretending?

Penelope Killigrew stood shivering in the hallway.

She realized she shouldn't have screamed like that, but she just couldn't help herself. When he'd exposed his wounds to her she'd been so overwhelmed. . . . Her relief at discovering Ferris still alive had prevented her from recognizing just how severe her husband's wounds really were. But now there was no turning away from it.

The half-starved creature that had found its way back home

was not the man she'd loved before the war. The Ferris Killigrew
that had returned was a mangled, incomplete copy of the husband that had marched off to war four years ago. But she owed
it to the memory of the man she'd adored to see to it that what
was left be looked after and treated well. It was the least she
could do.

Hester was walking home from school when she caught sight
of the wagon in her family's front yard. As she drew closer,
Hester recognized it as belonging to the man in town who bought
used furniture; the one who'd bought their old dining room set
the year before.

"Mama! Mama!"

Hester hurried through the front door, nearly knocking down
her mother. Mrs. Killigrew stood in the narrow foyer, Francis
resting on one hip.

"Land's sakes, child! What is it *now*?" she sighed.

"What are these men doing here?" Hester demanded, pointing
at the two men in the parlor. One of the men was laying thin
blankets on the floor, while the second prepared a heavy wooden
crate filled with excelsior.

"They've come to haul off some furnishings I've sold to Mr.
Mercer, that's all."

"What are they taking *this* time?"

"Don't use that tone of voice with me, Hester Annabelle
Killigrew!"

Just then there was the sound of a hundred angels laughing,
and Hester spun around in time to see one of the packing men
lower the crystal chandelier, winding the old-fashioned pulley
Grandpa Killigrew had had installed decades ago.

"No! No! I won't let you sell it!" shrieked Hester, throwing
her books to the floor.

"Hester! Hester, what's gotten into you?!?"

Hester propelled herself at the workman lowering the chandelier, hammering her doubled fists against his ribs. "I won't let
you take it! I won't! I *won't*!"

"*Hester!*"

The second workman grabbed the girl and pulled her away

from his companion. He cast an anxious look over his shoulder at the child's mother. "Mebbe we oughta come round later, Miz Killigrew, after she's calmed down some. . . ."

Penelope Killigrew's face was livid. "You'll do no such thing! You'll take the chandelier with you, just as I promised Mr. Mercer! Now if you'll kindly unhand my daughter . . ."

The workman let go and Mrs. Killigrew snatched her daughter's left ear, twisting it viciously.

"Mama! *Owww!* You're *hurting* me!"

"And you're *embarrassing* me, young lady!" Mrs. Killigrew dragged her daughter down the hall, away from Mr. Mercer's hired men. "How *dare* you act such a way in front of strangers!" she hissed. "People will think you were raised in a *barn*! I sold that chandelier to Mr. Mercer to help pay for your father's needs! We have another mouth to feed, and it will be some time before your father is well enough to contribute to the family's welfare! Now, would you care to explain yourself, young lady, as to what brought on that outburst?"

Hester shook her head, her tears finally catching up with her hurt. Francis, distressed by his older sister's sobs, began to whimper.

"Oh, don't you start in as well!" groaned Mrs. Killigrew. "Hester, go to your room! I don't want to see your face until supper time! Is that clear?"

Hester stormed up the stairs, clamping her hands over her ears to keep from hearing the chandelier's angel-song as it was packed away. She paused and gave her parents' bedroom a venomous look. Before she realized what she was doing, she'd kicked open the door and was shrieking at the Nutcracker.

"It's all *your* fault! She sold it because of *you*! I hate you! Why don't you go back where you came from and leave us *alone*?!?"

Mammy Joella sprang from the corner of the bed, moving faster than Hester had ever seen her move before. "Chile, get outta this room for I bust yore haid!" She flapped her apron at the girl as if she was an errant chicken, a wooden spoon clutched in one arthritic hand. Hester stumbled backward into the hall, but not before she caught a glimpse of the Nutcracker.

He was sitting up in bed, surrounded by pillows, one of Francis's old diapers knotted around his neck. A bowl of yellow grits and a pitcher of goat's milk rested on the dresser next to the bed. A length of rubber tubing hung from the middle of his face, a small metal funnel fixed to its end. A mixture of grits and milk dribbled from what passed for the Nutcracker's mouth.

The tube dangling from the Nutcracker's face reminded Hester of something she'd seen at the traveling circus in Arkansaw City before the war.

"He looks like an elephant!" she giggled.

Mammy Joella smacked her with the spoon, leaving a smear of porridge on Hester's forehead. "Don't you be callin' yore pappy names!"

Hester was taken aback by this new affront. As far back as she could remember, Mammy Joella had been a pleasant, if slightly decrepit, servant: loving, forgiving, and slow to anger. "You can't hit me! You're just a nigger!"

"I'm a nigger, awright; but I'm the only nigger y'all got!" Mammy Joella hissed back. With that, she returned her attention to the Nutcracker, closing the door in Hester's face.

The next day, Mrs. Killigrew loaded her husband into the buckboard and went in to town to see Doc Turner. Doc Turner measured Ferris Killigrew's head with a pair of calipers and studied the extent of his patient's wounds before showing them a catalog from a company up north.

"There's nothing they can't make nowadays," he explained cheerily. "Wooden legs, hook arms, glass eyes, tin noses. . . . Course it helps there's such a large demand! Now, what can I do you for, Ferris?"

The Sunday-go-to-meeting jaw came in the mail a month later. The Killigrew children watched as their mother unwrapped the parcel in the kitchen. While Francis was more interested in playing with the cast-off stamps and string, Hester's attention was riveted on the package's contents.

The Nutcracker's new jaw had its own special case that reminded Hester of the box Mama used to keep her emerald necklace and pearl brooch in, back when she used to have jewelry.

The jaw rested on a maroon velvet lining, a network of straps and buckles that resembled a dog's muzzle folded underneath it.

Mrs. Killigrew had sent the artificial limb company one of the few photographs she had of Mr. Killigrew from before the war. The custom-fitting cost more, but Doc Turner had assured them it was worth it. Seeing the replica jaw displayed like a watch in a jeweler's window flustered Mrs. Killigrew somewhat. Outside of noticing it had been painted to mimic European skin tones and was of a distinctly masculine cast, it was difficult to judge how closely the people at the artificial limb company had hewed to the photograph.

"Ferris, look! It's here!"

Ferris Killigrew stared at the gleaming piece of hard wood on its velvet cushion but did not move to touch it.

"Let's try it on," Mrs. Killigrew urged.

Killigrew grunted and slowly unfastened the straps that held his army-issue wooden jaw in place. Mrs. Killigrew did not allow her smile to slip as she averted her eyes.

When he'd finished adjusting the new straps, he shuffled over to the cheval glass his wife keep in the corner of the room and studied his new jaw.

He had to admit that it didn't look nearly as fake as the old one. It fit a damn sight better than his old one, too. However, its unnaturally rosy pigmentation made it look like he'd never washed his face above the jawline.

"Oh, Ferris! It's better than I thought it would be!" Mrs. Killigrew smiled. "It makes you look—like you!" She slid her arms around her husband's waist, pressing her head against his shoulder, like she did in their courting days. "Now you can go to church this Sunday!"

Killigrew clumsily returned her hug, trying hard not to cry again.

"I love you, Ferris," she whispered.

He wanted to tell her that he loved her, too; that it had been that love that kept him alive in the prisoner of war camp all those horrible months; that his love for her had drawn him back across four states, despite harsh weather, harsher treatment, and the threat of death by starvation or disease.

He wanted to tell her all these things, but that was impossible now.

As Doc Turner had warned them, weeks ago, the model Mrs. Killigrew had chosen for her husband, while expensive, was purely ornamental. All it was good for was looking natural.

"But Mama! Everyone will be *looking* at us!"

"So let them look, then," sighed Mrs. Killigrew, who was busy taking in a pair of her husband's old pants. She frowned at her handiwork. Even after all she'd done, Ferris would still need to wear suspenders *and* a belt.

"Mama! You don't understand!" The very idea of walking into the First Methodist Church of Seven Devils, Arkansaw, with the Nutcracker made Hester's stomach knot up.

"You're right I don't understand!" Mrs. Killigrew barked. "I don't understand why you're acting like such an ungrateful little monster! Here the Good Lord brings your daddy back from the war—"

"He's not Daddy! He's *not*!"

"See hear, young lady! You're not so grown up I can't take you over my knee! If I hear another outburst like that, I'll cut myself a switch and lash you bloody! You're going to church with us tomorrow even if I have to drag you behind the buckboard like a heifer bound for market!"

"You don't care! You don't care about me at all!" Hester bellowed, knocking her mother's sewing basket off the kitchen table with one sweep of her hand. "All you're interested in is that, that *Nutcracker*! You think you can turn him into Daddy and make everything like it used to be! But you can't! Daddy's dead!"

"*Hester!*" Mrs. Killigrew grabbed her daughter with her left hand, twisting Hester's right arm behind her back. "That's it, young lady! That's all I'm going to take out of you!" she spat, raising her right hand.

"Go ahead! Hit me! Slap me!" Hester taunted through her tears. "Beat on me all you like! It's still the truth!"

Mrs. Killigrew hesitated for a moment then lowered her hand, pulling her daughter to her bosom. Hester struggled for a moment, but her mother's grip was firm. After a few seconds, she began to cry—great, wracking sobs—while Mrs. Killigrew held her daughter tight, rocking her like she used to do, not so many years ago.

The Killigrew family always sat in the third pew on the left-hand side of the aisle. It was a tradition that dated back before Hester's birth. For as long as she could remember, her family always sat there during Sunday services.

As they walked down the aisle, everybody turned and *looked*. Hester's cheeks glowed like hot coals. She could feel Fanny Walchanski's greedy eyes on them, devouring every detail for later recitation. The thought of what she would have to face at school the next day made Hester tighten her grip on Francis' hand. Her little brother began to whine, but she quickly hushed him.

She could hear the members of the congregation mumbling amongst themselves; the ladies agitating the still air with their fans as they craned their necks for a better look.

Reverend Cakebread watched from behind the pulpit as the Killigrews approached the front of the church. He was a round, pink-faced man with heavy eyebrows the size and shape of caterpillars. Right then, the caterpillars looked like they were trying to crawl into his hair.

Aside from being keenly aware that everybody was watching them, the service went as usual; Francis curling up on the bench for a nap next to his sister halfway into Reverend Cakebread's sermon.

Bored by the minister's nasal drone, Hester found herself looking at the Nutcracker and was startled to glimpse the faint outline of her father's profile. Without realizing what she was doing, she brushed her fingers against his sleeve.

The Nutcracker turned his head and looked at her, breaking the illusion. The sadness in his eyes reminded Hester of the time she found a rabbit in the snare.

And then Reverend Cakebread was saying, ". . . and if there

are any announcements any of you in the congregation would
care to make right now?"

Mrs. Killigrew stood up, nervously straightening the shawl
around her shoulders. "I would like to make an announcement,
if I could, Reverend."

The minister nodded his agreement, and Mrs. Killigrew turned
to face the congregation.

"As you no doubt already heard, my husband—Captain Ferris
Killigrew, who I had thought lost to this world—has been returned to his rightful home, thanks to Our Lord. He is now once
more fit to reclaim his place in society. I would like to extend
an open invitation to all of you here today to stop by our place
after church and help my family celebrate God's mercy. There
will be food and drink for everyone."

After Mrs. Killigrew sat down, Mr. Eichorn stood up and an-
nounced that there would be a Ku Klux meeting that night at
the ruins of Old Man Stackpole's plantation house, then they
sang the benediction and church was over.

There was a fly walking on the potato salad. Mrs. Killigrew
waved a hand at the intruder, only to have it land on one of the
deviled eggs.

"Mama, can't we eat yet?"

"You know better than to ask me that, Hester! You know
we've got company coming!" She gave her son's hand a quick
slap, forcing him to let go of an oatmeal cookie. "Francis! No!"

Francis plopped down on the floor and began to cry, sucking
on his chastised fingers.

Ferris Killigrew sat on the parlor love seat, looking like a well-
dressed scarecrow, his hands folded in his lap. He could not bring
himself to meet his wife's eyes.

Mrs. Killigrew massaged her forehead, trying to stall the sick
headache she knew was coming. *All the money I spent on food.
Killing one of my best chickens. And no one has the decency to
show up. Not one.* She retreated into the kitchen, where Mammy
Joella was grinding Ferris' evening allotment of grits and black-
strap molasses into a fine mush.

"An' one show up yet?"

"Not yet. No, I take that back. Reverend Cakebread came by just after church."

"Tha's a preacher-man's job; payin' visits on folks no one else wants t' mess wif."

"That's not true! Ferris was born and raised in Seven Devils! He has plenty of friends! You know that!"

The old woman sighed wearily but did not halt grinding the grits into babyfood. "Tha's 'fore the war. Things different now. Folks herebouts usta thinkin' Mr. Ferris daid. They mo' comfortable wif him that way, I reckon."

"What are you babbling about?" hissed Mrs. Killigrew.

"If'n he'd come back whole stead'a crippled-up, things might be different. Mebbe. But he ain't. He reminds folks things ain't ne'er gonna be th' same. Like us black folks. He's embarassin'. He reminds folks of what they done lost."

Mrs. Killigrew stared, dumbstruck, at the gnarled negress. In the fifteen years since she'd become a member of the Killigrew home, this was the only time Mammy Joella had spoken to her about something besides housework and childcare.

The moment his mother left the room, Ferris Killigrew walked across the floor and helped himself to the oatmeal cookies. After satisfying his hunger, he waddled over to his father and offered him a cookie.

Killigrew accepted the offering, nodding his thanks and trying his best to smile around the jaw. It wasn't easy. He ruffled his son's curls and allowed his hand to linger, caressing the boy's cheeks and smooth brow with his trembling fingers.

When he looked up, he saw Hester standing in the parlor door, watching him the way you'd look at a bug.

He was found the next morning, hanging from the chandelier hook in the parlor, still dressed in his nightshirt. His face was darkened with congested blood while his lower jaw seemed to glow with rosy health. Although the Sunday-go-to-meeting jaw wasn't any good for eating or talking, it had proved adequate for suicide.

Mrs. Killigrew found him. She stared at her husband's body

for a long moment, then went upstairs and woke Hester. She told her daughter to take the mule and ride into town and fetch Mr. Mouzon, Seven Devil's undertaker.

After she made sure Hester had left by the back door, Mrs. Killigrew went to her room and dressed. When she returned to the parlor to await the undertaker's arrival, she discovered Mammy Joella standing in the doorway, staring up at her former master.

"Mammy Joella?"

The old woman grunted to herself and turned, brushing past her employer without looking at her.

"Joella!"

Her only answer was the slamming of the back door.

Hester sat on the love seat and watched the wax trickle down the sides of the thick white candles burning at either end of the Nutcracker's coffin. She was dressed in her best black dress, her hair fixed with a black velvet ribbon. She swung her feet back and forth, watching the tips of her shoes disappear then reappear from under the hem of her skirt.

She could hear her mother talking in hushed tones with Reverend Cakebread and Mr. Mouzon in the kitchen.

Francis was crawling on his hands and knees on the worn Persian carpet, pushing his little wooden train round and round in circles. Hester knew she should tell him to stop grubbing around on the floor in his good suit, but she also knew that would only make him cry, and she really didn't want to deal with that right now.

Hester wished Mammy Joella was still around so she wouldn't be expected to keep an eye on her little brother all the time. But Mammy Joella had disappeared the same day the Nutcracker hanged himself, walking away from her cabin with nothing but the clothes on her back, a gunnysack full of bread and goat's cheese, and a fruit jar full of sassafras tea.

Mama had complained to Sheriff Cooper about it, but he hadn't been of much help.

"What do you expect me to do about it, Nell? Set th' hounds on her? Niggers can leave whene'er they see fit, now."

Still, Hester thought her mother was holding up well, under the circumstances. In many ways, she seemed more tired than grief-stricken. To Hester's knowledge, her mother had yet to shed a tear. Whenever she responded to the condolences offered her, there was a hollowness in her voice. Hester knew that, secretly, her mother was relieved that it was all over; that she no longer had to pretend that the Nutcracker was her husband. Better to bury him and get on with the business of living. She wondered what new schoolyard taunt Fanny Walchanski would dream up to commemorate the event and was surprised to discover she no longer really cared what Fanny Walchanski thought or did.

Hester stared at the Nutcracker, stretched out in his narrow pine box, a lily clamped to his motionless chest. Mr. Mouzon had done a good job, for once. The Nutcracker's face was now the same color as his jaw, giving his appearance a continuity it had lacked in life.

As she stared at the Nutcracker's profile, a weird feeling crept over her, like the one in church two days earlier. For a moment, she found herself looking at the face of her father, Ferris Killigrew. Then the vision wavered and was gone. In its place was the dead Nutcracker; only now the rabbit was free of the snare.

Hester felt something on her face and touched her cheek. She stared at the tears for a long time before she realized she was crying.

Darker Angels

S. P. Somtow

S. P. Somtow was born in 1952 in Bangkok, Thailand, and grew up in Europe, where he was educated at Eton and Cambridge. After receiving his B.A. and M.A. degrees (with honors) in English and Music, he became one of Southeast Asia's most outspoken avant-garde musicians. He made his conducting debut at age nineteen with the Holland Symphony Orchestra, and later served as the director of the Bangkok Opera Society. His controversial career was the subject of a documentary on Japanese television.

He began writing fiction in 1977, quickly winning the John W. Campbell award as outstanding new writer in the SF field. He's been a frequent nominee for other major writing awards, and in 1988 his *Forgetting Places* received the Book of the Year Award for the Books for Young Adults Program. He has twenty books to his credit, several under his birthname, Somtow Sucharitkul.

Turning his talents to feature films, he wrote, directed, and composed the music to *The Laughing Dead,* which has had successful release in Europe and Asia. It is scheduled for distribution in the United States, though it is not yet available as of the writing of this introduction. With new film projects in the pipeline and various novels under contract, we are most pleased Somtow found time to pen this powerful and disturbing short story.

One day there'll be historians who can name all the battles and number the dead. They'll study the tactics of the generals and they'll see it all clear as crystal, like they was watching with the eyes of the angels.

But it warn't like that for me. I can't for the life of me put a name to one blame battle we fought. I had no time to number the dead nor could I see them clearly through the haze of red that swam before my eyes. And when the gore-drenched mist settled into dew, when the dead became visible in their stinking, wormy multitudes, I still could not tell one from another: it was a very sea of torsos, heads, and twisted limbs; the dead was wrapped around one another so close and intimate they was like lovers; didn't matter no more iffen they was ours or theirs.

I do not recollect what made me stay behind. Could be it was losing my last shinplaster on the cockroach races. Could have been the coffee which warn't real coffee at all but parched acorns roasted with bacon fat and ground up with a touch of chicory. Could be it was that my shoes was so wore out from marching that every step I took was like walking acrosst a field of brimstone.

More likely it was just because I was a running away kind of a boy. Running was in my blood. My pa and me, we done our share of running, and I reckon that even after I done run away from *him* and gone to war, the running fever was still inside of me and couldn't be let go.

And then, after I lagged behind, I knowed that if I went back they'd shoot me dead, and if they shot me, why then I'd go straight on to the everlasting fire, because we was fighting to protect the laws of God. I just warn't ready for Hell yet, not after a mere fourteen years on this mortal earth.

That's why I was tarrying amongst the dead, and that's how I come to meet the old darkie that used to work down at the Anderson place.

The sun was about setting and the place was right rank, because the carrion had had the whole day to bloat up and rot and to call out for the birds and the worms and the flies. But it felt good to walk on dead people because they was softer on my wounded feet. The bodies stretched acrosst a shallow creek and all the way up to the edge of a wood. I didn't know where I was nor where I was going. There warn't much light remaining and I wanted to get somewhere, anywhere, before nightfall. It was getting cold. I took a jacket off of one dead man and a pair of new boots from another, but I couldn't get the boots on past them open sores.

You might think it a sin to steal from the dead, but the dead don't have no use for gold and silver. There was scant daylight left for me to riffle through their pockets looking for coins. Warn't much in the way of money on that battlefield. It's usually only us poor folks which gets killed in battle.

It was slippery work wading through the corpses, keeping an eye for something shiny amongst the ripped-up torsos and the sightless heads and the coiling guts. I was near choking to death from the reek of it, and the coat I stole warn't much proof against the cold. I was hungry and I had no notion of where to find provender. And the mist was coming back, and I thought to myself, I'll just take myself a few more coppers and then I'll cross over into the wood and build me a shelter and mayhap a fire. Won't nobody see me, thin as a sapling, quiet as a shadow.

So I started to wade over the creek, which warn't no trouble because there was plenty of bodies to use as stepping stones. I was halfway acrosst when I spotted the old nigger under a cotton-wood tree, in a circle which was clear of carrion. He had a little fire going and something a-roasting over it. I could hear the crackling above the buzz of the flies, and I could smell the cooking fat somewhere behind the stench of putrefying men.

I moved nearer to where he sat. I was blame near fainting by then and ready to kill a body for my supper. He was squatting with his arms around his knees and he was a-rocking back and forth and I thought I could hear him crooning some song to himself, like a lullaby, in a language more kin to French than nigger-talk. Odd thing was, I had heard the song before. Mayhap my momma done sung it to me onc't, for she was born out Louisiana way. The more I listened, the less I was fixing to kill the old man.

He was old, all right. As I crept closer, I seen he warn't no threat to me. I still couldn't see his face, because he was turned away from me and looking straight into the setting sun. But I could see he was withered and white-haired and black as the coming night, and seemed like he couldn't even hear me approaching, for he never pricked up his ears though I stood nary a yard or two behind his back, in the shadow of the cottonwood.

That was when he said to me, never looking back, "Why, *bonjour*, Marse Jimmy Lee; I never did think I'd look upon you face again."

And then he turned, and I knew him by the black patch over his right eye.

Lord, it was strange to see him there, in the middle of the valley of the dead. It had been ten years since my pa and me gone up to the Anderson place. Warn't never any call to go back, since it burned to the ground a week after, and old man Anderson died, and his slaves was all sold.

"How did you know it was me?" I asked him. "I was but four years old last time you laid eyes on me."

"Your daddy still a itinerant preacher, Marse Jimmy Lee?" he says.

"I reckon," said I, for I warn't about ready to tell him the truth yet. "I ain't with my pa no more."

"You was always a running away sort of a boy," he said, and offered me a piece of what he was roasting.

"What is it?"

"I don't reckon I ought to tell you."

"I've had possum before. I've had field rat. I'm no stranger to strange flesh." I took a bite of the meat and it was right tasty. But I hadn't had solid food for two days, and soon I was a-heaving all over the nearest corpse.

He went back to his crooning song, and I remembered then that I had heard it last from his own lips, that day Pa shot Momma in the back because she wanted to go with the Choctaw farmer. I can't say I blamed her, because leastways the man was a landowner and had four slaves besides. Pa let her pack her bags and walk halfway acrosst the bridge afore he blew her to kingdom come. Then he took my hand and set me up on his horse and took me to the Anderson place, and when I started to squall, he slapped me in the face until it were purple and black, saying, between his blows, "She don't deserve your tears. She is a woman taken in adultery; such a woman should be stoned to death, according to the scriptures; a bullet were too good for her. I have exercised my rights according to the law, and iffen I hear one more sob out of you, I shall take a hickory to you, for he who spareth the rod loveth not his child." And he drained a flask of bug juice and burped, I did not hear the name of Mary Cox from his lips again for ten long years.

Pa was not a ordained minister, but plantation folks reckoned him book-learned enough to preach to their darkies, which is what he done every Sunday, a different estate each week, then luncheon with the master and mistress of the house or sometimes, if they was particular about eating with white trash, then in the kitchen amongst the house niggers. The niggers called him the Reverend Cox, but to the white folks he was just Cox, or Bug Juice Cox, or Blame-Fuckster Cox, or wretched, pitiable Cox, so low that his wife done left him for a Injun.

At the Anderson place he preached in a barn, and he took for his subject adultery; and as there was no one to notice, I stole away to a field and sat me down in a thicket of sugar cane and hollered and carried on like the end of the world was nigh, and me just four years old.

Then it was that I heard the selfsame song I was hearing now, and I looked up and saw this ancient nigger with a patch over one eye, and he says to me, "Oh, honey, it be a terrible thing to be without a mother." I remember the smell of him, a pungent smell like fresh crushed herbs. "I still remembers the day my *mamman* was took from me. Oh, do not grieve alone, white child."

"How'd you come to lose that eye?"

"It the price of knowledge, honey," he said softly.

Choking back my sobs, a mite embarrassed because someone had seen me in my loneliness, I said to him, "You shouldn't be here. You should be in that barn listening to my father's preaching, lessen you want to get yourself a whupping."

He smiled sadly and said, "They done given up on whupping old Joseph."

I said, "Is your momma dead too, Joseph?"

"Yes. She be dead, oh, nigh on sixty year now. She died in the revolution."

"Oh, come," I said, "even I know that the revolution was

almost a hundred years ago, and I know you ain't that old, because a white man's time is threescore years and ten, and a
nigger's time is shorter still." Now I wasn't comprehending anything I was saying; this was all things I heard my pa say, over
and over again, in his sermons.

"Oh," said old Joseph, "I ain't talking about the white man's
revolution, but the colored folks' revolt which happened on a
island name of Haiti. The French, they tortured my *mamman,*
but she wouldn't betray her friends, so they killed her and sold
me to a slaver, and the ship set sail one day before independence;
so sixty years after my kinfolk was set free, I's still in bondage
in a foreign country."

I knew that niggers was always full of stories about magic and
distant countries, and they couldn't always see truth from fantasy; my daddy told me that truth is a hard, solid thing to us
white folks, as easy to grasp as a stone or a horseshoe, but to
them it was slippery, it was like a phantom. That was why I
didn't take exception to the old man's lies. I just sat there quietly,
listening to the music of his voice, and it soothed me and seemed
like it helped to salve the pain I was feeling, for pretty soon
when I thought of Momma lying on the bridge choking on her
own blood, I felt I could remember the things I loved about her
too, like the way she called my name, the way her nipples tasted
on my lips, for she had lost my newborn sister and she was
bursting with milk and she would sometimes let me suckle, for
all that I was four years old.

And then I was crying again, but this time they was healing
tears.

Then old Joseph, he said, "You listen to me, Marse Jimmy
Lee. I ain't always gone be with you when you needs to open
up your heart." Now this surprised me, because I didn't recollect
telling him none of what was going through my mind. "I's gone
give you a gift," he said, and he pulls out a bottle from his
sleeve, a vial, only a inch high, and in that bottle was a doll that
was woven out of cornstalks. It were cunningly wrought, for the
head of the doll was bigger than the neck of the bottle, and it
must have taken somebody many hours to make, and somebody
with keen eyesight at that. "Now this be a problem doll. It can

listen to you when no man will listen. It a powerful magic from the island where I was born.''

He held it out to me and it made me smile, for I had oftentimes been told that darkies are simple people and believe in all kinds of magic. I clutched it in my hands, but mayhap he saw the disbelief in my face, for he said to me with the utmost gravity, "Do not mock this magic, white child. Among the colored people which still fears the old gods, they calls me a *boungan,* a man of power.''

"The old gods?" I said.

"Shangó,'' he said, and he done a curious sort of a genuflecting hop when he said the name. "Obatala; Ogun; Babalu Ayé. . . .''

The names churned round and round in my head as I stared into his good eye. I don't recollect what followed next or how my pa found me. But everything else I remembered just as though the ten years that followed, the years of wandering, Pa's worsening cruelty and drunkenness, hadn't never even happened.

It was as though I had circled back to that same place and time. Only instead of the burning sunlight of that summer's day there was the gathering cold and the night. Instead of the tall cane sticky with syrup, we was keeping company with the slain. And I warn't a child no more, although I warn't a man yet, neither.

"The *poupée* I give you,'' old Joseph said as I sat myself down beside him, "does you still got it?''

"My pa found it the next day. He said he didn't want no hoodoo devil dolls in his house. He done smashed it and throwed it in the fire, and then he done wore me out with his hickory.''

"And you a soldier now.''

"I run away.''

"Lordy, honey, you a sight to see. Old Joseph don't got no more dolls for you now. Old Joseph got no time for he be making dolls. There be a monstrous magic abroad now in this universe. This magic it the onliest reason old Joseph still living in this world. Old Joseph hears the magic summoning him. Old Joseph he stay behind to hear what the magic it have to tell him.''

Like a fool, I thought him simple when I heard him speak of magic. It made me smile. It was the first time I had smiled in many months. I smiled to keep from crying, for weeping ill becomes a man of fourteen years who has carried his rifle into battle to defend his country.

"You poor lost child," said Joseph, "you should be awaking up mornings to the song of the larks, not the whistle of miniés nor the thunder of cannon. You at the end of the road now, ain't nowhere left for you to go; that's why us has been called here to this valley of the shadow of death. It was written from the moment we met, Marse Jimmy Lee. Ten years I wandered alone in the wilderness. Now the darker angels has sent you to me."

"I don't know what you mean."

"Be not afraid," he said, "for I bring you glad tidings of great joy." I marveled that he knew the words of the evangelist, for this was the man who would not go hear my father's preaching.

He nibbled at the charred meat. For a moment I entertained the suspicion that it were human flesh. But it smelled good. I ate my fill and drank from the bloody stream and fell asleep beside the fire to the lilt of the old man's lullaby.

I had not told old Joseph all the truth. It warn't only the need to run that forced me from my father's house. Pa was a hard man and a drinking man and a man which had visions, and in those visions he saw other worlds. He was unmerciful to me, and oftentimes he would set to whipping the demons out of me, but everything he did to me was in keeping with holy scripture, which tells a father that love ain't always a sweet thing but can also come with bitterness and blows.

I had visions too, but they warn't heavenly the way his was. I would not wear my shoes. I played with the nigger children of the town, shaming him. I ran wild and I never went to no school. But I could read some, for that my pa set me to studying the scriptures whenever he could tie me down.

This is how I come to join the regiment:

We was living in a shack in back of the Jackson place, right next to the nigger burial plot. Young Master Jackson had all his darkies assembled in the graveyard to hear a special sermon from my pa, because the rumors of the 'mancipation proclamation was rife amongst the slaves. There was maybe thirty or forty of them, and a scattering of pickaninnies underfoot, sitting on the grass, leaning against the wooden markers.

I was sitting in the shack, minding a kettle of stew. Through the open window I could hear my pa preaching. "Now don't you darkies pay this emancipation proclamation no mind," came his voice, ringing and resonant. "It is an evil trickery. They are trying to fool you innocent souls into running away and joining up with those butchers who come down to rape and pillage our land, and they hold out freedom as a reward for treachery. But the true reward is death, for if a nigger is captured in the uniform of a Yankee it has been decreed by our government that he shall be shot without trial. No, this is no road to freedom! There is only one way there for those born into bondage, and that is through the blood of our savior Jesus Christ, and your freedom is not for this world, but for the next, for is it not written, 'In my father's house there are many mansions'? There is a mansion for you, and you, and you, and you, iffen you will obey your master in this life and accept the yoke of lowliness and the lash of repentance; for is it not written, 'By his stripes we are healed' and 'Blessed are the meek'? It's not for the colored people, freedom in this world. But the wicked, compassionless Yankees would prey on your simplicity. They would let you mistake the kingdom of heaven for a rebellious kingdom on earth. 'To everything there is a season.' Yes, there will be mansions for you all. Mansions with white stone columns and porticoes sheltered from the sun. The place of healing is beyond the valley of the shadow of death. . . ."

My pa could talk mighty proper when he had a mind to, and he had a chapter and verse for everything. I didn't pay no heed to his words, though, because there is different chapters and verses for niggers, and when they are quoted for white folks they do not always mean the same thing. No, I was busy stirring the stew and hiding the whisky, for Pa had always had a powerful thirst after he was done preaching, and with the quenching of thirst came violence.

After the preaching, the darkies all starts singing with a passion. They done sung "All God's Chillun Got Wings" and

"Swing Low, Sweet Chariot." Pa didn't stay for the singing but come into the shack calling for his food. It warn't ready, so he throwed a few pots and pans around, with me scurrying out of the way to avoid being knocked about, and then he finally found where I had hidden the bottle and he lumbered into the inner room to drink.

Presently the stew bubbled up, and I ladled out some in a tin cup and took it to the room. This was the room me and him slept in, on a straw pallet on the floor; a bare room with nothing but a chest of drawers, a chair with one leg missing, and a hunting rifle. He kept his hickories there too, for to chastise me with.

I should have knocked, because Pa warn't expecting me.

He was sitting in the chair with his britches about his ankles. He didn't see me. In one hand, he was holding a locket which had a picture of Momma. In the other hand, he was holding his bony cocker, and he was strenuously indulging in the vice of Onan.

I was right horrified when I saw this. I was full of shame to see my father unclothed, for was that not the shame of the sons of Noah? And I was angered, because in my mind's eye I seen my momma go down on that bridge, fold up and topple over, something I hadn't thought on for nigh on ten years. I stood there blushing scarlet and full of fury and grieving for my dead mother, and then I heard him a-murmuring, "Oh, sweet Jehovah, Oh, sweet Lord, I see you, I see the company of the heavenly host, I see you, my sweet Mary, standing on a cloud with your arms stretched out to me, naked as Eve in the Garden of Eden. Oh, oh, oh, I'm a-looking on the face of the Almighty and a-listening to the song of the angels."

Something broke inside me all at once when I heard him talk that way about Momma. Warn't it enough that she was dead, withouten him blasphemously lusting after her departed soul? I dropped the tin of stew, and he saw me and I could see the rage burning in his eyes, and I tried to force myself to obey the fifth commandment, but words just came pouring out of me. "Shame on you, Pa, pounding your cocker for a woman you done gunned down in cold blood. Don't you think I don't remember the way you kilt her, shot her in the back whilst she were crossing that bridge, and the Choctaw watching on t'other side in his top hat and morning dress, with his four slaves behind him, waiting to take her home?"

My pa was silent for a few moments, and the room was filled with the caterwauling of the niggers from the graveyard. We stood there staring each other down. Then he grabbed me by the scruff of the neck and dragged me over to the chair, lurching and stumbling because he hadn't even bothered to pull his britches back up, and I could smell the liquor on him; and he murmured, "You are right, I have sinned; I have sinned, but it is for the son to take on the sins of the world; the paschal lamb; you, Jimmy Lee; oh, God, but you do resemble her, you do remind me of her; oh, it is a heavy burden for you, my son, to take on the sins of the world, but I know that you do it for love," and suchlike, and he reached for the hickory and stripped the shirt off of my back and began to lay to with a will, all the while crying out, "Oh, Mary, oh, my Mary, I am so sorry that you left me . . . oh, my son, you shall bear thirty-nine stripes on your back in memory of our savior . . . oh, you shall redeem me . . ." And the hickory sang and I cried out, not so much from the pain, for that my back was become like leather from long abuse and warn't much feeling left in it. I gritted my teeth and try to bear it like I borne it so many times before, but this time it was not to be borne, and when the thirty-ninth stripe was inflicted, I tore myself loose from the chair and I screamed, "You ain't hurting me no more, because I ain't no paschal lamb and your sins is *your* sins, not mine," and I pushed him aside with all my strength.

"God, God," he says in a whisper, "I see God." And he rolls his eyes heavenward, excepting that heaven were a leaky roof made from a few planks leftover from the slaves' quarters.

Then I took the rifle from the wall and pounded him in the head with the stock, three, four, five, six times until he done slumped onto the straw.

Oh, I was raging and afeared, and I run away right then and there, without even making sure iffen he was kilt or not. I run right through them darkies, who was a-singing and a-carrying on to wake the very dead; they did not see a scrawny boy, small for his age, slip through them and out toward the woods.

I run and run with three dimes in my pocket and a sheaf of shinplasters that I stole from the chest of drawers; I run and I don't even recollect iffen I put out the fire on the stove.

And that was how I come to be with the regiment, tramping through blood and mud and shitting my bowels away with the flux each day; and that was how I come to be sleeping next to old Joseph, the hoodoo doctor, who become another father to me.

I did not confess to old Joseph or even to myself that I had done my father in. Mayhap he was still alive. I tried not to think on him. My old life was dead. Surely I could not go back to the Jackson place, nor the army, nor any other place from which I run. There was just me and the old nigger now, scavengers, carrion birds, eaters of the dead.

Yes, and sure it was human flesh old Joseph fed me that night, and again that morning. He showed me the manner of taking it, for there was certain corpses that cried out to be let be, whilst others craved to be consumed. We followed the army a safe distance, and when they moved on we took possession of the slain. He could always sniff out where a battle was going to be. He never carried nothing with him excepting a human skull, painted black, that was full of herbs—the same herbs that he always smelled of.

Oh, it was God's country we done passed through—hills, forests, meadows, creeks—and all this beauty marred by the handiwork of men. Old Joseph showed me not to drink from the bloodied streams but to lick the dew from flower petals and cupped leaves of a morning. As his trust of me grew, he became more bold. We went into encampments and sat amongst the soldiers, and they never seen us, not once.

"We is invisible," old Joseph told me.

And then it struck me, for we stood in broad daylight beside a willow tree, and on the other side of the brook was mayhap fifty tents and behind them a dense wood. The air was moist and thick. I could see members of my old company, with their skull faces too small for their gray coats, barely able to lift their bayonets off the ground, and they was sitting there huddled together waiting for gruel, but there I was, nourished by the dead, my flesh starting to fill out and the redness back in my cheeks. It struck me that they couldn't see me even though I was a-jumping up and down on the other side of the stream, and I said to old Joseph, "I don't think we are invisible. I think . . . oh, old Joseph, I think we have been dead ever since the day we met."

Old Joseph laughed—it were a dry laugh, like the wind stirring the leaves in autumn—and he said, "You ain't dead yet, honey; feel the flesh on them bones. No, your *beau-père* he nurturing you back to life."

"Then why don't they see us? Even when we walk amongst them?"

"Because I has cast a cloak of darkness about us. We be wearing the face of a dark god over our own."

"I don't trust God. Whenever my pa seen God, he hurt me."

Smiling, he said, "You daddy warn't a true preacher, honey; he just a *boungan macoute,* a man which *use* the name of God to adorn hisself."

And taking my hand, he led me acrosst that branch and we was right amongst the soldiers, and still they did not see me. We helped ourselves to hardtack and coffee right out of the kettle. In the distance I heard the screams of a man whose leg they was fixing to hack off. Around us men lay moaning. There is a sick-sweet body smell that starving men give off when they are burning up their last shreds of flesh to fuel their final days. That's how I knew they was near death. They was shivering with cold, even though it were broad daylight. Lord, many of them was just children, and some still younger than myself. I knew that the war was lost, or soon would be. I had no country, and no father save for a darkie witch doctor from Haiti.

There come a bugle call and a few men looked up, though most of them just goes on laying in their misery. Old Joseph and I saw soldiers come into the camp. They had a passel of niggers with them, niggers in blue uniforms, all chained up in a long row behind a wagon that was piled high with confiscated arms. They was as starved and miserable as our own men. They stared ahead as they trudged out of the wood and into the clearing. There was one or two white men with them two: officers, I reckoned.

A pause, and the bugle sounded again. Then a captain come out of a tent and addressed the captives. He said in a lugubrious voice, as though he were weary of making this announcement: "According to the orders given me by the congress of the Confederate States of America, all Negroes apprehended while in the uniform of the North are not to be considered prisoners of war, but shall be returned instantly to a condition of slavery or shot. Any white officer arrested while in command of such Negroes shall be considered to be inciting rebellion and also shot." He turned and went back into his tent, and the convoy moved onward, past the camp, upstream, toward another part of the woods.

"*Oba kosó!*" the old man whispered. "They gone kill them."

"Let's go away," I said.

"No," said old Joseph, "I feels the wind of the gods blowing down upon me. I feels the breath of the loa. I is standing on the coils of Koulèv, the earth-serpent. Oh, no, Marse Jimmy Lee, I don't be going nowhere, but you free to come and go as you pleases of course, being white."

"You know that ain't so," I said. "I'm less free than you. And I know if I leave you I will leave the shelter of your invisibility spell." I gazed right into the eyes of the prisoners, and tasted their rancid breath, and smelled the pus of their wounds, and seen no sign of recognition. There was something to his magic, though I was sure it come of the dark places, and not of God.

So I followed him alongside the creek as the captives were led into the wood, followed them uphill aways until we reached the edge of a shallow gully, and there was already niggers there, digging to make it deeper, and I seen what was going to happen and I didn't want to look, because this warn't a battle, this were butchery pure and simple.

Our soldiers didn't mock the prisoners and didn't call them no names. They were too tired and too hungry. The blacks and the whites, they didn't show no passion in their faces. They just wanted it to end. Our men done lined the niggers and their officers up all along the edge of the ditch and searched through their pockets for any coins or crumbs, and they turned them so they faced the gully and they done shot them in the back, one by one, until the pit was filled. Then the Southerners turned and filed back to the camp. Oh, God! As the first shots rung out, it put me in mind of my mother Mary, halfway across the bridge, with her old life behind her and her new life ahead of her, dead on her face, and the bloodstain spreading from her back onto the lace and calico.

And old Joseph said, "Honey, I seen what I must do. And it a dark journey that I must take, and maybe you don't be strong enough to come with me. But I hates to journey alone. Old Joseph afraid too, betimes, spite of his 'leventy-leven years upon this earth. I calls the powers to witness, *ni ayé àti ni òrun.*"

"What does that mean, old Joseph?"

"In heaven as it is in earth."

I saw the way his eye glowed and I was powerful afraid. He had become more than a shrunken old man. Seemed like he drew the sun's light into his face and shone brighter than the summer sky. He set his cauldron-skull down on the ground and said, again and again, *"Koulèv, Koulèv-O! Damballah Wedo, Papa! Koulèv, Koulèv-O! Damballah Wedo, Papa!"*

And then he says, in a raspy voice, "Watch out, Marse Jimmy Lee, the god gone come down and mount my body now . . . stand clear less you wants to be swept away by the breath of the serpent!" And he mutters to hisself, "Oh, *dieux puissants,* why you axing me to make biggest magic, me a old magician without no *poudre* and no herbs? Oh, take this cup from me, take, take this bitter poison from he lips, for old Joseph he don't study life and death no more."

And his old body started to shake, and he ripped off his patch and threw it onto the mud, and I looked into the empty eye socket and saw an inner eye, blood-red and shiny as a ruby. And he sank down on his knees in front of the pit of dead men and he went on a-mumbling and a-rocking, back and forth, back and forth, and seemed like he was a-speaking in tongues. And his good eye rolled right up into its socket.

"Why, old Joseph," I says to him, "what are you fixing to do?"

But he paid me no mind. He just went on a-shimmying and a-shaking, and presently he rose up from where he was and started to dance a curious hopping sort of dance, and with every hop he cried, *"Shangó! Shangó!"* in a voice that was steadily losing its human qualities. And soon his voice was rolling like thunder, and presently it *was* the thunder, for the sky was lowering and lightning was lancing the cloud peaks.

Oh, the sky became dark. The cauldron seethed and glowed, though he hadn't even touched it. I knew he were sure possessed. The dark angels he done told me of, they was speaking to him out of the mouth of hell.

I reckoned I was not long for this world, for the old man was a-hollering at the top of his lungs and we warn't far from the encampment, but no one came looking for us. Mayhap they was huddled in their tents hiding from the thunder. Presently it began to rain; it pelted us and soaked us, that rain. It were a hot rain, scalding to my skin. And when the lightning flashed, I looked into the pit and I thought I saw something moving. Mayhap it were just the rushing waters, throwing the corpses one against t'other. I crept closer to the edge of the gully. I didn't heed old Joseph's warning. I peered over the edge, and in the next flash of lightning I saw them a-writhing and a-shaking their arms and legs, and their necks a-craning this way and that, and I thought to myself, old Joseph he is raising the dead.

Old Joseph just went on screaming out those African words and leaping up and waving his arms. The rain battered my body and I was near fainting from it, for the water flooded my nostrils and drenched my lungs, and when I gasped for air I swallowed more and more water. I don't know how the old man kept on dancing; in the lightning flashes I saw him, dark and lithe, and the sluicing rain made him glisten and made his chest and arms to look like the scales of a great black serpent. I looked on him and breathed in the burning water, and the pit of dead niggers quooked as iffen the very earth were opening up, and there come a blue light from the mass grave, so blinding that I could see no more; and so, at last, I passed out from the terror of it.

*   *   *

When I done opened my eyes, the rain was just a memory: the sun was rising; the forest was silent and shrouded in mist. And I thought to myself, I have been dreaming, and I am still beside the creek where the dead bodies lay, and I never did see no old Joseph out of my past; but then I saw him frying up a bit of salt pork he done salvaged from the camp. Warn't no morning bugle calls, and I reckon the company done up and gone in the middle of the night, soon as the storm subsided.

Old Joseph, the patch over his eye again, was singing to hisself, that song I heard as a child. And when he saw me stir, he said, "Marse Jimmy Lee, you awake now."

"What is that song?" I asked him.

"It called 'Au Claire de la Lune,' honey: 'by the light of the moon.' "

I sat up. "Joseph?"

"What, Marse Jimmy Lee?"

"Last night I had the strangest dream . . . more like a vision. I dreamed you were possessed, and you pranced about and waved your arms and sang songs in a African language, and you raised up nigger soldiers from the grave."

"Life is a dream, honey," he says, "we calls them *les zombis*. It from a Kikongo word, 'nzambi,' that mean a dead man that walk the earth."

The fog began to clear a little and I saw their feet. Black feet, still shackled, still covered with chafing sores. We was surrounded by them. And as the sunlight began to dissipate the mist, I could see their faces; it was them which had been kilt and buried in the pit—I knew some of their faces. For though they stirred, they moved, they looked about them, there were no fire in their eyes, and didn't have no breath in their nostrils. Mayhap they wasn't dead, but they wasn't alive, neither.

They stood there, looming over us. Each one with a wound clean through him. Each one smelling of old Joseph's herbs.

"The magic still in me," old Joseph said, "even without the *coup poudre*."

I reckon I have never been more scared than I was then. My skin was crawling and my blood was racing.

"I never thought that old magic still in me," said Joseph again. There was wonderment in his voice. No fear. The dead men surrounded us, waiting; seemed like they had no mind of their own.

"Oh, Joseph, what are we going to do?"

"Don't know, white child. I's still in the dark. The vision don't come as clear to me no more; old Joseph he old, he old."

He fed me and gave me genuine coffee to drink, for the slain Yankees had carried some with them. I rose and went over to the pit, and it were sure enough empty save for the two white officers. "Why didn't you raise them too?" I said.

"Warn't no sense in it, Marse Jimmy Lee. For white folks there is a heaven and a hell; there ain't no middle ground. Best to forget them."

So we threw dirt over them and we marched on, and the column of undead darkies followed us. I could not name the places that we passed, but old Joseph knew where he was going. It was toward the rising sun, so I guessed it was southeast.

At nightfall we rested. We found a farmhouse. There warn't no people and the animals was all took away, but I found a ham a-hanging in the larder, and I feasted. In the night I slept in a real bed. Old Joseph sat out on the porch. The *zombis* did not sleep. They stood in a ring outside the house and swayed softly to the sound of Joseph's singing. As I looked out of the smashed window I could see them in the moonlight; there was still no fire in their eyes, and I recollected that they hadn't partaken of no victuals. What was it like to be a *zombi*? Iffen that the eyes are the windows of the soul, then surely there warn't no souls inside those fleshy shells.

We found plenty of gold in the abandoned house; they done hid it in a well, which was surrounded by dead Yankees. I reckon they done poisoned it so that the Northerners wouldn't be able to drink their water. But poison means naught to the dead.

And we walked on, and the passel of walking dead became a company, for wherever we went we found niggers that had been kilt, not just the ones in Yankee uniform but sometimes a woman lying dead in a ditch, or a young buck chained to a tree that was just abandoned and let starve to death when his masters fled from the enemy, and one time we found seven high-yaller children dead in a cage, with gunshot wounds to their heads; for they was frenzied times, and men were driven to acts not thought upon in times of peace. It was amongst the dead children that I found another cornstalk *poupée* like the one old Joseph gave me ten years before, a-sitting in a vial in the clenched fist of a dead little girl. After we done wakened them, she held it out to me, and I thought there were a glimmer in her eye, but mayhap it were only my imagination.

"Get up and walk," old Joseph said. And they walked.

And I said over and over to him, "Old Joseph, where are we going?"

And he said, "Towards freedom."

"But freedom is in the north, ain't it?"

"Freedom in the heart, honey."

We marched. For many days we didn't see no white folks at all. We saw burned hulks of farms and stray dogs hunting in packs. We passed other great battlefields, and them that was worth reviving, that still had enough flesh on them to be able to march, old Joseph raised up. He was growing in power. It got so he would just wave his hands and say one or two words, and the dead man would climb right out of the ground. And I took to repeating the words to myself, soundlessly at first, just moving my lips; then softly, then—for when he were a-concentrating on his magic, he couldn't see nothing of the world—I would shout out those words along with him, I would wrap my tongue around them twisted and barbarian sounds, and I would tell myself, 'twas I which raised them, I which reached into the abyss and drawed them out.

Still we encountered no sign of human life. The summer sun streamed down on us by day, and seemed like I sweat blood. It warn't at all certain to me that we was still alive and on this earth, for the land was a wasteland, spite of the verdant meadows and the mountains blanketed with purple flowers, spite of the rich-smelling earth and the warm rain. Sometimes I think that the country we was wandering in was an illusion, a false Eden. Or that we was somehow half-in, half-out of the world.

Though I didn't know where the road was leading, yet I was

happy. I trusted old Joseph, and I didn't have no one else left in the world. The only times I become sad was thinking on my pa and momma's death, and wondering iffen my pa was with God now, for he said he done seen the face of God before I smashed his head. Sometimes I dreamed about coming home to see him well again. But they was only dreams. I knew that I had kilt him.

On the seventh day, we come onc't more into the sight of living men.

The road become wider and we was coming into the vicinity of a town. I knew this was a port, maybe Charleston. There warn't no signs to tell us, but Pa and I had been booted out of Charleston once; I remembered the way the wind smelt, wet and tangy. A few miles outside town, our road joined up with a wider road that come in a straight line from due north. On the other road, straggling down to meet us, we saw a company of graycoats.

Not many of them, maybe three dozen. They warn't exactly marching. Some was leaning on each other, some hobbling, and one, a slip of a boy, tapped on the side of a skinless drum. Their clothes was in tatters and most of them didn't have no rifles. They was just old men and boys, for the able-bodied had long since fallen.

They seen us, and one of them cried out, "Nigger soldiers!" They fell into a pathetic semblance of a formation, and them which had rifles aimed them, and them which had crutches brandished them at us.

I shouted out, "Let us pass . . . we don't have no quarrel with you." For they were wretched creatures, these remnants of the Southern army, and I was sure that the war was already lost, and they was coming back to what was left of their homes.

But one boy, mayhap their leader, screamed at me, "Nigger lover! Traitor!" I looked in his eyes and saw we were just alike, poor trash fighting a rich man's war, him and me; and I pitied the deluded soul. Because I knew now that there warn't no justice in this war, and that neither side had foughten for God, but only for hisself.

"It's no use!" I shouted at the boy who was so like myself. "These darkies ain't even alive; they're shadows marching to the sea; they ain't got souls to kill."

And old Joseph said, "March on, my children."

They commenced to fire on us.

This was the terriblest thing which I did witness on that journey. For the nigger soldiers marched and marched, and not a bullet could stop them. The miniés flew and the white boys shrieked out a ghostly echo of a rebel yell, and *les zombis* kept right on coming and coming, and me and old Joseph with them, untouched by the bullets, for his magic still shielded our mortal flesh. The niggers marched. Their faces was ripped asunder and still they marched. Their brains came oozing from their skulls, their guts came writhing from their bellies, and still they marched. They marched until they were too close for bullets. Then the white boys flung themselves at us, and they was ripped to pieces. They was tore limb from limb by dead men which stared with glazed and vacant eyes. It took but a few minutes, this final skirmish of the war. Their yells died in their throats. The *zombis* broke their necks and flung them to the ground. Their strength warn't a human kind of strength. They'd shove their hands into an old man's belly and snap his spine and pull out the intestines like a coil of rope. They'd take a rifle and break the barrel in two.

There was no anger in what the *zombis* done. And they didn't make no noise whilst they was killing. They done it the way you might darn a sock or feed the chickens; it were just something which had to be done.

And we marched onward, leaving the bodies to rot; it was getting on toward sunset now.

Oh, I was angry. The boys we kilt warn't no strangers from the North; they could have been my brothers. Oh, I screamed in rage at old Joseph. I didn't trust him no more; the happiness had left me.

"Did you hear what he called me?" I shouted. "A traitor to my people. A nigger lover. And it's God's plain truth. If you wanted freedom, why didn't you go north into the arms of the Yankees? You spoke to me of a big magic, and of the coils of the serpent Koulèv, and the wind of the gods, and the voices of darker angels . . . to what end? It were Satan's magic, magic to give the dead an illusion of life, so you could kill more of my people!"

"Be still," he said to me, as the church spires of the port town rose up in the distance. "Your war don't be my war. You think the Yankees got theyselfs kilt to set old Joseph free? You think the 'mancipation proclamation was wrote to give the nigger back he soul? I say to you, white child, that a piece of paper don't make men free. The black man in this land he ain't gone be free tomorrow nor in a hundred years nor in a thousand. I didn't bring men back from the outer darkness so they could shine you shoes and wipe you butts. The army I lead, he kingdom don't be of this earth."

"You are mad, old Joseph," I said, and I wept, for he was no longer a father to me.

We marched into the town. Children peered from behind empty beer kegs with solemn eyes. Horses reared up and whin-nied. Women stared sullenly at us. The Yankees had already took the town; half the houses was smoldering, and we didn't see no grown men. The stars and stripes flew over the ruint courthouse. I reckon folks thought we was just another company of the conquering army.

We reached the harbor. There was one or two sailing ships docked there: rickety ships with tattered sails. The army of dead men stood at attention and old Joseph said to me: "Now I under-stands why you come with me so far. There a higher purpose to everything, *ni ayé àti ni òrun.*"

I didn't want to stay with him anymore. When I seen the way *les zombis* plowed down my countrymen, I had been moved to a powerful rage, and the rage would not die away. "What higher purpose?" I said. And the salt wind chafed my lips.

"You think," said old Joseph, "that old Joseph done tricked you, he done magicked you with mirrors and smoke; but I never told you we was fighting on the same side. But we come far together, and I wants you to do me one last favor afore we parts for all eternity."

"And what sort of favor would that be, old sorcerer? I thought you could do anything."

"Anything. But not this thing. You see, old Joseph a nigger. Nigger he can't go into no portside bar to offer gold for to buy him a ship."

"You want a ship now? Where are you fixing to go? Back to Haiti, where the white man rules no more?"

Old Joseph said, "Mayhap it a kind of Haiti where we go." He laughed. "Haiti, yes, Haiti! And I gone see my dear *mamman,* though she be cold in her grave sixty year past. Or mayhap it mother Africa herself we go to. *Oba kosó!"*

And I remembered that he had told me: *My kingdom is not of this earth.* He had used the words of our savior and our Lord. Oh, the ocean wind were warm, and it howled, and the torn sails clattered against the masts. The air fair dripped with moisture. And the niggers stood like statues, all-unseeing.

"I'll do as you ask," I said, and I took the sack of gold we had gathered from the poisoned well, and I walked along the harbor until I found a bar and ship's captain for hire, which was not hard, for the embargo had starved their business. And presently I come back and told old Joseph everything was ready. And the niggers lined up, ready to embark. Night was falling.

But as they prepared themselves to board that ship, I could hold my tongue no more. "Old Joseph," I said, "your kingdom is founded on a lie. You have waked these bodies from the earth, but where are their souls? You may dream of leading these creatures to a mystic land acrosst the sea, and you may dream of freeing them forever from the bonds of servitude, but how can you free what can't be freed? How can you free a rock, a tree, a piece of earth? Dust they were and dust they ever shall be, world without end."

And the *zombi* warriors stood, unmoving and unblinking, and not a breath passed their lips, though that the wind was rising and whipping at our faces.

And old Joseph looked at me long and hard, and I knew that I had said the thing that must be said. He whispered, "Out of the mouths of babes and sucklings hast thou ordained strength, O Lord." He fell down on his knees before me and said, "And all this time I thought that *I* the wise one and you the student! Oh, Marse Jimmy Lee, you done spoke right. There be no life in *les zombis* because I daresn't pay the final price. But now I's *gone* make that sacrifice. Onc't I done gave my eye in exchange for knowledge. But there be *two* trees in Eden, Marse Jimmy Lee; there be the tree of knowledge, and there be the tree of life."

So saying he covered his face with his hands. He plunged his thumb into the socket of his good eye and he plucked it out, screaming to almighty God with the pain of it. His agony was real. His shrieking curdled my blood. It brought back my pa's chastisements and my momma's dying and the tramping of my bare feet on sharp stones and the sight of all my comrades, pierced through by bayonets, cloven by cannon, their limbs ripped off, their bellies torn asunder, their lives gushing hot and young and crimson into the stream. Oh, but I craved to carry his pain, but he were the one that were chosen to bear it, and I was the one which brung him to the understanding of it.

And now his eye were in his hand, a round, white, glistening pearl, and he cries out in a thunderous voice, "If thine eye offend thee, pluck it out!" and he takes blind aim and hurls the eye with all his might into the mighty sea.

I clenched the *poupée* in my hand.

Then came lightning, for old Joseph had summoned the power of the serpent Koulèv, whose coils were entwined about the earth. Then did he unleash the rain. Then did he turn to me, with the gore gushing from the yawning socket, and cry to me, a good-for-nothing white trash boy which kilt his own father and stole from the dead, "Thou hast redeemed me."

Then, and only then, did I see the *zombis* smile. Then, as the rain softened, as the sky did glow with a cold blue light that didn't come from no sun nor moon, then did I hear the laughter of the dead, and the fire of life begin to flicker in their eyes. But they was already trooping up the gangplank, and presently there was only the old man, purblind now and like to die, I thought.

"Farewell," he says to me.

And I said, "No, old Joseph. You are blind now. You need a

boy to hold your hand and guide you, to be your eyes against the wild blue sea."

"Not blind," he said. "I *chooses* not to see. I gone evermore be looking inward, at the glory and the majesty of eternal light."

"But what have I? Where can I go, excepting that I go with you?"

"Honey, you has lived but fourteen of your threescore and ten. It don't be written that you's to follow a old man acrosst the sea to a land that maybe don't even *be* a land save in that old man's dream. Go now. But first you gone kiss your *beau-père* goodbye, for I loves you."

My tears were brine and his were blood. As I kissed his cheek, the salt did run together with the crimson. I saw him no more; I did not see the ship sail from the port, for my eyes was blinded with weeping.

So I walked and walked until I come back to the Jackson place. The mansion were a cinder, and even the fields was all burnt up, and the animals was dead. The place was looted good and thorough; warn't one thing of value in the vicinity, not a gold piece nor a silver spoon nor even the rugs that the Jacksons done bought from a French merchant.

I walked up the low knoll to where the nigger graveyard was and where our shack onc't stood. The wooden markers was all charred, and here and there was a shred of homespun clinging to them. I thought to myself, mayhap the Yankees come down to the Jackson place not an hour after I done run away, whilst the slaves was still a-singing their spirituals. That cloth was surely torn off some of the slave women, for the Yankees loved to have their way with darkies. And I thought, mayhap my pa is still laying inside that shack, in the inner room, beside the locket with Mamma's picture, with his hickory in his fist, with his britches down about his ankles.

And so it was I found him.

He warn't rank no more. It had been many months since I run off. Warn't much left of his face that the worms hadn't ate. At his naked loins, the bone poked through the papery hide, and there was a swarm of ants. It was a miracle there was this much left of him, for there was wild dogs roaming the fields.

I set down the *poupée* on the chair and got to wondering what I should do. What I wanted most in life were a new beginning. I spoke to that doll, for I knew that old Joseph's spirit was in it somehow, and I said, "I don't know where you come from, and I don't know where you are. But oh, give me the strength to begin onc't more. Oh, carry me back from the land of the dead."

Without thinking, I started to murmur the words of power, the African words I done mimicked when I watched him raise the dead. I knelt down beside the corpse of my pa and waited for the breath of the serpent. I whispered them words over and over until my mind emptied itself and was filled with the souls of darker angels.

I reckon I knelt all night long, or mayhap many nights. But when I opened my eyes again, there was flesh on my father's bones, and he was beginning to rouse himself; and his eyes had the fire of life, for that old Joseph had sacrificed his second eye.

"You sure have growed, son," he says softly. "You ain't a sapling no more; you're a mighty tree."

"Yes, Pa," says I.

"Oh, son, you have carried me back from a terrible dream. In that dream I abandoned you, and I practiced all manner of cruelty upon you, and a dark angel came to you and became your new pa; and you followed him to the edge of the river that divides the quick from the dead."

"Yes, Pa. But I stopped at the riverbank and watched him sail away. And I come back to you."

"Oh, Jimmy Lee, my son, I have seen hell. I have been down into the fire of damnation, and I've felt the loneliness of perdition. And the cruelest torture was being cut off from you, my flesh and blood. Oh, sweet Jesus, Jimmy Lee, it were only that you made me think on her so much—she which I killed, she which I never loved more even as I sent the bullet flying into her back."

And this was strange, for in the old days my pa had only spoke of heaven, and of seeing the face of God, and when he done seen God he would wear me out, calling on His holy name to witness his infamy and my sacrifice. But now he had seen hell and he was full of gentleness.

And then he said to me, "My son, I craves your forgiveness."

"Ain't nothing to forgive."

"Then give me your love," says he, "for you are tall and strong, and I have become old. And it is now for you to be the father, and I the child."

It were time to cross the bridge. It were time to heal the hurting.

"My love you have always had, Pa."

So saying, I embraced him; and thus it was our war came to an end.

Roll Call

Jerry Ahern and Sharon Ahern

No accounting of the worldwide sale of Ahern novels can be accurate, but it is fair to say that with eighty published books and translations into most of the world's major languages, the combined sales exceed ten million copies. That's a lot of books.

The direct descendants of such hero pulps as *Doc Savage* and *The Shadow*, their novels have continued the best traditions of action-oriented storytelling, with frequently outrageous situations and bizarre scientific extrapolation dashed together at a frenetic pace. The most popular Ahern series, *The Survivalist*, is now approaching thirty titles, but it is in their non-series efforts such as *The Takers* that you'll find their strongest writing. Among their writing awards, they've been honored by the Second Amendment Foundation for their novel *The Freeman*, an effective parable against the dangers of the erosion of the liberties guaranteed in the United States Bill of Rights.

They are Chicago natives who left the urban congestion for the pastoral countryside of Commerce, Georgia. Their steamboat gothic house stays in a constant state of renovation. What I remember most about my visit there is Jerry's revolver with the laser bullets—an absolutely essential technological improvement if you want to set up a couch-to-television shooting range in your living room.

Jerry has a great deadpan sense of humor. When I offered to have a convention staff member stay with their school-age children while the Aherns took a friend to dinner, Jerry told me it wouldn't be necessary. "Samantha can talk her way out of most situations, and if she can't, Jason knows which suitcase has the guns."

Later, when I told that story at another convention, Sharon expressed concern people would think she and Jerry have an inordinate obsession with guns. "Yeah. That'd be wrong," interrupted Jerry. "We like knives, too."

Rain filled his mouth, and he tilted his head back slightly so the natural gutters formed by the brim of his hat would flush the water back. The rubber lining of his canvas poncho was worn, mostly over the shoulders, and his uniform tunic was dampening there more and more as the rain drove down still harder. There were sheets of the rain, black as ink except for the gold shadows where a sheltered lamp made its reflection; the rain so solid a wall that the icy cold water held the light, forcing it back.

The three lamps that still functioned were shielded behind shelter halves so that their meager light could only be seen from the river, if at all, but not from the road. On the other side of the river, across a bridge that gave him shivers when he looked at it, there was still freedom, yet for how much longer he was afraid to guess. The bridge was well downstream from where he stood. And here, on this side of the usually quiet, meandering little river which almost but not quite marked the border between Georgia and Tennessee (it was just south and east of the actual line, according to the maps), Union troops were the only ones who were free—free to loot and ransack and only God knew what else.

Preston Hollings had lived North, gone to school there. And he knew that some of the things folks said about the Yankees were lies—lies born out of fear and dread. But he knew soldiers, too, and these men whom the 10th Georgia Militia had fought throughout the day and long and hard into the night were hardened campaigners, men whom blood and death had numbed to their own humanity.

There was no sniper fire, and the rain's heaviness was a blessing that way. Even one of the .45 caliber Whitworth rifles, which some Southern boys claimed could reach out accurately to better than a thousand yards, would have been hard pressed to find its mark tonight with the visibility so bad and the walls of water in between so unremitting.

"Lieutenant Hollings?"

Hollings had been watching the bridge for quite some time, walked downriver along the bank to where it was impossible to continue because the bank was flooded over. He walked upriver, then, the quarter mile or so toward the camp. But there was nowhere to cross but the bridge, no answer but the bridge. When he heard his name called, he turned around too quickly, and water poured down from his hat for his trouble, bathing his face and running down under the neck of his poncho and soaking the front of the linsey-woolsey shirt he wore beneath his tunic. The face under the beak of the kepi belonged to Platoon Sergeant Rawlins: a good face, broad and generous, character lines etched into it by hardship and anguish. Tonight, like all the faces, when faces could be seen at all in some stray shaft of lamplight, Rawlins' face was a mask of exhaustion and despair.

But there was none of that in his voice. "Captain Sterett requests that y'all join 'im in his tent, Lieutenant."

Rawlins saluted and Hollings returned it, Rawlins slogging off through the clay and mud and into the night, evidently on some other errand or another for the captain.

Hollings took one more look downstream toward the bridge, then tucked the muzzle of his rifle more closely against his side beneath the poncho. The rifle was a Zuave carbine he'd picked up on the battlefield today, his own privately purchased Henry repeater lost along with all the rest of his gear, even the letter from Molly, when his horse was shot out from under him early in the afternoon.

Hollings' right knee was still a little stiff, but there was nothing broken, no permanent damage. He'd gotten far enough along in school to know that at least.

The ground, so saturated with rain that every depression was a pool, sucked at his feet as he left the bridge and started across their encampment. He couldn't even see the pickets, but told himself they were still out there. And he could no longer see the road.

The road.

It wasn't much of a road, not much of a road at all. It was wide enough for a carriage, of the kind in which a beautifully dressed lady might ride or the kind which drew an artillery piece.

There were no ladies tonight and the 10th's one piece of Yankee ordnance got mired in the mud and was abandoned, but not before Rawlins and he had packed the muzzle hard and lit a long fuse, ringing the piece and blowing it off the mounts.

The road, cut off by some of Sherman's men, about a hundred or so infantry and two score of cavalry, was the only way out.

Hollings stepped the wrong way, his right boot heel slipping and he went down, into a puddle deep as a shell hole, pushing his rifle clear of it so rapidly he almost threw his right arm out of the shoulder socket.

He scrambled up and out, onto his knees, the lower half of his body soaked through. Hollings patted at the holster for his belt pistol, grateful once again for the Smith & Wesson's waterproof metallic cartridges, and to the dead Yankee officer who'd supplied the revolver. As he stood up, the knee he'd twisted when his horse was put down from under him gave him a twinge of pain. But, by using the butt of the Zuave and grasping the muzzle end like a cane, he was able to stand. The gun's action was doused beyond redemption now and would have to be emptied and cleaned before firing.

He resumed, boots awash with muddy water, his already wet stockings wetter, walking toward Captain Sterett's tent.

When the rain let up, or when dawn came, whichever occurred first, the Union Cavalry would cut through their camp, and the Union Infantry would be right on their horses' heels.

Eight horses remained in the camp tonight, the ninth—the beast stepped in one of the water-filled holes and broke off its hind leg clean through to where the bone protruded—butchered so the men would have something to eat.

The cook fire, nearly out now, was just visible as glowing red embers, some of the men huddled around it for its meager warmth against the unseasonably chilly night. The fire had been built on a broad flat rock which rose several feet above the banks of the river, but well below where the ground dropped off and, hence, safe enough against attracting enemy fire.

In the reddish glow, Hollings could see the water, risen well over two feet from earlier, churning fierce and fast and white along the bank.

At midstream, the water would be moving so fast, no horse or man could swim it.

And the bridge, the bridge he'd been watching for an hour at least, would not hold against it much longer.

The bridge was a trestle, not very high, but not very sturdy either, its wooden braces creaking audibly, like old men's voices in the night. Sometimes, like old men, too, it shook. . . .

The nurse's face was prettier than he'd remembered it being. "Mr. Hollings?"

If he said something to her, maybe he could close his eyes again, maybe she would go away. "Ma'am?"

"Mr. Hollings. The lady from the Daughters of the Confederacy is here. She said you promised to talk to her today, when she came last week."

He closed his eyes, hoping the nurse would think he'd drifted off again. But, in his mind's eye, he saw the very earnest face of the pretty young woman from the Daughters of the Confederacy. Research, she said. She was doing research on the 10th Georgia Militia and he was the only man surviving.

He knew that right enough.

And it was this young woman—Mrs. Mary Elizabeth Hubbard—who started him thinking about things again after all these years. After meeting up with that Illinois corporal who was in Crook's outfit there past the North Platte along Rosebud Creek and talking with him about that night back in '64, Preston Hollings vowed never to think about that night again.

Hollings could see the wrinkled-up, freckled face even now when he closed his eyes really tight, and after a while he could hear the terrifyingly punctuated night stillness. The red-skinned men who killed George Custer were still out there, and even the wild things were afraid to speak when the Sioux called back and forth like wolves and prairie dogs.

It was the Fourth of July, and the country was one hundred years old and there were lots of men wearing blue who used to wear gray. You say strange things on guard duty, get close to a man in the darkness whom in daylight you wouldn't get close to at all, let someone inside you because it's even darker in there than the night that surrounds you. . . .

"Officer, wasn't ya?"

Hollings looked down at his sleeve, and even though he couldn't see the two stripes, he could feel them without touching them. "Wasn't much to do at home, Jim. Either join up to fight Indians or sit on the porch rockin' until some Yankee banker comes along with the sheriff and some blue bellies backin' them all up to tell a man he doesn't own the porch anymore, or the rockin' chair for that matter." Jim Bodkin had just been shipped west after four years in the East, just missed being assigned to the 7th and maybe being one of the 215 men Crazy Horse massacred at Little Big Horn.

"Crazy thing, ain't it, you an' me?"

"What?"

"I mean, reckon after all the men got theyselves killt back there that night in Tennessee—"

"It was Georgia, Jim."

Bodkin grunted something, spat some juice from his chaw and readjusted the way he hugged his rifle, then leaned back against the wagon.

They had drawn guard duty together three times now, and the first night out, a night like this, the air so still it clung to you like a shroud, they'd realized they fought together in the same battle, but on different sides, twelve years before.

Hollings hadn't asked, but each time he ended a tour with Bodkin, he had promised himself to draw up the courage and bring it up. Tonight, it just happened. "When y'all's unit got hit by our boys, what happened?"

"What happened? Hell! Ya Johnny Rebs took us all by surprise, ya did. Ya jes' kept up a comin' no matterwise how damn many we'd a shoot, they was always more o' ya, they was. Never seen no soldiers in my life was braver, an' I'll be givin' ya that."

So, it had happened . . .

"Mr. Hollings?"

Different voice, but a woman.

Blurry a little, then after a blink or two not that blurry at all. Pretty face. Dry throat. "Ma'am." He realized suddenly that his chest was showing and, after all, she was a gentle lady. "Forgive me, ma'am."

"Oh, Mr. Hollings, maybe I should come back another day, sir. Y'all seem tired."

He tried to sit up, succeeded in raising one shoulder. "It's a genuine pleasure, ma'am. Y'all and y'all's ladies do fine work, keepin' memories alive, ma'am."

"It's men like you, Mr. Hollings, who make our labors a pleasure, sir."

"Y'all's too kind, Miz Hubbard, ma'am."

"It was First Lieutenant Hollings, wasn't it, sir, of the 10th Georgia Militia? I sometimes wonder if all the gallant men of the South came together for one moment of history." She had a lovely smile, lovelier when she talked, because her eyes were so bright and full of wonder and interest, like a child's eyes. "It was called the Battle of Bugle Ford, what I wanna ask y'all some things about, Mr. Hollings."

He felt himself starting to laugh, remembering suddenly that he hadn't laughed for a long time and it was a good feeling, despite the pain in his left arm that started like a toothache and radiated upward. He held his arm but said nothing about the pain.

"Why, y'all's laughin' at me!" And her smile broadened and she pushed a lock of hair away from her forehead with the back of her hand, just the way Molly always had, her forehead glistening slightly.

It had been a warm summer; he'd heard some of the new boys complaining about it sometimes when they wheeled him into the recreation hall. And then he thought about the gas they were using in Europe, and he felt like crying, instead.

"Mr. Hollings?"

"How's that young soldier?"

"Young soldier?" There was genuine bemusement in her eyes, and then suddenly her eyes went a little hard and she looked away.

He remembered now. The boy with the burned-out lungs died,

a week ago, a day ago, an hour ago, but dead regardless. "I fought with ol' Teddy, y'all know, down Cuba way. Was a sergeant major. That's where I lost my leg, ma'am." And Preston Hollings felt sudden embarrassment, because he'd made a direct reference to a portion of his anatomy in front of a lady. He charted it off to old age. He was born in 1840 and here it was, 1917—or was it 1918? He could have asked Mrs. Hubbard, of course, and she would have told him. But Hollings didn't bother.

"Did y'all always wanna be a soldier, Mr. Hollings?"

"No, ma'am. I wanted to be a doctor, and my family sent me north to study, in 1859 it was. But then . . ."

There was always the talk about slavery in the smoky hours near twilight, and he never defended it because he never believed that a man was anything less than a man because his skin was dark, or anything more than any other man because he said he was an Abolitionist. After a while, he'd walk the commons by himself rather than sit on porches with empty-headed boys who knew nothing about what lay in store for them. Somehow—and he didn't know why—he had always known.

Then word of Lincoln's election came, and of South Carolina leaving the Union, and he went to Professor Masterson and told him, "I am afraid, sir, that responsibility to my house must come before the pursuance of a medical career."

"I would expect no less of you, Mr. Hollings. But you would make a fine surgeon, the speed with which you can act, the deftness of your touch. I see that in few young men, Mr. Hollings. It is a gift. Do not throw it away."

He promised Doctor Masterson he would not throw it away. . . .

Jim Bodkin was pumping blood all around the arrow shaft, bloody pink drool dribbling down from the left corner of his mouth and oozing through the wide gaps between the dozen or so brown teeth in the lower half of his jaw. Hollings' useless single shot rifle was jammed and his Colt revolver was empty. As he knelt beside Bodkin, he took the old Smith & Wesson Model 2 Army from under his blouse, stabbing it toward the Indian who'd shot Jim Bodkin through, pulling the trigger, cocking the hammer, pulling the trigger again.

The Sioux warrior, rawhide thongs wound through his braids, iron jaw set hard over the bear claw necklace round a neck with stretched taut tendons, face painted, skin gleaming sweat over muscles that Michelangelo could have used to model David, fell over dead with a cry.

Their horses' hooves throwing up a wake of turf, two of the other soldiers from the foraging party came over the rise and opened fire on the remaining Sioux warriors, Colt revolvers belching tongues of orange flame and great puffs of gray smoke. The other three Indians returned fire, two of them with Winchester repeating rifles that were better and faster than anything the Army could afford, the other with a bow and arrows.

One of the ones with a Winchester fell, and Hollings shouted to Jim Bodkin, "I will be back, Jim!" And he ran toward the fallen Sioux, working the lever of the modern Winchester just like the lever of the old Henry he'd lost in the war, snapping it to his shoulder, twitching back the trigger and watching one of the redmen fall. "Goddamnit!"

He stood there, the two of his boys—My God, blue bellies were his boys!?—riding after the two Indians.

The rifle hot to the touch of the barrel, he set it down as he returned to Jim Bodkin's side.

Jim opened his eyes. "I gotta—gotta—"

"Jim! What?"

"Yo! Bodkin, James T., sir!"

Jim's eyes never closed, except under Preston Hollings' fingers. . . .

"Mr. Hollings?"

"Ma'am?"

"I said, why were y'all laughing before, Mr. Hollings?"

He remembered. "Bugle Ford is the name y'all gave it, ma'am. We called that ol' river fork the Cherokee Wife, ma'am. There wasn't any 'Bugle Ford' or anythin' like that back then."

"How many men were on the bridge when it went down? Do y'all remember?"

Asking him if he remembered that night was like asking him if he remembered his name. . . .

"Lieutenant Hollings reporting, sir!"

Captain Sterett looked up from the wash of candlelight which made the yellowed surface of the map he studied look somehow yellower. "At ease, Lieutenant." Captain Sterett wasn't the sort of man who looked to be a natural leader, but he was. His face was puffy-looking in the cheeks, his eyes smallish and pale, a watery blue, his shoulders sloping almost as much as a woman's would and his size not imposing. He was tall, but almost wraith thin. "Sit down, Pres."

"Thank you, sir." Hollings pulled the emptied upended powder keg a little way from the tent wall, taking off his hat, more rain water washing down inside his poncho.

"Drink? Tennessee whiskey, best there is."

"Thank you, sir." Hollings took the offered bottle and took a short swallow, never having developed much of a taste for liquor. But it was hot going down and his insides were cold.

"Sherman's going to reach Atlanta, Pres. I feel it in my bones. But that don't mean we ain't gonna try an' stop him."

Hollings didn't know what to say. He handed back the bottle, and Captain Sterett took a swallow, the captain's Adam's apple bobbing crazily in his skinny neck as the whiskey went down.

Amos Sterett had been a dentist and his family owned Fields of Elysia, acre upon acre of cotton and timber, sawmills and graineries, a teamstering business that carried goods all up and down through the mountains through the Carolinas and Tennessee and sometimes all the way over into Birmingham on the other side of the Alabama line. He'd raised the company himself, as was the usual thing, the boys all volunteers, the officers elected, Captain Sterett the hands-down choice not just because he paid for the rifles and the uniforms and the horses and provisions, but because he was Amos Sterett, a man other men counted on. Most of his slaves had been freed years before the war, except the ones too old to find homes and work or the ones who wanted to stay on to look after aging parents.

And Hollings thought about the boys up at college, how Amos Sterett didn't fit their preconceptions.

"That road is our only way out, unless y'all think that bridge'll take us."

"No, sir, I think it would collapse."

"Then we are surely doomed, Pres."

Surrender was out of the question, and if Captain Sterett were right about Atlanta, every man who could be saved would be needed to fight, and then someday to rebuild. "I have been thinking, Captain."

"And?"

"One man might be able to make it across, Captain. I am a good swimmer, if it comes to that, sir. And there must be units of our boys nearby on the other side of the river. If I could find such a unit, then we could counterattack the Union force along its western flank; that could gain us enough advantage so there would be time to get down the road and out. The road narrows through that rocky pass about two miles to the west. A handful of men could cover a withdrawal there, then use what powder we have to block the road with rockslide. The Union Infantry could scrabble over the rocks for certain, but the Union Cavalry would be cut off from pursuin' our boys, sir."

"I agree, Pres, that there certainly must be plenty of our lads on the other side of this damnable river, and y'all's plan is a good one. But it hinges upon a man bein' able to get across that confounded bridge. I've been helpin' my family build things at Fields of Elysia since I was old 'nough for one of the darkies to show me which end of the mallet was used to hit which end of the peg, and I know that old bridge is gonna collapse first time somebody sets a foot on it there near the middle. The underpinnings are all washed out where they were shored up with dirt and rock. That dirt and rock is gone, the water jes' carryin' 'em away, Pres." Captain Sterett struck fire from a tinder box, putting the flame deep within the bowl of his pipe. Tobacco was something the captain hadn't had for many weeks, and the smoke from his pipe smelled like burning leaves because that was all it was. And he looked across the bowl of his pipe, pale eyes squinting against the smoke when he said, "Carry y'all away, that water will, to y'all's death sure as I know, Pres."

"If no one crosses that bridge, we are done for sure, sir."

Sterett nodded soberly. "Y'all's a valuable officer, Lieutenant. That young subaltern, Mr. Caruthers, is sincere but not very adept. Although y'all might be too charitable to agree to that openly, in y'all's inner thoughts the conclusion is obvious."

"Captain Sterett, sir, if we are agreed that someone must try to cross the river, then I am, sir, the logical choice. I have no wounds to inhibit me physically"—Hollings had been careful about not limping on his right knee when he entered the tent, keeping the leg stretched out now so he would be able to arise without calling attention to it—"and many of our boys do not swim a single stroke, sir. As an officer, I am more likely to be able to rouse support on the other side of the river, more so than an ordinary soldier of any sort. I know the countryside to a degree, so there is little chance that I will wander off in the wrong direction, wastin' valuable time and energy. I am, Captain Sterett, the logical man to undertake this mission."

Captain Amos Sterett leaned forward over his map, the smoke from his pipe and the candle mingling as they drifted upward into the gray cloud already clinging in the shadows above the yellow light. "I will not deny y'all this chance to save the men of our company, Lieutenant. And I shall read my Bible for y'all's safe return. And, should that not occur, then I shall make every effort to inform the Hollings family how bravely their son died in the service of our cause."

The interview was over.

Preston Hollings stood, a stab of pain in his right knee. But he dropped his hat, bending over to recover the sodden headgear and masking the difficulty with which he fully straightened his leg. He redonned his hat.

Captain Sterett saluted him. . . .

"Mr. Hollings?"

He turned his head, pain and stiffness in the left side of his neck.

"Sir? I can come back another day if y'all's feeling tired."

"I thoroughly enjoy y'all's company, ma'am, if I may be so bold."

She smiled, a smile of genuine warmth, and again she made that gesture—the gesture that Molly had made so often, gently nudging away a lock of silken hair with the back of her hand. . . .

She brushed back a lock of her dark hair. Her eyes were brighter blue than a clear sky on a windy morning, long-lashed lids fluttering downward like the wings of summer butterflies, her cheeks flushing, yet her soft, smooth skin white and cool like marble against his fingertips.

"It ain't right; it certainly ain't right, Preston Hollings, that a man who is almost a doctor of medicine should be goin' off to Lawd knows what carryin' some silly gun! And, I love y'all so hard it hurts." She leaned her head against his chest.

In the arbor, the strong scents of the honeysuckle beyond and the roses within were as nothing—it was supposed to be evil to think of it, he knew. But they were as nothing to the heady scent of her as he bent his face and placed his lips to her bare shoulder, and she trembled beneath his touch.

Her body seemed to melt and remold itself against him. "Pres!" And he felt a tear as it fell from her eye against his hand.

"Everyone is tellin' that the war will not last long, Molly. And if every Southern boy has a girl one-tenth as beautiful as y'all waitin' at home for him, the Union boys won't have a chance against us." Preston Hollings believed the opposite of his words, of course. Not about Molly's considerable charms, but about the war. Northern boys had sweethearts waiting for them, too. And the vast industrial power of the North was a weapon no amount of Southern valor could, in the long term, stand against.

His father had once told him, though, that a man did what he had to do, could do no less, regardless of the cost.

That summed up this war; he had known that before the first shot was fired at Fort Sumter, known that his world was about to end forever.

"Y'all must swear to me, Preston Hollings, that y'all will come back and make a good Christian woman out of me."

"I swear," Hollings whispered, daring to kiss her lips. He had kissed her like that before, many times, but never quite like that.

And never would he do so again. . . .

"Molly died of a fever."

"Who was Molly, Mr. Hollings?"

He flexed the fingers of his left hand against the growing stiffness. "She was why I tried crossin' that—" He almost used profanity in front of a woman. But he caught himself, saying instead, "—that godforsaken bridge, ma'am."

But, had God forsaken the bridge? Or had God merely taken more active control of his destiny than he had ever imagined possible?

His left hand began to shake violently, and no matter how hard he tried, he could not stop it from shaking.

Preston Hollings could not be sure about the bridge, except that what had happened had really happened. But he felt deep within him that soon, very soon now, he would know.

He could not stop the shaking. . . .

It shook violently.

The bridge.

It rattled and shook and pulsed, the trembling so pronounced for long moments at a stretch that he was almost certain that the bridge would collapse and be washed away down the river and into oblivion before he could even set foot upon it.

But the bridge merely waited, warning him not to tempt it, daring him to try.

"Lieutenant Hollings, sir, ya'll's gonna git pitched into that ole river for certain sure."

Hollings forced a smile as he looked over at Rawlins. "Y'all might just have a talent for predictin' the future, Tom."

"Beggin' the lieutenant's pardon, sir, but I reckon it wouldn't hurt none if I was to—"

"Try it?" Preston Hollings couldn't see Tom Rawlins' face, but he knew the look that would be there, an earnest smile. "Sergeant, y'all outweigh me by fifty pounds if it's an ounce. And this was my damned fool idea, anyway."

Rawlins said nothing. Thunder had begun rumbling heavily through the sky, so loud it was like the roar of cannon fire, and there were occasional brilliant flashes of lightning. In those flashes, he had watched the bridge. Now he watched Tom Rawlins' face. It was as he had predicted it would be: well meaning, full of friendship and concern.

There was a clap of thunder, so loud that Hollings' ears rang with the sound.

Hollings had given over the rifle to Corporal Scoggins. The rifle's fate did not matter to him and was too heavy to take along. He would need both hands along the bridge rail and, should the structure collapse with him on it, both hands to hold on. He could have slung the rifle over his shoulder, but that would only be extra weight with which to deal should he be thrown into the current and be forced to swim for his life. The weapon he removed now, however, was of considerable value to him. "Take my saber, Tom. If I should not return and it is within y'all's power to do so, I would appreciate it being given to Miss Molly Abercrombie, the daughter of Mr. Titus Abercrombie, of Stonewood."

"Yes, sir. But—"

There was a flash of lightning, and Hollings knew that Rawlins would be able to see his face, so he merely shook his head as he placed the saber into the platoon sergeant's open hands.

Hollings drew the Smith & Wesson, inverted the revolver first, and broke it open at the latch where barrel met frame. Six cartridges were loaded, and there were twenty more in a drawstring bag secured inside his uniform.

He closed the weapon, reholstered it, and secured the flap.

The Sheffield-made long-bladed Bowie knife was tied into its sheath on the same side as his pistol.

As if, somehow, he and the bridge were actors in a stage play, lightning flashed and the bridge took its cue when he stared at it once again, twisting and rolling, yet still standing.

"As soon as I am across, Sergeant, inform Captain Sterett. Should I fail in my attempt, please inform the captain of that as well."

Lightning flashed again, and Hollings saw Tom Rawlins clearly in its glow, the saber shifted to his left hand, his right hand extended. Hollings clasped hands with the older man, then Rawlins stepped back, saluting.

Hollings returned the salute as smartly as he could.

Hollings looked at the bridge. There was no lightning to cue his adversary this time. Thunder rumbled round about them, sounding somehow as though time and the world were being ripped asunder.

Preston Hollings took his watch from its pocket, already knowing the approximate time, but checking that it was wound tight. He replaced the watch securely.

Lightning flash.

The bridge takes its cue.

He set foot on the nearest whole board and the bridge twisted and vibrated, repelling him.

He took a step further.

Between the sounds of the thunder, there was a sound more familiar; a human voice, a cry of warning. Hollings turned his head in time to see Tom Rawlins stepping back as a dark shape lunged out of the trees.

A soldier. A rifle. A fixed bayonet. A shot. A miss.

Rawlins' LeMat belt pistol spoke with authority, not one of the eight .41 caliber balls from the revolver's cylinder, but the twenty-gauge shotgun barrel beneath. But there was only light, no sound of the shot audible above the thunderclaps which came now one after the other after the other.

The soldier—all uniforms would be darkened to the same color with rain—had to be Union. And, where there was one—

Hollings jumped from the bridge to the embankment, nearly losing his balance, coming down hard, his right knee twisting but holding.

More man shapes came from the trees on the downstream side of the bridge, infiltrators, perhaps looking for a live prisoner to interrogate, perhaps intent on demoralizing the enemy with close-range harassing fire.

There was no further time to consider motivation. The Smith & Wesson revolver was already out of its holster and clenched tightly in his right fist. Hollings fired from the hip, not knowing where he hit the Union soldier (one of four now visible) but certain that he had hit him. The man stumbled back, rifle flying from his hands, hands clasping his left breast, face turned down toward his hands, mouth moving as though he were shouting. But the thunder rumbled continuously now, and not even the sound of the shot from the pistol in his own hand had Preston Hollings heard.

One of the three Northern boys still standing charged toward him. Hollings fired and missed.

But the Union soldier slipped in the Georgia mud, sprawling across it, sliding toward the bridge.

There was no time to shoot at him again. Lightning flashed continuously. Hollings wheeled left, just in time to see Tom Rawlins taking a Union bayonet square through the chest in the same instant as Rawlins fired his revolver into his killer's neck. Blood sprayed from the Union soldier's neck; that an artery was struck clear from its volume and force. Tom and the Union boy collapsed into each other's arms, like lovers embracing.

The last of the Union soldiers still on his feet brought his rifle to his shoulder, the yawning cavern that was its muzzle pointed at Hollings' chest.

Hollings fired the Smith & Wesson from shoulder level, at extended arm's length, like a duelist in a romantic novel, then fired it again.

The Union boy plunged to his knees; a tree chopped through in woods too dense would fall this way, just dropping, the perfect balance point attained. The dead soldier didn't move again.

It was clear that Tom Rawlins was dead, the point of the Union soldier's bayonet protruding from his back so equidistant between the shoulder blades that it could have done nothing but sever the spine.

Then Hollings remembered the Union boy who had gone sprawling into the mud and turned so quickly back toward the bridge that his knee nearly went out from under him.

The Union boy was gone from sight. Perhaps the infiltrator had slid all the way over the embankment and into the swirling waters of the river.

Smith & Wesson revolver clenched tight in his fist, Hollings started toward the bridge. Lightning seemed to swirl around him, the night was bright as noon. Yet the sound of thunder, curiously, was now abated, wind rushing loudly, but somehow he could still hear the smallest sounds: the bridge creaking and the water roaring beneath it, battering the trembling supports. It seemed reasonable to conclude that the Union party was only those men he had seen here by the bridge, no more; and, therefore, there was no immediate danger to the camp. If he delayed now, ran back the half mile or so and informed Captain Sterett about what had transpired, by the time he would be able to return to the bridge, the bridge would be out. All hope of finding any means by which to counterattack and thus save the men of the 10th Georgia would be dashed.

Preston Hollings holstered his revolver and set foot upon the bridge, and as he did so he heard two sounds almost simultaneously, both striking fear into his heart: the sound of one of the boards which comprised the bridge snapping in two and the sound of a revolver being cocked.

Hollings wheeled round, his left hand going to the bridge rail, his right hand groping for the flap which closed his gun into the holster. The Union boy whom Hollings had assumed had slipped into the stream was standing there, a big Colt aimed straight for Hollings' chest.

Hollings knew he had to move or die. He vaulted toward the Union soldier, the big bore Colt revolver discharging, Hollings feeling the bullet as it cracked just past his left ear. Hollings' right hand held the Bowie knife, and he stabbed it downward, the point biting flesh along the boy's back, then the blade flat skittering off over the shoulder blade.

Hollings' left hand vised over the boy's Colt, the hammer falling with a loud click, but biting into the fleshy web between Hollings' thumb and first finger rather than striking the cap set into the nipple on the other side of the frame. He remembered something he'd first seen done when one of the darkie boys he'd played with as a boy had gotten into a fight with a Cherokee. The Cherokee did it and nearly crippled little Ben, doubling him over. Hollings did it now, smashing his right knee upward into the Union boy's private parts.

There was a rush of foul-smelling breath, and for an instant all the weight of the Union boy's Colt was hanging from Hollings' flesh. Hollings rammed his knife inward, catching the enemy soldier under the ribcage, and there was a terrible howl. Flesh tore from the web of Hollings' hand as the boy fell against him. Hollings lost his balance, his right knee finally failing him.

And he collapsed, the Union soldier's weight smothering him. They fell onto the bridge.

Boards split, fell away, Hollings' upper body was hanging over the raging waters. The Union boy, blood streaming from his mouth, had his big Colt pistol in his right hand, twisting its muzzle toward Hollings' chest.

Hollings swung his left fist up, hammering it into the middle of his opponent's face, the blow apparently stunning the Union soldier. The boy fell back, Hollings' knife still protruding from his left side.

Hollings grabbed onto a section of bridge flooring, more of the boards giving way beneath him as he clawed with his right hand for the flap of his holster. He had it, tore it open, his fingers closing over the butt of the revolver.

The Union boy shouted, "You have killt me, Rebel!"

The Union boy and Hollings fired their revolvers in the same instant, the Colt's muzzle so close to Hollings' chest that, in the next instant, as Hollings lay there, his own revolver still smoking in his hand, he could not understand how the Union soldier's round missed him.

It seemed impossible.

But there was no pain.

Hollings had not missed: one neat hole in the center of the Union boy's face, just at the very bridge of the nose, rain washing over wide open eyes.

The bridge.

The trembling of the bridge persisted, but for some reason, Hollings no longer feared its collapse beneath him. He had survived this life and death encounter. He would survive the next, he knew.

The rushing sound of the wind increased. The lightning was coming so rapidly now, the bright light from it was continuous.

Preston Hollings stood up. Whatever he had done to his knee was better now, because he could move it with ease.

He looked down at his left hand, where his flesh had stopped the Colt's hammer from falling.

There was a wound, but the bleeding had stopped and it no longer hurt.

He nodded to himself.

Rain rolled from the brim of his hat and crossed his face, and he was momentarily surprised that his hat had not been lost during the fight.

Preston Hollings holstered his gun, reminding himself to reload once he was across.

And he started forward, picking each step, both hands grasped to the right side rail.

The light was gradually dimming. . . .

It wasn't that nice Mrs. Hubbard's face now, but the nurse's face again, hovering above him, seeming to float there. "Mr. Hollings? Can you hear me? Blink your eyes if you can hear me, Mr. Hollings? Preston Hollings! Can you hear me?"

Only a dead man couldn't have heard her, Hollings thought. That night, the Union boy stopped hearing forever. . . .

Behind him, the very second that his feet touched the ground, the bridge collapsed into the raging river below it, the supports washed away like twigs, the bridge splitting right at the center, both halves of it falling into the water with simultaneously great splashes, battering against one another, for a moment blocking the river's course itself.

There were tearing sounds, popping noises like small explosions, and the bridge sections rose and snapped, then sank under the white-frothed waters.

Preston Hollings stood there, shaking as he watched it.

He drew his revolver: one shot remaining of the six.

He would reload it beneath the shelter of one of the massive live oaks some yards distant, back from the swollen rivercourse.

Killing men in battle, when everyone around you was killing or being killed, wasn't like it had been back on the other side of the bridge. That was personal, somehow more real, more terrifying.

The mud was deep here, but he managed walking better than he had before, and soon he was beneath one of the trees. The lightning persisted, but not coming so rapidly now, and the cacaphonous rumble of thunder was louder here. As a boy, every time there was a storm, someone would always warn him not to hide from it under a tree, because trees seemed to attract lightning. Oaks worst of all. But he would only be a moment, then on his way again.

From beneath his clothes he untied the small sack with his spare cartridges, opened it, removed five, reclosed, and secured the precious ammunition again. Carefully, he broke open his revolver, waiting for the light of a lightning flash. He discarded the spent cases, putting five fresh with the one remaining from before. Then he closed the action.

A fully loaded gun, he felt better now, although six .32 rimfires would do little against a Union force if this side of the river were in enemy hands as well.

"Tempus fugit," he reminded himself aloud, having totally lost track of just what time it was. He took his watch, the one given him when he went off to study medicine, from its pocket. He opened the case, and in a flash of lightning could see the face right enough. The hands seemed not to have moved. He held the watch to his ear but could hear no ticking. Yet, it was fully wound, just as before. Clearly, the watch had been damaged during the fight.

Hollings put the watch away carefully. Someday, when this war was over, he might be able to find someone who could restore it.

He marched away from the trees, the rain falling more heavily than before, it seemed, yet probably because of his exertion at the bridge it no longer chilled him. As best he could judge, he made good time, moving briskly along a steep hillside, but at a diagonal, minimizing the effort needed to reach the top. The body, his professors had told him, had a remarkable way, at times, of rising beyond its normal capabilities. Men—and sometimes women—had been known to perform near-Herculean feats of strength during a crisis situation, which under normal circumstances would have been impossible for them.

Such was the case now, he realized, but such added vigor

would ebb quickly, and he must find help as rapidly as circumstances allowed.

Hollings attained the crest of the hill and there was, stretching before him, the carriage road he had expected. To the west, there should be a settlement. Westerly up the course of the river there was a small falls, and logic dictated that a grist mill would be set there to utilize the natural force of the water. Where there was a mill, there was usually a town nearby. To the east, he was uncertain how many miles might need to be traveled. It was possible, even likely, that if help were not immediately available, he could find a telegraph and send word somehow for help.

To the west it was, and he turned right, starting down the carriage road.

The trees on either side of the road rose high and were densely clustered, the result being that the road was in almost total blackness, little illumination from the still persistent lightning flashes able to penetrate the foliage. But, the rain was also less forceful beneath this natural shelter, and the surface of the road beneath his feet seemed admirably firm. He was able to walk even faster than before, his steps not seeming to tire him at all.

Hollings walked on that way for some considerable time, his pace as fast as prudence dictated. The road rose, following the natural contour of the terrain, Hollings supposing that he had to be near to the likely mill site. He quickened his pace in anticipation.

At the crest, however, he stopped.

To his left, toward the south, well beyond a wall of the same trees which had sheltered him all along, Hollings saw light.

A farmhouse?

If this were the light from a farmhouse, he might be able to borrow a horse or even a mule. And he could travel faster still. The source of the light did not appear to be terribly far beyond the trees, so he left the road, making his way toward it. At once, as soon as he left the protective canopy, the rain returned in its full intensity, and he pushed his hat down lower and hunched his shoulders higher against it, marching on.

The ground was not only less uniform than the road, but

rougher still than the hillside he'd originally mounted in order to reach the road. At one point, wild grasses reaching nearly to his waist, he put his foot into a hole and nearly fell. But he didn't twist anything. He pressed on, toward the light, a glow which seemed somehow to be floating in the middle of the night.

Hollings held his pistol more tightly.

The terrain he traversed quite suddenly began to rise, and he followed its topography upward, toward the light. He realized with some considerable relief that the light source did not float at all, but merely appeared to do so because it was situated on higher ground, and the otherwise total blackness—the lightning had now ceased—did not allow the eyes to distinguish features.

As he neared the source of the light, he was better able to discern its specific nature. It was some sort of a bonfire.

The fire burned so brightly, he deduced, because the logs which served it were immense: felled trees dragged to one single location, for one purpose only. It was an old woodsman's trick to lay a single tree trunk into a fire and, as the night progressed and the fire devoured the wood, merely force the log deeper into the flames, feeding them. But this fire carried that practice to the extreme. As he came closer still to it, he could see at least six such massive logs set around the blaze much like spokes were set in a wheel about a central hub.

And he flexed his fingers on the grip of his revolver, because he saw men huddled round the fire, the silhouettes of arms—rifles, some fixed with bayonets—outlined against the blaze.

There were other shapes at the boundary circumscribed by the light: monoliths with squared off or rounded tops, oddly defined figures, crosses, too. He realized what these were as he nearly fell over one of them.

These were headstones and this was a cemetery.

A curiously formal voice called out to him from the darkness, challenging, "Halt! Who goes there? Friend or foe?"

Some of the silhouettes moved against the firelight.

For a moment, Hollings was dumbstruck as to the wording of his reply. At last, however, he called back, "First Lieutenant Preston W. Hollings, 10th Georgia Militia!" If these were Union boys, his fate was sealed. He readied his revolver.

But a voice, formal sounding but different from the first in both accent and modulation, called out to him, this time emanating from near the fire. "Approach, Lieutenant. And put away your pistol."

Whoever the speaker was had keen eyesight, because by contrast to the light from the fire, where he stood was as black as pitch.

Hollings eased down the hammer of his revolver, holstered it, but did not close the flap in the event he might require quick access to this his only weapon.

He walked toward the fire, and as he did the silhouettes seemed to grow, not in size but dimension, with form and substance beyond what he had seen before. Some of them, who had apparently been sitting on headstones near to the flames, rose.

And one of them, taller than the others, approached him, meeting him by the boundary between the darkness and the light. The voice—cultured-sounding, confident and resonant—was the same voice which had welcomed him to this company. "And what are you doing here this night, lad?"

Hollings had not been called "lad" for many years, but he answered, saluting as he said, "I am on a mission of grave importance for my commander, sir, Captain Amos Colton Sterett. Perhaps y'all have heard of him, sir."

The salute was returned. "I regret that I have not, but if what brings you here this night is of grave importance, lad, then surely you have come to the right place." And one hand made a sweeping gesture toward the headstones surrounding them.

There was laughter, hearty, loud, from the persons still beside the fire.

"This is no jokin' matter, I assure y'all, sir. The boys are cut off by the river, the only road being one which has been overrun by Union forces. If the rain stops tonight, or when the sun rises, regardless of the rain, the enemy forces will sweep down on our encampment. We have very few men, sir, only eight horses, no field pieces, and several boys who are seriously wounded."

"I find your use of the word 'enemy' very interesting, lad. Come and warm yourself by the fire, and then you can ask me what it is you want to ask me, but only then."

He moved away.

Hollings followed him, still not quite certain that this was not a Union force, the speech pattern of the man not at all like anything he had ever heard in the South, but not quite Northern, either.

As Hollings neared the bright center of the firelight, he could see most of the others quite clearly. A more raggedy uniformed group would have been hard to imagine, some of the clothes all but tatters, and no rhyme or reason to them, either. Much the same could be said for the weapons, too; guns of such widely ranging age and description as to defy an arms historian. There were Gallaghers, Burnsides, Enfields, but older pieces as well: long rifles of the kind one only saw in these days hung with a powder horn above a fireboard, both percussion and flintlock.

He sat down by the fire, feeling as though he were desecrating some dead person's memory by using a headstone thusly, but keenly desirous not to offend this strange band. Perhaps they were irregulars. There were such units, often operating in civilian clothing or mixed uniform parts, using hit and run tactics against Union supply trains and the like.

Once seated, Hollings noticed that nowhere was there sign of any food or drink. These soldiers seemed almost in worse straits than the 10th.

"There was something you wished to ask me, lad."

Hollings could see his host quite clearly now by the firelight. The man's uniform tunic was Tuscaloosa gray, but there was no black piping. His badges of rank, set on the open high collar of the garment, showed him to be a colonel, but their design was unique. The man had hair nearly as long as a woman's, well past his shoulders, but pushed back from his face, dark and full beneath a broad-brimmed equally dark hat with a low crown, a plume, somewhat bedraggled with the rain, rising from the left side of the hatband. The hat was cocked low over his right eye, and his left eye was covered by a black patch.

One finger touched the patch, then the hand drifted over his massive chest to rest on his thigh. Two Colt Army Models of 1860 were thrust into the broad belt at his waist, the holster for a smaller revolver of some sort suspended at his right side, a knife nearly the size of a Roman short sword at his left hip.

Hollings was drawn back to the face, lean to the point of haggard, but the good eye—in the firelight to tell the color would have been impossible—was almost inky in its blackness and seemed keen enough, following Hollings' eyes.

It was hard for Preston Hollings to draw his gaze from that eye, to break its hold. But, with considerable effort, he turned his attention briefly to the other men, all of their faces visible except for that of a bulky man sitting on the opposite side of the fire, head bent down, the flames between them a barricade denying closer scrutiny.

"Your question, Lieutenant Hollings."

"Sir, I request the aid of y'all and y'all's men in order that a counterattack might be launched against that portion of the Union force which denies the 10th access to the road, the only route to survival. Surely, there must be a means by which this wild river to the north can be crossed. We can double back, striking unexpectedly against their weak flank.

"They will fall back to reorganize," Hollings continued. "My captain will move the men out before the Union forces can rally against y'all's unit. Y'all can withdraw, then. Captain Sterett will be able to block Union access along the road through the use of our remainin' gunpowder, and in so doing securin' our line of withdrawal. Y'all's swift interdiction is the 10th's only chance, sir."

"We have been fighting for a very long time, Lieutenant Hollings, longer I daresay than any soldiers you have ever encountered."

Hollings would not dispute such a statement; these men looked every word of it, and then some. "Sir, I appeal to y'all's sense of decency."

"And what will you do, lad, if you can find no help?"

Hollings felt an emptiness, and stood as he said, "Failin' that help can be found, sir, I shall rejoin Captain Sterett and the men, fightin' beside them against the enemy as long as breath remains to me."

"Fine sentiments, lad. You use that word again, a word which I find curious in great measure. Describe for me this 'enemy.' "

"The Union soldiers, sir."

"Are they not men like you?"

"Certainly, but they fight against us."

"Then you hold no personal animosity toward this enemy?"

Hollings shook his head. "That is war, sir. Under other circumstances, who is to know if these Union boys might not be friends or y'all the enemy."

At this the colonel laughed heartily.

Hollings was about to take offense, but the colonel's laughter abruptly ceased, and he said, "We will march with you, Lieutenant, because the answer you gave was the only correct answer." And the colonel looked skyward into the night. "But we will have to move quickly." He stood up, taller seeming now, or perhaps it was just that Preston Hollings had not taken notice of his height before. In a loud command voice, those men still seated around the fire rising at his words, those already standing stepping forward, all taking up their motley collection of arms, the colonel ordered, "It is time to fall in lads! There is bloody work to do this night!"

Hollings had not realized that so many men were encamped here, the soldiers ranking themselves into two files, the rear of each file extending so far back into the darkness that Hollings could not clearly discern any approximation of their numbers.

The colonel turned to Hollings, bidding him, "March beside me, lad."

Hollings fell in.

As if some silent command had been given, they moved out, the silence total except for the noise of the rain and the thrumming of boots on muddy ground and the rattling of saber chains and rifle slings. . . .

"Mr. Hollings is not responding, Doctor Carew."

"Let's see if we can rally him. Mr. Hollings? What's his first name?"

"Preston. He used to be a lieutenant in the War Between the States."

"Right. Mr.— Er, Lieutenant Hollings! We need you to respond, sir. Lieutenant Hollings? Can you hear me at all?"

"His pulse is erratic, Doctor."

"The heart. The old, strong ones like this fellow—it's usually the heart."

Preston Hollings wanted to tell them that they were right, but it was as if a fist were tightening and twisting inside his chest, and he didn't have the breath to form the words. . . .

There were shoals above the falls which powered the grist mill. Under normal conditions, the water here would have been mere inches deep, Hollings realized, so gentle that its current would hardly have been noticeable. To cross it, you would jump from one flat rock to another, careful to mind the footing lest a misstep should cause a slip and douse your boots in a shallow pool. This night, however, as they linked hands to keep each other upright, the water rose to Hollings' thighs and tore at his balance, trying to catch him off guard for the slightest second, drag him along in its raging current, pull him over the edge, and into the falls and down to his death.

The colonel walked at their head with such apparent ease, however, that the pace and force of the water seemed not to affect him, and curiously Hollings' own movement required less effort than he would have supposed. Both the colonel and the man behind Hollings had hands even colder than Hollings' own, and he knew that he and all of the colonel's men should be chilled to the bone by now. Yet, he was not, nor did anyone else evince that condition.

These men were battle-hardened.

The colonel, to Hollings' thinking, was of indeterminate age, but moved with the agility of a boy, scrambling up the embankment, Hollings hard-pressed to keep from falling behind. Hollings looked back across the river, but he still could not see where the column ended. "You have a sizable force, sir."

"Yes, indeed, lad." And there was a note of something like sadness in that sonorous voice. "The ranks grow even as we speak." And the colonel's pace quickened now. . . .

*   *   *

"Rapid pulse. Erratic."

"Labored breathing."

"We're losing him."

There was a perfectly good reason for heavy breathing, of course, and he wanted to tell them that, but the fist that clenched within his chest would not allow it, was in fact closing tighter. . . .

They marched to the east. Hollings wished that his watch still functioned, because he was certain every time that he looked horizonward that the sun would be there and he had lost all track of time.

They marched on, the physical appearance of the colonel's men belying their freshness, their fitness. Not only did no man break ranks, not a one broke step, albeit the pace was a killing one.

Then the colonel stopped. "The Union lines are there." And he looked toward the north.

Hollings stared into the darkness. He could see nothing.

The colonel's words were not a question, it seemed, but more a statement of obvious fact.

"Where, sir?"

The colonel looked at him, the rain falling so intensely that Hollings could barely discern the colonel's outline. "A gun emplacement—rather hastily dug, it would appear—five hundred yards just at the edge of a stand of white pine. From that point as an apex, the Union lines extend both southeasterly and northeasterly. The obvious object of the position is to allow your lads access to the road, then close in behind them, the numbers pursuing them increasing the more deeply the road is penetrated. Midway long the southeasterly tangent there is cavalry. When your lads have reached a point one hundred yards up the road along which we travel, the artillery will saturate the road. With your lads stalled, the cavalry will swoop down, driving them into the woods there." And the colonel pointed to his right, to the south. "There is infantry positioned in those woods, nothing your lads could not handle if they did not have a cavalry unit at their heels. To neutralize this situation, we must first silence that gun before it speaks, then cause the cavalry to withdraw. Once your lads have reached this point, if they are unmolested by the gun, the infantry hidden in these woods will not dare attack. Your lads will escape with their lives for now."

Hollings just stared, wishing he could see that solitary eye, and perhaps through it some insight to this strange man's tactical genius.

"Do you choose to fight with us for now, or return to your unit? At this point, you have the choice. Choose wisely."

"I will fight with y'all, sir, to make certain that all goes as planned, beggin' the Colonel's pardon. Then I will be able to rejoin my unit as they pass."

"The wise choice, lad. Stay close." And the colonel turned away. Without a sound from his lips, he merely gestured and about two dozen of his company fell out from one column, starting up the rise toward the gun position. The colonel raised his right hand, his sword clenched there, then pointed the blade in the direction where he had said the cavalry was lying in wait.

"Sir?"

"Hollings."

"Are we—"

"We must attack the cavalry. But we will drive them back. Follow me." They began to move at a slight tangent to the road, just above it, toward a darker darkness that Hollings assumed would be a treeline. He would keep his cavalry there. The Smith & Wesson was in his hand without his consciously drawing it, right elbow tight to his side.

The rain fell unremittingly, relentlessly, but he was past cold; he felt nothing, except a thrill that was not physical, welling up inside of him. Captain Sterett would hear the shots, would rouse the boys and start them out along the road, the other seven men on horseback keeping to the north side of the road in a posture for instant defense from a cavalry strike, the wounded well to the center of the column.

They neared the darker darkness and it was a treeline.

None of the others of the company brandished weapons. What a well-trained lot, he thought.

Hollings strode beside and a pace behind the colonel; he noticed the large man he had seen across the fire in the cemetery encampment fall in to his immediate left. In the darkness, he could see no face. Evidently a senior noncommissioned officer prepared to fight and die at his commander's side, or perhaps aid a first lieutenant in staying out of trouble.

And Hollings thought of Tom Rawlins, platoon sergeant extraordinaire, a soldier's soldier, but a farmer, a husband, and a father a few short years ago.

The pace quickened, the treeline less than fifty yards off now. Still no repositioning of weapons, still no orders.

These men had to be regulars, despite their uniforms, the discipline unlike anything Hollings had ever experienced. Despite the pace—they were at a full run now—the step was not broken.

Into the trees, horses picketed there, but fully tacked. A rifle shot.

This would start it.

Yet there was no shot, no sound from the men who now surrounded him. Hollings raised his revolver, making to fire at a Union soldier visible in the flash of a rifle. But Hollings could not take the shot with no clear field of fire, the colonel's men blocking him.

Hollings ran on.

Gunfire was general now.

Horses and men fled from the onslaught.

Rifles and pistols were fired, but none by the colonel's men.

They ran, in perfect step.

A wall of Union soldiers, cavalrymen afoot. Pistols were fired, sabers brandished.

The wall crumbled.

Hollings could get no clear field of fire.

Behind them and to the north, Hollings heard the sound of an explosion, not a gun being fired, but spiked instead.

He had heard that sound early that day, when he and Rawlins had destroyed the field piece which had to be left behind.

In perfect step, the colonel's men ran forward.

A line of riflemen, a volley of Union fire, the flashes blindingly bright against the darkness. . . .

*   *   *

"Lieutenant Hollings. This is Doctor Carew. Blink if you can hear me."

Hollings looked up.

His eyelids did not want to close, despite the brightness. . . .

They ran on.

The Union boys were in a rout.

Then the burly sergeant beside Preston Hollings turned to face him; perhaps there was a lightning flash, but regardless Hollings could see the face clearly. Unmistakably, the face was that of Tom Rawlins. "Lieutenant Hollings, sir. It is time for y'all to rejoin Captain Sterett."

The running had ceased and they all stood there, Hollings walled in by the colonel's men.

All gunfire had ended and the wind-driven rain no longer lashed Hollings' face. "Tom. Y'all are dead."

"Yes, sir. With all respect, sir, y'all must rejoin the boys, sir. It is now or never, sir."

Hollings stared. He could feel the wall of soldiers which was surrounding him opening to give him passage. "Tom?"

"Hurry, Lieutenant."

"Tom!"

"It is now or never, sir."

"Tom—I—"

"Lieutenant, do not y'all think I know?"

"Come back with me, Tom."

"I cannot obey y'all's order, sir, even if I wished."

"We—"

"We will fight together another day, sir."

Hollings could not feel himself moving, but Tom Rawlins and the colonel and the colonel's men were moving, away from him, their images now like something seen when looking through the wrong end of a telescope, growing more distant by the instant.

There was gunfire, more thunderous than before. The colonel's men began to run again, charging to the guns.

The shroud of night closed around them, covered them, darkness everywhere.

Preston Hollings closed his eyes against it.

He opened his eyes.

He saw the river of wild white froth careening beneath him.

Above him, darkness, then a face. "Pres? Speak to me, Pres!"

The face was that of Captain Sterett.

There was a terrible pain in Preston Hollings' chest. He looked down across his body. His right hand held his revolver, was clenched over his chest. In the light of a torch held in Captain Sterett's hand, Hollings could see that the hand which held the Smith & Wesson was bathed in blood.

"Captain?"

"I sent the men on ahead, Pres. There's a force attacking the Union flank. I do not know how y'all did it. God, you could not have done it, because you are here. But y'all must have."

Preston Hollings looked to his right.

The bridge was gone.

He was on the side of the river where he had started.

"I came back for y'all, thinkin' there was somethin' wrong."

"Tom—Tom Rawlins."

"Run through the backbone with a bayonet by a damned blue belly, boy."

Captain Sterett's hand reached out to him. . . .

Hands touched at his face.

He could feel that.

The doctor and the nurse were trying to be kind, he knew, trying to close his eyes against the light.

But the light did not go away, became only brighter.

And now there was something visible in the light, far away, but coming closer by the second, then suddenly there.

It was the colonel's eye. "I missed you at roll call, lad, that night when first we met, and later when Jim Bodkin took that Sioux arrow instead of you. And again on that hill in Cuba when that bullet missed the artery in your leg. Are you ready now?"

Preston Hollings looked down across his body. Both legs were there.

His stomach was flat.

In his holster was the old .32 rimfire.

And his uniform was Confederate gray.

Thousands of faces were ranked behind the colonel, in column of twos, going on, it seemed, forever. Somewhere near the rear, he saw the soldier who died of bad lungs from the gas in the trenches in France, saw the Union boy who had shot him through the left breast beside the bridge he never crossed that night in 1864. The Sioux warrior was there, too, proud and defiant, war-bonnet fresh, warpaint gleaming.

"Hey, Reb!" To his left stood Jim Bodkin.

"Welcome, sir." Preston Hollings looked to his right. Tom Rawlins. "I told y'all, Lieutenant, we would fight together again."

The colonel ordered, "It is time to fall in, lads. There is bloody work to do this night!"

> When the trumpet of the Lord shall sound,
> and time shall be no more,
> And the morning breaks,
> eternal, bright, and fair;
> When the saved of earth shall gather
> over on the other shore,
> And the roll is called up yonder,
> I'll be there.
> —James M. Black

The Crater

Doug Murray

Doug Murray has impeccable credentials to appear in an anthology of stories about the Civil War. While completing his B.A. in history at Columbia University, Doug walked many of the battlefields and other historical sites of the war, including the one where this story is set. Much of his career has dealt with military historical settings—for example, his much-acclaimed series "The Nam" for Marvel Comics.

Doug has a versatile set of credentials, as eclectic as they are dissimilar. He's worked on *Famous Monsters of Filmland*, scripted numerous comics, including *Conan the Barbarian,* and written the graphic novel *Batman: Digital Justice*. In addition, he has scripted *Savage Tales* and Isaac Asimov's *Robot City*. So what's Doug doing these days after a steady diet of cyborgs, savages, superheroes, and famous monsters? As unlikely as it sounds, he's having a lot of fun scripting "Roger Rabbit" and "Toon Town" for Disney. All this, plus an increasing number of anthology appearances to go with several pseudonymous paperbacks.

After reading "The Crater," it was easy to understand why Doug is in demand within today's increasingly adult-oriented comics industry. He writes with a visual flair that enables the reader to illustrate without printed pictures. A native New Yorker, Doug now resides in Deltona, Florida.

The man in gray looked around, his head moving nervously from side to side. Somebody was watching him, he was sure of that, but from where? And whose side was the watcher on?

He took one more peek over his shoulder and then bent down

to his work. He'd be dead if he was in the sights of a Union sharpshooter, it *must* be his imagination. Best to finish what he had to do and get back to his own lines.

He bent back to the blue-clad corpse in front of him, working to get those long cavalry boots off the feet. . . .

Three hundred yards away, Sergeant Joe Scroggs peered through his battered little pair of binoculars. Son of a gun! It *was* the Rebs! They were grabbing off the bodies, stripping the corpses, and then hiding the remains God knew where.

"Lieutenant Gaines is gonna love this!" Scroggs pulled his attention off the binoculars for a moment to glance at Corporal Dan White, lying in the trench just to his right.

"He's been worried to death that *we* were misplacin' all those bodies! This'll just make his day!"

Scroggs brought his binoculars back up, watching as the Confederate soldier got the first of the boots off the dead cavalryman and started working on the second.

"Before we go back to tell the lieutenant," Scroggs nodded toward the little tableau in front of him, "let's make sure that this particular body doesn't disappear."

Scroggs glanced over as White got to work. The corporal was the best shot in the company, and Scroggs had worked hard to get him one of the new Sharps rifles—the long barrel looked odd with the tin telescope mounted on top of it, but it sure did the job. Scroggs had seen White hit targets at near five hundred yards.

The Reb soldier was a whole lot closer.

White let his cheek rest on the polished guard of his rifle, turned all his concentration onto its knife-edged sight: *Wait for it*, he told himself. *Get a good sight picture, just the way Pa always told you back home in Massachusetts . . .* The Reb was turning around now, sitting down on the ground to pull on the boots. *Perfect! Now, just let the sight settle onto the chest, take a deep breath and squeeze, ever so slightly, until . . .*

The Confederate troop fell without a sound.

"Nice shooting, Dan." Scroggs slipped his binoculars into their worn leather case. "Now, let's go tell the lieutenant."

"Hey—Sarge?"

Scroggs turned to the other men in his little unit. The 5th Colored Division was newly formed, and black noncommissioned officers like Joe Scroggs were rare. Joe had been lucky—born and raised in free Ohio. His light skin had always allowed him to pass for white, so when the war broke out, Joe was quick to join up with the army, finding a spot in the 104th Ohio. He'd done pretty well there, moving up through the ranks until he attained the rank of sergeant—he'd probably have been made an officer by now, but when the Union Infantry of African Descent had been formed in January, Joe had arranged to be transferred to them.

He felt that it was his duty to fight with his own kind.

Unfortunately, Union officers seemed to have other ideas about coloreds fighting. The 5th had arrived in Petersburg with the rest of the army, ready to participate in the continued assaults on the Reb lines.

But they'd yet to have a shot fired at them in open battle.

They seemed to spend all their time doing the shit details— digging latrines, standing picket duty, even recovering the dead. Joe kept hoping they'd see some real action soon, but who could tell. . . .

"Sarge?"

"What's up, Roskins?"

Most of the troops in the 5th Colored were too scared and nervous to talk much, but Roskins was an older man—and a good trooper. It was usually a good idea to pay attention to what he said.

"We put four bodies out there, didn't we?"

Scroggs looked out into the field where the birds were already beginning to circle over the fallen Reb trooper.

"That's right, Roskins. Four. Why?"

Jimbo Roskins settled a little deeper into the trench as he motioned out into the open field. He'd heard that this place was haunted, maybe.

"Sarge, there's not but three there now."

Joe Scroggs pulled his binoculars back out and started to curse in a quiet and deadly earnest tone.

*   *   *

Before Petersburg,
July 1, 1864

From: Colonel Henry Pleasants, 58th Pennsylvania
To: General George Meade, Commanding

General:

I ask you again to consider my report of June 21. It seems plain that further assaults on the Rebel positions will be as fruitless as our most recent attacks. However, an attack preceded by the destruction of one of their salients from underground might well succeed and allow us to move immediately on Richmond and end this war.

I have the men necessary for such a plan—coal miners from Pennsylvania who have wide experience in the digging and shoring of such tunnels—and my own experience as a civil engineer is quite adequate to the planning and supervision of such a work.

At least let us try. This siegework causes too great a delay and results in too much hardship for our soldiers.

Pleasants

Washington City
July 5, 1864

To: General Meade

George:

Go ahead and let Pleasants dig his hole. Burnside thinks he might be able to do it, and at the very least, it'll give him something to do other than write more letters and bother us.

U.S. Grant

"Sure! We'll be glad to dig a tunnel, Colonel Sir. What else could we *possibly* want to do!" Bob Gallagher pulled a shovelful of sand from the tunnel face in front of him, dumping it in the little wooden wagon that sat just behind him. Then he watched as the hole he'd just made disappeared as the surrounding grit settled.

"Hell, Bob. Why complain?" Darrel Walker threw his own shovel load into the wagon, and stopped to wipe sweat and sand out of his eyes. "It could be worse."

Gallagher thrust his shovel back into the face. "Worse! How could it be worse?"

Walker shrugged his beefy shoulders, then jabbed his own shovel back into the working face—and winced as it struck something hard. "Shit. That felt like rock!"

Gallagher stood stock-still for a moment, then started laughing. Walker was right. It *was* rock.

Things *had* gotten worse.

Four hours later, things were worse still. The *band* of rock they had struck turned out to be more than just a band. Gallagher had dulled three picks, and they hadn't gotten more than another six inches. The colonel wasn't going to like this.

July 10, 1864

From: Major Thomas J. Feeny
To: Colonel Henry Pleasants, Commanding

Sir:

I have just inspected the tunnel. Work has slowed considerably since the men struck rock five days ago. It now appears that our estimate of twelve feet a day is much too optimistic. Perhaps it would be best to suspend planning of the actual assault until the tunnel is complete.

Feeny

11 July, 1864

Tom:

The assault is scheduled for 30 July. The tunnel will be completed on the 29th. No delay will be countenanced.

Pleasants

*   *   *

Joe Scroggs motioned a halt. His platoon needed a moment to stop and catch a blow. Besides, the moon was high, the area all around them silvered in the soft light—not a good time to be moving around—there were too many trigger-happy men on both sides of the line. Scroggs didn't want to be killed by his own side any more than he wanted to get shot by the Rebs.

They'd wait a few minutes, catch their breath, and hope that those clouds up there would oblige them by moving across the moon.

The job could wait—it was a stupid one anyway. Bodies! Who in hell cared about bodies aside from some pencil-pushing rear echelon types who wanted nothing more than to balance their books!

Still, a job was a job, and Joe Scroggs wanted to prove to the rest of the Army that the 5th Colored was just as brave as any of them.

Even if that wasn't true.

Joe's men had been nervous for days. Joe had heard some of the stories, tales of white things gliding across the ground, grabbing men, both dead and alive, and dragging them off under the ground somewhere—he'd always hated stories like that. Ghosts! Hauntings! His folks had taught him that there were no such things. That stories about them had been told by the old mammys on the plantation to scare slaves so they wouldn't run away.

Joe had always believed that—but now he was beginning to have second thoughts. He still didn't believe in ghosts, but there was sure something wrong out here; too many of his men had seen things, and he had to believe the evidence of his own ears—and nose.

Scroggs had been hearing things all night—all of his men had. Funny noises, scrapings, echoing moans. . . . And then there was the smell—faint but there. The sort of smell he remembered from his days in Ohio—he'd smelled it there when he walked down Sutter Street and passed old Bender's Slaughterhouse; a carrion smell.

The smell of something rotting.

Joe took another deep breath, thinking about that smell—but

there was nothing there now. Nothing but the mossy smells of the earth and the faint reminders of the huge Union camp only a mile or so away.

Big Dan White tapped Joe on the shoulder and pointed to the sky. Joe looked up just as the moon started to disappear behind some clouds. Its fading light touched the gold of Dan's two front teeth, making them glow in the dark like some Halloween jack-o'-lantern. Joe nodded to the other man; yes, it was time to move now. Use the darkness to get where they were going and, if they were really lucky, to get back to friendly lines.

Joe motioned to his men and said a little prayer that the moon would stay covered. Just a couple of hours of this pitch dark and they would be safe. At least, he kept telling himself that.

Even if he didn't believe it.

July 11, 1864

My dearest sister Marie:

Well, they got us digging again. Colonel Pleasants came up with this idea to tunnel under the Reb lines. That'll let us put a whole bunch of gunpowder and explosives right under their feet—we can blow a big hole in their line and walk through. Finish this siege off.

We've been working away for nearly two weeks now—they've got a couple of hundred men working in relays, twenty-four hours a day—we've already gone nearly two hundred feet, but we've got to average more'n twelve feet a day if we're going to be able to attack when the colonel's got it planned.

The ground here is real strange. At first we thought it was all sand and clay, but as we got in a ways, we found it was honeycombed with rock—we can't blast because the Rebs'd find out what we were doing, so we got to manhandle it out with picks and shovels—we're used to that, but every now and then we come upon what seems to be a tunnel—a real narrow channel that seems to come from below and go up. My friend Darrel Walker thinks they're natural chimneys—says he's seen such things back home, but I don't know—they don't *seem* natural—they're too smooth, too regular! Darrel's right about one thing, though—they couldn't have been dug by men—they're way too narrow, no way a man could fit into one of them.

As if that weren't bad enough, we also got to put up with this smell—every time we dig into one of these chimney things, this *stench* comes out of it. It's like there was a slaughterhouse under us or something.

But we haven't found nothing like that—nothing at all.

Maybe it's just me. Maybe I've been out here too long. Three years. It seems like forever.

I just hope it all ends soon. If we *can* bust through the Reb lines here, we can be in Richmond in a week, and the war'll be over.

And I can get back to digging tunnels for money rather than to kill people.

Give my love to Ma, and tell Catherine Ann that I haven't forgotten her and that I hope to see you all real soon.

Your loving brother,

Bob Gallagher
58th Pennsylvania

Joe Scroggs signaled his men to hurry up. The lines weren't too far ahead now. Not more'n a couple of hundred yards. If they could make it there, they *should* be safe.

He peered up at the sky for the hundredth time, the moon was still safely behind clouds. There was just enough of a glow coming through to let Joe see the ground to about fifty feet in front of him.

There wasn't enough to see what was making the noises that were coming from all around.

Joe started as another little shuffle came, off to the right this time. He squinted into the silver and black, trying to pick out some movement, anything that would tell him what was out there. But he couldn't see anything beyond the scrub in front of him.

He could smell it, though. That carrion stench was really getting to him now, making him nervous—making him scared. Especially since he *knew* there weren't any dead things left out there—he'd just *checked* that area.

Still, his nose kept telling him different.

He and his men *had* found some bodies—but *they* weren't causing that smell, Joe was sure of that.

His men had found four bodies out on the field—four men in Union blue—but Joe didn't know how they'd died—gunshot wounds, cannon fire, whatever—it was impossible for Joe to tell.

The bodies were stripped clean. Their flesh flensed off the bones, stripped bare.

Joe knew what bodies *should* look like—he'd seen enough of them in Antietam, Chicamauga, Gettysburg—dozens of battles— he'd seen thousands of bodies by now. But these . . .

What was left was barely recognizable as human. No face, white bones staring out of the chest, the legs . . .

Joe'd seen that kind of thing before. When he was growing up, he'd stumbled across a dead man in the fields—the body'd been there for days, and the birds and carrion eaters had been at it. Joe remembered staring at that body, looking at the face without eyes, the chest without flesh or muscle . . .

He'd had nightmares about that body for years, dreams in which he was the man on the ground, looking up without eyes, seeing the wolves move in, their jaws opening and closing on his arms, his legs, then moving in, closer, closer . . .

But now, here, on a battlefield, there just weren't any animals to do such a thing. They'd all been scared off by the noise—or shoved into the pot by men tired of rancid bacon and wormy meal—Joe was sure that there wasn't anything big enough left to do *this* to a dead man—and even if there was, it just wouldn't have had the *time*. These men had fallen within the past two days—there wasn't a creature on earth that could strip a body *that* fast.

At least, there wasn't anything that Joe had ever heard of.

He checked his rifle. The percussion cap was in place and intact. Joe quietly pulled the hammer off half-cock, holding the trigger back so there'd be no loud click of metal to draw the attention of any Southern pickets as it settled into position.

Joe wanted to make sure the rifle was ready if he needed it.

The bodies were a puzzle, all right, but not Joe's puzzle. All he had to do was get them back behind the lines and let the officers figure out what happened to them.

He strained his eyes forward—yep, that was one of the Union

bulwarks just ahead; only a little further and everything would be fine. Joe turned, motioning for his men to pass, as he took one last look around. He heard more shuffling to his right and swung his musket around, ready to fire in that direction if he saw . . .

Nothing. Maybe he was letting the look of those corpses get to him. Maybe he'd been out here too long.

He watched as his men began to pass. He was proud of those men. The 5th Colored Regiment may not have gotten into any real fights yet, but they certainly had done their duty.

He didn't know how many white men could have done what his boys had just accomplished: going out between the lines, searching out the corpses, then carrying them back. All without firing a shot or losing a man.

He watched as Kingston and Stratton passed him. Only two more to go. He looked back for White and James; they couldn't be too far behind—he'd seen the two of them just a couple of minutes before when he'd settled one of the bodies into the sling they were carrying between them. Could they have had a problem with the sling? Dropped the body?

But they would have called for him. Wouldn't they?

He froze in place for a moment, searching for some movement, some sign of life. Anything.

But there was nothing but silence, and the silver glow of the moon on the ground. Even the smell was gone—that smell of death and blood.

White and James were gone, too.

Bob Gallagher swung his pick into the surface in front of him, grunting as it clanged against rock. The head had turned, sliding over the surface without penetrating.

Damn! Got to do better than that! Make it hit straight. . . .

He pulled the pick back over his shoulder and tried again, putting his shoulders and back into the action now, striking the rock face with all the anger and frustration that was bubbling in him.

"Hey, Walker! Look at this!" Gallagher pulled the pick out, yanking rock towards him, uncovering a large, open space. He held his breath for a minute, waiting for the stench to waft out around him.

"Hell, Bob. It's just another of them chimneys we've been coming across!"

Gallagher swung again, causing a little avalanche of dirt and rock. The hole in front of him was definitely getting bigger!

"I don't think so. This goes *way* back—look how black it is in there! And take a sniff—there's no smell! Maybe we should call the lieutenant."

Walker moved forward, holding his lamp up so it shone into the large dark area Gallagher had uncovered. The light went back fifteen or twenty feet, then dissipated into the surrounding darkness. Gallagher was right. This was no chimney.

"I'm tellin' you, Howard, there's some kind of cavern in there! It goes on forever! Our lamps don't even show us the roof!"

Major Thomas Feeny was a big man, six foot two and near two hundred fifty pounds. His men called him "Bullhorn," because when he bellowed an order on the field, *everyone* heard. He wasn't bellowing now, though. He was talking quietly and precisely as he tried to convince his commander that orders had to be changed.

"I don't care if there's a damn ocean down there, Tom! I want that tunnel finished and packed with powder by midnight of the twenty-ninth!"

Colonel Howard Pleasants was a small man, just two inches over five feet, never weighing more than 120 pounds. Still, he did not suffer from comparison to the bigger man. Pleasants seemed to grow when he talked, the sheer power of his personality adding inches to his height, pounds to his demeanor.

And when Howard Pleasants was angry, even the biggest of men would hesitate to face him.

"I promised Burnside that we'd be ready to attack on the thirtieth! Everything is planned for that day! I *won't* go back and tell him to reschedule now!"

"But, sir . . ."

"No buts, Feeny. If that damn cavern is so big, it should make your job easier, not harder! Use it! Get an engineer down there to figure out the direction you want to go in and follow the damn cavern!" Pleasants headed for his desk, dismissal in his every move. "Now get out of here!"

20 July, 1864

My dearest sister,

Darrel Walker died yesterday. He was my best friend among the men here. The surgeon says he died of a brain fever, brought on by spending too much time in the tunnel.

I don't believe that. I think he died of fright.

Darrel and I were together nearly the whole day yesterday, shoveling up all the rocks and gravel that block the entrance to a cavern we found. We kept hearing funny noises the whole time we were working there—now, you've got to understand, we've been hearing noises for weeks—shuffling sounds, muffled thumps that *might* be footfalls but darn sure aren't shoes or boots. The tunnel's just been full of sounds, 'specially around those chimney things I wrote you about.

These new sounds were different, though. Louder, closer—different, that's all I can say.

They got so loud yesterday that Darrel decided that he was going to go take a look. He took one of our lanterns—a really good one, powerful, with a directional lens so he could see twenty or thirty feet in front of him—and set off into the cavern to see what was going on. I stayed behind to make sure that the lieutenant didn't find out what he was doing—the cavern's off limits until it gets checked out by Major Feeny. We were sure there wasn't any danger, though. I mean, I could see Darrel's light the whole way—if there was trouble, he knew he could just call out and I'd go to him.

I stood there and watched for a while as the light moved along, getting deeper and deeper into the darkness of the cavern—then I saw it stop—I couldn't see what it was pointed at, but I heard Darrel give a little yell, then the light started back my way, moving lickety-split.

Darrel was white! I don't mean just the skin—his hair was white, too! It was as if he had seen something that just scared him half to death—he was trembling so bad that he dropped the lantern—the lens broke on the rocks below—but I wasn't worrying about that then. I was only worried about getting him some help.

I yelled at the other guys working a couple of yards away to get a doctor or something, then I just sat with Darrel and tried to get him to tell me what he'd seen—tell me what had scared him so much.

He wouldn't say a word, though. Just sat there, arms wrapped tight around his kneecaps, staring back into the dark, trembling and sobbing away.

Nobody came, so finally I picked him up and carried him to the surgeon's tent—but he was dead before I got him there. He never said a word the whole way. Never a word.

Tomorrow, Lieutenant Gaines, Major Feeny, and a bunch of colored boys from the 5th Colored are going to explore around inside—try to find where the cavern ends and figure out where we have to dig to finish our tunnel. But I'm not going to wait for them—I'm going to find out who killed my friend. I'm going to take a lantern and my rifle and go take a look into that cavern.

I'll find out what really killed Darrel Walker.

Your loving brother,

Robert

24 July, 1864

From: The Department of the Army
To: Miss Marie Gallagher

Miss Gallagher:

It is my unhappy duty to inform you of the death of your brother Robert. He, along with several of his comrades in the 58th Pennsylvania, apparently contracted a rare form of brain fever while working on siege works around the Confederate city of Petersburg.

With all respects,

James K. Roberts, Maj.
Adjutant, 58th Pennsylvania

*   *   *

Joe Scroggs was scared to death. He'd always been uncomfortable in small, closed spaces—carriages, railroad cars, even sitting in a honey house made him uncomfortable.

This was worse.

He felt like he was buried alive. And the fact that there were twenty men with him didn't make it any easier.

The tunnel was so small they couldn't even walk upright—Major Feeny practically had to go on hands and knees! Still, they went, the major cursin' away, Joe sweatin', seein' the walls close in further every step he took.

But he couldn't back down. He had to show his men that there was nothin' to be afraid of. Had to show the officers that his colored troops were every bit as good as their white soldiers.

Maybe better.

It was easier when they got into what the major called the "cavern"—*that* was big—so big that even with his light held high, Joe couldn't see the ceiling. So big that even the major could walk straight and tall. Still, there was somethin' wrong here. The floor, for one thing—it wasn't rough and gravelly as Joe expected a cave floor to be. This one was smooth, level, as if someone had *cut* it right out of the rock.

And then there was the smell. Joe smelled it as soon as they were inside. It was the same smell that he'd been smelling for *weeks* above—that carrion odor that had scared him so bad the other night. It was here, faint though, as if it were far away, barely reaching him in the motionless air of the cave.

Joe sighed. He didn't like it, but there was nothing he could do about *that* now. He just kept walking forward, lantern held at arm's length, musket tight against his back, his free arm holding the sling so that the weapon didn't slap against his back or bang against the wall of the cavern.

Besides, that way he was always sure it was still there.

They kept trudgin' along for what seemed like hours, the major and the lieutenant takin' turns peerin' at their compasses, pointin' this way and that. Finally, they came to a halt, the officers huddlin' up around the light of their lanterns, pullin' out maps and makin' lines this way and that on the paper.

Joe motioned his troops to circle around the two preoccupied men. They'd all been hearing noises, and Joe wanted to make sure they were ready for anything—maybe the Rebs had found the cavern. Hell, maybe they'd known it was there all the time.

Joe couldn't just stand there, though. If he did, he'd start feelin' the walls closing in. He had to move, had to keep walking around. He began to check on his men, inspectin' their weapons, makin' sure they were ready for anything.

Time passed. The two officers kept arguing about where they were. Joe realized he couldn't just keep walking in circles forever—he was just making the other men nervous. He'd been hearing those familiar shuffling noises for a while now—out there, in the dark. He was sure they were gettin' louder, as if someone or something were moving just as close as they could, waiting for the men to venture outside of the circle of light—or waiting for the lights to go out.

Joe didn't *want* to leave that circle of safety, but if he stayed where he was, those walls were going to come crashing in and he'd run away screaming. He couldn't let that happen; it was better that he do *something*—even if what he did was the wrong thing. He checked the oil in his lantern, decided there was enough, checked the load in his musket, decided that was all right, too—and realized that he was stalling. He snugged the sling on his rifle back over his shoulder and walked away from the little knot of nervous men, whispering to Corporal Watson that he was going to scout around a bit and that he'd be right back.

As the lights behind him got further away, Joe realized that the sounds were getting fainter, too—it was as if whatever was out there just wasn't ready to be seen. Maybe it *was* some kind of animal after all; a bear or cougar would keep his distance unless . . .

Joe's foot touched something—something big and round. He froze for a moment, mouth open to cry out, stopped only by the realization that the two white officers would carry the story of the terrified *colored* soldier back to the army. He took a deep breath, and turned his lantern down, looking to see what he had stepped on.

And nearly screamed.

He was surrounded by the dead—he could see them clearly, his lantern light reflected all around by a gleaming white skull at his feet. There were dozens of bones here, scores. . . .

And they were all human.

Major Feeny swept his light around the scattered groups of ivory that almost surrounded him. "Yep, these are human bones all right! I guess we know what's been happening to those missing bodies now."

"But how did they get down here?" Lieutenant Gaines kept swinging around, sweeping his torch in little circles as if to prevent the darkness from sneaking up behind him. "Did someone bring them here?"

"I doubt it." Feeny swung his torch toward the ceiling, although its light didn't quite reach. "I suspect that it's those chimneys the miners have been telling us about. We know they extend to the surface. Perhaps wounded or dying men crawl into them for protection, then, as time passes and the flesh rots away, they just slip down to . . . here."

Joe Scroggs was standing a few feet away, his back to the two officers. They were wrong—he knew they were wrong—he held the proof in his hands. It was another skull—this one a man with two gold teeth right in front. Scroggs knew those teeth—knew that smile. It was Dan White, and he sure hadn't had the time to rot out and slip down here—he'd been alive just two days before.

Besides, there wasn't any flesh at all on the skull—even bones that had been here for months would have a little gristle left on them. This one seemed to have been scrubbed clean, just like the ones above. Looking close, though, Joe saw there were a couple of marks—deep indentations here and there on the surface of the bone.

Joe recognized those marks—he'd seen them just the night before when he'd discarded the leftovers from the special dinner his men had caught and cooked.

It was the first chicken he'd had in nearly six months, and he'd been careful to eat every scrap of meat. He'd left some really deep gashes in those bones, grooves where his teeth had dug in.

Marks just like the ones on this skull.

*   *   *

"So, that cavern of yours *does* save us some time, doesn't it?" Colonel Howard Pleasants was in his element now, proved right, ready to be the gracious winner.

"Seems so, sir." Major Feeny planned to go easy here; after all, there was no reason to jeopardize his career. "However, there *are* the bones . . ."

"I thought you had an explanation for that." Pleasants lit up a cigar. "And one that might well keep the Inspector General off our backs!"

Feeny turned away from the other man for a moment, trying to get his thoughts in order. "Well, I *think* that the chimneys are the reason for the bones. But there's a sergeant from the 5th Colored that thinks—"

Pleasants exploded off his chair toward Feeny. "You're listening to some negra troop? You know damn well that they're here as cannon fodder—nothing else!"

"But sir, I thought Mr. Lincoln said . . ."

"Abraham Lincoln can say whatever the hell he wants! Out here in the field, *we* make the decisions! Is that clear?"

Feeny's shoulders sagged. He knew he had lost, but he had felt honor-bound to make the attempt. "And what does the Colonel want me to do?"

Pleasants sauntered back to his chair, taking his time while he savored his cigar. "I'd like you to . . . *use* the colored troops. Use them to fill that cavern with the powder we've set aside. After that, Brigadier Ferrero will do the rest—the colored troops will be the first through the hole, and we'll follow up their assault with a full-scale attack of our own."

Pleasants puffed the cigar hotter and hotter as he warmed to his subject.

"Once through the Reb lines, it's only a two-day march to Richmond and then—the end of the war!"

Feeny heaved a sigh and brought himself to attention for a salute. He hoped the colonel was right; he hoped it would all be as easy as the smaller man said.

But the image of that skull with the gold teeth kept running through his mind—and the marks on it. Scroggs had pointed them out—claimed they were tooth marks.

Feeny had tried, but he just couldn't think what else they could be.

Joe Scroggs sighed heavily. He'd hoped to avoid going down into that hole again, but Major Feeny had insisted. Said it was important that the men who knew their way around help the others along. Scroggs hated the idea, but Feeny was going, and Joe just couldn't bear the idea of being shown up by the big officer.

Besides, there'd be plenty of men this time—and lots of light. 'Course, all that light wasn't going to do them a whole lot of good if someone got careless with it—the kegs of gunpowder they were carrying would sure see to that.

Joe sighed again and hefted his own keg of black death. Time to go inside. He took a last look around at the moon and the stars, then bent his back and started down the tunnel the Pennsylvanians had dug.

Brigadier General Edward Ferrero took another swig from his whisky bottle. Imagine! They wanted him to lead *Negro* soldiers into this battle! And through some damned tunnel! As if he were a darkie himself! Well, Edward Ferrero always obeyed his orders—after taking a little time to get himself ready.

He looked at the bottle. Still a couple of drinks left—sure wouldn't do to waste them. . . .

Major Feeny called Joe Scroggs to his side as soon as they reached the cavern: "Sergeant Scroggs." The big officer gestured into the blank darkness in front of them. "Do you remember the way to that point we marked?"

Scroggs squinted ahead, lifting his lantern to dispel some of the darkness in front of him. "Reckon it was that way, sir. Maybe two, three hundred yards."

Feeny nodded, following the other man's line of sight. "That's the way I see it, too. I'll lead off with these men, you and Lieutenant Gaines wait here—keep the men moving and . . ." Feeny made a face. "If you happen to see General Ferrero . . ."

Joe grinned. General Ferrero's penchant for having a drink or ten on the eve of battle was well known.

Feeny saw the smile and realized Joe understood what he was thinking. He smiled in return. "Tell the good brigadier that I'll be supervising the positioning of the charge."

With that, Feeny turned on his heel and, gesturing to the head of the column to follow, strode into the thick darkness of the cavern.

Above, the siege went on as usual. Sentries patrolled, pickets kept watch over their posts, while the bulk of the two opposing armies slept, undisturbed by the slithering sounds that had become a part of their environment.

Two sentries would be found missing in the morning, but their disappearance was put down to desertion—a common enough occurrence.

No one took notice of the fact that the "desertion" rate had increased by some twenty percent since the start of the Petersburg siege.

Even if they had, they wouldn't have considered it important.

The last man in the long line of powder bearers staggered past Joe Scroggs and Lieutenant Gaines. Joe had lost count, but the lieutenant assured him that nobody was missing; all the men assigned to them had indeed gone into the cavern.

It was time for them to follow.

Joe checked his lantern, touched his rifle butt for reassurance, and followed the lieutenant into the mouth of the big cave. It didn't seem quite so dark this time—probably due to the fact that the light from nearly fifty lanterns was just a couple of hundred feet ahead. Joe couldn't help but notice that the light from those lanterns still didn't reach the walls or the ceiling.

And he noticed that the carrion smell was back, too, stronger than ever.

It took just a couple of minutes to reach Major Feeny. The major was kneeling, looking at something on the ground. Around him, the men of the 5th were milling around, eyes wide as they stared, lanterns pointing this way and that, some of them dangerously near the bags of gunpowder each man was carrying.

They were scared—just like Joe—and just like Joe, were determined not to show it.

"What's up, Major?" Gaines didn't understand why the men hadn't started placing their explosives—they'd certainly had enough time. Was there some problem?

Feeny looked up, motioning for Gaines and the sergeant to join him. "Take a look at this, Bill, Sergeant. Have you ever seen anything like it?"

Joe crouched down for a better look, and blinked as he realized what he was looking at. It was a trail of slime, perhaps two feet wide—it looked like the kind of things slugs left behind them, and the smell, so familiar. . . .

Joe started to reach out to touch it, see what it was made of, but the major brushed his hand aside.

"Better not, Sergeant. Look."

Joe's eyes followed the major's gesture to Private Roskins, who smiled nervously and showed Joe the toe of his boot—or where the toe had been. There was nothing there now, the tough leather dissolved away for about the length of a finger.

"Roskins stuck his toe into that stuff." Feeny nodded toward the slime. "I don't know what would have happened if we hadn't managed to get the boot off and his foot washed down with some water. As it was . . ."

Joe pointed to the slime trail. "Have you noticed the smell, sir? It's the same carrion odor we've been smelling for weeks— the same smell that was on those bodies we found."

Feeny stiffened his jaw and nodded. "That's what I thought, too. We've got to follow this trail—see where it goes."

He turned to the lieutenant. "Bill, you have command for now—see that the powder is placed properly. Sergeant Scroggs and I will follow this up." Feeny looked at Joe. "Right, Sergeant?"

"Whatever you say, sir." Joe unslung his rifle to check it. "Whatever you say."

Colonel Jake Warden hated his job. Staff officer—what a joke. Sure, it had gotten him quick promotion and kept him out of real danger—but it also meant that he had to deal with some really distasteful characters.

Like General Ferrero.

Warden had learned months ago that the good general liked to take an occasional drink—later he had learned that the good general *kept* taking those drinks until he couldn't lift a hand to take another—especially on the eve of a battle. After all, battles were dangerous, and the general didn't like being in dangerous places.

That made Warden's job tonight extra hard. The general was supposed to be leading the 5th Colored Division in tomorrow's assault on the Reb line. He was supposed to be down in the tunnel with them now, getting them ready to attack right after the explosives went off.

Of course, he wasn't doing any of those things. He was in his tent, having taken "one last drink" over and over until he "last drank" himself into a stupor.

Now Warden had to get him up, get him sober, and get him into the tunnel.

Warden accomplished the first part easily enough. The general wasn't *that* big and, fortunately, he wasn't *that* drunk—the bottle hadn't been full when he started. It only took the colonel a couple of minutes of frenzied activity to get Ferrero to his feet, eyes open (Warden took that as a good sign even if they were bloodshot and bleary).

Twenty minutes, and a dozen mugs of coffee later, the general was actually showing signs of intelligent life. Warden decided it was time to start the long walk into the tunnel entrance, and, sure enough, marching the general through the fresh air finished the job the coffee had begun—the general was just about sober by the time they returned the salute of the sentry at the entry point. Now, if Warden could only keep him that way for another couple of hours. . . .

Below, Sergeant Joe Scroggs was wishing he *wasn't* sober. While Lieutenant Gaines supervised the placement of the explosive charges, Joe and Major Feeny explored around, trying to find the source of that unclean trail.

"I'm sure there's some logical explanation, Sergeant." Feeny was very earnest, as anxious to convince himself as Joe. "Perhaps some watercourse badly polluted by one of the new Reb factories in Petersburg."

"And how could it get *here*, sir?" Joe wasn't going to accept any more half-assed explanations; he was going to find the *truth*.

"Well, there are the chimneys . . ."

"Which are dry as a bone." Joe turned to the big officer, gesturing down at the trail in front of them. "Hell, sir. I'm not just one of those ignorant ex-slaves. I've got an education! And this isn't factory spill—you know that as well as I do!"

Feeny sighed. He knew the negro was right—and he knew that if they didn't find *some* explanation, they'd never get anybody to come down this tunnel again. Colonel Pleasants wouldn't like that—and he'd make sure that Feeny suffered for it.

If there was just some other explanation. . . .

Then both men stopped dead in their tracks. They'd been down here so long that they'd actually stopped hearing the shuffling noise that always seemed to fill the cavern—but now they heard a new noise, a high-pitched keening, almost a wail, that came from right in front of them.

Then there was the scream.

Colonel Warden had gotten the general all the way to the cavern entrance. He could see the faint glow of Major Feeny's party some distance ahead. If he could just keep the other officer walking for a little while longer . . .

Then he heard it. A high-pitched wail, just ahead of them, near the cavern wall.

Warden left the general by the rough-hewn entrance and stepped inside, his lantern pointed toward the apparent source of the noise. For a moment, he didn't see anything; then, as his eyes adjusted, he could just make out . . .

Jake Warden screamed. And kept on screaming as his body was caught around the ankles and dragged away, the lantern shattering against the rock floor.

Behind him, General Ferrero saw something white and cancerous flash out of the darkness, then the light shattered and Warden's scream shattered the everlasting night. That was enough for the brigadier. He dropped his own lantern and scurried toward the entrance, trying to remember where that other bottle was hidden. . . .

Scroggs and Feeny froze for a second as the hideous scream knifed through the air of the cavern. Then Joe pulled his rifle off his shoulder and started forward, the major right behind. As they raced toward the receding sound, Joe marveled at what he was doing. He'd never been so scared in his life, yet it seemed completely natural to be running *toward* his fear—he shook his head and kept on moving.

It was about fifty yards before their lantern began to show them the wall ahead. It was the first time they'd seen the outer edges of the cavern, and he was astonished at what the light revealed. There were holes everywhere, probably the outlet points of those "chimneys" everyone had been talking about— and there was something else.

Joe stopped as he reached the wall, holding his lantern up as he tried to keep breathing regularly. The walls were painted with gleaming ichor trails—flows of the same foul slime that Joe and the major had been following—and the smell! It was all Joe could do to keep from retching, the major wasn't quite so lucky; Joe could hear him emptying his stomach a few feet away.

Joe stared at the walls, frozen in place as he tried to think of what could have left all these trails: *What kind of creature could it be? And how many are there?*

Then he jumped at another of those ungodly screams—louder now, closer . . .

Joe turned and found Feeny in front of him, the officer's lantern flashing toward the point those tortured sounds seemed to be coming from, the cold light moving across the floor until it revealed the source of the sound.

It was a man—or what had once been a man. He was wearing the tattered remains of a Union uniform, but that wasn't what Feeny and Joe were staring at—it was his face.

Or the place where his face should have been.

There was nothing there except the gleaming white of teeth

and the staring hemispheres of his eyes—eyes that continued to roll in the gleaming sockets of his skull while his teeth kept gaping open in silent echo to the screams that had brought the two soldiers running.

Joe stared in horror—the thing in front of him was still alive! The man's face, upper chest, hell, half his body was gone and yet he lived! Joe could see the ultimate agony in those eyes and realized there was only one thing he could do. He pulled the hammer on his rifle back off half-cock and aimed carefully at the staring eyes of the *thing* that had once been a man.

He was sure he saw a look of thanks as he pulled the trigger.

The echoing *boooom* of Joe's rifle brought Feeny back to himself. He dragged his eyes away from the thing on the ground and looked around, trying to make some sense out of what had happened—then he saw them.

It was the shufflers, the things that had made the sounds in the night, the things which had taken the missing bodies. There were just a few of them in the circle of illumination that Feeny's lantern cast, but he could see other shapes in the darkness behind them—dozens of shapes, perhaps hundreds.

Feeny's fingers dug into Joe Scroggs' shoulder, and the black sergeant looked up to further horror. The holes in the walls, the "chimneys," had disgorged their contents—and those contents were terror itself. They moved closer, blind white shapes gliding on slime somehow excreted from sluglike bellies, glowing white tentacles outstretched. Joe watched in horror as tentacle ends moved closer to his face, their ends puckering slightly, then opening to reveal tiny white teeth, gnashing open and closed as he watched.

Then, adding horror to horror, a tiny white tongue appeared, hanging over those teeth, slavering and dripping a steaming ooze to the ground, the drops burning tiny holes in the hard rock.

Joe backed up, staggered by the horror, half-strangled by the strength of the odor they emitted—it was the smell! That carrion smell magnified a hundredfold! He took another step back, then another. The horrible, slobbering things kept *shuffling* forward, closer, closer . . .

Joe had heard that sound before—he'd been hearing it for weeks. Now he knew what it was. The tentacles reached for him, teeth moving, ten feet away, five, three . . .

Joe brought his rifle up, squeezing the trigger, then, as the hammer clicked on a spent cap, he realized that it was empty—he'd used his only shot! His head jerked around then, looking in panic for the major, catching sight of the big man just as a tentacle flashed toward him.

That was enough. Reputation or not, laughter or not, Joe Scroggs turned and ran for the glow of his comrades' position.

Major Feeny was right behind him.

Lieutenant Gaines had heard the screams and the loud retort of Joe's rifle. He hadn't been sure what to think—perhaps Major Feeny had been forced to shoot the black sergeant—but Gaines had heard a rifle, not a pistol.

He cocked his own weapon and settled down to wait. With Feeny gone, he was in command, and there was a mission to be completed. Gaines had almost completed the setting of the explosives; the bags of powder were in position and the men were setting the fusing now. There would be no difficulty in meeting the colonel's timetable for the morning's surprise attack, and Lieutenant Gaines was going to make sure that the right person got the credit for it.

After all, *he* had done all the work while the major went off on some half-assed expedition of his own; it was only fair that he take the credit—he didn't plan to remain a lieutenant forever.

Joe Scroggs could hear the shuffling close behind him. He was only a hundred feet or so from the glow of the company's lanterns now; if he could just reach them, he knew he'd be safe. He could hear Major Feeny just to his right and behind. The bigger man was puffing away, unable to match Joe's speed over such a distance. *Only fifty more feet . . .*

Joe could see the rest of the men now—see them sitting around, lounging against the piles of gunpowder that were stacked ten high all around them. There was the lieutenant; it looked like he didn't know what the hell he was doing—like always.

Then Joe noticed that the lieutenant was raising his pistol. Were the creatures that close behind him? He started to look over his shoulder just as the pistol *cracked*.

Major Feeny saw Gaines fire his pistol, saw Joe Scroggs take the ball in the belly and tumble to the earth, then he was on top of the black man. He slid to a halt, pushing panic to the back of his mind: *Got to get him . . .*

Feeny gritted his teeth, expecting one of those tentacles to grab him any second; but he didn't look back, just reached down, grabbed the sergeant's webbing, and started moving toward the safety of the lights, dragging the smaller man behind him.

"What the hell did you shoot for?" he bellowed at the gape-mouthed Gaines.

"But sir . . ." Gaines was shocked. He'd heard the shot some minutes before, and when he'd seen the black sergeant running his way, rifle at port, eyes white and wild, he'd naturally assumed that the NCO had gone crazy, murdered the major, and was on his way to kill Gaines. What else could he do but shoot first? "I just naturally assumed—"

"You ass! Take care of this man!" Feeny laid Scroggs gently on the ground, glaring at Gaines until the lieutenant kneeled by the wounded man. "The rest of you! Stop staring at me and look out there! Make sure nothing—"

His warning was too late. Before the men could begin to react, tentacles began to appear out of the stygian darkness. Tentacles that grabbed men around the face, the arm, the leg—men fell, screaming. Everywhere those tentacles touched, flesh began to burn, liquefying and running off. The remains were caught by the snapping teeth, swallowed, digested even before it reached the creatures' stomachs.

Men sobbed, watching as their flesh sloughed off their bones, fighting with fading strength as the shamblers dragged them off to their fate.

They tried to rally, tried to use their muskets on the intruders, but it was not to be. The weapons fired, minié balls thumping into the skin of the creatures, but they did no harm—simply passed through and disappeared into the darkness beyond. And as the soldiers worked to reload, questing tentacles appeared out of the darkness, grabbing, burning, killing. . . .

Major Feeny was everywhere, trying to organize a defense here, fighting off an attack there—but it was a losing battle. More and more of his men were disappearing, dragged away by the shambling horrors. Others, their courage shattered, tried to run, only to be cut off and grappled before they could get fifty yards.

Then Feeny himself fell, firing his pistol over and over into the thing whose grasping member was slowly turning his waist and chest into liquefied gore.

Joe Scroggs regained consciousness then, eyes opening just as the major began screaming. Joe saw Feeny pulled away, his ribs gleaming white in the light of the few remaining lanterns, and as Feeny disappeared, Joe fought to get to his feet: *Got to die like a man* . . .

Then Joe saw the bags of powder all around, and realized that there *was* something he could do—if he could find . . .

He saw Lieutenant Gaines then, not ten feet away, mouth hanging open as he gaped at the carnage all around him. The lieutenant's pistol was hanging in his hand, and Joe grabbed it, pulling it away from the terrified officer.

Scroggs knew what he had to do, knew there was only one way to prevent these things from decimating both armies, killing blue and gray alike. He dragged himself toward the stacks of gunpowder, barely slowing when the lieutenant was grabbed around the face and neck and dragged away, his eyes and chin falling almost at Joe's feet.

Got to make it! I'm the only one who can. . . . Joe pulled himself to the first of the gunpowder bags, clawing at its side, trying to get the thing to burst. *Come on! Come on!*

He barely felt the pain as one of the tentacles grabbed his ankle, the flesh rolling off in seconds, the bare bone held tight in the shambler's grasp. The bag had to give! It just had to!

And then it did. Black grains of gunpowder poured onto the

floor, and Joe calmly drove the pistol into the opened bag, making sure it was deep in the powder.

Then he pulled the trigger.

The New York Herald
July 30, 1864

TELEGRAPH FLASH FROM PETERSBURG

Onlookers witnessed the most awesome spectacle of the entire conflict this morning when more than four tons of gunpowder were detonated beneath Confederate lines here.

An immediate assault was launched into the confused remnants of the Rebel front. The 5th Colored Regiment, under the command of Brigadier General Edward Ferrero, rushed into the breach, and fighting was heated and close, neither side giving or asking for quarter.

"Why did the explosives go off so early?" General George Meade hated failures—especially failures that cost him men. He was determined to find out who was responsible for this fiasco. Two hours early! And he'd lost nearly four thousand men trying to follow up! Four thousand!

"General Ferrero was in charge of the operations, why not. . . ." Colonel Henry Pleasants was equally determined to avoid any blame for this. After all, his plan had been sound; it was the execution that was at fault.

"General Ferrero was found lying in a bomb proof, roaring drunk! He's been telling us some wild story about huge white creatures *eating* our troops!"

Pleasants snorted, brushing a speck of dust off his uniform—the whole camp was full of dust, the remnants of yesterday's explosion. "Well sir, surely I can't be held responsible for someone else's lack of discipline. Perhaps there's still something more we can do, though. My Pennsylvanians tell me that there was some kind of cavern under the tunnel; if we were to run a new shaft . . ."

"Enough of this!" Meade stood up so fast that his camp chair fell to the floor. "I thought this was a bad idea before! Now I'm sure of it!

"Get out of here, Pleasants! And don't let me see you again!"

Henry Pleasants stood up and saluted smartly, then about-faced and left the general's tent. *Typical. Can't face the fact that it was his execution at fault, not my plan.*

Pleasants stopped to light a cigar, a slight smile on his lips. *Besides, we only lost the coloreds.*

He tossed the match away. *Too bad about Feeny, though. He was a pretty good man.*

Pleasants started strolling back to his regiment. *Maybe if I try writing directly to Grant . . .*

3 August, 1864

From: Colonel Jerome Wilhite
To: General George Montgomery

Sir:

I have to report that we seem to be having further problems with our casualty reports. Again, bodies found and tagged are far fewer than those reported killed or wounded in action. In addition, desertion seems on the rise, with many soldiers assigned to picket or guard duty disappearing each night.

Reports of odd noises and smells around our lines continue. Could the Confederates somehow be infiltrating and attempting to damage morale? I'd like to request an additional fifty noncommissioned officers so I can double the number of sergeants of the guard and keep a closer eye on sentries.

In addition, could we bother some colored troops to search for the dead? It would do wonders for the morale of our troops.

Jerry

Sons

Charles Grant

Charles Grant has lived in New Jersey all his life, which might set you to wondering why he was given the Phoenix Award—Deep South Con's life achievement for Southern professionals. Charlie likes Southern conventions. Southern fans like Charlie, adopting him as one of their own. Charlie's specialty is serving as emcee for the costume class, his well-practiced patter and quick ad libs earning repeat performance invitations year after year.

Charlie has written or edited nearly a hundred books, winning three World Fantasy awards, two Nebulas, and one British Fantasy Award. Although best known for such dark fantasy novels as *The Pet, For Fear of the Night,* and *Stunts,* he has occasionally ventured into other genres, most notably with his post-holocaust novels *The Shadow of Alpha* and *Ascension.*

What makes Charlie both critically respected and popular with readers is his ability to work comfortably in a variety of styles. Under the name Geoffrey Marsh, he wrote the novelization of the Bruce Willis movie *Hudson Hawk,* significantly improving the source material. His "Kent Montana" series, which he writes as Lionel Fenn, displays the same sort of humor that has made him popular with convention goers.

Charlie lives in a one-hundred-year-old Victorian house with his wife, Kathy Ptacek, and their three cats. In his spare time he likes to shoot down enemy planes on his computer screen.

There's nothing to it, Momma, nothing to it at all. So you just sit down there, don't bother your head about nothing, and if you're real good, I don't guess I'll have to kill you.

Now for heaven's sake, stop that fretting. I know it's a terrible thing to say about a man's momma, I truly do, but I can't have you carrying on like that. People hear, they come running, I'll have to leave again, and you don't want that. You don't want me back in the woods again so soon.

Do you.

I didn't think so, Momma. I didn't think so.

So just calm yourself, the tea's brewing, and soon as it's done I'll get us some, and some of them corn biscuits too, just the way we used to do it, remember?

Here. Take this cloth, wipe those tears.

I still love you, Momma, you know.

In spite of everything, I still love you.

See, the thing is, I don't mean to be rotten, you know I'm not disrespectful, but O *Lord,* I'm tired. So damn tired. Moving around all the time, not having a real bed to sleep in, coldest winter that I can remember . . . it's so nice now just to sit here for a while, not have to worry about anything. Listen to the birds, feel the sun, kind of close my eyes a little, blur things so all there is left is green and brown and a touch of sunlight gold and that rainbow in the garden down by the road. Feel the breeze. Even now it's only April, it gets so hot out there sometimes, Momma, you wouldn't believe it. And the only time the birds sing is just before the sun comes up and there's that mist from the river moving along the ground, the trees growing out of all that white like they was growing out of clouds. The birds would do their singing, the ground would be kind of damp and cold, and it was like there was nothing wrong in the world, Momma, nothing wrong at all.

So nice just to sit here.

So nice not to run.

Reminds me of the way it was in the beginning. Me and Jake and Ram. Piss and vinegar, you said we was, three of the damnedest sons you ever had. So damnfool excited sometimes, you had to practically beat us with the skillet to keep us from running off without our boots.

Remember that, Momma?

Yes, I see you do.

Oh God, Momma, you don't know how good it is to see you smile again. Had that picture of you in my bedroll don't know how long. The men said, That your girl, Goldy?—they called me Goldy on account of my hair being so much like yours, Momma—and I'd say, No, that's my momma, Mrs. Vangeline Rooten, of Hart's Bend, Tennessee. They did so say that, they really did. They just couldn't believe you look so young. Made me proud. 'Course, Ram, being the way he is, he thought they was making fun and got into a lot of fights until the sergeant— he's from down Chattanooga—took hold of Ram's collar and dumped him in the nearest creek like he was putting out a fire. Jake too, because he couldn't let Ram take on all them folks on his own. But I knew better. I knew they wasn't making fun. I knew. I could see it in their eyes.

Like I could see how all the fun was gone the day after the Federals finally drove us out of Fort Donelson. It was horrible, Momma. I had no idea it would be like that. So much smoke, so much fire, people screaming and hollering like the Devil himself was walking through the fighting. Man next to me—didn't even have time to learn his name—had his arm torn off, and one time I fell over a captain who didn't have the top of his head and he wasn't dead yet and kept trying to push himself up to his knees.

It was red, Momma.

The world had turned red.

They tried to keep us together when we left, but some of us saw how it was, saw how it was going to be from now on, and we knew this wasn't the place to make a stand. Not with the officers we had, strutting around, trying to pretend they knew what they were doing, praying to God and Davis and not getting any answers. Some of the boys, they stayed to fight anyway. Stayed to die. Stayed to get caught. Not me. You know I ain't no coward, but there wasn't a way in the world I was ending up in some damn camp or other like I was some dog you tie up in the shed. And I wasn't ready to die, either. No sense in it. Can't fight if you're dead. Can't do Davis or God any good at all getting picked on by crows. So Jake and Ram and me, we lit out north and east, thinking we could hit up somewhere with someone else, another unit, one that knew what it was doing and could stop them bastards. Went back into the hills for a while. Ram had taken a good nick in the upper arm from a ball, Jake wrapped it, and we rested for a while. But by the time we got around to Nashville, they was already marching out.

I couldn't believe it, Momma.

Federals spit on the ground, look at you cross-eyed—them crawl-bellies, they took off, I don't even know if anyone bothered to fire a single shot.

That's the first time I really got mad.

That's the first time I really hated.

And I got to admit it, that's the first time I was really scared I wasn't going to come home.

Ram didn't think the bluecoats would bother with us, twitch a tail like a mule at a fly, that's all. Jake, though, he said they probably knew damn well we were the ones who blew up some of the supply wagons that first night after Nashville. We did, too. They're fools, you know. Figure they got it all in the palm of their hand, and we slipped in there, slipped out again . . . like shadows, Momma, just like shadows. Just like you taught us. Next thing you know, there's fire and light in the sky and the earth is shaking and Jake has us running so hard, so long, so fast, I thought I'd died before morning.

Didn't, though.

Maybe I should have.

No, Momma, don't start crying again. I ain't crazy, truly I ain't.

You don't understand yet.

It snowed that night, you see. Not hard, but enough to turn all that red to white in a couple of quiet hours. We had the blankets you gave us, but we didn't dare light a fire because we had no idea how many of the Union boys were sneaking around the hills, looking for us. So we kept moving, must've been two days, until Ram couldn't take another step. Damn arm wouldn't stop burning and bleeding. Be fine for a while, then it'd start again, so we found this pretty deep cave up off a ledge. Didn't have a bear, just dead leaves and some bones in the corner. Tell you the truth, I've never been so cold in my life. Teeth chattering so hard, I thought they'd fall out. Ram's arm stiffened up. Jake just sat there, looking out at the trees down in the valley. I could tell what he was thinking.

"You don't want to fight," I said.

He shook his head real slow.

"You think we're wrong."

He didn't move at all.

"So why didn't you ever tell Momma? This'll kill her."

His head turned so slow I didn't know he was looking at me until I saw his eyes, bloodshot and wide. "Momma ain't got nothing to do with this, Goldy," he said. "Momma don't know about this at all."

"You're crazy!"

His smile then, so sad I nearly cried. "You're only fifteen, Goldy, you don't understand. You don't know."

"Well, if you don't like it so much," Ram said, trying to yell, ending up coughing, "how the hell come you helped blow up them wagons?"

Jake didn't answer.

He looked back at the valley, at the snow, and when the sun went down, the wind came up to dance with our fire.

I didn't sleep much that night, listening to the wind. It talked to me. I didn't understand it at first. Whistling a little. Sighing a little. Sometimes coming down from the top of the mountain and screaming into the cave. After a while, though, it all started to make sense.

It really did.

It made me remember that night last summer.

Remember, Momma?

You showed me things. Me! 'Cause I was your favorite, you always said that, and you showed me things I didn't believe them, and you just smiled like Jake did that night in the cave, and you kissed me and said the wind would tell me when.

It did, Momma.

I never believed it before.

But that night, I was so scared, I didn't want to end up like Ram and all them others that turned red . . . I was so scared. . . .

So after a while I took some of them old bones—possum, I

guess, and a couple of squirrels, maybe—and tore off a bit of Ram's bandage. He was sleeping, moaning, sweating so bad you'd think it was July out there beyond the cave, and he didn't even know what I'd done. Jake had fallen asleep in the mouth, leaning up against the rock, musket on his shoulder just like he was standing guard. He didn't see me tie the bones up, didn't see me stuff it into my shirt. Didn't have string or rawhide to hang it around my neck, so I just tucked it in good.

And listened to the wind.

Next day, Jake said we had to get Ram to a doctor or he'd lose that arm. I didn't say anything. I guess I knew even then Ram was going to die. You could see it in his face—there was no color there, even with the cold that made Jake and me turn red on the cheeks and forehead. No color at all. He didn't talk either when we stood him up. Just looked at us like he didn't know who we were. Jake cursed a lot and made me take hold of Ram's waist to help him down off the ledge into the trees.

We walked forever.

Slept in a field that night.

Slept in a barn night after that.

Ram was dead. He was walking and all, but I could see that he was dead, so it didn't make any difference that Jake found a doctor that afternoon. His place was right outside a little town that looked like it didn't have nobody in it at all. The man, he called himself Anthrop and claimed he wasn't fighting because he thought war was a sin even if all the other men had already gone to be at Davis' side . . . that man wouldn't even let us bring Ram inside. We had to lie him down in the front yard, keep some dogs away with a stick while that fat little bastard unwrapped the bandages. I couldn't look.

Black.

Ram's arm was turning black, and he screamed when the doctor touched it with his cane.

"Have to take it off," he said, shaking his head, covering his nose with a handkerchief. "Don't think it'll do any good, though."

It didn't.

Ram died before Anthrop came back with the liquor and the saw.

He just lay there, looking at Jake, looking at me, then closed his eyes.

Just like that.

Man took one look at him and said, "That'll be a dollar, boys."

Jake spat at his shoes and walked off, dragging his musket behind him.

"Dollar," the man said to me.

I wanted to cry, and I wanted to kill him, but I said, "Jefferson Davis says every man's got to do his part."

"Jefferson Davis," the doctor said, "don't have to feed my family. A dollar. A real one."

I slung my musket over my right shoulder, picked up Ram and slung him over my left. The doctor, he just looked at me like I was something that come up from the bottom of the river, and when I started after Jake, he said, "You ought to go home, boy, go back to your momma before you end up like your brother."

He laughed.

I hated again.

But I kept on walking, up the road to where Jake was sitting on a rock, looking mad enough to split the sky with a wink. Ram wasn't heavy at all, so I didn't mind when Jake said we had to go into the field yonder and bury him.

The ground was hard, but we used our hands anyway.

Jake said some words, and I held the bones against my stomach.

I had my first dream that night, Momma.

Later, Jake and me, we found another barn falling down like some old woman, but at least it was out of the wind and the snow that started up again, and that's where I had my first dream. I guess it was a nightmare, because when I woke up, Jake was holding me just like you used to when I was a baby and dreamed that Daddy was coming back from the dead to get me. He said I was yelling a lot, but I don't remember. I just remember that it was so cold, there in the barn and there in the dream, and it was so dark that I couldn't see the end of my nose. I guess I thought I was dead. I don't know. Then it got to be light and I knew it was dawn. I wanted to sleep—God, I was tired—but Jake said we had to move on. He heard wagons passing along the road in the night, dragging guns. He didn't know whose they were, but he didn't figure they were ours.

I knew they weren't.

I pointed to the barn door.

It all happened so slow, it was like I was back in the dream.

One of the doors had been swung open, and a man stood there, black against the dawn light, the snow so bright it hurt my eyes and made them water.

He had a gun.

Jake dove for the musket in the straw next to us, but the man was faster. It sounded like everything blew up. A flash, thunder, birds flying out of the loft, Jake flying backward into the wall of an empty stall. The wood gave way and he fell through it and didn't get up. I knew he was dead. I saw parts of his face hanging in the air.

Slow.

It was slow.

Then the man saw me.

But I already had my musket up and aimed.

"I'm not the only one out here," the man said, and there was white in the dark place where the shadows hid his face. He was grinning at me.

I shot him.

He didn't fly; he just fell where he stood.

I kind of ran and crawled at the same time, grabbed his shoulders and dragged him back inside. Closed the door. Reloaded and waited.

Listening to the snow scratching against the barn.

Listening to the wind talking to me out there.

Waiting for the rest of the Union patrol to bust in and try to kill me.

I waited until dark.

Holding the bones.

I don't mind telling you, Momma, I was so scared I thought I'd go crazy. Every sound, every creak of the barn, every bird that shifted in the straw up in the loft . . . I thought it was them, coming to get me. So I held that packet of bones and prayed all night, just like you taught me. I prayed, I cried a little, I maybe even fell asleep for a little while, I don't know; but when the next sun came, I was still alive. Damn near frozen solid, but I was still alive. I could hear, off in the distance, horses snorting, straps and spurs jingling, so the Federals were still around. Sounded to me like they was getting ready to move out, so I made my way over to where Jake was lying, and I thought about burying him there in the barn. Pull some boards up from the floor and slip him under. The ground was too hard to dig by myself, and I didn't dare go out there anyway because I knew I'd get caught.

Poor old Jake.

So I did just like you taught me.

Yes, I did.

All right, Momma, that's enough! Goddamnit, if you didn't want me to make the bones, you should have kept your mouth shut. If you didn't want me coming back here, you should have picked someone else, Jake or Ram, to be your favorite. I never asked for it! I never did anything so special you should pick me instead of one of them. So just shut your mouth and listen!

You started it.

I'm gonna finish it.

Oh, God. Oh, God, I'm tired. It's making me say things I don't really mean.

Forgive me, Momma.

Or not.

Right about now, I don't give a damn.

'Cause that next night I left the barn. They weren't ever going to find Jake, and I made sure they weren't ever going to find Ram, either. I was stronger. I could dig. And when it was done, I went back into the hills, but not so deep that I couldn't keep up with that Union patrol.

That's when I truly believed you, Momma.

That's when I knew whose bones were in *your* little bag.

So the weather started to warm, sun got brighter, there were some skirmishes once in a while, people on one side or the other getting killed.

I did my part.

Mr. Davis, he'd be proud of me, don't you think?

'Course, I feel a little sorry for the mommas of some of them boys, don't you? I mean, they come marching all the way from up Massachusetts or New York or someplace like that, and their mommas pretty soon stop getting letters and they won't ever know what happened to their babies. I heard one Federal lieutenant, hardly looked older than me, he was complaining that half his men were running off west, figuring it was better to fight the Indians than their own kind.

Some of them did.

Some of them didn't.

Hey, I think the tea's about ready, you want some?

No, you just sit. I'll fetch it. You want some of them biscuits I smelled coming up the road? Good. You look like you could use some good food now and then, Momma. You're much too rail-thin, if you don't mind me saying so.

No.

You know I won't eat them, but thank you anyway.

I'll eat later this week.

Heard some rumors about lots of movement up by Pittsburg Landing. Seems like it's gonna be a hell of a fight.

Lots of smoke.

Lots of fire.

Lots of . . .

No, Momma, don't worry, they ain't gonna catch me.

You know they won't.

When I have to be, I'm just like a shadow.

Slip in, slip out.

And if they see me, what the hell, I'm just some dirt-poor fifteen-year-old boy with a bag of his brother's bones hanging around his neck. Addlepated. Who the hell's gonna be scared of someone like me?

There's that smile again.

Lord, you're pretty, Momma!

Hey, Momma, I have an idea. You ain't had much to eat since I left, I can see that, what with the biscuits and all, and you're looking a little older, please don't take offense. You want to go with me? We'd have someone to talk to then, and they surely ain't gonna stop a pretty lady with her weak-minded boy.

No, Momma, I don't hate you no more, and I'm sorry for the way I spoke to you. I see what it's all about now.

So why don't you come with me?

Just like old times.

In and out like shadows, Momma.

And a long time before we're ever hungry again.

Butternut and Blood

Kathryn Ptacek

Kathryn Ptacek was raised in the southwestern United States and attended the University of New Mexico, where she received a B.A. in journalism. She's been a full-time writer since 1979, with eighteen novels and three anthologies to her credit.

Her official bio says she has worked in a number of genres. That's perhaps an understatement. She may be the only person ever to publish a historical romance and a giant gila monster novel in the same year. Kathy's best known for such novels as *Ghost Dance* and *Shadoweyes,* and for her frequent short story appearances.

In the introduction to her much acclaimed *Women of Darkness* anthology, Kathy cites the scarcity of women writers in the horror genre as a motivating factor for her project. The success of that project led to her 1991 anthology, *Women of the West.* Kathy also edits a monthly newsletter, "The Gila Queen's Guide to Markets," which lists opportunities for writers and artists.

As mentioned in the introduction to Charles Grant's story, Kathy and Charlie live in a Victorian house in Newton, New Jersey. While Charlie sits at his computer monitor and protects the family from airborne assault, Kathy spends her spare time tending to her very fine collection of tea pots.

He first saw her on the autumn night when the temperature plunged toward freezing, and the stink of smoke combined with that of dying leaves and dying men.

John Francis Foster had himself been wounded just three days ago in battle, and after laying a full day and a chill rainy night on the blood-soaked field—there were not enough able-bodied men to collect the wounded and dying—he had finally been located and brought in.

The first evening there in the relative comfort of the hospital tent, Foster had done nothing but sleep and occasionally moan. The second night he had slept less heavily, and once he woke, fell back to sleep quickly, hardly aware of his injuries, for the moment.

The third night he was fully awake, fully aware of the pain in his side where the minié ball had puckered his flesh, and where a fall had broken his arm in two places; and it was then he saw the woman.

She stood at the far end of the tent talking to one of the patients there, a young dark-haired man whose left leg had been shattered by shot and then later amputated. The man's condition was fair because he was young and in good health overall, and he was expected to leave the hospital in a week or so. The man was far luckier than many other of his comrades in this place, Foster thought.

A woman in this hellish place was an odd sight, Foster realized, for all the nurses, save one, were male, mostly Marines assigned to this duty. Perhaps this woman was one of the civilians from a nearby farm or town, come to visit the wounded, come with gifts of food, come to cheer them up.

He shifted his head slightly, closed his eyes when the nausea hit him, then once he was all right, looked to his right. A boy, surely no older than fourteen, lay curled on the cot. A smell of pus and urine came from him. Foster, too long accustomed to the sharp smells of battlefield and hospital now, scarcely noticed the stench. On the far side of the boy—Foster thought the lad's name was Willy—slept an overweight man with a reddened countenance.

A drinker, Foster thought, and envied the man his liquid escape. Now, though, the drinker snored heavily, spittle bubbling on his plump lips. Foster didn't know what was wrong with the drinker, but he'd been there the longest of any of the patients, and he did not seem likely to leave any time soon.

To Foster's left lay an old sergeant; the man must have been all of fifty or so, but he looked elderly now. His skin was gray and hung in folds upon his body where he had lost so much weight. Since Foster had been there, the sergeant had not opened his eyes; his breathing, scarcely audible, never varied. Across the narrow walkway between rows of cots, Foster could see others similar to him—men with bandages on heads, across their eyes, around stumps of arms and legs, swathing torsos.

During the day some of them talked—those in less pain—but at night it was bad. While some slept, oblivious to their pain and the anguish of those around them, most of the wounded suffered more through the long dark hours. Few spoke at all, but Foster heard much groaning and sobbing and cursing and whimpering, while others wordlessly tossed in their fevered states; occasionally a plaintive voice prayed to die.

At the end of the tent, just a few feet away from the woman, stood a tall movable screen. It had once been white cloth, but now was spotted with red and yellow and black, from all the patients who had faced the surgeon's desperate ministrations behind it. A sturdy table upon which operations were conducted sat behind that barrier, and one modest cabinet which stored the surgeon's meager supply of drugs and tools.

The woman glanced up now and saw Foster watching, and she smiled, and he thought how beautiful she was—quite the loveliest he had seen in a long time. Her waist-length hair, caught at the nape of her slender neck, appeared to be a reddish gold, or so it seemed in the dim light. He could not see the color of her eyes, though they seemed dark. Her lips were red and full, her skin pale, but that was the way of many of our Southern ladies, he reflected. She wore a gown of good cloth, a sober gray in color, much like the uniforms of Foster's army.

Or the uniforms that we once had, he thought, as he noted the appearance of each of the patients. Some still wore the remnants of their uniforms—the gray with butternut trim, but most had only discolored rags, and even those with nearly whole uniforms had added a color; the men wore gray and butternut and blood.

The woman was bending over the young amputee now, holding his hand. Foster looked away. Perhaps she was a sister or the man's fiancée.

He fell asleep soon after that, and when he woke again, the woman was gone.

The next day the young man died.

The doctors came by that afternoon and examined each man. They told Foster that he must rest more and spooned down some awful-tasting medicine. His meals that day were several mouthfuls of a thin gruel over which a chicken had been passed for flavor, or so he suspected, and in which floated a few wild onions. It was all that his stomach could tolerate.

That night he felt much worse than he had the night before, the pain radiating out from his side, coursing down his legs until he thought his limbs were on fire; his arm throbbed each time he took a breath. He forced himself not to think about his condition, forced his mind to other matters, such as his family.

His family waited for him at home in eastern Tennessee, and God willing, he would be with them soon. He wished he could get a letter home to his wife, but no one had come by, asking if he wanted to write letters; no one in the tent had pencil or paper for him to use. So he wrote the letters to Sarah, and to his parents, in his mind. Each night he revised the letter from the night before; he concentrated on each word, each phrase. He thought it was the only way to keep the pain at bay.

He was not always successful.

The night he slept fitfully, and once when he woke—or perhaps it was simply a dream—he saw the titian-haired woman again, and this time she was at the second cot from the door, and she had somehow *crawled* up onto the body of the sleeping soldier there, and she seemed to be leaning over his chest and whispering to him. Her hair hung in long burnished folds, and all Foster could see through that curtain was the tips of her breasts pushing at the confines of her gown. He blinked, his vision blurred, and when he awoke, the man in the second cot— an Irishman with flaming red hair—lay alone.

The next day as Foster struggled to sit upright, he thought of his dream the night before. How curious it had been. He'd never dreamt anything like that before; never. And what did this most peculiar dream mean?

Perhaps it meant, he thought with what passed for a grin, he had been too long without a woman.

He saw that a man across from him was awake and spooning down the gruel the nurses brought them, and he decided that he would visit a little.

"John Francis Foster," he said when he had caught the other man's attention.

"Webster Long," the other said.

They exchanged information on their individual companies and their fighting experiences real and exaggerated, and that last battle which had sent them to the hospital. Long, a private who'd volunteered as had Foster, had lost an eye to a bayonet, and his head was nearly encased with dressings so that Foster couldn't tell what color the man's hair was. Long had a fair moustache, though, and a pale blue eye. Foster shifted slightly, wincing at the jab of pain.

"Did you see something odd here last night?" he asked when he'd settled himself more comfortably.

"Odd?" Long paused, a piece of cornbread in his hand. "What do you mean by that?"

"A woman was here. I saw her last night and one night before."

Long shook his head. "Didn't see no woman. You must be dreaming." He smiled. "Wisht I had those dreams."

Foster grinned back. "No, brother, I tell you; I saw a woman. Down there." He pointed with his chin where the red-haired Irishman lay.

"No, didn't see it." Long popped the last of the cornbread in his mouth, then brushed the crumbs from his moustache. "Was she purty?"

"Beautiful."

"Tell me," Long said as he leaned back against the wall.

Foster proceeded to describe the woman in great detail; it was true that after a moment or so he began to embellish the description. It was the look in Long's remaining eye that made him do it. Long wanted something out of the ordinary, something to keep him from thinking of his condition, and Foster decided he would give it to the other man.

"An angel," Long breathed.

"I would think so," Foster said. It was true he had never seen a woman as lovely as this one. His Sarah was right comely, but not the way this other woman was. Sarah, too, worked the farm with him, and she had red, roughened hands and skin darkened by the sun. She was just as lovely, he thought, as the day he'd first married her three years before.

At that moment one of the nurses, a husky man—they had to be, Foster knew, strapping and strong so that they could hold down the screaming men whose arms or legs were being sawn off without the benefit of anesthesia—entered the tent. He was here to check each convalescing man; he began at Foster's and Long's end, and then when he reached the other end, he shouted for another nurse, who rushed in.

"This man's dead." And the first nurse pointed at the red-haired Irishman.

Foster had thought the man was simply sleeping.

The two nurses managed to take the corpse out; Foster and Long looked at one another, but said nothing. An hour later another man, freshly injured in the fighting that continued, had claimed the vacant cot.

Foster spoke a little more with Long and several others who were that day more alert; and when nightfall came, and their last meal was being served, he knew he was ready to sleep.

Still, it puzzled him that Long hadn't seen the woman, and neither had the two other men Foster questioned. He could see that Long might not have seen her because of the bandages across that side of his face. Still . . .

Foster ate his cornbread, slightly greasy but still tasting the best he'd ever had, and quickly slurped up his broth and called for more. It was the first time he'd ever wanted more than the one bowlful.

After using the chamberpot held by one of the nurses, a great ugly fellow who looked as if he much preferred to kill each one of the wounded men rather than wait upon them, Foster eased himself down onto his cot and pulled up the coarse sheet. The sun had long ago gone down and a light chill had set in. From outside he could smell newly mown hay, the last of the year, and he wondered if the hospital lay close to a farm still being worked. There were so few left intact since the war had begun.

He missed his own farm and wondered how it fared. He had men to work it, but had they left for the war as he had done? What had his wife done, left with only her old infirm father and the handful of slaves they owned?

He caught a scent of something else now, a smell almost of spice, some exotic fragrance that seemed to have no place in this place that reeked of urine and loosened bowels and unwashed bodies, and he opened his eyes and saw that the woman had returned. She was sitting primly in a chair alongside the bed of Patrick DeLance, a lieutenant in Foster's own company. De-Lance had been injured a day or two before Foster, but his wounds were healing rather nicely. DeLance was talking intently with the woman, his eyes never once straying from her face. Their voices were low, so Foster couldn't make out too many words, but once he thought he heard the name "Ariadne."

Foster was a man of some education, having gone two years to college before returning home to the farm where he was needed, and he knew the name was classical in origin. The daughter of King Minos, as he recalled, the woman who had loved Theseus and had helped him find his way out of the labyrinth.

Ariadne. A beautiful name. He murmured it aloud. It set right on his tongue and lips.

Ariadne. It fit her. A beautiful name for a beautiful woman. He glanced once more at her, and like that one other time she seemed to have crawled atop the other man. He blinked; surely he could not be seeing what he saw, and yet even though the light in the tent was dim, he could make out the outline of the woman straddling the prone DeLance, the skirts of her gown spread out. She rocked back and forth and murmured all the while, and he could hear DeLance groan.

Embarrassed, Foster still watched; he couldn't look away. De-Lance cried out in release, and the woman whispered and bent down over DeLance's lips and kissed him long.

Foster felt a warmth suffusing his body, and he closed his eyes tightly and thought of Sarah, good-hearted Sarah. Sarah who was just a little too thin because of their hard times, not with a voluptuous body like this woman . . . this Ariadne . . . here in the tent.

A woman in the hospital. Impossible, he told himself, and he looked once more, and Ariadne was rising from DeLance, straightening her skirts. Foster watched as she ran a hand down DeLance's chest to his groin, and DeLance shuddered.

He glanced across at Long, but the man was asleep. Foster looked up and down the double rows and saw that of the other men he was the only one awake, the only one to see . . . what he had seen. But what was that?

The woman—Ariadne—had done something to DeLance. She had climbed atop—no, Foster decided, climbed wasn't quite the proper word. Slithered? No.

She had seduced . . . no, that wasn't the right word. Nothing was right, he decided, nothing tonight.

He closed his eyes and willed sleep to come, but stubbornly it refused.

The following day it rained, and the dampness seeped through the canvas walls into the bones of the men, chilling them to their very souls. Foster felt the worst he had since coming to the hospital. The flap to the tent had been left open, and he could see the grayness outside, the dripping leaves, the subdued colors, and remembered what autumn was like at home.

He and the other farmers in the area would be done with their harvesting, and the wives and mothers and sisters would have been cooking all day long, and then toward sundown would come the dances in someone's barn. Some man would bring out a fiddle and maybe a mouth harp, then maybe a bucket or two or even some old jugs—they didn't much care what they used as musical instruments as long as it made noise—and William, Foster's oldest slave, a man who'd worked for his father, would bring out his banjo. They'd all dance, too, the slaves and their owners in their own separate circles. The barn would smell of drying apples and old manure, of new hay and dust which rose under the stamping of their feet on the dirt floor. A cow, somewhere down the line in a crib, would low in response, a bird in the eaves might flutter briefly, and in the flickering yellow light of the lanterns they would sing and laugh and drink homemade brew and celebrate the good harvest.

Only the past two years there'd been no good harvest; times had gotten rougher, and there'd been no dances. There'd been setbacks in the planting, he'd lost a crop or two, and several times army companies had marched through the farmland and taken what food they wanted. They'd also hurt Nell, William's granddaughter, and William had grabbed a pitchfork before Foster could stop him and had run after the retreating soldiers. He'd been shot in the head, and he'd simply sunk to his knees, lifeless already; when Foster had finally reached the old man, his skin was already cooling.

Sarah had cried when Foster and Tom and George, William's sons, buried the old man out on the hill behind the house.

And for a long time after that, Foster had sat upon the porch thinking. It had been Confederate troops who had come through his farm, who had hurt Nell, killed poor old William.

His own kind, Foster kept saying. His own kind did this. But it was war, one part of him said. That doesn't excuse it, another argued. And he knew then that if the Southern troops would do such awful things, what could he—and Sarah and the others— expect if the Yankees were to come down here, to come through these bountiful farms? What sorts of horrors could they expect at these Northerners' hands? What would these Yankees who hated them so much do?

And so the next day he'd kissed his wife goodbye, taken his best hat and best rifle and a pouch full of shot, and had left the farm to volunteer. He would fight, and he would keep the Yankees and the others away from his family. It was the only thing he could do.

But that had been a year ago, and he didn't see that the Yankees were being pushed back. Sometimes the Union forces won a battle, sometimes his people did. And even when they did, there didn't seem to be an advantage. More men got killed and injured, some lay in the fields for days, some were never found. And the officers didn't seem to care for their men, as he thought they would. They weren't the ones at the beginning of the charges. It was the young men like him, some men hardly more

than boys, or the old men who should have been at home being
waited on by their sons and daughters. It was these men who
died and whose bodies the horses of the mounted officers picked
their way over.

Foster rubbed a hand across his face, felt the dampness at the
corners of his eyes. A year of fighting, of eating off the land,
and mostly that meant not eating, of being either too hot or too
cold, and mostly too wet had soured him on the army—Northern
or Southern.

He knew now that he should have stayed home, should have
laid in as much food as possible, as many supplies as he could
find, should have barricaded the house, and kept Sarah and the
others together, and maybe they could have fought off anyone
who approached.

Maybe it wasn't too late now, though; he had to believe that.
As soon as he got out of here, he was going home. The doctors
might say he was fit to go to the front lines again, but he wasn't.
He was going back to Sarah. He would worry about the Yankees
when and if they came.

He had no appetite that day. He knew his fever was returning,
and nothing tasted good. He laid on the cot, never opening his
eyes, hardly moving.

All he could think of was his family, and he wondered if he
would ever see them again.

That night Ariadne returned. She was closer now to Foster,
and he could see the darkness of her lovely eyes; they looked
almost as if they'd been lined with something black; Sarah had
called it kohl and said all the fancy ladies wore it. Ariadne's
bodice was lower than he'd seen before, and her breasts were
full and pale in the dimness.

She murmured to the young man three beds down from Foster,
and he responded lethargically. She kissed the man, caressed the
back of his hands with her curling eyelashes, and Foster once
more felt the stirrings inside him.

He turned his head, though, so he wouldn't watch, but he
couldn't escape the sounds of the couple's passion. Illicit passion,
he told himself, but those were empty words. What did illicit

mean anyway, when he'd seen men blown to bits by cannon, horses that screamed in their death agonies?

Once more Foster smelled the scent of Ariadne. Some spice almost like cloves, or perhaps cinnamon mixed with musk, and he licked his lips. That strange perfume almost overcame the stench of blood and pus and sweat that pervaded the tent.

When he looked back, she was gone.

The next day when the doctor came, Foster asked when he could leave the hospital. The doctor seemed preoccupied and merely said soon. Still, those few words heartened Foster, because before then the doctor had refused to say.

The nurses came in and carried out the body of the young man he had seen the night before.

Foster looked across at Long, who was sitting up once more. "Another one."

"Yeah," Long said. He was chewing a wad and leaned over his bed and spat into the chamberpot.

"She's getting closer," Foster said, his voice low.

"What's that?"

"The woman I saw."

"You on that agin?" Long shook his head. "You need a woman, boy; I can see it plain and simple."

Foster nodded, slightly distracted, then said, "But there was one. I saw her. She was at the sides of those three men—one of 'em that Irishman—and now they're all dead."

"Plenty o' men here are dead, and there ain't been no woman with 'em."

"Not this time."

Long shook his head again and pushed himself down and rolled over, and Foster knew their conversation was over.

That night the woman brought with her the scent of wood smoke and spices, and she knelt beside the red-faced man.

In the morning he was dead. And when the nurses hauled him out, Foster could see that the drinker was no longer red-faced. The dead man was pale, paler than he should have been even in death, and he seemed to have shrunk down upon himself, as if something—his blood, his soul—had been . . . sucked . . . out of him.

Foster looked at Long. "She's coming down this way."

"You're crazy, you know. Crazy." Long concentrated on drinking his broth.

Foster pushed back the sheet and swung his legs over the side. Momentarily he felt lightheaded, and his arm pained him. He tried to push up from the cot to stand, couldn't and fell back. He couldn't escape, not even if he wanted to. He managed to get under the covers again, and saw that Long was watching him.

"You could help me," Foster said. He hated to ask for help— it wasn't his way—but there was no other choice.

"Help you?"

Foster nodded. "To escape."

"You're here to heal, boy, and that's good enough for me. I'll be out in a day or two, or so the docs say. You need to stay a little longer and rest up."

"You don't understand," he said bitterly.

"No, I guess not."

Two nights went by and the woman didn't appear. Then on the third night, she was across from Foster, by Long's bed.

"No," Foster said, struggling to sit up, but his limbs were entangled in the sheets and they dragged him down. His head was spinning, and he could hardly keep his eyes open, and yet he saw the woman, so beautiful, *slithering* atop Long, who was staring wide-eyed at her. She caressed and kissed the one-eyed man, and delicately nipped at the skin on his chest. Foster watched as her mouth slid lower and lower, and suddenly Long moaned, a loud sensual sound.

She spread her skirts around them and rode Long like he was a horse being broken, and Foster could hear Long's cry of lust, the cry that was almost a scream.

Foster struggled once more to sit up; he had to help Long. But he couldn't manage, and every time he moved, his arm throbbed so fiercely he momentarily blacked out. He could only lie back and watch helplessly.

When it was over, Ariadne smoothed her skirts, kissed Long upon the lips and left.

In the dimness Foster stared at Long. The man was pale, too pale.

"Long?" he called.

No response.

And when morning came, the nurses took Long away.

"I don't understand it," Foster called to them. "He was getting better. He was going to be out in a day or two. He didn't have no killing disease."

The burliest of the two nurses shrugged. "It happens sometimes. They seem all right and then just up and die."

"No, no, not Long. He was all right, I tell you." Foster labored to sit. "That woman came for him. I warned him, I did, but he wouldn't listen. No one would." He looked around the ward, but most of the patients were sleeping or had slipped into their own private hells. "Long didn't listen to me—he didn't believe—and now look at him."

"Calm down," one of the nurses said, and he glanced across at the other. They called for a third nurse, and between the three nurses they restrained him and tied him down with ropes to the cot.

He fought and screamed and shouted at them, but they told him it was for his own good, that he was too violent to be left on his own.

He tried to undo his bonds but couldn't, and after a while, he stopped fighting. He closed his eyes. Some time later, one of the nurses came back and fed him some broth, this time with a little bit of potato and onion in it. He tasted nothing.

He simply lay there, his eyes closed, and waited and felt the coolness of the air when the sun went down. And when he smelled the spices, he opened his eyes.

Ariadne stood at the foot of his cot.

She was smiling at him.

She whispered his name, and he realized then what that strange odor about her was.

It was the smell of death.

Strawman

Nancy Holder

Nancy Holder comes to this anthology by way of recommendation from Kathy Ptacek, having contributed to Kathy's *Women of Darkness* and *Women of the West* projects. No wonder I wasn't familiar with Nancy's work. Of her seventeen novels, thirteen were romances and most appeared under pseudonyms. Since then, I've made it a point to seek out Nancy's more than three dozen short stories, many appearing in such series anthologies as *Shadows, Borderlands,* and *Pulphouse.*

Her stories are often daring and inventive, and I wonder how someone with such outrageous ideas could place seven novels on the Waldenbooks Romance Bestseller lists and receive awards from *Romance Times.* Then again, maybe her romance fans wonder how she can be so successful writing horror.

When I met Nancy in Chicago at the 1990 World Fantasy Convention, her story had already been selected for inclusion in this book. It was Saturday night, and we were at a rather outstanding ice cream social honoring the 100th birthday of H. P. Lovecraft. The party was in full swing, and the guest list included a large number of well-known writers, publishers, artists, and editors. I had another activity planned between 9:00 and 10:00 plus more parties afterwards. Nancy and I spotted each other's name badge, but it was nearly 8:50, and I didn't want to cut the conversation short despite the other plans. Not to worry. Nancy looked at her watch, and said, "It's almost nine. I have something else I'd like to do for a little while." "So do I," I replied, "and I'll bet we're probably thinking of the same thing." Nancy smiled. And thus we exited the really fabulous party, found a television set, and watched "Twin Peaks."

Strawman, strawman, on the tree
Strawman, harken to my plea.

Mandy Prather's pa was dying, and the air clanged with thunder. Blue soldiers on their way, and everybody's pa was dying. The world churned with blood and thunder, shrieks and screams, and widow's weeds—blue and red and black, the new colors of the Confederacy. Sorrow, the anthem. Six months before, the men pranced away on white chargers, feathers in their hats and the women waving lily-white handkerchiefs. And six months later, the feathers was charred ash and the handkerchiefs soaked in blood, and the dashing young men committed to the Lord in fresh gouges in the earth.

Mandy sat on the ladder in the middle of the bean patch and stared at the house. Tallow candlelight flickered on the thin burlap curtains, the shadows of Ma and Aunt Maryneal moving and shifting, sliding and weeping. Mandy's throat tightened and she imagined the shadows was blue soldiers, come to steal her pa away. Or darkies; Ma said the neighbors' darkies was the ones come and broke the window. But the children at school taunted her and called her a darkie-lover because her daddy didn't go and fight; so how's come the darkies would break their windows?

Strawman, strawman, on the tree
Strawman, harken to my plea.

Closer now, a cannon boomed, rattling the bones in Mandy's spine. She shifted on the wooden crossbeam and put her arm around the scarecrow, guardian of the bean patch.

"Pa's dying," she told him. "They killed him."

The scarecrow stared straight ahead, but Mandy pretended he was listening. Through spring and fall and summer and winter, he had listened. With his eyeless, mouthless face of straw, his corncob pipe, his overalls and weathered straw hat, he let Mandy put her arms around him and talk out her heart. He was her friend, had always been. And now that all the other children was forbidden to speak to her, and she couldn't go to the school, he

was her only friend. Even though she was nine now, and knew
he wasn't real and that she was too big to pretend, she laid her
head against his temple and he listened to her sobs.

"It's because he wouldn't defend us," she said. And a sure,
horrid pain slashed her heart, because she was ashamed of her
pa, even as he lay burned and cut in his bed. Because he should
have fought. The neighbors was right to shun them; he was a
coward, or worse.

And it wasn't for love of the darkies, oh no. She knew he
didn't care if they was slaves or not. As far as she could figure,
he didn't go to war because he didn't want to, simple as that.
Awful as that. He was a disgrace to the South, and to her, but
she loved him. She had always loved him, and he had always
loved her. He was her pa.

Now she wasn't going to have no pa. Ma had taken Mandy on
her lap and held her hands in hers, and cried and cried. Aunt
Maryneal came up the stairs then, to where they sat at the landing, and said, "Elizabeth, go see to Richard and I'll take care of
Mandy." And it was Aunt Maryneal who told her Pa was not
going to make it, not get better, ever. Aunt Maryneal had waited
for her to cry, but Mandy stood hard against her tears. She didn't
like Aunt Maryneal, and never had, not since she came to live
with them when Mandy was six. That was the same year they
put in the bean patch, and Pa made the scarecrow.

"I wish it was her instead," Mandy told the scarecrow. He
made no response. She put her hand over his chest, wishing for
a heartbeat. Since her pa had crawled to the porch three nights
before, Ma had not said a word to her. Aunt Maryneal did all
the work, did the talking, sent for the preacher. Now they was
trying to keep her pa alive until the preacher came, so he could
have a blessing before he died. Ma had said no funeral, but Aunt
Maryneal said yes, there will be one. She had sent word to the
undertaker as well.

A tattoo of rifleshot. Mandy's stomach tightened around itself
and she hugged the scarecrow. The smell of red dirt and pine
filled her nose. Dusk was coming on, and she thought she saw a
flash of blue among the trees. Magnolia blossoms like explosions
masked her view. She clung to the strawman, her heart pounding

into her wrists, her head, the crown of her head. The blue soldiers stole what they wanted, burned everything else, shot the men and hurt the women. They was demons from the North, and the Confederacy didn't have the magic to stop them. Ma had wept for the South, but Pa had said nothing about it either way, only tended the crops. He spent long nights alone on the back porch, rocking on the mammy bench and staring out at the bean patch. Mandy sat at his feet, and he stroked her hair and called her his beauty.

Sometimes Aunt Maryneal came out and sat with them, fragrant with lavender water, murmuring something about Ma being "at it again," and the three sat there like a family. But Mandy trembled beneath her pa's hand, not understanding if she was angry or frightened or something else. She sat and looked at the scarecrow, and made wishes on him—about the rustling behind her of Aunt Maryneal's petticoats, and about the hand that stroked Mandy's hair.

Strawman, strawman.

He was hung up on some old boards Pa found in the barn, like a stuffed Jesus on a cross, except he was too heavy for the pieces and fell over a couple of times. So they moved him back a little, Pa and Mandy, and propped him up against a peach tree. Mandy left the ladder beside him after harvest time, and now it was weathered and gray from the years it had remained there.

And even though Pa had changed the scarecrow's thatch hide many times, he had remained there too, the same, her friend.

"Oh, strawman," Mandy groaned, and hugged him.

"Child?"

Aunt Maryneal stood on the back porch with a glass in her hand. Her blond hair was pulled back tight in a bun, though she usually wore it loose over her shoulders. Her face was sunken and there was rings around her eyes, and a streak of something red on her cheek.

Another cannon boomed. Aunt Maryneal jumped, spilling the liquid in the glass.

"Lemonade, child," she said, extending her hand. Mandy said nothing, only held the scarecrow and shook her head.

Aunt Maryneal looked at her for a long time, then sighed and went back into the house.

Oh, strawman, strawman.

It grew dark. The moon sliced the branches of the peach tree into snakes and fingers; and Mandy huddled beside the scarecrow as the world boomed and rattled, and far away, men in fresh graves saluted with honor and their widows sat in windows and prayed for the South's deliverance. And Mandy prayed, but for what she didn't know, and found herself thinking about Jackieboy Anderson, the little deaf boy, who had died when she was six. Pa had found him and carried him to the Andersons' farm, and sat up for three days in a row with his head in his hands, saying nothing. And Ma had gone upstairs and closed the door, and she had never been the same since.

And Pa's sister, Aunt Maryneal, had come, and they had built the scarecrow.

Mandy didn't know how Jackie-boy had died, but people whispered, and it was something horrible. Something ladies pretended never happened.

"Amanda Jean?"

A man stood on the back porch, in black with his black hat, and his face was dark in the moonlight. Mandy squeezed the scarecrow's neck until she realized it was the preacher. The Prathers never went to church, so he was hard to recognize.

Without a word, she let go of the scarecrow and climbed down the ladder. The preacher put his hand on her shoulder and led her into the house. The kitchen stood in shadow, plates and dishes neatly stacked. No one had eaten all day.

Mandy swallowed, tried to ask if he was here because her pa was dead. Solemnly he led her up the stairs. His tread was hard on the stairs, *boom boom boom,* matching the cannon fire in the hills. As Mandy passed the window, a flare of red lit up the treetops, and she thought, *Pa is gone. He's gone.*

But when they came to the door to her parents' room, cries and moans seeped beneath it. The preacher said, "I don't think you should come in, but your father demands it."

Mandy said nothing. The door opened, and Aunt Maryneal stood on the other side. The glass of lemonade was still in her hand. Mandy wished for it to be poison, and that Aunt Maryneal would drink it.

The preacher stood on one side of her, Aunt Maryneal on the other, and they led her toward the bed.

Oh, strawman.

And her ma sat in the black shadows, her face buried in a white handkerchief, lily white, as Pa's eyes rolled back in his head. He shouted: "Stay back. Stay back!"

"He has a fever," the preacher explained in a somber voice. He strode to the center of the room, a distance from Pa, and opened his Bible.

Aunt Maryneal said, "Go to him, child."

Mandy walked alone to the bedside. The sheets was wet and sour; and a smell rose from the fissures in her pa's body where he'd been burned and cut. His face was gashed and there was holes in his cheeks; Mandy reached out a hand and touched his chest, where his heart wrestled with the Angel of Death.

Pa's neck arched and he screamed once, loudly. Mandy stood beside him with her hand on him. Her own heart shook.

Then he whipped his head toward her. "My beauty. My beauty," he moaned. "Stay back!"

Frightened, Mandy pulled her hand away. The preacher started reading from his Bible: *Yea, though I walk through the Valley* . . .

Her father stared at Mandy. She stared back. She thought about his hand on her. Hers on him. She thought about her wishes.

Then Ma jumped up from her place in the corner and lunged at her. "It's because of you!" she shouted, making fists and pounding the air. "You're the cause!"

It wasn't until the preacher pulled Mandy away from the bed that she realized Ma was screaming at *her*. There was no love on her face, nor sorrow, but a long-smoldering hatred.

"I know what he did to you!" Ma shouted.

With a cry, Mandy ran from the room.

"Child!" Aunt Maryneal shouted, but Mandy raced down the stairs and out the back door, flew off the porch, and ran to the arms of the strawman.

"Oh, oh," she said, over and over again. Because she couldn't make sense of it. Ma hated her. Hated *her*. If there was anyone in the house who should be hated, it was not Mandy. Not Pa's beauty.

Mandy wept until her ribs ached. Miserably, she rested her head against the scarecrow's shoulder and listened to the cannons, and the crickets, and the echo of Ma's words.

In the distance, the blue demons marched toward Mandy's house. She smelled gunpowder. And blood.

A cry from the house. Mandy started. Then someone appeared in the window, a woman, and raised her arms toward the midnight-red sky. Another figure came and pulled her away. Mandy watched, her stomach tight and sick. Pa was dead. Pa was dead, and Ma hated her.

Strawman.

Mandy cringed beside the scarecrow, wishing.

The South was dying, and the air clanged with the laughter of the damned.

Mandy woke coughing. Thick, soggy smoke settled on her lids and pushed down hard on her chest. Her eyes watered and she waved wildly at the hot, dank fog with both hands, falling back against the limbs of the peach tree.

The scarecrow was gone.

The ladder was also gone.

And the peach tree was on fire. Hot orange flames shot up from the roots, licking the trunk. The fruit sizzled and split, broiled jam oozing down leaves that curled into charred ash, the feathers of dead heroes. Sparks shot up and ignited other parts of the tree, and sped along the dry, old wood.

Mandy shrieked and scrabbled to her feet. Rolls of smoke wrapped the trunk and chased her as she climbed the branches that ripped her skirt and tore at her fingers and hair. She stumbled and a twig pierced her cheek with a red-hot stab. In her terror, she barely noticed it. Higher and higher she climbed, until she balanced in the delicate, topmost branches, high above the bean patch.

The house was on fire! A furious torrent devoured the boards of the house, gunpowder fast. The windows exploded. The chimney bricks blazed and shattered.

The fire traveled along the porch, crackling and destroying; and within it, a man rocked on the mammy bench in the center of the red-blackening wind.

"Pa!" Mandy shrieked. "Pa!"

The figure's head raised. Grasping a branch, she leaned toward it. "Pa!"

The figure slowly stood. Flames flared from the top of its head, a tallow torch that jerked stiffly toward the stairs. Mandy screamed.

Aunt Maryneal ran from the side of the house. She was naked, her blond hair flying around her shoulders like a veil. A streak of red dripped from her throat to her stomach, as if she'd just butchered a hog.

"He's dead!" she shouted, running to the figure. "We're free!" She danced in a wild circle, her breasts flopping. Mandy pulled back her hand and covered her mouth. The smoke poured into her lungs and she fought to keep from falling.

The figure stopped and faced Aunt Maryneal. It made a noise. Mandy choked hard, straining to keep her eyes open.

"We're free!" Aunt Maryneal said again.

At the window in Pa's bedroom, Ma appeared. Flames shot behind her; she pummeled the glass, leaving bright red smears. Her mouth opened and closed like a dying catfish. *Help, help.*

"Help!" Mandy cried aloud, horrified.

Aunt Maryneal stopped. She shielded her forehead with her hand and looked up at the peach tree.

"You're not dead yet?" she asked savagely.

The smoke whirled around her and the cannons boomed close. The house guttered and cracked, broke in two like a dishonored sword. The earth trembled beneath the footfalls of a thousand Union soldiers.

Aunt Maryneal's teeth drew back. Fangs sprang from her gums like bayonets. She turned *blue*. Blue hair, blue skin, blue horns that sprang from the crown of her head.

In the window, Mandy's ma slumped against the glass and slid downward, out of sight.

Mandy swayed from side to side, hacking and sobbing. She was going to faint. She was going to die.

"No matter about you. The one who held us is dead." She put her hands on her hips and laughed. "Your pa was a brave man, but he was stupid. We got him, and we'll get all of you." She pointed at her. "Take her," she told the burning strawman.

The scarecrow advanced. Mandy launched herself into the crotch of the branches. The world shook as the smoke curled around her. She whimpered. Pa had been magic. Pa had been a jailer of something evil. He didn't go to war because he had a war to fight to home.

He was a martyr to the cause. But he was gone now, and he couldn't help her.

She reached a hand to the window. Ma. Ma. Had she known? Or had she been a part of it?

And which side had she been on?

The scarecrow reached the base of the tree. Mandy's tears steamed around her temples. She scrabbled backward, ripping the skin from the heels of her hands. Coming for her!

He stopped and looked at Aunt Maryneal, who raised her arms and chanted:

Strawman, strawman, now you are free!
The rebel is vanquished, now harken to me!

He began to climb, hand over hand, foot on branch, finding Mandy's well-worn handholds. There was nowhere to go, and there was too much smoke, and Mandy . . . and she . . .

His burning hand grazed her bare foot. A howl of terror ripped out of her burning lungs. But his flames didn't hurt her!

"Come on!" Aunt Maryneal shouted.

His fingers closed around her ankle. She grabbed the nearest branch, sobbing and coughing, holding on with all her strength. But his pull was steady, sure; the scratchy straw scraped her raw, but there was no burns.

He yanked her down, and she collided with his chest. For a moment he teetered, and she kicked wildly, pummeling him, but he grabbed her and held her, then leaped to the ground.

She screamed; he landed on his feet, with her in his arms. Through the flame, the same, unseeing face. The head that had listened to her, all those years.

"Throw her into the fire!" Aunt Maryneal shouted.

"Strawman," Mandy begged. "Strawman."

He lifted her high, raised her over his head, took a step back. A funeral pyre; she remembered a story she had read, how Hindu women got burned like this, after their husbands died. . . .

She remembered then how Pa had loved her, years and years before, loved her more than daddies and daughters did, but he said it was something different, because he had a special task and he needed the power of her youth and beauty. She remembered it all now, in a flood, and how she had hated him for it; only six, and she had wished, and wished . . .

And loved him, and wished that Ma . . .

The power of her youth and beauty. To keep the evil at bay.

"Strawman!" she pleaded.

The strawman hesitated. Then he bent down and lowered Mandy to the earth. For a moment she was held against him; and for the first time, she heard his heart.

"No!" Aunt Maryneal cried. "No, kill her!"

But the strawman shuffled away from Mandy. She fell to her knees, forward into the dirt.

"All right, then," Aunt Maryneal snapped. "She's *everyone's* darling. Let's go."

He crouched down, and Aunt Maryneal climbed onto his back. Wings sprouted from her shoulders; her voice was a rage, a roar as the strawman carried her away, toward the cannon shot and the deadly angels from a Northern, blue hell.

Her arms outstretched, as Mandy's had been when Pa had loved her, when Pa had loved the Confederacy:

"Sherman, Sherman, Sherman! We're on our way! We'll lead you!"

And as they shambled away, and Mandy ran, the world clanged with smoke and thunder.

And wishes.

A Dress for Tea

Wendy Webb

The credits of our contributors are wide and varied, but not many people have starred in a motion picture and served on the editorial advisory board of *Nursing News Today.* Actually just one, Wendy Webb.

Wendy had a principal role in S. P. Somtow's *The Laughing Dead,* and also appeared in *Blood Salvage,* the horror film produced by boxing champion Evander Holyfield. As a writer her work has appeared in *Women of Darkness, The Sea Harp Hotel, Where the Black Lotus Blooms* and in the *Shadows* series. Acting and writing are perhaps the two most difficult fields to break into, but Wendy seems to be doing well with each.

She lives in Stone Mountain, Georgia, near the famous Confederate Memorial, and is a founding member of the Science Fiction Writers of Cobb County, the Atlanta area group that has done much to help develop new talent in the deep South. Most of our contributors were interested in writing about the latter stages of the Civil War. Wendy's story is appropriately set in the gathering days of the conflict.

The fever had broken.

She opened her eyes slowly, so very slowly, and blinked at the single window that allowed summer afternoon light to fall softly across the pieced quilt and her now painfully thin body. She tried to raise her head, fought weakness, and turned instead to check for it. To be sure. Was it . . . ?

Yes.

She sighed deeply. A faint smile touched her lips as she scanned the little reed sewing basket and the wrought iron scis-

215

sors, ribbon securely attached, waiting for her skilled hands to put them to use. Two framed samplers from childhood practice hung on the walls and reminded her of the early attempts. Her name, Prudence Maris, done in neat, even stitches was blocked by a simple design in reds and blues. Sewing the little samplers was just the beginning. Now it was a skill that she loved and helped to feed her family.

A slight motion beyond the window caught her eye. Prudence twisted toward it so softly that the old pine-framed bed forgot to groan under her weight.

There. On the top of the knoll. Six-year-old Wesley stood motionless except for the scant movement of his lips. He tucked his fingers into the suspenders that held up his gray cotton trousers, kicked clumps of Georgia clay with his bare feet, and continued his one-sided conversation. He was talking to his father. Or maybe the three babies.

Four, she remembered suddenly, and wiped away a tear from the corner of her eye.

Mrs. Graves had helped with the last child as with all the births, and shook her head sadly at the delivery. There was no need for words. The large woman's tight jaw and deep-set, saddened eyes spoke instead. She patted Prudence's work-hardened hands, stroked her damp brown hair, changed the blood-stained clothes, then went about setting the household straight with deliberation, and typically few spoken words.

The hours following the stillbirth faded into days of pain and fever, of nonsense thoughts and cool towels applied to a sweat-covered forehead by the caring neighbor lady. Mrs. Graves never left the house, and was even now still here. Prudence watched as the stocky, mirthless woman guided little Wesley down from the knoll toward the house with a firm but gentle hand on his shoulder.

The smell of corn bread, coffee, burning candles, and lye soap filled the three-room house.

Prudence saw it bare and empty in the corner, and covered her face with callused hands to stifle a sob. The handmade cradle, with its worn knobs on either side, was sullen and lonely as if it, like her, had arms outstretched to receive the new one only to have it snatched away by a dark insatiable cold.

Wesley was their only surviving child, and now would forever remain so.

She took a deep breath, dabbed her eyes with an edge of quilt, and smoothed the worn, white cotton gown that covered her.

White. Not as white as if the sun itself was inside. How she would love that. Brilliant white. Silk. White as winter snow. And made into a dress.

A dress for tea. A fancy tea, with cakes, fine china, and handsome women wearing their beautiful white dresses. There would be color in the sashes and bows. Colors from the new dyes that rendered violet and fuchsia. Bright colors to set off the white and make it that much brighter. And hoop skirts that measured six feet across.

But Prudence was not to wear one. Not now. For her there were only simple black dresses—three folded neatly in a trunk—that she would continue to wear. When she was better. When she was up and around.

Black cotton dresses. Dyed black. The faded flower pattern faintly visible underneath. A simple plaid barely noticeable under the dye. Black for death. Death and mourning.

Black for those who survived. Never for the ones who passed on.

She missed her husband. Missed him terribly. His quick smile, his joy at their son and plans for other children, his appetite for her bread and stews cooked over the open fireplace. Now he was gone, and she was scared. Scared of so many things.

Loneliness. Money. Getting by.

War.

It was talk. Only talk. But the idea of war had frightened her while it gave him a sense of duty and pride. He held his head high, indignation pulled at the corner of his lips as he relayed the latest news. He had sneered at the prospect but vowed he would fight if the need arose.

He would never have the chance.

Wooden wheels splashed through muddy water when the neighbors brought him home. Rain dampened the blanket that covered his bruised and broken body. The horse that had thrown him and trampled him underfoot, bucked and snorted at the end of the reins tied to the cart.

That night, laying the body out for burial in the front room, she felt stillness. On the knoll where he would join the babies in rest, and deep in her womb.

She worked the land from early morning to sundown, but it was barely enough. Sewing for Mrs. Talbott over near Stone Mountain provided her with a little extra money, an occasional remnant of cloth, a sash and hat, and a fierce pride in her work. A joy.

Even if her hands bled and scarred from the day's work, and sun crept under the brim of her bonnet to freckle her skin.

Her fingers twitched and she could almost feel the fine imported material. Slick green taffeta, dress-length Brussels lace, grosgrain ribbon, soft blue velvet that would become a pelisse . . . white silk. She could almost feel her hand curving closed as if it held scissors. She cut the imaginary material carefully, so very carefully so as not to waste even the tiniest bit. Next the fittings, and then the delicate stitches that held it all together. Months and months of work until she stood back, the breath caught in her throat, and admired the beauty of it.

A white dress. Made of silk.

The one she would wear to tea.

The sound of bare feet on pine floors followed by clumping footsteps forced Prudence up in the bed. She pulled the pillow under her head to see better and smiled at their entrance to her bedroom.

Mrs. Graves wiped her hands on her apron, then reached wordlessly for the water-filled pitcher and basin by the bedside. She turned to leave, then caught sight of the necklace on the tiny dresser. She paused, touched it, recoiled, then slid it into a pocket with a shrug. Her heavy steps to the front room echoed, then fell silent. A door closed.

Prudence opened her mouth to question, then turned to her son.

"Can I read to you, Mother?"

"I'd like that."

"You'd like it." He opened a primer and stared at the words. He picked a few out, then added some she knew weren't there. He closed the book suddenly and fell quiet. "I miss you."

"I've missed you, too. But I'm all right now."

"I'm afraid."

"Don't be. We're together. Just the two of us."

Confusion etched little wrinkles across his forehead. "Is Father lonely? Is that why?" He fought with the words. "I'm lonely, too."

Her heart jumped in her chest and she reached out to him. He stepped away from her and walked slowly to the door. He squeezed his eyes tight, stood that way for a few seconds until the urge to cry had passed. She recognized the sign and patted the bed. "Wesley. Come here. Sit by me."

He shook his head and rubbed his face with clenched fists. He turned suddenly and bolted out the door and up the narrow steps to his room in the loft. The ceiling reverberated with his weight thrown suddenly into his bed.

"Wesley." She sat up and swung her legs to the floor. Dizziness surrounded her, blurred her vision. She grabbed the side of the bed, thwarting a fall to the hard wooden floor. Nausea picked at her stomach. She sat still a minute, two, and felt a little better.

Mrs. Graves appeared at the door. "Poor child. All alone."

Prudence balanced herself carefully on the bed and could almost feel some color return to her face. "He's upset. I'll talk to him. It will be all right."

The large woman mopped her face with the apron, and tugged at her plaid gingham housedress. "It's too much for a child. And one as young as that. Don't know what will happen to him. Wish I did." She threw open a trunk and rummaged through it. She pulled out a hat and laid it carefully on the dresser. A knock on the front door pulled her attention. She mumbled under her breath and went to answer it.

Muffled, low conversation, their words lost, filtered to Prudence's ears. The talk continued to a door that opened, then shut behind them, masking the topic even further.

She shrugged, willed her strength to reach for the hat, and fell back heavily in the bed with it. She rubbed the curved brim across her cheek and breathed deep the aroma of expensive material. An ostrich plume tickled her nose and she giggled. It was beautiful. A fine hat for tea. She leaned forward in bed, grimaced at the pain, and spotted her other prize. The pink silk sash. Folded with utmost care, it peeked out from under her black cotton dresses.

She twisted the plumes on the hat so that they fell fashionably down the side and back, and slipped it over her head. Her long brown hair was pulled over her ears and tucked under the back of the hat in a hasty knot. She wished she could see herself in the hat, but settled for the simple pleasure of just wearing it right now.

She eased it gently off her head for a closer look. Flowers, maybe, or a bow to match the sash. Something special. Her own touch. But, she decided, that could wait. She was more than thankful to Mrs. Talbott for this treasure, and the woman's generosity in other things as well. She pulled the quilt up under her chin and remembered the day Mrs. Talbott had given her the hat.

Mrs. Talbott had turned this way and that while Prudence molded the material to her frame. Material, pattern pieces, dresses, and hats had been draped over the furniture and dropped carelessly in piles on the floor as the woman alternately admired and discarded.

"Remember, Prudence, three tiers on the skirt."

"Yessim, I haven't forgotten." She knelt on the floor and began to work on the hem.

"And a little longer in the back."

Prudence eyed Mrs. Talbott's flat shoes. The woman's long feet and weighty ankles seemed wedged and distorted in the delicate white satin shoes. She glanced at her own feet, little, slender, covered by black high-topped shoes, and tucked them further under her skirts.

"Be quick about it, Prudence. I hear my guests arriving."

"I'll work harder, ma'am."

"They're coming for tea. Minerva has been cooking all morning." Mrs. Talbott bent over to check the progress. "Never mind. This will just have to do for now." She shimmied out of the dress and turned to Prudence for assistance with another. "There now. A little tighter, please. Good. Yes, they are here. So I'll be leaving you now." She threw open the door.

The women converged on the hallway almost all at once in a rustle of crinolines. Open fans snapped shut and light, animated conversation, sprinkled with airy laughter, filled the room.

Prudence slipped to the door and stared out into the hallway with open admiration. She watched the women flounce and toss their skirts this way and that, and committed to memory every detail of the styles, and color of their clothing.

Mrs. Talbott greeted them graciously, then spotted Prudence from the corner of her eye. Without missing a "hello" or "good to see you," she eased over to the door and reached for the knob.

"They're all so beautiful."

Mrs. Talbott surveyed the hall as if seeing it for the first time and turned back to the awestruck young woman.

"So beautiful. And they're here for tea. I wish . . ." Prudence caught herself, blushed, and stepped back into the room. "I'm sorry. I shouldn't have . . . I'm sorry."

The older woman's face softened. "Maybe one day." A glimmer caught in her eye. "I'd like to give you something." She glided over to a discarded pile of clothes and dug through them. "Yes. Here it is." She turned and thrust the curved brim hat in outstretched arms. Then, in an afterthought, she snatched a pink silk sash from the top of the pile and added it to the offering.

"I couldn't."

"But you must."

"No, I . . ." Prudence gazed lovingly at the objects and felt herself weakening.

Mrs. Talbott glanced out at the hallway and tapped her foot impatiently. "Take them, child." She pushed them towards Prudence and let go.

Prudence caught them before they fell to the floor.

"Oh, and I have something that may be of interest to you. In the trunk there. Take a look. Mr. Talbott brought it to me from his last trip. You of all people will appreciate it." She walked briskly to the door and began to pull it closed behind her. "Look, but don't touch." The door clicked shut.

She held the hat and sash tighter, walked to the trunk, opened it, and gasped in pleasure. She looked over her shoulder to make sure Mrs. Talbott hadn't returned and knew she had to touch it. Just once.

Wheeler and Wilson Mfg. Co. A brand-new sewing machine.

The first she had ever seen. And in 1860. She'd heard of such a miraculous thing, of course, but wondered if it was really true. So it was. She ran her hand over it, closed her eyes as the cool of it tingled her fingers, and imagined the work she could do if she only had one. With reluctance, she lowered the trunk lid slowly, peeping in one final time before it closed, and turned to leave.

She carried the sash and hat as if they were the rarest and most fragile china. The three-mile walk stretched interminably until she could get home and fully admire her new things.

Mrs. Talbott had been generous in giving up the clothing. More generous than anyone had ever been to her before or since. Prudence stirred restlessly in bed and recalled every minute of that wonderful day. To think that Mrs. Talbott would part with such lovely things—it must have been very difficult.

But best of all, the promise of tea. "Maybe one day." She still heard that special invitation.

Prudence rolled the hat around and around in her hands to see it from every angle, then laid it carefully at the foot of the bed for perspective. A pink silk bow would do it. And if she was very careful, she could take the material from the sash and no one would be the wiser. The two of them would be just right for the white silk dress she would make. One day.

Then, she would go to tea. No doubt about it.

A door opened and spilled the two talking women out into the hall. Prudence cocked her head to listen, then called out. "Mrs. Graves? Who's there? I will take visitors." Snatches of conversation drifted to her.

". . . least I could do . . ."

"Of course."

"The boy?"

". . . sad . . . we'll have to see . . ."

Prudence twisted in bed and pulled herself up to a sitting position. "Mrs. Graves?" And the other voice? Familiar.

Mrs. Talbott? Yes, she was sure of it. But calling on her?

No. Not possible. It wouldn't be right. Not a woman of her social position. Unless it was something, well, important.

Of course. The unfinished dress. Mrs. Talbott would be wanting it soon.

The front door squeaked open, then closed. The woman gone.

Mrs. Graves clumped into the bedroom and stopped at the dresser. Her face turned worried. She wrung her hands, scanned the room, and spotted the hat lying at the foot of the bed. The lines of her face smoothed, then turned to a glare at the sight of the ostrich plumes. She shook her head as if chastising a child, snatched up the hat, and plucked the feathers out. With an uncharacteristic deftness, she swooped the pink sash from the trunk and was out of the room before Prudence could speak.

A door opened and closed and the woman's steps were silenced.

Outrage filled Prudence at the act of her neighbor. "How dare you? Mrs. Graves, may I speak with you, please?" No answer. Her voice heightened and tensed. "Mrs. Graves?" She teased her feet onto the bare wood floor. Her legs trembled with weakness. "Mrs. Graves? A word with you, please."

A shadow outside her window danced across the room. She turned in time to see Wesley trotting past on his way to the knoll.

The orphaned plumes floated to the floor.

Enough. Things were out of hand. She could no longer stay in bed and allow her responsibilities to be relegated to her neighbor. Mrs. Graves had done more than anyone could ask, and Prudence was appreciative more than the older woman could know. But something was wrong.

Wrong. With both of them, with Mrs. Graves and with Wesley.

She couldn't put her finger on it, but she could feel it. Sense it somehow.

Her legs stopped trembling, and she dared to push herself up to a stand. Her knees buckled, then locked, and she grabbed hold of the dresser to steady herself. It wobbled under her weight and tapped a staccato beat on the floor. It settled, finally, to an ominous silence.

"Mrs. Graves?"

Activity in the front room, closed off by the shut door, stilled, then gradually resumed. Water sloshed on the floor met by stifled mumbling. She's ignoring me, Prudence realized with growing anger.

She took a tentative step and measured her strength for another. Her hand slid from the dresser and touched, palm open, the pine paneling. Breathing in ragged gasps, she fought to remain conscious. She stood still, rigid until the sickness passed.

Better. A little better.

She eased a foot over the rough flooring and caught the movement out of the corner of her eye. Wesley had reached the knoll, was talking again.

Crying?

He bent over to reach for something.

Sweat formed beads on her forehead and ran in trickles down her face. She leaned her cheek into the cool wood and saw it.

In the hallway. Crisp and clean. White.

Cotton.

The dress.

Her hat—naked without its ostrich plumes—pink sash, and the only necklace she owned, lay beside the dress. A small smile played at her lips. Her heart skipped a beat.

The dress was hers. It had to be. A gift from Mrs. Talbott to quicken the mend. The invitation to tea.

But why? The question loomed dark in her mind.

Body bent in pain, she stepped slowly into the hall. Her eyes never wavered from the dress.

Touch it. Feel the material under her fingers. And soon, so soon, wear it.

The front room door opened. Mrs. Graves stepped out, took a deep breath, and swatted a single tear from her stoic face. She cleared her throat and gathered up the clothing, then turned back to the room.

One last time.

Prudence shook her head of the fragmented thoughts that tried to gather there, and stared beyond the bulk of her neighbor. Where was the woman going with her fine things? Bring them back. They're mine. Please.

Mine.

She saw then, and closed her eyes against the sight.

No. Can't be. No.

Her mind was playing tricks. That's all. And if she refused to accept it . . .

The window. Wesley. She whirled around to see him.

Her little boy's lips moved. Talked. Pleaded. A single clump of damp, red clay clenched tight in his fist, dropped silently into the open hole.

Her eyes widened in realization and were forced back to the front room.

The hands callused from a long day's work—motionless. Brown hair pulled back to receive a hat.

Mrs. Graves tugged and smoothed the pretty white dress over the frail, still form.

Her strength left her and she clawed at the wall.

The scream fell hollow and quiet as the wind in the empty house.

Foragers

Richard Lee Byers

If you are one of the very few people fortunate enough to come across *Deathward,* the first novel by Richard Lee Byers, then you already know the depth of writing his ten years' experience working in an emergency psychiatric care facility has given him. Richard is well trained, with a B.A. from Ohio State and an M.A. from the University of South Florida. His background as administrator of a hospital inpatient unit, and its twenty-four-hour telephone counseling service, was what made the patients in *Deathward* chillingly believable.

Richard's first two novels suffered a most unfortunate fate. They had barely hit the newsstands when their publisher folded, leaving them unavailable and mostly unnoticed. It's a shame, because both *Deathward* and *Fright Line* were deserving of better fortune. They're worth the effort to locate, though I'm uncertain where to suggest you look. The good news is that Richard has found new publishers and his novels *The Vampire's Apprentice, Dead Time,* and *Dark Fortune* have already hit the stands.

One thing the several Florida writers presented here share in common is that I first met each of them somewhere other than Florida. Richard and I met at the 1985 Deep South Convention in Huntsville, though it was two years before we really got to know each other. He lives in Riverview, a rural community just east of Tampa, with six other lovers of fantastic fiction, and a huge backyard populated with assorted cats and horses, not to mention a mule and a monkey.

When we marched back into the forest, last year's dead were waiting to greet us. Some we'd buried too shallow, and

rain and animals had dug them up. Others, I suppose, we'd
missed burying at all. Now skeletal arms jutted from the carpet
of pine needles, and broken skulls grinned from the shadows
under the trees. A faint stench hung in the air.

Most of the regiment were so green they were still simmering
down, discarding quilts, overcoats, knapsacks, Bibles, and every
other sort of baggage to lighten their loads. When they saw the
bodies, some turned pale. A few stumbled into the bushes to be
sick.

We veteran volunteers despised the new men for a rabble of
conscripts and bounty jumpers, so it amused us to add to their
discomfort. We started merrily discussing how the dead men
died. This fellow with the extra hole above his eye sockets was
lucky. It had happened in an instant. The wretch with the shattered knee had probably suffered for hours.

But even though I chatted with the rest, and had seen my share of
carnage, for some reason the spectacle bothered me, too.

That evening we hooked up with the 2nd, learned that they'd
fought earlier that day and that we'd probably fight alongside
them in the morning. My friends and I set up our mess in a
corner, where outsiders wouldn't come tramping through, and
after supper I tossed my letters on the fire.

I should have waited till Josh had gone to sleep. He considered
himself the wisest man in the Union army, and thought it was his
duty to help his poor, befuddled comrades manage their affairs.
"Don't!" he squawked, then tried to snatch the bundle off the
coals. I caught his wrist, and he started to tussle.

I'm a farmer's son, with the kind of muscles you develop pushing a plow. Josh had been a schoolmaster. Campaigning had
toughened him up considerably, but it still wasn't much of a
contest. After a few seconds, he realized it and stopped squirming. "Get them out," he pleaded, "or you'll hate yourself in the
morning."

"I never look at them anymore," I answered, which was true
enough. "And I don't like the thought of some plunderer reading
them over."

"What's gotten into you?" he asked.

I couldn't tell him that seeing the corpses had rattled me. They

all would have ragged me unmercifully. Nor could I say that
planning for death was only sensible when most of the men who'd
enlisted with us were dead already. We didn't talk about that.
"Nothing. I just don't feel like carrying them around anymore."

Being Josh, he couldn't let it drop, not till he thought I'd
bucked up. "Deep down inside, you must sense you'll be all
right. Otherwise, you wouldn't have reenlisted."

The letters had charred to black curls of ash, so I let him go.
"Sure I would," I said solemnly. "I had to stay on, to preserve
the Union."

"Amen," he said, then the rest of us burst out laughing. For
a moment he scowled, then smiled and shook his head pityingly,
like we were a bunch of particularly dull-witted pupils.

The first time I enlisted, I *did* do it for our country, and so
had most of the others. But when I signed up again, it was for
the furlough. I was afraid that if I didn't get home then, I might
never make it at all.

The sad thing was that when I did get there, I couldn't enjoy
it. My mother was a mover and a shaker in the Methodist Church
and the Sanitary Commission, and she turned into a one-woman
prayer-meeting-cum-war-rally whenever she opened her mouth.
She was always exhorting me to "stand by the flag," and to avoid
"corruptions" like card-playing, drink, and foul language. As
near as I could make out, it never occurred to her to worry about
my ability to avoid minié balls, grapeshot, and canister.

I wished that she and all the other stay-at-homes could experience the war as it truly was. After they'd marched in the rain
and slept in the mud, caught a case of lice or the itch, taken a
wound and grown a crop of maggots inside it, then we could all
have a nice long talk about how important it was to subdue the
Rebels, emancipate the Negroes, and maintain our moral purity
during the process.

But of course I didn't tell her that. I just kept to myself as
much as possible, kept what I felt bottled up inside. I came back
to camp three days early, and when I arrived, I felt like I'd
returned to the only place in the world where I really belonged.

Thinking about it then, I started feeling glummer than before.

But I figured I knew a remedy. I still had quite a bit of my bonus, and a sutler I knew sold whiskey on the sly.

Unfortunately, the supply wagons were on the other side of the camp, and I'd never seen the place by daylight. It took me an hour to find him, and when I finally did, the bastard wanted two dollars a bottle.

I considered telling him to go to the devil, but it occurred to me that I might never get another chance to spend my money. So I paid with the best grace I could muster, and hoped I'd be around the next time he needed his wagon dragged out of a mire or hauled across a river. Then it would be my turn to rob him.

I planned to share with my mess mates, but it had been my money and my trouble, so I didn't see any reason why I shouldn't start nipping on the way back. Perhaps the liquor addled me, or perhaps I was so busy watching out for officers that I neglected to pay attention to where I was going, but before long I realized I was lost.

I blundered down rows of dirty tents, stepped around men sleeping on the ground. Haggard faces, all strange to me, looked up from the camp fires, and a faint drone, compounded of low-pitched voices, sighs, and snores, murmured incessantly.

I asked directions twice, but either the men I questioned didn't really know where my outfit had settled or I didn't understand what they told me, because I still didn't reach my destination. Instead, I found my way to the surgeons' tent.

It was dark inside; evidently the butchers had finished their work for today. I quickened my pace, anxious to forsake the vicinity, and something thudded softly on the ground.

I turned, peered. Beside the tent, almost invisible in the gloom, a shadowy figure crouched over a heap of firewood. Apparently he'd dislodged a stick, and when it fell, it made the noise I'd heard.

As near as I could make out, he was wearing a Federal uniform, but his manner was so furtive that I couldn't help but suspect he was up to no good. I shouted, "You there!" He didn't straighten up or turn to face me, and then I was sure of it.

I strode toward him. He leaped up and fled, still hunched over. As I started to run, I caught a whiff of stink, much like the stench of the corpses up in the forest. Then I tripped over a guy rope and fell face first into the woodpile.

Only it wasn't wood. It was softer than sticks, and it didn't clatter. Wallowing in the clammy midst of it, I could see it was a litter of amputated limbs.

I yelped, scrambled backward, brushed myself off frantically. By the time I remembered I was supposed to be pursuing someone, he was long gone.

I considered reporting what I'd seen, but I didn't understand it and certainly couldn't have explained it. Besides, as far as I could tell, no harm had been done, and I had whiskey on my breath. So I decided to forget about it, and finally located our campsite a few minutes later.

I slept fitfully, awoke knowing I'd had nightmares, though I couldn't remember what they were. Before long, our officers formed us up, and the colonel told us he'd appointed file followers to shoot skulkers and skedaddlers. Evidently he disdained the new men as much as we did. Then we marched through another thick patch of woods and halted where the trees began to thin.

Beyond that point, the ground sloped upward. A long way off, at the top of the ridge, stood earthen breastworks, with Rebel flags flying behind them.

"Jesus, Mary, and Joseph!" I muttered. We'd have some rocks and trees, some cover, as we advanced, but we were still in for a long, straight run at a fortified position. Three years, and our generals hadn't learned anything. Either that, or they didn't care how many of the rank and file they slaughtered.

Josh swallowed, wiped the sweat off his brow. "Just play your part, and you'll be fine. The Lord wouldn't bring you through all our other battles just to take you now."

I felt like telling him what an idiot he was, but he was my friend, and he meant well. "Don't worry, I won't run. If I have to take a bullet, I'd rather it be a Southern one."

They made us stand and wait for quite a while. Some fellows checked their muskets, over and over again. Josh probably spent the time in prayer, or reciting poems and Scripture to himself. I looked at the dew sparkling on the grass and the branches swaying in the breeze. Birds twittered until some artillery started booming off to our right.

It was really too pretty a place to turn into a battlefield. If I were God, I'd protect it by striking all the Rebels dead. Come to think of it, I'd smite the bulk of the Federal forces, the stupid, arrogant officers and the craven conscripts and substitutes, too. I'd destroy the politicians, the businessmen, the Abolitionists, the newspaper writers, the carpet knights, the slaves, and the slave-owners, everyone who cared to have the war fought for any reason whatsoever, and then my friends and I could go home for good.

A bugle call aroused me from my reverie. The sergeant barked the command, and we all trotted forward, a prodigious mass of meat pouring into the grinder.

For a few seconds, nothing moved but us, nothing sounded but the huff of our breath and the thud of our footsteps. Then the enemy howled their Rebel yells. Rifles cracked, cannons thundered, and suddenly blue smoke veiled the hilltop. The air around us seemed to shiver, as though we could feel the shot whizzing by.

Josh and I threw ourselves down behind a boulder. I leaned around the side of it, fired at a tiny head sticking up over the rampart, jerked myself back without waiting to see if I'd hit it. As always, my fingers trembled when I reloaded. Josh waited till I was nearly finished, then took his shot. When he'd reloaded too, we jumped up and dashed on.

By now, men were falling all around us, a few screaming, most just grunting or dropping without a sound. We pressed on, firing, reloading, availing ourselves of whatever cover we could, until, halfway up the hillside, we ducked behind a stump.

I peered around, trying to make sure I still understood what we were supposed to be doing. I was hoping someone had given the order to retreat, but no such luck. The rest of us, those who remained on their feet, were still working their way up the slope.

I aimed at another Rebel, and a bullet punched into the bark just inches from my face. I snatched myself back, huddled down. Perhaps I cried out or looked panicky, because Josh gripped my arm and said, "We're going to be all right."

Another cannon roared, and an instant later, the stump exploded into a hail of splinters. Something smashed into my forehead. I toppled backward, rolled a few feet down the hill, and passed out.

When I awoke, it was dark. A layer of clouds dimmed the moonlight, and groans and whimpers sounded all around. My head ached, I was thirsty, and a crust of something itchy adhered to half my face. The night seemed horribly cold, as though someone had rolled the calendar back to January.

For a while, I just lay there in a daze. I understood that I'd been wounded and was still lying on the battlefield, but I couldn't think of anything to do about 't. But eventually my thoughts began to clear, and I decided I'd better make my way back to camp.

So I attempted to sit up, and the soreness in my temple flared into a sharp pain. The world spun, and I flopped back down.

As I gathered my strength to try again, someone mumbled. The grass swished, people coming closer. The one in the lead limped badly, stepping out on his good foot, then dragging the lame one behind.

I started to call, then caught myself. Just because I wanted them to be a band of Union soldiers, that didn't mean that was what they were. They could just as easily be Confederates, or civilians out for an evening of robbing the fallen. I decided I'd better play dead till I got a look at them.

As they shuffled closer, their muttering grew louder, but no clearer. I could tell they were speaking English, but the sounds were garbled, like they'd been born with malformed throats and tongues. The air began to smell of rot. I wished I could believe that it was just the normal reek of a battlefield, the stink of fresh, bloated bodies, but I could tell it was an older, mustier stench: the same smell I'd encountered on the march, and outside the surgeons' tent the night before.

They were only lopsided shadows until they were nearly on top of me. Then the moon slipped out from behind the clouds. My eyes were already slitted, and I tried to close them all the way. I found that I couldn't.

There were eight them, all withered, all missing parts, and

all with patches of mold flourishing on their skins. The ones with two functional hands carried muskets. Some looked slimy and some dry as dust; some wore filthy blue tatters and others relatively presentable Federal uniforms. Some were so riddled with worm holes that their original wounds were nearly lost among them.

I don't know how I managed not to scream, not to jump up and run. But I'd already discovered how weak and dizzy I was, and I was afraid I *couldn't* run, at least not fast enough to get away.

One bent over a man sprawled on my right, prodded him in the ribs with his toe. Evidently half-conscious, the fellow whimpered, and the dead thing kicked him in the head.

The one with the limp crouched over me, studied me, pressed his fingers against my neck to feel my pulse. Somehow I made myself keep still. His skin felt like dry, flaking leather; in places, bone had rubbed through.

He slung his rifle over his shoulder, then stepped behind me and gripped me under the arms. Another took my ankles, and together they lifted me up.

Before long, they'd all picked up someone. One of those selected was a skinny soldier whose tunic was stiff with blood. When his head lolled toward me, I saw that it was Josh.

They carried us off the hillside into the woods. Our weight didn't seem to trouble them, and they shambled along faster than I expected. They stayed pretty quiet till they were clear of the field, then became more talkative. I still couldn't understand them, but I could tell that the one with the empty right sleeve and the bayonet wound under his left eye was the platoon comedian. Whenever he made a remark, the others laughed.

We seemed to travel for a long time. I had the mad notion that perhaps I was dead too and just didn't know it, that my captors were never going to put me down till they'd carried me all the way to Hell.

But at last we emerged into a fire-lit clearing. Six more dead things, including some missing feet or entire legs, gabbled greetings. Dismembered bodies lay scattered on the ground, and another dozen wounded prisoners, all seemingly unconscious, sprawled in one corner. A guard missing his jaw and an ear kept watch over them, no doubt ready to bludgeon any who stirred.

Our captors deposited us by the others, then palavered briefly with their fellows. Evidently, they decided they'd procured all the live men they needed for the moment, because now they began to make use of the ones they had.

They dragged a stocky, freckled boy with a chest wound away from the rest of us, pulled off his shoes, and unbuttoned his coat. Some of the ones who were still wearing rags passed his garments around, appropriating them if they deemed them suitable, but no one took his eyes off the boy for any length of time, and it was obvious that the clothing wasn't what chiefly interested them.

Once he was bare, they started crouching down beside him, lying down beside him in some cases. One set his hand on top of the boy's hand, and another measured first his own leg and foot, then the prisoner's, with a knotted string. Each was comparing the living body to his own.

When everyone had finished, they talked a little more. Then the joker took off his tunic. His maimed arm ended just below the shoulder. A ring of tiny holes encircled the stump.

Someone pulled the boy's arm out at a right angle to his torso; someone else handed the limping man a haversack. He opened it and removed a surgical saw, perhaps stolen from the 2nd's field hospital, then knelt down and started cutting.

About that time, I surmised what was going on.

The dead men didn't like being incomplete, and one of them, perhaps someone familiar with chimeras, or merely with dentures and peg legs, had hit on a scheme to improve their situation. They'd procure new limbs and organs, to graft on in place of the old.

They'd begun by mutilating corpses and rummaging through the surgeons' refuse, but those parts hadn't melded with their bodies. Reckoning that perhaps the material wasn't fresh enough, they proposed to try again with the freshest possible.

All my notions about life, death, and nature had turned upside down, but I still couldn't believe that such an experiment could succeed. If the dead things still reasoned like ordinary human beings, they probably didn't believe it either. But they were willing to carve us anyway, just on the off chance that it might.

The saw grated bone; blood spurted. When the arm came off, the limping man pressed it to the joker's stump. The two didn't fit together well, so, working hastily, he took a knife and trimmed them till they did. When the join was as good as he could manage, he sewed the limb in place, wrapped it in splints and bandages, and finally suspended it in a sling.

Meanwhile, a one-legged thing attempted to stanch the flow of blood from the boy's stump. But he died anyway, and the creature, who must have wanted a piece of him also, pounded the ground in frustration. One of his comrades patted him on the shoulder.

The mass of them turned, studied the rest of us prisoners once again. For some reason, I was sure I was next, but I wasn't. Josh was.

Once they'd stripped him, finished their measuring, comparing, and discussion, a pair of them pulled his legs apart. The limping thing took his manhood in his mummified hand, and then Josh's eyes snapped open.

He saw the blue tunics and the knife, but I don't think he saw that they were dead. Perhaps his mind refused to see it. "Don't!" he bawled. "I'm a Federal, too!"

A couple of them tried to grab his arms.

He realized they weren't going to heed him and started thrashing. I've heard that desperation can make a man as strong as an ox, and evidently it's true, because he tore his legs free, knocked the limping man away, and leaped to his feet.

But he was surrounded and couldn't flee. The pack surged in on him, muskets upraised to cudgel him back into unconsciousness. Momentarily distracted from his responsibilities, our provost guard hobbled closer to the action.

I sprang up and raced for the trees. My temple throbbed, the landscape whirled again, and for a second I was horribly certain I was going to fall. But then I caught my balance and could feel that I'd recovered at least a measure of my strength.

A dead thing shouted; rifles barked. A horned owl flapped up from a branch, and footsteps thudded behind me.

As the clearing and fire receded, the night grew black, and blacker still when the moon slipped back behind the clouds. Roots tripped me, and twigs lashed my face; occasionally, I slammed right into a tree trunk. Whenever I had to pause to catch my breath, I listened. For a few moments, I only heard my own panting, and dared to hope they'd abandoned the chase. Then shoe leather creaked, or dry leaves rustled. Once I smelled rot and realized that one had nearly caught up with me. When I bolted, he fired. The shot whined past my ear.

I tried to move quietly, changed directions as frequently as possible, but I couldn't shake them. Soon I felt myself weakening again. I wondered if I ought to stop running while I was still strong enough to fight and force them to kill me so they couldn't cut me up alive. I'd just about scraped up the sand to do it when something flickered.

At first the light was so faint that I wasn't sure it was really there, but after I staggered a few more paces, I saw it clearly. Ahead in the dark maze of forest burned a fire.

I sprinted toward it, praying that I hadn't traveled in a circle, that I wasn't rushing back into the dead things' camp. My pursuers' feet pounded after me.

Up ahead, a figure stepped into the firelight, a live man, upright and whole. But his uniform was gray.

Crazy as it sounds when you say it outright, during the early days of the war, we were on cordial terms with the enemy. We paroled prisoners. Made truces to swap newspapers and our coffee for their tobacco. Sometimes even cheered when a soldier on the other side displayed extraordinary nerve.

But that sort of thing didn't happen anymore. These days we concentrated our fire on the heroes and color-bearers, and felt only satisfaction when they fell. Men on both sides had taken to bushwhacking as a kind of sport.

And so I feared the Rebel would shoot me even if he recognized my harmlessness, but it didn't slow me down. As I'd said to Josh, better a Southern bullet than a Northern. Better a live man's than a walking corpse's.

"Truce!" I bellowed. "Truce! Truce! Truce!"

The Rebel jumped, spun, peered, and aimed.

But before he could pull the trigger, another man stepped from behind another tree and said something I couldn't catch. The first man growled a curse but held his fire. A few seconds later, I blundered up to them, clutched at the bole of a pine to keep from collapsing. I tried to speak a warning, but I couldn't catch my breath.

Now that I'd reached my goal, I could see the others, a dozen ragged, weary-looking soldiers lurking behind the trees, pickets posted to warn of a flanking movement. Evidently they'd scavenged the battlefield earlier that day. One wore blue trousers, and another had been trimming a rind of blood off a piece of Union hardtack.

The lad pointing his gun at me was on the short side, with a pocky face and big, dark eyes. Lacking shoes, he'd wrapped his feet in cloths. "All right," he said, "now we're sure he's a Federal."

The man who'd stopped him from shooting me before was a corporal, with spectacles, bushy, gingery side-whiskers, and a high crown going bald. "And so we're taking him prisoner," he replied.

"Why bother? Does he look like he knows anything? I say kill him and divvy up his things."

"I'm with Gabe," another fellow said.

"Ghosts," I finally gasped, not knowing what else to call them. "Chasing me. Please—"

"What did I tell you?" said Gabe. "Wounded in the head and crazy as a loon. No point questioning a madman."

"Ghosts," I said again. "Get ready, they'll be on us in a second."

"I didn't see them," said the man with the hardtack. "Wasn't nothing running around out there but you."

I turned, peered into the darkness. Everything was still.

"Valuable or not, lunatic or not, we can't just murder him," the corporal said. "Take anything you want, but then a couple of us will escort him back to camp."

Gabe grimaced. "I've said it before and I'll say it again: you need to harden up. But all right, we'll do it your way. Come on, Billy Yank, peel off that coat."

I said, "Something terrible is happening. You—"

"By God, I *will* shoot a prisoner who resists."

"You'd better do as you're told," the corporal said.

Despairing, I began to unbutton my tunic. Two shots rang out; one burned into my shoulder and the other cracked into the tree trunk beside me. An instant later, two dead men lunged out of the night.

They must have been as stealthy as Indians, to creep so close without anybody spotting them. Perhaps, like me, they didn't see most of the pickets till they were right on top of them, or they might not have charged into their midst.

I hurled myself backward. Bayonets stabbed, narrowly missing my face and stomach. The corpses lurched at me again, and then the Rebels fired.

The dead things staggered; one fell. The other, a noseless creature with half its scalp flapping loose, kept after me. I backed into a tree, and he lifted his weapon for another thrust.

The corporal sprang in behind him, drove his rifle butt into the back of his head. Bone crunched, and the dead thing fell to his knees. My rescuer struck him again, kept striking until finally he sprawled inanimate at my feet.

"Dear God," someone moaned.

The corporal asked, "Were those the only ones chasing you?"

"I don't know. I suppose so. Some of them move around sprier than you'd imagine, but most aren't fast enough to run down a man."

"All right, then. Take off your tunic and I'll see to your wounds. While I'm about it, you tell your story. The rest of you, listen, but make sure you keep watch, too."

And so I explained, as best I was able. When I finished, Gabe asked, "So all your devils are dead Federals?"

"They seem to be."

"It figures."

"I reckon they were hell-bent on killing you because they figured you could lead us back to their camp," the corporal said. "Can you?"

"I made a lot of turns running through the dark," I replied, "but . . . which way's your camp?" He pointed. "And which way's mine?"

He pointed again. "Over yonder."

"Then, yes, I think I can find them."

"Now just a damn minute!" Gabe exploded. "If all the spooks are Federals, and all their prisoners are Federals, then it's no skin off my ass whatever they do."

"They only restricted themselves to our wounded because they would have had to climb over your earthworks into the heart of your camp to take yours," I told him. "If we don't stop them now, they might come after you some other night."

"This is bigger than Union and Confederate," said the corporal. "This is an abomination. We can't claim we're Christian men if we let it go on."

"I'd rather not have any part of it," said the soldier in blue trousers, "but you're right. Haunts cutting up live folks, that's pretty bad."

Gabe frowned. "So what do we do, report it?"

The corporal shook his head. "Would you believe it if you hadn't seen it yourself? We'll have to take care of it alone. Don, Robert, you stay here, so we'll have someone on guard like we're supposed to." He turned to me. "Are you ready to guide us?"

Though the bullet had only creased me, I felt pretty puny. But I doubted that another few minutes would help, so I dragged myself to my feet. The earth wobbled, then settled again. One of the men who'd remained behind handed me his rifle.

As we set out, Gabe scowled and shook his head, and a couple of others whispered back and forth. I figured they weren't going to follow, but after a moment they fell in at the end of the file.

We crept through the woods for at least an hour. I was shaky with fear, fatigue, and injury. Groping through the darkness, doubling back when I thought we'd gone too far, spying in vain for a glimmer of firelight, I started to wonder if I actually would locate the camp.

I wasn't the only one. Gabe strode to the head of the line, asked, "What the hell are you doing?"

"Keep your voice down," the corporal said.

"What for? We're not going to find them. The damn Yank's running us in circles."

"I'm doing the best I can," I said. "They have to be right around here somewhere."

"Do they? Not if you caught cannon fever and headed in the wrong direction."

The suggestion enraged me, partly because I *was* afraid. I clenched my fist, shifted my weight, and stepped on an object that crunched.

I'd been treading on twigs and stones throughout the march, but some instinct whispered that this was different. I stooped and picked up something stiff and greasy, like a stick of jerky. Felt the knuckle and the nail, and sensed that the dead things were right in front of us. Perhaps they'd set up the ambush because my pursuers failed to return quickly, or perhaps we'd made more noise than we realized, and they'd heard us coming far away.

I yelled, "Get down!" and most of them did. Gabe froze, so I grabbed his belt and yanked him down. Muskets cracked, and one of us cried out.

The corporal jumped up and shouted, "Charge!" We sprang up after him, dashed at the spots where we'd seen their rifles flash. The idea was to get on top of them and shoot point-blank before they could reload.

It was so dark, I ran right past them, then caught a flicker of motion at the corner of my eye. The provost guard, his head bandaged as though he had a toothache, knelt behind a pine ramming a bullet down his rifle barrel. As I wheeled, he scrambled to his feet.

I aimed at his head, squeezed the trigger. His new chin broke loose and tumbled out of the bandage. He hissed like a viper and lunged.

I struck his bayonet out of line, plunged my own into the center of his chest. It would have finished any normal foe, but he pulled back his musket and stabbed again. My own weapon immobilized, I had to release it and grab the muzzle of his to keep his point from my throat.

I could tell at once that he was stronger than I was. I strained with all my might, but the blade jerked closer and closer to my neck.

Then Gabe came out of the shadows behind him and shot him in the back of the head. Chunks of bone and brain blew out of his brow. He stopped trying to spit me, gurgled, and collapsed.

Gabe started to say something, then yelped and dropped too. A thing with one arm and no feet and a burnt-black creature with one leg had crawled out of the brush and tripped him. The one-armed one had a knife and started slashing; the burnt one pounded with a rock.

The three of them made a writhing tangle. I snatched the guard's rifle, thrust again and again, scared every time that I'd stick the Rebel. But I didn't, and at last the dead men stopped moving.

Gabe tossed them aside, clutched my hand, and hauled himself erect. He swayed, blood streaming from his cheek, shoulder, and thigh. I asked if he was all right, and he spat a cuss word.

So we double-timed through the trees, toward the stamp of feet and the clash of steel, spotted the corporal and another two of ours fighting four of theirs. We slunk around and took them from the rear, and in just a few seconds we cut them down.

And then things were quiet.

The corporal called to the Rebels we couldn't see, and those who were able shouted back. Then we reformed and prowled over the scene.

Two Rebels were dead and three more wounded, none grievously; Gabe's cuts weren't as bad as they appeared. We'd destroyed twelve dead things, which accounted for all I'd ever seen. They were hard to kill, but we were quicker and made our bullets count, and that had won us the battle.

We were glad it had, but not jubilant, partly because of our casualties and partly because, even after we'd prevailed against them, it still frightened us that such ghastly things could exist.

Gabe gazed down at the limping man, his nose crinkled up against the stink. "I wonder if they'll stay dead this time."

"And I wonder if this has happened to anyone else," said the corporal. "I wonder if it could happen to us."

I remembered how I'd wished I could kill every last Rebel with a wave of my hand. It made me feel queasy.

We tended the men who were hurt, reloaded our guns, and marched on. Finally found the clearing a few minutes later; they'd extinguished their fire to conceal it. Poor Josh was dead, as I'd known he would be, but five of the other prisoners were still alive.

So we ministered to them, then picked them up and carried them off toward the Federal camp. Not long before sunrise, as birds started singing and the eastern sky turned gray, we came to a stream. There the Rebels set their burdens down.

"This is as far as we go," the corporal said. "Keep on a little farther and you'll find some of your own pickets."

I felt like I should make a speech, but I couldn't find the words. The best I could manage was "Thank you."

Gabe said, "Don't get killed." Then they went their way and I went mine.

Perhaps the strangest thing about the whole adventure was that it didn't change me much. Another man might have turned religious. Brooded till he went insane. Become a drunkard. Or at least deserted.

But none of that happened to me. I slept poorly and flinched at sudden noises for a couple days, and then my nerves got steadier again. The next time we fought, I killed Rebels the same as always.

I did befriend some of the new men. The way I figured it, it didn't matter why they'd wound up in the army, or why it had taken them three years to arrive. We were all in the same boat now, and we might as well treat one another like comrades.

And I discovered I'd softened toward civilians.

Three months, several battles, and a couple hundred miles later, I led a foraging party up to a farmhouse. We knocked and shouted, but no one answered the door. It was locked, so we finally kicked it in.

In the parlor we found a girl with long, black hair. She would have been pretty if she hadn't been glaring so fiercely. "Get out of my home and off my land!" she screeched.

"We can't," I answered. "We're under orders to commandeer provisions." We started toward the kitchen and she spat at us.

One of the new men rounded on her. "You know what you just did? You just burned this pigsty down."

I gripped his shoulder. "Take it easy. Nobody told us to start any fires."

"Nobody will care, either. She probably shelters guerillas."

"It doesn't matter. No matter how ugly things get, you have to remember what you're supposed to be, and that other folks—*all* other folks—are human beings, too. The war won't last forever."

Not for me it won't, whatever happens.

Spoils of War

Owl Goingback

Owl Goingback lives in Winter Park, Florida, a little over an hour's drive from my home in Clearwater. So where did we meet? In Seattle, Washington, just about as far as it is possible to travel from Florida and still be in the continental United States.

The occasion was the 1989 World Fantasy Convention. Owl was there as a featured speaker on Native American folklore. He told me a story about how Seminole Indians frequently adopted runaway slaves, hiding in the sections of the Everglades that were, for all practical purposes, impenetrable to the white man. Many slaves imported to the United States came from areas of Africa and Haiti where Voodoo was openly practiced. One Seminole legend has it that a group of the escaped slaves settled in central Florida and resumed cannibalism. While such stories can not be documented as history, when we began this project, Owl was one of the first people I asked to contribute.

Samual Parker sat with his back rigid against a pine tree, his eyes tightly closed. He didn't want to watch what was happening around him, but knew that sooner or later he would have to open his eyes. When he did, he would witness the terrible things Captain Crawford and his soldiers had done.

The screams and cries for help had ripped through Samual like a hot knife, bringing tears to his eyes. He wanted to stop them, but dared not try. What could one Negro slave do against twenty Confederate soldiers? He wanted to run away, but they would only hunt him down and hang him, like they had poor George.

When he finally did open his eyes, what Samual saw was far worse than what he imagined.

Eight Seminole Indians lay dead along the east bank of a tiny spring, their blood mingling with the clear rushing water. The three men had been killed outright, their bodies blown apart by a volley of bullets. The women weren't so lucky. Four of them—the young ones—had provided entertainment for twenty soldiers, a moment of perverted pleasure for men who had long ago forgotten what it was to be compassionate or merciful.

Their sexual appetites appeased, most of the soldiers lounged around in the shade, talking, laughing, some even sleeping. Two of them were busy stripping the hide from the back of a Seminole warrior. There was a severe shortage of leather in the Confederacy. Many of the soldiers were in dire need of boots. Indian skin wasn't as durable as cowhide, but some figured it was better than nothing. Samual knew to keep his mouth shut about what he saw, lest he end up as a pair of boots himself.

But why hadn't the Indians fled? On the west side of the spring was an abandoned village, beyond that more forest. They could have easily gotten away. But the Indians had stopped at the spring, refusing to cross it. Why?

Samual studied the village. Of the dozen or so buildings, only four still stood. The others had long ago rotted and collapsed. Three of the four buildings were of Seminole design: little more than open-air huts set above the ground on poles. The other building was a log cabin, about fifty feet long, with a wooden shingle roof. It didn't look Seminole to Samual. Instead, it resembled something he would see on a plantation—something designed for multi-families. Negro, perhaps.

Samual's interest picked up. Could this have been a village belonging to his people? It was possible. The swamps and pine forests of Florida have long provided havens for runaway slaves. If this was a Negro village, perhaps there were others nearby.

Freedom.

But Samual knew better than to get his hopes up. Freedom was an elusive thing, not easy to come by for a Negro. With a sigh, he looked away from the village.

Captain Crawford stood about twenty feet away, his quality Virginia uniform a sharp contrast to the soldiers' tattered, homespun wool jackets. Blood dripped from his saber, dark red in the light of the fading sun. He stared down at the woman lying at his feet. She had been young—sixteen, seventeen at the most— her breasts still firm, her dark body unscarred from the burden of childbearing. After raping her, he'd cut her from abdomen to pelvis, spilling her guts like wet snakes upon the ground.

The captain was once an officer with the 1st Virginia Cavalry, but at the battle of Shilo, a Billy Yank bullet shattered his left arm and ended his career. He'd gone from being a first class cavalry officer, with a promising future in the Confederacy, to being a reserve officer in charge of a motley crew of militia men whose job it was to search the unoccupied wilderness of the Florida frontier for deserters, draft evaders, and runaway Negro slaves.

When they amputated the captain's arm, Samual figured they must have also removed all the decency from within him. Without a doubt, Captain Crawford was the meanest man Samual had ever known. Even old Lucifer couldn't be much meaner.

The captain looked up, noticed Samual watching him.

"What you looking at, boy?"

Samual quickly lowered his gaze. He didn't like being called boy—he was almost nineteen years old—but said nothing. He knew better than to answer. The captain could be as mean as a bobcat when riled. In the four months since being bought off the auction block in Atlanta, Samual had been whipped seven times for minor violations. His back was a painful maze of scars.

Captain Crawford sheathed his saber and slowly approached Samual, stopping in front of him. Samual looked up.

The captain towered over Samual, daring him to say something. When Samual didn't respond, he smiled. There was no warmth in the smile. It was the hard, deadly grin of a predator.

"What's the matter, boy? You upset 'cause nobody would share a woman with you?" Captain Crawford taunted, grabbing his crotch. "You've got to be a man to get a woman. You a man, boy?" He slowly looked Samual up and down. "No, I think you're just a boy. I think that slave trader in Atlanta got the best of me. He said you was a man, so I paid top dollar for you. But damn if you ain't just a boy."

The captain scratched his blond beard in thought. "I know.

Maybe you're upset about the way we treated them Indians. Is that it, boy?" He didn't wait for an answer.

"Well then, let me set you straight. Those Indians ain't supposed to be here—they lost *their* war—they're supposed to be out West with the rest of their murdering kin. The way I figure it, we saved the state some money by killing them. And if we happened to take something from them before we killed them—well, that's just the spoils of war. But don't you worry; I didn't forget you. No sir. You're my Negro. I'm gonna treat you right. Got you a little something to keep under your pillow."

Captain Crawford reached behind his back, pulling something from his belt. He dropped it in Samual's lap. It was hairy and wet with blood. A scalp!

Samual cried out and jumped to his feet. The scalp tumbled to the ground.

He scalped her. The bastard scalped her. Wasn't bad enough he raped and killed her, he had to go and scalp her, too. Dear God.

The captain roared with laughter. Stepping forward, he drew his saber and pinned the scalp to the ground.

"I want you to clean this saber real good now. I want the blade spotless. It's not good leaving blood on a blade. Rusts the metal. Lord knows it would be damn near impossible to find a decent replacement now that the Union's got the coast blockaded. Damn state is practically cut off from the rest of the Confederacy. Be quick about it. It'll be dark soon, and I want to set up camp on the other side of the spring."

A tingle of fear danced up Samual's back.

Surely the captain wasn't serious. He wasn't planning on spending the night in the village, was he? Samual turned and looked at the village.

You're in a world of trouble now, Samual. If ever there was a place for haints, that's it.

With a shudder of disgust, Samual put his foot on the scalp and pulled the saber out of the ground. Removing a handkerchief from his pocket, he began to polish the blade. As he did, he wondered what it would feel like to drive it deep into Captain Crawford's vile heart.

*   *   *

The sun was sinking low by the time they moved to the other side of the spring. The move was necessary. The bodies of the dead Seminoles were beginning to smell. The stench would attract predators: bears, panthers, and other creatures of the woods.

Leading the captain's horse, Samual walked behind him as they crossed the spring. Captain Crawford was the only one with a horse; the soldiers walked. Actually, the captain did more walking than he did riding. There were few trails in the woods, few places where one could ride a horse, but the captain insisted on bringing it along anyway.

The closer they had gotten to the village, the less Samual had liked it. It was as uncheerful a place as any he had ever seen. A thick, tangled mass of intertwined shrubs gave an impenetrable appearance to the surrounding forest. Overhead, the crowns of tropical broad-leaved trees made a canopy through which the sunlight barely trickled. Air plants, orchids, and bromeliads decorated the trunks and branches of several trees, while vines grew wild up the sides and over the roofs of the buildings. No wind caressed the village. No birds sang. Instead, a foreboding atmosphere hung heavy over the area, like the calm before a summer thunderstorm.

Where are the birds? There's supposed to be birds. Something's not right.

Samual's skin tingled. It felt as though he was being watched. He looked around, expecting to see a face peering out of a doorway or window. But the village was deserted, as it apparently had been for years.

Approaching the log cabin, Samual noticed that its roof and walls were decorated with peculiar carvings of circles, rainbows, and other designs. Someone, perhaps a Seminole craftsman with nothing better to do, had gone to great lengths inscribing the images. Above the building's only door was an intricate carving of a large serpent. Samual stopped to look at it.

Were Seminole Indians afraid of snakes? Could that be the reason for the carving? Lord knew there were plenty of snakes in Florida, many poisonous. Or did they worship the reptile, consider it some kind of god?

Something about the carving tugged at Samual's memory. There was something vaugely familiar about the pattern on the snake's back, about the oblong shape of its head. Where had he seen such a snake before? He searched his memory for a clue, thought all the way back to his early days of childhood. And then he knew:

Damballa!

Though Samual was born a slave in Georgia, his grandmother had been born and raised on the island of Haiti. When he was a little boy, she'd told him all about a religion called Voodoo. It was a strange religion, brought over from the old country—from Africa. It was a religion steeped in magic, secret ceremonies, possessions and strange gods. One of the voodoo gods was Damballa Quedo, the supreme mystery, whose signature was the serpent.

This is bad . . . real bad. There's voodoo magic protecting this village, or there was. Captain Crawford shouldn't be here. I shouldn't be here.

Captain Crawford noticed Samual had stopped. "Something wrong, boy?"

Samual tore his gaze away from the snake carving. He wanted to tell Captain Crawford about the voodoo stories, but was afraid he wouldn't understand.

"No, sir, nothing's wrong," Samual said. "I was just looking."

Captain Crawford stared at Samual. "You don't have permission to look. Now tie my horse over there to that tree and come with me. I want to have a look inside this building."

The tree Samual tied the horse to was at the edge of the clearing. Beyond the tree, practically hidden by palmetto bushes, were three large iron kettles. Samual was curious about the kettles. What were they used for? Was anything in them? He turned to see if anyone was watching him—nobody was—and quickly walked over to the kettles to look inside. He wished he hadn't.

Inside the rusty kettles were bones. Human bones. Shiny white they were: skulls, leg bones, arm bones, ribs, and backs. Samual jumped back as though burnt.

Lordy, Samual. You were right. This is a bad place. These poor people were cooked in a pot. Made into soup. Eaten.

A man would have to be powerful hungry to eat another man. Unless . . .

Cannibals! There were cannibals here. No wonder the Indians wouldn't come near this place.

Samual looked around nervously. Were cannibals lurking in the shadows of the trees, their faces painted, their lips wet with blood? The forest seemed to close in around him. He jumped when his name was called.

"Samual!"

Turning his back on the kettles, he hurried back to join the others. Captain Crawford had just opened the door of the log cabin. Two soldiers stood beside him. One held a lit lantern.

"Hurry up, boy. I ain't got all night."

Pushing past the soldiers, Samual ran up to the captain, grabbed him by his armless left sleeve.

"Please, Captain, listen to me. We have to get out of here. This is a bad place—"

The slap caught Samual by surprise, knocking him to the ground. He lay there, stunned.

Captain Crawford looked at the sleeve of his uniform as though the fabric was soiled. Tainted. His voice trembled with anger.

"Damn you, boy. Don't you ever grab me. Don't touch me. Never."

The slap brought tears to Samual's eyes, but he refused to cry. He wouldn't give the captain the satisfaction of seeing him cry.

"Now you get up and get your black butt inside. Do you understand me?"

Samual nodded. With lowered head, he stood up, brushed the dirt from his clothes, and stepped through the doorway.

The cabin was one big open room on the inside, like a large dining hall. Only there weren't any tables; no furniture at all. Nor were there any windows. The room was cloaked in darkness. The soldier carrying the lantern stepped forward and raised the light high, forcing the shadows to recede into the corners.

Samual wrinkled his nose. The room was dusty and smelled

like moldy vegetation and dead mice. Spiderwebs hung like crystal chandeliers from the ceiling. In the center of the otherwise bare room stood a large, ornately carved wooden post. Its purpose might have been to support the roof, but Samual suspected there was more to it than that. It appeared to be the centerpiece of the room, as if it was something very special. The carvings on the post, like those on the outside of the building, were of circles, rainbows, and snakes.

A crude plank shelf ran the length of both sides of the room, the walls above it painted with symbols similar to those on the post. Upon the shelves were bottles, plates, clay jars, wooden bowls, gourds, small cooking kettles, stones of various sizes and shapes, several handbeaten metal crosses, and what might have been the skeleton and feathers of a chicken.

Voodoo things.

Samual's legs trembled with fear. He remembered his grandmother saying how powerful voodoo priests were. Why, they could change into animals if they wanted to, or kill a man just by looking at him. Some could even call up evil spirits and demons. Samual didn't want to see a demon. If it was up to him, he'd turn around and get out of the building as fast as he could.

But Samual didn't run back outside like he wanted to. Fear of getting a bullet in the back stayed his legs. Instead, he stood and watched as Captain Crawford and the others began examining the items displayed on the shelf along the right side of the room.

Please, Captain, don't touch those things. It's dangerous. Grandmother says if you touch the things of a voodoo man, he can come and steal your soul out the top of your head. It don't even matter if he be dead and long buried; he can still come and get you.

Captain Crawford picked up one of the metal crosses, wiped the dust from it, and examined it closely. He turned and held it out for everyone to see.

"Look at this. It's silver. Now why'd you suppose someone would go off and leave something like this lying around. Mighty foolish, if you ask me." The captain smiled. "Guess I'll just have to keep it till the owner shows up to claim it. Spoils of war, you know."

Captain Crawford handed the cross to one of the soldiers, instructing him to gather up the rest of them.

Samual was mortified. Silver or not, did the captain really intend on taking the crosses? It was wrong. They were sacred. Was it his imagination, or did the room moan in protest?

Turning back to the shelf, Captain Crawford picked up one of the tiny clay jars, removed its lid, and looked inside. The jar was empty. He checked three more. They, too, were empty. Or were they? Samual remembered his grandmother describing similar jars. "Spirit jars" she called them. In them were kept the souls of the victims of a voodoo priest. The souls were kept in jars while the bodies did the priest's bidding. Dead bodies . . . zombies.

Something moved in the corner of the room, Samual was sure of it. But when he turned to look there was nothing there. Only shadows. But the shadows seemed blacker than before, larger.

Giving up on the jars, Captain Crawford walked across the room to the other shelf, a new prize in mind.

Samual watched the captain cross the room, watched him pick up a shiny metal plate from the shelf. He heard him whisper:

"Gold . . . by God, it's gold!"

Please, Captain. Put it down. Let's leave this awful place.

Samual was afraid, more frightened than he had ever been in his whole life. He looked around the room. The shadows were closing in on them, talons of blackness spreading out from the walls, spilling down from the ceiling. Couldn't the captain see what was happening? Didn't he feel that their presence in the room had awakened something . . . something best left sleeping?

"Spoils of—"

Captain Crawford stopped in mid-sentence.

The sound of a drum beating suddenly echoed through the room. It was a haunting, hollow sound, like the throbbing of a giant heart.

Ka boom . . . boom . . . boom. Ka boom . . . boom . . . boom.

Voodoo drums.

The drumbeats were immediately followed by shouts of warning from the men outside. Shots were fired.

Captain Crawford drew his saber and raced to the door. The two soldiers followed, taking the lamp with them.

Darkness engulfed Samual, swallowed him, attempted to smother him. He felt something move toward him, reaching out to grab him. There was a rush of air from behind him, the creaking of floorboards. Something brushed against the back of his neck.

Samual screamed and ran outside. He didn't stop running until he reached the captain's side, well away from the cabin. Only then did he turn around and look back. The blackness of the open doorway was like the mouth of some great beast wanting to devour him. He expected something to leap out after him, but nothing did.

The drumming grew louder, the tempo more hectic. Samual looked around, trying to figure out where it was coming from. He found the source—

The drumming came from inside the log cabin.

That's impossible. We were just in there. There's no drum in there. No one to play it.

But that's where it was coming from. The beating grew even louder, like the fist of God crashing down upon the world.

BOOM . . . BOOM . . . BOOM. KA BOOM.

More shots rang out. Soldiers rushed past. Samual turned to see what was going on. Were they being attacked?

The soldiers were lined up at the edge of the spring. They were down on one knee; firing, reloading, and firing again.

Across the spring, Samual saw a flicker of movement in the tiny clearing where lay the bodies of the Indians. Shadows. More movement among the trees.

Someone stepped into the clearing. Another person followed. They were too far away to see them clearly. Samual couldn't tell if they were Indians, Negroes, or white men. More people appeared: lots more. Captain Crawford shouted for the soldiers to hold their fire, trying desperately to maintain order.

People continued to emerge from the forest, crowding into the tiny clearing. They approached the bodies.

What are they doing?

Between drumbeats, Samual could hear sounds coming from

the clearing, chilling sounds: the ripping of flesh; the snapping of bones; slobbering, gurgling noises.

They're eating the Indians—eating them raw. Cannibals!

The cannibals were engaged in a feeding frenzy. Bodies were snatched up, torn apart; pieces of flesh hungrily sucked down. Fights broke out over what remained.

As he watched in horror, Samual saw several of the cannibals start across the spring toward the soldiers. They didn't hurry but moved with a slow shuffling gate, as though movement itself was painful.

"Open fire!" Captain Crawford yelled.

Twenty rifles fired. The cannibals twisted and jumped as .58 caliber bullets tore into them. Samual saw them go down . . . then saw them get back up again.

"What the hell?" Captain Crawford turned, noticing Samual for the first time. There was bewilderment in his eyes.

The first of the cannibals made it across the spring. A soldier jumped up and stabbed the man in the stomach with a bayonet. The blade went clean through, stuck out his back, but it didn't stop him—didn't even slow him down. He grabbed the soldier by the throat, fingers digging deep, choking off a scream. Another soldier stood up and fired his rifle. The bullet tore the top of the cannibal's head off, but still he did not fall, refused to die.

Oh, my Lord. They're not just cannibals; they're zombies. Dead men. Grandmother's stories are true. Captain, what did you disturb in that room? What did you awaken?

More zombies crossed the spring, attacking the soldiers. Screams of pain shattered the night. With no time to reload, the soldiers fought with knives and bayonets. But the zombies pushed forward, forcing the soldiers back.

"Hold your position, men," Captain Crawford shouted. "Don't fall back. I mean it. Don't you dare fall back. I'll shoot the first man who retreats."

Don't retreat? He's crazy. He thinks he's back at Shilo. But those aren't Billy Yanks his men are fighting. They're zombies . . . walking dead people.

The fighting drew nearer. Samual got a good look at some of the attackers. They were Negroes—or at least they had been—

their bodies wrinkled, withered, and long dead in the ground. Worms crawled in their rotting flesh, and in some places bone showed. Their smell was of the grave: nauseating, overpowering.

One of the zombies turned and looked straight at Samual. His face was rancid, leprous, oozing yellowish pus. The left side of his face had rotted away, revealing bone, teeth. The left eye was also gone, leaving an empty socket in which a fat cockroach played. Samual screamed and stepped back.

Looking down, Samual spotted a burlap bag lying at the captain's feet. It was the bag filled with the items taken from the building. Voodoo items.

Put them back. Put them all back. Those things belong to a voodoo man. Those are his zombies. They'll go away if you put everything back.

But to return the items meant going back inside the building and maybe facing things far worse than zombies.

Knowing he had no other choice, Samual snatched up the bag and started for the building. But before he could take two steps, he was grabbed from behind.

Zombie's got me!

But it wasn't a zombie who held Samual, it was Captain Crawford. The captain had dropped his saber in order to grab Samual's shoulder.

"Where are you going with those, boy?"

Samual saw madness in the captain's eyes.

"I'm going to put them back, sir," Samual answered. "They belong to the voodoo man."

Captain Crawford shook his head. "They belong to me, boy. Same as you." He released Samual and reached for his .44 caliber revolver.

He's going to shoot me.

"EEEIIIYAAA . . . !"

A soldier screamed and staggered past. Clinging to his leg was a child—a boy of bony fingers and rotting flesh, with a face that had seen better days. The nose was missing and the skin was festered pustule. The zombie child grabbed the soldier just above the calf of his leg, biting him behind the knee. Blood trickled over rotting lips and ran down the soldier's pants.

Captain Crawford turned to look at the soldier. When he did, Samual kneed him in the groin.

"Ugh . . ."

Captain Crawford dropped to his knees with a groan. Samual threw a quick glance in the direction of the fighting. The dozen or so soldiers still standing were only about twenty feet away. Twice as many zombies surrounded them. Knowing what must be done, he turned and ran back into the building.

Samual did not look around, dared not look around, afraid of what he might see. Going by just feel in the darkness, he raced to the right wall. Pulling items from the sack, he placed them back on the shelf as fast as he could. The last item was the gold plate. Samual could tell what it was by its feel. The plate was important; it had been kept in a special place. But where?

Think, Samual. Think. It has to be placed back where it was taken from. Where does it go?

He heard something move in the darkness. A heavy scraping sound. It drew nearer, approaching him. Terror prickled his scalp. He started to run, then remembered where the plate went.

The other side of the room! In the center of the shelf.

He rushed across the room to the other shelf. He was about to replace the plate when the door burst open.

"Samual!"

Captain Crawford stood in the doorway.

"I know you're in here, boy."

Samual didn't move, barely breathed. The captain looked around, but apparently couldn't see him in the darkness. For the first time in his life, Samual was glad to be black.

Captain Crawford stepped back and reached behind him. When he stepped forward again he was holding the lantern.

I'm dead.

The light forced the shadows back, exposing Samual. Captain Crawford smiled.

"There you are, boy." Captain Crawford set the lantern on the floor and drew his revolver. "You disobeyed me, Samual. I'm gonna have to punish you for that. Nobody disobeys me, especially a Negro."

Captain Crawford walked toward him. He spotted the plate in Samual's hands.

"You trying to steal from me, boy? You a thief?"

Samual shook his head. "I wasn't trying to steal it. I was returning it."

Captain Crawford laughed. He raised the revolver, aimed it at Samual's head.

Samual knew he was about to die. But before the captain killed him, he had something to say:

"Captain, coming here was wrong. Your being here has awakened something that's better left alone.

"A voodoo man lives here, Captain. He must have died. But when a voodoo man dies, it ain't like you or me dying. No, sir. He's still got his servants. Zombies. You've seen them outside. The bodies of the Indians drew them. They smelled the blood. Maybe the voodoo man's got something else. Maybe he's got himself a demon."

Captain Crawford slowly cocked the revolver's hammer. But Samual didn't care, hardly noticed. There was something going on behind the captain much more frightening than the threat of death.

While Samual spoke, the pole in the center of the room began to glow from within with a flickering red light, like someone had lit a fire inside of it. As the glow became brighter, a faint mist started forming near the top of the pole. At first the mist was light gray in color, like an early morning fog, but it quickly grew darker.

Sweat slimed Samual's neck. As he watched, the mist churned and swirled like an angry thunderhead. It began to mold itself into shape. Legs formed. A head. Ears and tusks. Eyes appeared.

The churning slowed, stopped. The mist became solid. Flesh and blood. The transformation was complete.

It's not real. It can't be real.

But it was. As Samual stood watching, the mist formed into a giant gray pig—an incredibly mean-looking pig—with sharp white tusks and eyes of fire.

It's a demon! Voodoo man's got himself a baca. We're dead.

The baca hung upside down near the ceiling, its legs wrapped tightly around the pole. It lifted its head, staring straight at Samual and the captain. Watching them. Perhaps it wondered what they were doing in its home. Perhaps it knew exactly what they were doing.

Slowly, like a spider descending a strand of web, the baca started climbing down the pole.

Samual wet his pants but didn't care. He tore his gaze away from the baca, looked back at Captain Crawford. The captain was speaking to him, but Samual could not lock his attention on what was being said.

The baca continued down the pole. It was a mind-numbing sight: a giant pig moving with the grace of a cat and the fluidness of a snake.

Not taking his eyes off the baca, Samual slowly leaned forward and placed the gold plate at Captain Crawford's feet. The captain started to retrieve the plate, when he caught a glimpse of movement behind him.

The captain spun around, gun at the ready . . .

And screamed.

The baca squealed and lunged. Captain Crawford tried to jump out of its way, but he wasn't quick enough. The baca crashed into him, knocking his legs out from under him. He went down. The baca whipped its head to the right. Tusks tore flesh. Blood flowed.

Run! Get out! Get away!

Samual sprinted for the door. Behind him, the room erupted in a series of gunshots, squeals, and screams. He reached the door, flung it open, started out—

"Samual!"

Samual stopped.

Don't stop. Run. Run. Run.

"Samual, for God's sake, help me!"

He turned.

Captain Crawford was running toward him, his arm outstretched. Blood flowed from the captain in a dozen different places. The right side of his face had been ripped open, exposing bone. A flap of flesh hung down over his jaw. His right ear was also missing. Racing to catch the captain was the baca. Blood dripped from its tusks.

"Samual, please help me!"

Captain Crawford was going to make it. He was going to outrun a half-ton of killer pig.

Samual reached out to help him, to pull him to safety. But then he remembered all the bad things Captain Crawford had done. He remembered the beatings he had received, remembered the screams of the Indian women and how their bodies had looked all naked and bloody.

Raped, murdered, and scalped.

Samual let his arm fall to his side. He looked the captain straight in the eyes and said: "Go to hell, sir."

Stepping through the doorway, Samual closed the door behind him and locked it from outside.

"Samual. Noooo . . . !"

The cry ended in an agonizing scream. Something struck the door from the inside, shook it, but the latch held.

Samual felt his body break out in goosebumps. A shiver touched his spine. He closed his mind to what was going on inside, blocked out the sounds of Captain Crawford being torn apart. He took a deep breath, exhaled. Took another. He turned away from the door . . .

And froze.

There were at least thirty of them, maybe more. Dead, each and every one of them, but not knowing they were dead. Their bodies soulless; their minds responding to only one stimulus— food. Human flesh.

The zombies formed a solid barricade around the front of the building. Escape was impossible. Samual looked around for any of the soldiers but saw none. He let out a sigh of despair. It would be useless to put up a fight. He was hopelessly outnumbered. Unarmed.

With a silent prayer, Samual resigned himself to whatever fate was in store for him.

Lord, please let me die quick. Don't let me suffer.

He wondered if the zombies would eat him right away or save him for some future meal.

I hope you all get sick.

But the zombies made no move to attack. Instead, they stood silently before him—walking apparitions of rotting flesh and bone—watching him with vacant eyes.

What are they waiting for?

The drumbeats stopped suddenly. The night grew deathly still. Samual was wondering what was going to happen, when, from inside the building, there came a long, high-pitched squeal. A series of low grunts followed.

As the grunts faded to silence, the zombies began to move. Apparently, they had been waiting for instructions, and the baca, voodoo man, or whatever that thing was inside had just given them some.

Oh, Lord. This is it.

Samual prepared to die.

But instead of moving forward, the zombies were backing up, stepping aside, opening up a path between them.

A way out!

Samual took a hesitant step forward. Was it a trick? Perhaps, but none of the zombies moved to intercept him. He took another step, and another.

He kept walking, passing between the horde of zombies. He stepped over bodies of Confederate soldiers but did not look down. He didn't want to know what the zombies had done to them. He didn't look back, either, afraid of what he might see.

Samual stopped long enough to untie Captain Crawford's horse from the tree. He led the horse out of the village and across the spring, not stopping to mount it until he reached the clearing on the other side. The zombies stayed by the building, watching him. None made any move to stop him.

Climbing into the saddle, Samual wondered why he alone had been allowed to live. Was it because he had returned the voodoo items to their rightful owner? Perhaps. Or did the zombies feel a certain kinship toward him? After all, they had been Negroes—men and women with the same dreams as himself, the same desires. They had probably fled the cruelty of plantation life, seeking a safe haven from men like Captain Crawford, searching for freedom. But freedom had eluded their grasp and they had again become slaves, guardians of the village. For eternity.

The voodoo priest that enslaved them was probably long dead, but his magic still lingered in the village. It had been awakened by Captain Crawford. Evil feeding evil.

Samual smiled.

It was almost ironic that Captain Crawford and his men had ended up as zombie delicacies, booty to be fought over, plunder—

Spoils of war.

Squaring his shoulders, Samual turned the horse to the east— toward the coast of Florida that was firmly under Union control.

He turned toward freedom.

Red Clay, Crimson Clay

Brad Linaweaver

My personal political philosophies favor neither of the two major parties. Most Democrats have never met a spending program they didn't like, while the Republicans' long-standing effort to weaken the Bill of Rights has moved us dangerously close to the "Big Brother" style central government envisioned by George Orwell. I was bemoaning this problem on a convention panel—appropriately, the topic was "The Uses of Science Fiction as a Cautionary Tale"—when one of my panelists said, "Oh. You're a libertarian!" My tendency is to disdain labels, but I'm willing to accept the small "l" designation as generally reflective of my viewpoints.

Brad Linaweaver is a big "L" Libertarian, actively committed to providing voters a meaningful alternative to traditional politics. Brad sent me an issue of *Prometheus,* the quarterly journal of the Libertarian Futurist Society, where he had an article discussing libertarian themes in horror fiction. Brad makes his case well, but what caught my eye was a separate piece on science fiction books in the Libertarian Hall of Fame. Robert Heinlein and Ursula LeGuin I expected to find there, and my only question about L. Neil Smith's credentials is whether anarchy constitutes a workable form of Libertarianism. On the other hand, finding Jerry Pournelle and Tom Clancy among those honored surprised me until I considered the works for which they were selected. The entire issue was thought provoking, though I'm still willing to espouse only the small "l" version of libertarianism, just as I'm willing to espouse the small "r" usage of republican.

Brad's stories have appeared in *When the Black Lotus Blooms, The Ultimate Werewolf,* and *Psycho-paths.* His first novel, *Moon of Ice,* has been widely praised. He's another of the Atlanta products in this anthology, though he presently splits his time between Georgia and Hollywood.

D o not fear me, although I was one of only two survivors. Sometimes we cannot help staying alive. It is not that we choose these things. Life chooses us; or sometimes, it is a matter of death passing us by.

Oh sir, I am real flesh and blood, as I will prove to you soon enough. I would think you were already well satisfied in that area, after the way you've been pawing poor Maria there. . . . I'm sure she enjoys your company as much as I hope you'll enjoy mine. But then, I must remember that you are interested in more than my body.

The madam suggests you are a most sophisticated gentleman. You wouldn't come to a house of this character if you didn't prefer our variety. . . . Yes, it is true that I'm fluent in both English and French. You could say I've two other languages as well—the degenerate French of our fair city and plain old colored English. Yassuh, or *Oui, monsieur.* What is your pleasure? . . . I appreciate the compliment. I'd rather speak in this fashion, kind sir. You're right that I find time to read novels and plays. I even write letters as a service to my more decadent clients.

Well, if you are finished running your fingers through Maria's blond tresses, it is best we have privacy. I don't tell the story very often. No one has ever believed it before, but I have confidence that you will be my first exception. . . .

Now that we're alone, where should I begin? Of course, you want to hear about my mother. . . . No, she was not as light-hued, since you ask. A "High Yellow," as they call me, takes time to bloom in this old black and white world. Mama was a quadroon and my father was white. That's how we, to put it delicately, breed an octoroon. . . . There are social disadvantages, to be sure, but in my line of work there are advantages. If you'd be a bit more generous with your champagne, sir, I'll tell you what the customer really wants when he asks for something *exotic.* Here, let me pour your glass. For a fine Yankee

gentleman to travel so long a distance to New Orleans just to
see me, a girl might think he's after more than memories. . . .

Why, how flattering! Let me sit here by the window and you
may have a better view of the sunset in my hair. You can see
the water from here; it's so beautiful this time of day.

. . . Now don't pretend with me. Talk like that will get you
nowhere. It is true that I'm outspoken, but you can't blame that
on the end of the peculiar institution. I haven't been a slave for
many years. The late unpleasantness had nothing to do with it.
But please forgive my tone; you are master here, so long as you
pay the price. And you will.

Mother was born in the West Indies, where the races mix as
easily as rum and love, at least on the good days. She learned
the craft of *Voudon*. Perhaps you know it as Voodoo. There's
not a lot to it, really. The spells are all very simple. People are
made well or ill, happy or sad. It makes use of the four basic
elements: fire, air, earth, and water. Mama was especially adept
at using earth. She knew it all, from the meaning of a buzzard's
wing on your doorstep to the uses of a pail of water under the
full moon. She had opinions on every variety of doll and zombie.
She was a *mamaloi,* or mambo, the highest female position. She
even knew the Queen herself, Marie LaVeau, who introduced
her to other things.

As for me, I was born right here in New Orleans. Mama initi-
ated me at a very early age. I was so young, I got the mistaken
impression that you couldn't prepare a meal without saying incan-
tations over the food! She used the same pots for the magic, you
see. What's that, sir? She must have raised some spicy demons?
Why, imagine that—a Yankee with a sense of humor.

. . . Please don't misunderstand. I mean no disrespect. Here,
let me fill your glass again. I know you find it difficult to believe
that I could have any sympathy for the Confederacy. It's not
easy to explain, but my loyalty has always been to people and
places. I am very much my mother's daughter in this.

There's not much more to say about Voodoo. You should not
make too much of it. It doesn't take long to penetrate the mysteries of Damballa and the lesser spirits which serve the serpent.
As easily as those names tripped off Mama's tongue, she would

say very little about other knowledge she had acquired over the years, beginning with her discovery that the Queen of Voodoo turned elsewhere when need was greatest. The most I could get out of Mama was that there were great forces beyond the dreams of human will, powers that could never be commanded or cajoled but only obeyed. To even put a name to these things was to court disaster, and the names—she assured me—were very difficult to pronounce. Voodoo was child's play in comparison: playing with matches compared with trying to hold the sun.

My education in such occult matters was brought to a close by a change in fortune. Our family (for that is how we thought of them) went bankrupt. Mama was sold to an old friend in Atlanta. She had already determined the best course for my future and used her considerable influence to see it brought to fruition. I was sold here, to the best bordello in New Orleans, where it was understood that if I proved myself, I would be set free. It was frankly more economical for me to be an employee. It was even standard practice in this house. Mama wanted to broaden my horizons, and promised me the world by this means.

. . . You would ask that, wouldn't you? I began my career at the age of twelve. I was very popular. . . . Thank you for not feigning disgust. A taste for young girls is not always restricted to the connoisseur.

I have since given much thought to this subject. My situation was hardly unique in world history. For many women, the only road to economic independence was to become a courtesan. In this business, youth comes at a premium.

. . . You flatter me again, kind sir. I will not tell you my true age except to say I plan to be in my early to mid-twenties for a very long time. And Voodoo has nothing to do with it.

. . . You're right about there being a link between sex and magic. Magic draws its powers from the interplay of all sorts of human tensions. But only one human activity allows for the release of the most powerful forces. War has no substitute. The darkness of the heart is exalted when good people are being patriotic.

. . . You wonder why I came back from Europe? My, my, you have been checking up on me. Perhaps I was foolish to return from Paris during the war. It was no small feat returning to this place, but I knew I'd always be welcome here. Besides, the French at peace are more dangerous than Americans at war. (No, Maria is not French, I assure you of that. She doesn't speak because she has nothing to say. Her language is English.) The gentleman who had taken me overseas became tired of me about the same time I tired of him. And the streets of Paris are never safe.

I had to come back, even with war clouds obscuring the horizon. Mama guided me. From the earliest I can remember, she could communicate by words and pictures in my mind. As I grew older, she could reach over longer distances. She wouldn't call me back without a reason. And it's not as if I had much choice. She had a way of invading my dreams if I were not the dutiful daughter. I would have to go to her to receive the family legacy.

. . . I can't answer that. I don't know if I loved her. We were linked. It goes beyond mere relationship. Do you love your hand?

. . . No, I'd never met the Swains, but I felt as if I knew them. Mama showed off the new family in my dreams. The father had a dignified quality, a man who was moderate in most things. His family had originally come from Charleston. The mother was a quiet-mannered woman of old Atlanta stock. Neither was very large and their health only middling. But they had produced three children: two boys and a girl. Mama was most taken with the daughter, of course. She could never look at a female without considering the potential.

Mama made me see their home, as well. I could tell that she approved of the Swains' taste. The house was all white and blue, the front door surrounded by classical posts and a lintel. Inside, there were beautiful hardwood floors, polished to reflect the lights of a hundred parties. As for the rest—furnishings, carpets, tapestries, even the least detail of the chandelier—it all had just the right touch.

Do you know how you can tell a house that has become a world in itself? The strongest impressions come from children. They leave so much of themselves behind, and I don't mean their fingerprints on the brass fittings. There is a thin layer of emotion, as if a fine dust, left over all the surfaces where children play; and from this you can extract joy or melancholy. Mama was very good at what she did. She helped me to feel that she was living in a happy home. She liked their masquerade parties best because she could dress up Sarah—that was the little girl's name—as a witch.

. . . You want to hear about the trip? I admit that I don't like remembering it. It was worse than I'd expected. Shadows in the mind can never have the same raw impact as being there. I'd already seen pieces of the war. Only men could call something so bloody by its proper name and not even notice the word: *pieces*. If only those who brought about this war could witness every horror up close. . . .

Oh, please sir, let us not be distracted by anything so tawdry as politics. You can't seriously consider the opinion of someone in my station, now can you? . . . Well, if you insist, I'll admit that I don't believe the war was fought to free the slaves. The late President made it clear from the start that his goal was to save the Union *at any cost*. All other issues were secondary. But surely this is not the time to discuss American statecraft. I read a lot, and have traveled some, but I wouldn't pretend to match my thoughts against a graduate of Harvard, such as yourself.

. . . The trip was terrible, with one exception. I started up the Mississippi and soon discovered a river of wounded men whose spirits had been torn out of their bodies. Your religion doesn't understand how bound to flesh is the spirit. I will never forget the faces, especially the ones missing features. It made no difference, whether going by water or by land; there were always those faces to haunt the soul.

. . . You want to know how I arrived at my destination in so timely a fashion? Maybe I flew on one of my mother's broomsticks! Well, I'll tell you, I'm only half joking about that. There is good fortune attached to the trade we practice in this establishment. I made the acquaintance of a Confederate signal corps officer. He'd already paid his respects to me when he found out that I'd been present at a certain event before the war, an event he'd regretted having missed. It was when Monsieur Petin of the French Academy conducted his famous balloon flight from

Lafayette Square right here in New Orleans. After that, it was the next best thing to love. Despite the risks, my dashing officer in gray took me with him. The wind was most obliging, but I don't know that Mama had anything to do with it.

This was the only part of the journey where I didn't see any wounded. But even in the heavens one remembers Hell. Images in my mind were growing stronger as we neared the destination until, finally, the red glow on the horizon became as bright as freshly spilled blood. It was the first time I'd ever seen Atlanta, Georgia.

. . . Oh, I am pleased to learn that you don't approve of Sherman. I've yet to meet a Yankee who thinks the burning was a good thing; although a surprising number will argue that it was necessary. To be fair, I agree there were plenty of atrocities to go around. You've certainly followed the Andersonville Trial. I don't dispute that Union soldiers were ill treated as prisoners of war in that Confederate hellhole. Yet couldn't a case be made for extenuating circumstances? . . . I mean that when supply lines are cut off, prisoners of war are the first to feel the pain. . . . I don't deny that justice was done, or will be done. I only ask what military justification was there for General Sherman's pyromania? I hadn't thought that he was so noble a man as you make out, only dedicated to shortening the war and saving the lives of his troops. Well, as I said before, despite my unusual education, I am still but a woman, and a darkie at that. You can't expect me to see the picture whole, as you do.

You must remember that I saw Southern life from an unusual perspective. The Old South was not so much a system as a set of attitudes, of personal faith and subtle hatreds. If the goal of the late unpleasantness was to reduce the oppression of man by man, then I'm afraid someone in authority made a miscalculation.

. . . As for the carpetbaggers who have lately joined my clientele, I won't say that they fail to measure up, but they do lack something one came to expect from Southern gentlemen. The old way had its problems, but at least it developed manners to a high art. Mama always taught me to love ritual for its own sake, as well as for the practical side of getting a formula right.

But there's no point lamenting over things that are gone with the wind. You want to know how I found the Swain estate.

. . . It was on the outskirts of Atlanta, and outside the perimeter of Sherman's flames. With a bit more luck, it might have escaped notice altogether. Mama had used her Voodoo for spells of protection. As you have gathered, it didn't work. The other, darker powers could only be used destructively, but at least they *always* worked. In matters of revenge, Mama had lost her faith in the power of pins and dolls and all that rigamarole.

. . . You're right. I still haven't told you how I found the house. Can't a girl keep any secrets? Shadows in my mind were all the guide I needed. In that chaos of fire and death, of murder and rape and looting, I was reluctant to ask for directions. Yet surrounded by all that danger, I felt queerly safe the nearer I came to my mother.

These feelings of confidence and purpose were shattered the moment I saw what had happened on the Swain property. I realized Mama had withheld the most recent events from her messages. The house was strangely untouched, except for a few broken windows in the front and some bulletholes in the walls. I say strangely, because it seemed almost indecent that it was still standing. It should have been in mourning for the Swains, who lay butchered out in what remained of the side yard. The earth had been torn up around them, as if in sympathy with their torn and ruptured bodies—or as if graves had been begun and then abandoned. The children were the worst, whole pieces of them lying about the grounds, as if discarded toys. The blood had drained out and mixed with . . .

You don't look well, sir. Shall I continue? My aim is to please. The customer is always right. Here, let me pour you another glass to settle your nerves.

Well, as I was saying, the blood had seeped into the ground. Are you familiar with the topography of Georgia? There are places in that state where the soil is very red; and this was so even before the arrival of Union troops. The Swains had a stretch of the reddest clay I've ever seen in that side yard. Of course, I never saw it completely dry. I won't try to describe the odor.

. . . You wonder what had become of Mama. So did I. The

next thing I remember was hearing voices from the house. And laughter. The most pleasant sound in the world becomes the most terrible when heard in an abattoir. They were male voices. Young voices. Soldiers' voices.

It didn't seem possible that Mama could have been bested by such as these. Yet strewn before me were the remains of those she would have protected; the red spots turning brown on the charnel flesh, the skin a pale white terrain on which insects carried out their own military sorties. The impossible was real: Mama had failed.

It was late afternoon. The sky was overcast with clouds that seemed to be made of smoke. No birds sang. I knew that when night fell, not a single cricket would be heard. It was more unnatural than any witchcraft. But when men have done such things, they set the stage. What nature cannot restore may be restored in other ways.

I did not yet realize that Mama was dead. You see, she was still communicating with me. I wanted to scream at her: How could you let this happen? Why didn't you protect yourself? The only trouble was that I knew the answers as soon as anger flashed through my brain.

Powers of protection never match powers of revenge. She had sensed that her time was coming if she intended to pass on the legacy to me. Turning to the greatest powers she knew, and uttering the names that must not be spoken, meant that she would have to let go of this existence and join with *them* if she were to avenge the Swains and pass on to her daughter a higher understanding. Her body was nowhere to be found. *They* had taken it and left something behind in the ground where the slaughtered family lay unburied and unmourned.

I realized then the role I had to play. Mama needed me to finish it. Walking up to the house, I let myself in the front door. There were ten of them.

They were all privates. I never did find out how they had become so cut off from the command structure. It really didn't matter, though, as one named George had come to dominate the rest. He was the idealist of the group, constantly quoting Robespierre from the French revolution. The rest had fallen in line behind this thoroughly evil bastard, all except one fair-haired lad who hesitated to offer up the full measure of his devotion. This boy was named Mark.

. . . Oh, *monsieur,* you seem upset again. Here, have some more of your excellent champagne. As I say, this George had worked them up to a killing frenzy against the Southern plutocracy, as he put it. Mark had been uneasy about the gruesome business, but he hadn't resisted. No more did he resist when the other nine took turns with me. George was quite the ringleader. His rationalizations were nothing short of remarkable. As this was the only time in my life I'd been raped, much less raped by a mob, his fine words about my personal deliverance fell on deaf ears.

They kept at me until I was bleeding profusely. That's when Mama began whispering again. My blood was the missing ingredient, the catalyst, now that she was gone.

When my education was finished, theirs began. The sky darkened, and with it came a deeper silence. I was left unguarded, except for Mark who sat crying in a corner. The rest had been drunk when they raped me. Now they got drunker on the last of the Swains' liquor. George was arguing loudly with two others about the necessity of burying the bodies before morning. The stench was becoming hard to ignore. In the absence of officers, he had seized the baton, so to speak, and showed a natural skill for delegating responsibility. Everyone was so preoccupied that they failed to notice my going over to the window, where I opened it and let some of my blood drip outside. This was on the side of the house next to the bodies.

That's all there was to it. The rest happened very quickly, as when the last pinch of seasoning has been added to a stew and there is nothing else but to bring it to the boiling point. There was a rumbling sound, then an explosion. One of the soldiers ran to the front door to see what had happened, but something was blocking the door on the other side. The young soldier, Mark, had moved over to the side window and he saw it first.

Swain blood, red clay, my blood—they had come together to make a reddish mass. In the failing light, it looked as if a side of raw beef was being dragged across the pane, making a horrid streaking sound. And while this was happening, the rest of it was bubbling up and spreading around the house.

I knew that I was safe. That's what my mind said. Mama said it. I hadn't been required to speak any of the forbidden names. Despite these assurances, however, it was the most terrifying experience of my life—just watching what happened to those men.

None of them had any idea what it was. How could they? It came through three windows at once. The presence or absence of glass in the panes was entirely irrelevant. It started off like a cascade of mud pouring into the room, but as the volume increased, it took on a more recognizable form. The thing grew tentacles, and they were redder at the tips than the remainder of the bulk that kept pushing through the windows until I feared we would all smother. But no one was to have that merciful a death.

George was the first to go. I liked that. Dozens of the tentacles struck him all at once. At every point of contact, he began to bleed. This was no mere trickle but a human being turned into a crimson fountain. He fell to the floor without uttering a sound, it had happened so quickly. But his men—for that is what they had become—had time to scream.

The others tried to escape, but all they managed to do was trample one another up against the front door. Mark and one other soldier managed to flee upstairs. From where I stood, I had an unobstructed view of the carnage; it still seemed incredible to me that I was spared by the flailing tentacles.

There was still a spasm of life in the first victim's body, and I watched George slither across the floor before coming to a stop, sliding in his own blood. The skin was as pale white as the corpses outside, but it didn't stay that way. Even as I watched, it changed—the skin dried and then cracked, like clay baking in the sun.

Suddenly a clear path opened to the stairs. I walked in that direction, fearing that to run would mean slipping on the wet floor. Once on the stairs, I hurried to the top floor, where I found Mark and his friend, huddled together as if they were Siamese fetuses dreading birth into an unknowable world of pain.

. . . Speaking of which, I see pain in your expression again. Dear sir, it seems you are upset every time I mention this young man, Mark. We needn't fence any longer. I know why you're here. You almost restore my belief in the power of love. Only the most dedicated father would have followed so unlikely a trail to the bitter end. . . . When you first heard stories of monsters and witchcraft, you must have dismissed them. But the disappearance of your son must have been agony you couldn't abide. . . . As we agreed, there are different kinds of love. Only love would inspire you to give credence to stories of a New Orleans prostitute who had something to do with the mysterious disappearance of Union soldiers. What made you believe your son was still alive? An instinct? Perhaps love is another form of magic.

Your son was the only one who didn't rape me. Clearly, Mama intended that all of them should die. I decided to be merciful. I don't believe your son participated in the murder of the Swains, but he passively stood by, as he did in my case. But the other one was guilty of the acts. He had to die. It wasn't easy prying them apart, but I managed. The pulsing red mass was already pushing its way up the stairs by then. I fed it the last one.

While this other soldier was writhing in the tentacles, I placed myself over your son's body. By the time the thing reached us, I had decided what to do. It searched for a way around me, but it was too difficult to touch Mark without also touching me. Mama spoke again, and we had our final argument. Her years of being a mambo helped develop her sense of humor. We reached a compromise about what should happen to Mark.

. . . There's no point in threatening li'l ol' me. You'll discover shortly that you cannot take any action against me. The champagne you've been drinking has a special ingredient from an old southern recipe—the southern hemisphere, that is. It eliminates undesirable initiative. *You cannot lift a hand against your new companion.*

. . . Now we understand each other better. As I say, Mama and I were of one mind on what was to be done. Your son, Mark, was touched in three places by the thing. Twice on the chest, and once in a more delicate location. He bled, but the flow was allowed to stop. As for his body, there were changes, but nothing so drastic as what happened to his comrades. The shock was severe and he was granted a loss of memory. There might have been a suicide otherwise.

"He" still doesn't remember. And it can stay that way, unless you want me to change it. If you are very good, and do exactly what I want you to do when we consummate the evening, I'll be kind, dear sir, and allow *you* to forget.

You'll want to forget everything you did . . . with Maria.

Beneath a Waning Moon

Brad Strickland

Brad Strickland began writing science fiction and fantasy in 1982. He frequently uses Southern settings in his work, most notably in his novel *Shadowshow*. His novels *Moon Dreams, Nul's Quest,* and *Wizard's Mole* are each part of his Jeremy Moon series, humorous fantasies involving an advertising specialist loose in a world of magic. Of his more than fifty published short stories, twice his work has been selected for inclusion in *The Year's Best Horror Stories*.

He has gained acclaim for his dark fantasy, typically dreamlike and off-center, but is quick to point out it is not reflective of his ordinary life as a professor at Georgia's Gainesville College.

Talent runs deep in the Strickland family. While Papa Strickland is a popular guest at Southern conventions, his wife Barbara, and children Jonathan and Amy are the ones who typically walk away from the gatherings with awards in hand. Jonathan and Amy (with lots of help from designer Barbara) won Best in Show in the children's division at the costume contest at the 1986 World Science Fiction Convention, dressed as Daffy Duck and Marvin Martian. It is, however, their occasional appearances as Danger Mouse and the Easter Penguin that are my favorites.

This is one of six stories by Georgia residents in this book—seven if Michael Bishop's introduction is included, plus co-editor Ed Kramer gets credit as the eighth Peach State resident contributing to the project. (And I suppose we could count both Aherns separately, getting the total up to nine.) That's not a coincidence. Atlanta is a burgeoning center of literary activity, especially in the areas of fantasy and science fiction. This story is reflective of that momentum, a finely crafted story from a writer well skilled in atmosphere and foreshadowing.

The moon betrayed him.

Charles Martin lay face down, unmoving, his telltale white face pressed to the long grass, but the pale light of the crescent moon, not yet at first quarter, must have revealed him to the searchers. Martin did not even hear the one on his right approach before he felt the hollow cold of a shotgun barrel pressed against his jaw.

"Who is it?" The voice came from the other side, his left side, but Martin was so sick and scared that he could not look.

A hand seized his hair and forced his head back, turning his face to the night sky. "Hit's a stranger," a second voice said. "What you reckon we ought to do with him?"

"Take him to the master's," the other said. His *r* was hard, a hill sound, and the *t* was not the slur of the voices farther to the south: *master* the voice said, not *massa*. For a moment Martin wondered if he had made it close to the Union camp at Chattanooga, but then they picked him up, roughly, not minding his wounded arm, and he fainted.

He woke in a bed, woke to candlelight and the face of an angel bending over him. "Where did you find him?" she asked.

One of the hill voices said, "Up top o' Tesnattee Ridge."

"He's hurt. Go tell Dr. Anderson."

"Yes, Miz Ada."

Martin's head swam. The woman had an ageless oval face, pale as ivory, framed by soft black hair. Her arched brows were the same inky hue, and in that dim wavering light even her wide eyes seemed black. Her lips were full and red, the one touch of color about her, for she wore a dress the color of midnight. He tried to rise, but the soft pressure of her hands on his chest kept him down. "What shall I call you, young gentleman?" she asked.

As he had staggered north beneath a waning moon, Martin had prepared an elaborate lie, one to tell the Union troops when he reached Chattanooga, about how pain had taken his memory. But lying there, gazing into her face, he heard himself speak the simple truth: "Charles Wesley Martin."

She smiled. "Christened a Methodist, Mr. Martin?"

He nodded.

She smoothed his sweat-stiffened hair away from his forehead. "How old are you, Charles Wesley Martin? Sixteen?"

"N-Nineteen. Where am I? W-who are—"

"I am Ada Linton. You are safe on Blackstone Plantation—"

Martin gasped at the last word. He tried again to rise, but the effort was too great and he fell back. "I have to go—"

"No. You are hurt. You must rest until the doctor comes."

"But—your husband—a plantation owner, a Southerner—"

She averted her face. "Sir," she said, "my husband is in hell."

He might have fainted again, or he might simply have lapsed into restless, fitful sleep. He awakened to find a man bending over him, gaunt, gray-bearded, wearing a homespun white shirt with no collar to it. The man pressed a glass to Martin's dry lips. "Drink."

He swallowed something sharp—brandy—with a bitter undertaste. The bearded man took away the drained glass and squinted down at him. Hot though the night was, a small fire burned on the hearth across the room. The flickering light played on the man's thin, worried face, pooled darkness in the hollows beneath his cheeks. "I'll have to do something about that arm, son."

Martin struggled to move, felt that his legs and arms were bound to the bedstead. "No," said Ada Linton. "We had to tie you so you wouldn't thrash about."

"You can see for yourself," the man said. "It's about to mortify, son."

Martin squeezed his eyelids shut, turned his head, and opened his eyes all at once, forcing himself to look. The wound was smaller than he thought it would be, a furrowed scarlet gouge the size of a pencil in the meat two inches below his left elbow. But the flesh around it swelled black and puffy. Bile rose in his throat. "I—I—"

"Hush," the woman said, coming to his side. "This man is Dr. Anderson. He can help you." Her palm felt cool on his brow.

"Get your instrument ready, Doctor. Now, Charles Wesley Martin, open your mouth."

He did, and she put a damp cloth between his teeth. Bending close, so close he could smell verbena on her, she whispered, "You bite this hard if it gets too bad. And holler all you want." Gazing into her face, he realized with a shock that she was not more than twenty-five. Before, he had thought her somehow much older than he.

Martin heard the doctor stirring the fire. He tried to turn his head, but the woman clasped his face with her hands. "No, don't look. It will be worse if you look."

Strong hands undid the cord binding his left arm, and he felt his forearm pinioned between the doctor's elbow and chest. He heard the hiss of the red-hot iron eating into his flesh, then he smelled it; and then he felt it. His back arched as though from a galvanic shock, and he chewed the cloth, screaming through it, his voice rising to a wordless wail of pain. Even when the hissing ceased, he could not stop his shrieks, until at last sheer exhaustion quieted him. "There," the woman said, taking the cloth away. It was stained red. "Oh, Charles, you've bitten your tongue badly."

His head lolled toward the white-washed wall. His barking exhalations of breath sprayed it with a fine red mist. Martin passed out again.

And woke to a blue summer morning. Ada Linton sat next to the window at the foot of his bed, her elbow resting on the sill, her cheek resting on her half-closed fist. "Well," she said. "You have a little color today."

"Where am I?" he asked, his voice a rusty squeak. Pain stabbed his bitten tongue, and he winced.

"You're in the plantation house, of course," she said. "This is Blackstone Plantation. And that," she added with a gesture, "is our reverend, Mr. Wilvern."

Too weak to rise up, Martin rolled his head on the pillow. A tall man, clean-shaven, scarecrow-thin, stood in the corner with his hands clasped behind his back. He wore a somber black suit with a long coat. "Ma'am," he said in a voice that reverberated like a moan in a sepulchre, "as he seems clearer in his mind, I shall leave you now." With a bow, Wilvern turned and walked out.

Turning back to the woman, Martin swallowed. "You had the preacher in. Did you think—was I about to die?"

Ada had risen. She walked to the door and closed it softly. "No, Charles Wesley Martin, you were not. But Mr. Wilvern does see to our spiritual needs here in the valley, and he is involved with our lives. I asked him to call, and his visit was simply a courtesy to me."

Cords no longer bound Martin's wrists and ankles, though beneath the sheet his left arm had been lashed to a board. With an effort he raised his head, felt the room spin, and fell back. "So this is a plantation house. I thought we burned 'em all," he said.

"Whatever for?"

"The war."

She laughed. "The war never got this far."

"My arm—will I lose it?"

"Dr. Anderson says no. How does it feel?"

"Dead."

"It will be better by and by. You are very thin, Charles. You have been living on brandy and laudanum. Shall I have the servants bring you a bite to eat?"

He mused. His hollow and aching belly wanted food. "I'd surely appreciate it, ma'am."

She laughed. "Don't you ever call me that. 'Ma'am' makes me feel older than the hills. I tolerate it from Mr. Wilvern only because he is a man of the cloth. You call me 'Miss Ada.' " She leaned close, so close that he could see only her face, her wide dark eyes, a deep blue in the light of morning. "Or just Ada will do."

He did not glimpse the servants, for she met them at the door and brought the tray of food to the bed. He struggled to sit up, realizing only then that he was naked beneath the one sheet. She put the tray on a table beside the bed and said, "Let me help you."

With his free hand, Martin clutched the sheet to his chest.

"I've seen you naked once already," Ada chided. "Who do you think cut that blue uniform off you?" With no waste motions, she helped him to a sitting position, placing pillows behind him. He held onto the sheet, decorously covering his lap with it. He dared to look at the wound again then.

At first he thought it had suppurated, for a white film covered it. But he felt his stomach rise as the film moved and resolved itself into a hundred blind pulsating bodies. He retched.

"The doctor put them there. They'll only eat the bad flesh," Ada said. "Don't think about them."

But Martin, his mind full of maggots, could touch no morsel of the food she brought. He did choke down some brandy laced with laudanum, and afterwards he slept.

In feverish dreams he wandered long through a vast and endless red-brick city, the walls of innumerable low houses all blind, all windowless and doorless. Bare streets the exact color of brick dust stretched infinitely in all directions, and he was the only soul moving on them, unrestful, desperate, seeking some nameless destination in this place where all destinations were the same. It came to him that he roamed a city of the unknown dead, a necropolis of mausoleums, and he screamed forever until he awakened again.

The wound was clean.

At the doctor's urging, Martin had looked at it when he came out of the latest laudanum dream, had looked at it expecting to cry out in revulsion and terror; but now it was clean, a hollow hemisphere of slick pink flesh the size of a walnut.

"I wanted you to see it," Dr. Anderson said, "before I dressed it. It's mending, son. You won't have full use of that arm for a long time, but you won't lose it, either."

"Thank you," Martin said.

Anderson scowled and shook his head. "Don't thank me. It's my job to save the lives of young fools." He busied himself freeing the arm from its restraining board, then reached into his bag for lint and bandages. The two men were alone in the room. Through the open window at the foot of the bed, morning light spilled in, and warm July air.

As he wrapped the bandages carefully in place, the doctor said, "I suppose you deserted?"

Martin nodded.

"Come from down Atlanta way, I expect?"

Martin turned his face to the wall. The blood he had breathed out, brown now, still speckled it. His tongue still hurt from the bite, though it, too, was healing. "We were on a patrol. Six of us. Some Rebs jumped us. I got shot, fell down a hill, and fetched up with my head against a rock. When I came to, the other five were dead and stripped. The Rebs must not have found me."

"So you ran. How long, son?"

He shook his head. "At first I had the mare. She was running loose, trailing a halter rope. I caught her and I rode her bareback. I followed the Little Dipper north every night, six, seven nights, as long as I could ride, and then I hid up in the woods by day." He felt moved to elaborate, moved to explain how he and the mare had traveled north through a dark, ruined land, the smell of burned wood and rot strong in their nostrils. He lacked the strength. "Finally," he finished, "the horse died on me. I walked on north until one boot wore out. I lay down to die, and that's when they found me."

The doctor grunted, evidently satisfied with the bandage. "Eight or nine days on the road with that chunk gone out of your arm, and you never bandaged it nor cleaned it. It's a wonder you have any arm left, young fellow."

"Doctor, when—when may I leave, sir?"

Anderson shrugged, repacking his battered leather bag. "I couldn't say, son. You've been here a week—"

"A week!"

"I know, it don't seem that long. Laudanum does that to you. But you've been here a week, and except for an occasional egg beaten up in brandy and some milk, you've had nothing in your belly. You're going to have to eat some, to build up your strength, before you can start to think about leaving us."

"Can I at least have some clothes?"

The doctor's eyes twinkled. "Miss Ada don't stand on ceremony, does she? I'll see what I can arrange, son."

That afternoon she brought him a nightshirt—white cotton and just a little large on him. He struggled into it while she averted her eyes. He had eaten some already, but she made him eat again: chicken broth with diced chunks of white meat, green beans cooked with pork seasoning, coarse corn bread. Martin was ravenous once he began, and she sat watching him with approval.

"Where are you from, Charles?" she asked him.

"Ohio," he said.

His callused left hand lay palm up. She touched it tentatively. "You've done work in your time. A farm boy?"

He nodded. "But my uncle is in the railroad business. He was putting me through college when—before I enlisted."

"Oh. You mean to be a lawyer, I expect?"

"A poet," he confessed, then grinned foolishly.

She rose to take the tray from his lap. "Finished for now?"

"Yes, thank you, m—Ada." He swallowed. "You've been kind to me. I want you to know that I'm grateful."

"Nonsense. It's only what one person would do for another."

"But we're enemies," he said.

Her eyebrows arched as she smiled. "Oh? Are we?"

"We're at war."

"You and I? I am not aware that we are."

He sighed. "Our countries."

"Well, we don't worry much about any country in this valley." Having put the tray aside, she stood smiling down at him. "I take it war was not all you believed it would be."

"I thought the battles would be glorious. But it's only boredom and misery, bad food and chiggers, heat rash and mosquitoes, and then it's powder and blood and death." He shook his head, feeling that he had grown decades older since the onset near Kennesaw Mountain. "Did—was Mr. Linton killed in the war?"

She took a moment before answering: "Linton is my own name. I chose not to take that of my husband when we married."

Martin blinked. "I—I never heard of that before."

"Well. You haven't been out of Ohio very long, have you?" Taking up the tray, she paused in the doorway, her back to him. "My husband is in hell, Charles," she told him for the second time. "That is all you need to know."

*   *   *

His dreams did not quit him. Night after night he lived in agonies of illusion, crossing charnel landscapes that stretched on without end, passing eons of time drowned beneath stagnant waters, walled within suffocating caverns. By day he ate and grew stronger, and the night fears receded during the hours of sunshine. Every evening he drank an ounce of brandy and then sank into hellish slumbers.

A week passed, and he felt able to totter out of the bed and sit in the chair by the window, looking out over a quiet valley. He sat there as Ada knelt beside him with a basin of water and a bright straight razor, shaving the downy golden beard from his cheeks and chin with slow sizzling strokes. Martin did not trust himself to look at her from that close, and so instead he gazed out the window.

He saw a cedar-bordered stream with a mill, its dripping wheel lazily turning in the July sunshine; a scatter of whitewashed houses; fields furrowed and tended; and at the head of the valley a blocky unpainted structure that was, he supposed, the church. He thought the valley an enchanted place, untouched by war or the world outside. He could not help contrasting it with the terrible lands of his dreams—or the landscape of war that he had come to know too well.

Ada sat with him from time to time, listening to him talk, to his reminiscences of Ohio and of college, to his ambition of becoming a writer. She spoke little herself, but regarded him with a quizzical tilt of her head, an indolent smile. She answered his every request easily: when he could walk, she brought him trousers, shirt, and slippers to wear.

On a memorable day in his second week of convalescence and with Miss Ada's help, he made it to the privy and back, though on his return he fell onto the bed exhausted and panting. He felt triumphant, for more than once the sight of Ada Linton silently removing the reeking thunder-mug from beneath his bed had caused him the deepest shame.

On the morning after that, she helped him downstairs and out onto the veranda, where he sat in the morning sun and listened to the songs of mockingbirds in the pines. She sat nearby, her hands folded in her lap. She rocked in a rocking chair, as Martin's spinster aunts had done in Ohio, but despite her mourning dress, Ada Linton looked anything but spinsterish.

Their time together seemed almost a fragile illusion, for even awake, Martin felt dreamy, removed from himself. He found talking to Ada easy. At her urging, he spoke to her of his studies at school, of his growing eagerness to see the war. He poured out to her his conviction, held with all the passion that only a nineteen-year-old could muster, of the wrongfulness of slavery. Breaking off in confusion, he stammered, "I meant no offense to you—"

She tossed her head and laughed. "You think we keep slaves at Blackstone?"

"You said—the servants—"

"Some people choose to serve, Charles. None live in my husband's valley against their will." And that was that; though when Martin thought about it, he had seen no servants in the big stone house, nor about it. In fact, aside from Ada, he had seen no one in the valley at close range except the doctor, the minister, and his two captors, and they had all been white.

He tried to get from her some sense of where he was, but Ada teased him: "Away from war, my brave Private Martin. Is that not enough? It is for the rest of us." He smiled and pretended to be satisfied with that answer, though inwardly he wondered. He had no energy to press the point or to question her too sharply. It was easier to drift and speculate.

He knew that he had passed from the hilly country outside Atlanta, at any rate, and had come to the land of long, pine-clad ridges and deep valleys, where even high summer passed with nothing more than a pleasant drowsy warmth. Storms came over the mountains now and again, breaking from clouds the greenish-purple hue of a ripening grape, but their thunder no longer had the power to dismay Martin, who had seen man-made lightning sweep his friends from his side. The rains washed the valley and made it sparkle, and nothing seemed more kindly to him than the scene he viewed each morning, shining with dew and fresh as creation.

Looking at it hurt him.

For a long time he probed the hurt, like a man touching a hollow and aching tooth with a tentative tongue. At last he located the cause of the pain, and it was guilt.

For sitting near Ada, her lovely face calm and provocative, Martin thought of his comrades to the south. He had fled before the assault on Atlanta, but by now that surely was underway. Sherman's army might even now be in possession of their prize.

Or perhaps they were straggling back in defeat.

Perhaps his friends lay in unmarked graves, or fed the vultures.

While he rested safe here.

The pain sharpened whenever he touched it, biting more keenly than the healing wound in his arm ever had.

He could not stop probing that inward pain, increasing it, almost savoring it.

So most of another week passed, with Martin suffering through nights of wild dreams and fantasies and days of lassitude and regret. He ate as though famished, drank what seemed to be gallons of cold well-water, and slowly felt his strength returning.

"I shall not have to help you upstairs again," Ada said to him one evening as they went up to the second floor together. He had to lean on the banister, had to stop and rest twice, but she was right: he could now get up and down stairs without having to clutch her shoulder for support. She saw him to his room, where he sat on the edge of the bed, gasping for air.

She stroked his damp hair. "My poor Charles. War has been unkind to you."

"It's unkind to everyone."

"Is it? I think not. The war has brought people to our valley, people tired of the hell that man makes for himself. And you are the latest and the best."

He dropped his gaze. "I deserted," he muttered.

From far off he heard a sound, a rhythmic musical swell and fall. He heard her breathe, heard the rustle of her black dress, and behind it all that farther music. "What's that?" he asked.

Ada became absolutely still, tilted her head, and listened. "The choir. Mr. Wilvern's services are tonight."

He shook his head. "I didn't know it was Sunday."

She stroked his hair again, her fingers soft on his forehead.

She traced the line of his jaw, smooth now since she had been shaving him every other morning. "Don't worry yourself about the day. You lose track of time when you're ill." She sat beside him on the bed, her face radiant in the soft evening glow coming from the window. "You look so pure, dear Charles Wesley. Tell me, have you ever known a woman?"

He felt his cheeks go fiery red. "I—I—"

She laughed. "Hide your face," she said. "I see the answer there." She pulled him to her, cradled his head against her bosom, rocked softly back and forth on the bed, cooing. Martin smelled the fragrance of her again; sweet verbena, and under that a duskier, musky scent. With his face pressed to the yielding softness of her breasts, he felt like weeping.

He reached to hold her, but she pushed him gently away and stood. "I am keeping you awake too late," she said. "I forget how ill you have been. Good night, my dear innocent Charles."

She left him alone. After a time he stood and undressed. He went to the casement and stared out across the dark valley, only a candlelit window showing here and there, and directly across, the tall twin windows of the Reverend Wilvern's unsteepled church, illumined by oil lanterns. The droning music lulled him, and before he knew it, he had fallen asleep leaning on the sill, into more of his feverish dreams of infernal landscapes, of fleeing through illimitable vistas. He climbed endless stairs; he followed tortuous rivers of molten fire; running, always running. But this time he thought he had a goal: for he knew that somewhere Ada stood clad in shining white, magnificent in the darkness, her bare arms outspread for him.

He awoke hours later, stiff and aching from the straight chair he had sat in. He stretched, feeling a cool breeze on his face. The night insects had ceased their buzz and chirr, and the peeping frogs had fallen silent. The valley was all dark now, save for the church. A thin crescent moon shone over the structure, centered in the sky above its two red-lighted windows.

The wind brought again to him the faint sound of unaccompanied voices singing a dreary hymn, making him wonder how late these people held services. But he forgot about that as he stumbled to his bed and collapsed there to sleep, this time, blessedly, without dreams.

Dr. Anderson came the next morning to change the dressing on his arm. Martin could make a fist with his left hand now, and when the bandage was off he saw that the flesh had begun to fill in the wound, to pucker it closed. It no longer looked raw, but had scabbed over and oozed only a clear fluid.

Dr. Anderson grunted his satisfaction. "Coming along nicely. And you've put on flesh, too."

"Yes, sir."

"Walking much?"

"Some."

The doctor rebandaged the arm, then sat on the foot of the bed. "Son, will you take some advice?"

"Sir?"

"Leave," Anderson said.

Martin nodded. "I have to turn myself in."

"Damnation, boy. Just leave, that's all."

"No, I've thought about it. I must turn myself in—to the Union forces, preferably—and beg for—"

Dr. Anderson rose, his gaunt face red, his gray beard bristling. "Hellfire, son. Listen to me. Leave the house. Leave the valley. Let her bring somebody else in, somebody who lives here and knows. You get out. Then worry about where you'll go and who you'll surrender to. Tomorrow night's the dark—"

"What, Doctor?" It was Ada; she had come silently into the doorway.

The doctor turned. "I was just telling Mr. Martin that he should get more exercise. He has recovered enough to do a little walking."

"I am glad to hear he is doing so well."

With a stiff bow, Anderson picked up his bag and approached her. She stepped aside, letting him out of the room. Martin heard his steps clumping down the stairway; a moment later the front door opened and closed. Ada came to sit on the foot of the bed. "You *are* doing well, are you not?"

"Yes," he said.

"You know, the doctor recommended that I stop your doses of laudanum," Ada said.

He felt cold. Getting to his feet, he croaked, "Stop them? You haven't yet?"

She shook her head. She was only a few inches shorter than he, but she seemed to look up at him from a distance. "You were in pain, Charles. You had to have something to make you sleep. You've had some every evening before bed, in your tot of brandy. Do you think you can sleep through the night without it, dear Charles?"

He nodded, but his throat felt tight.

"We shall see. Tonight I will leave a glass with brandy and tincture of laudanum on the table beside your bed. If you feel that you need it, it will be there for you." She stepped close to him, turning her face up, and quickly, primly kissed him on the lips. "If you need something else . . ." she whispered, and then she kissed him again, lingeringly. He felt her teeth catch his bottom lip. She tugged playfully, then released him and pushed him back from her. "Well, if you need something else, you have only to ask."

He ached for her, but she turned and left him there. Martin's legs trembled as if they could no longer hold his weight. He forced them to move anyway, followed her into the hall. She was not there. Nor did she respond to his tentative knock on her bedroom door.

Martin was irresolute that day. He told himself that he did not need the drug, did not want to suffer the dreams it brought. But as evening fell, he became more and more agitated, his heart pounding in his chest, his mind whirling with a thousand inchoate thoughts. He would get no sleep without the oblivion of the drink. By nightfall his limbs all shook as though from ague. Ten times, a dozen, he started up from his bed in panic, fearing he knew not what. Finally, near midnight, he drank the draught and delivered himself to accursed dreams. When he awoke before dawn, he stumbled to the window.

The waning crescent moon, a red sliver, rode so low in the east that its horns seemed to crown the dark church. For a moment, Martin even thought he heard the droning music of a hymn, but it was only the blood singing in his ears.

Weeping, he pounded the windowsill with his good right fist.

They ate breakfast together that morning, Ada and he, in the cool dining room. The walnut table could have seated a dozen, but they were alone, except for—Martin finally saw her—the old cook. A wizened, white-haired woman, she came silently in with the food, set it before them, and then retired.

"Fresh eggs," Ada said. "Home-churned butter. Biscuits and syrup. Cold milk. You didn't eat this well in the army, did you, my Charles?"

He shook his head. "No. Nor did your people, after we came through."

Though still wearing a mourning dress, Ada looked different. She had done something with her hair, had let it down from its customary bun. It cascaded to her shoulders now, lustrous and soft and black as a moonless night. "My people are here in the valley," she said. "Your army has not harmed them."

She reached to touch his hand, but he withdrew it. "I'm leaving Blackstone Plantation today," he heard himself say.

Her smile was quizzical. "Oh?"

He looked down at his plate. "I have to. Honor demands that I—"

She laughed, once, softly. "Honor." Her voice made the word a mockery. "The honor of a murderer?"

He flushed. "Of a soldier," he said.

"Oh, Charles Wesley Martin, what quaint ideas you have. Why flee back to that wicked world of death and hatred when you could so easily stay here with me?"

"I have to go," he whispered. "Can't you understand that?"

She reached to caress his cheek, but he flinched away. "You have disappeared from your war," she murmured. "They probably believe you are dead—your friends, your officers, perhaps even your family by now. There is nothing to hold you to the outside world, no one who would miss you. And I so dearly want you to stay with me."

He dared not meet her deep blue eyes. "I couldn't live with myself."

"Couldn't you live with me?"

Despite himself he began to weep. "Don't."

"Then you do not want to be with me, here, tonight?"

"Oh, God," he said. "I want it more than anything. But I cannot. In all honor, I cannot."

She rose, her voice cool: "If my desires have upset you, I am sorry, Charles. I shall not importune you further." She turned her back on him. "But pray consider your decision well. Sleep on it tonight."

Before she could leave him alone, he blurted, "I don't want any more laudanum."

"Very well," she said without looking back.

July had faded into August to the accompaniment of buzzing cicadas. The day was hot, not with the sweltering heat of the flatlands, but still oppressive. This, Martin told himself, kept him from setting out in the forenoon. It would be better to travel in the cool of night, to follow the Little Dipper until it led to whatever redemption he could hope to find.

That afternoon, thinking himself alone in the house (for Ada had apparently deserted the plantation house and him), Martin wandered from his room to her bedroom door. Driven by impulse, he tried the knob and opened the door silently. A man stood with his back to Martin. As Martin watched, the man stacked kindling on the grate of an enormous stone fireplace. He turned for more wood, and seeing him in partial profile, Martin recognized him as one of the two who had captured him nearly a month earlier. He closed the door silently, undiscovered.

The aged cook brought him supper at sundown. Martin ate it without relish, already feeling a trembling in his limbs. As soon as he finished, Martin rose from his place and walked out the front door of Blackstone Plantation. He did not mean to return.

The valley lay mostly east and west, but at the eastern end, where the church was, it seemed to bend more northerly. Martin lowered his head and began to walk through dense twilight heat.

He passed the mill, then followed the course of the stream. It led through a little scattering of houses, where candlelight gave him occasional glimpses of people seated at dinner tables. The road beneath his feet was a red dust, dry and powdery. Drops of his sweat fell onto it and formed tiny dark spheres of salty mud. Trudging along the roadway, Martin began to have the feeling that he was back in one of his damnable dreams. The thought made him shudder.

He was weaker than he thought, or the valley was longer. Full night had fallen when he reached the church. Its unpainted boards weathered almost black, its two tall windows flanking a door left invitingly open, the dark structure reared before him. Martin rested on the bottom step, chest heaving. The hot and humid air filled his lungs but brought him no relief.

He must have dozed, for he started from sleep when a hand touched his shoulder. "Easy," a deep voice said. It was the preacher, Mr. Wilvern.

"I—I—"

"I know who you are." The tall old man sat down next to Martin, his knees popping. "Dark night to be out, boy. Dark of the moon tonight."

"I'm leaving."

Martin heard the other man take a long, slow breath. "Uneasy, are you?"

"Ashamed."

The preacher sighed. "Man has much to shame him. And seldom does he recognize the sacrifice he must make to sponge away that shame. Where are you heading, boy?"

"Chattanooga. Union lines."

"Well. You ain't going to make it tonight."

"But Ada—Miz Linton—"

"Hush," the preacher said. "You don't know all about her, and you can't guess the burden she bears. She is a strong woman, and on her rests the welfare of all the souls in this valley. She wants you to return. Can you make it back to Blackstone on your own? No? I thought not. You wait here."

Huddled on the step, Martin shook and wept for the brandy and the laudanum. The preacher was gone a few minutes; then he was back, leading a sable horse. "Here," he said, gesturing to the horse. "When you get there, just let him go. He knows the way home."

Somehow or other, Martin found himself in the saddle. Reeling, barely keeping his seat, he let the horse trot him back through the dark village. In the night ahead of him, he saw one red spark: a window, a second-floor window of Blackstone Plantation.

It grew as he came closer. He smelled smoke on the wind, realized that the fire in Ada's bedroom fireplace had been lighted, that it blazed there now, even on this sweltering evening. He had the feeling that she had lighted it as a beacon for him.

Fleetingly the thought of escape crossed his mind, the thought of riding the black horse over the ridge, turning northward, seeking his own people. But then he saw her.

She stood at the closed window, looking out over the dark valley. She wore a thin nightgown. The firelight behind her defined the shape of her body through it, the softness and the curves. He remembered how her breasts had felt against his fevered cheek. He knew, then, what would get him through the night without brandy, without laudanum.

He urged the horse forward.

Martin fell off more than dismounted, and the stallion turned and galloped away behind him. On unsteady legs he took the steps up to the veranda. He heard the mournful melody of the hymn on the air again, swelling stronger than before; a dismal sound but somehow welcoming, triumphant. He shook the phantom music from his ears.

The stair seemed to stretch away endlessly, like one of the stairs he had climbed in delirium. He finally reached the top, finally opened the door to the room and to her.

Ada still stood at the window. A wave of heat broke over him, for the fire on the hearth raged high, its voice roaring in the chimney. She turned to him. He saw that she was sweating, that the thin gown clung to her damp shoulders, to the underside of her breasts. "You came back," she said. "I am so glad."

He could not answer. He stepped to meet her, and they embraced before the shouting fire. He kissed her, tasting the salt of her perspiration. "I couldn't stay away," he said, panting.

"Oh, my dear Charles. You came back to give yourself," she murmured against his throat.

"Yes. Kiss me again." Her mouth was sweet, spiced with some exotic taste he could not name. He felt her breasts rise against his chest, hot through the thin nightgown and through his shirt, hotter even than the furnacelike air in that darkened room. Her hips thrust her against him.

He heard her gasp, felt her moist lips roll away from his. "Please, Charles," she said, her curiously demure voice all breath, "my husband—"

He laughed. "Your husband, madam, is in hell."

She turned her face away from him. Firelight gleamed on her long neck, made a golden track in the light sheen of sweat across her cheek. Behind him he heard the door open.

He felt a blast of even hotter air.

She turned, her eyes catching the light, glowing as though from within, and she smiled at him then, the expression wild, capturing his gaze, captivating it so that he could not, could not look at what had come into the room.

The gusts of superheated air smelled of sulfur.

"No, sir," she said, looking over his shoulder. "He has come home."

The Master's Time

Anya Martin and Steve Antczak

One of the drawbacks to fiction editing is that you have to keep up with your slushpile. Magazine editors are particularly vulnerable, and even an invitational anthology such as this one will receive unsolicited manuscripts. Rejecting stories isn't easy, even when the submission comes from an unfamiliar name you are unlikely to ever meet. Fairly often, as word gets around, you'll receive inquires as to whether your project is open. That's a double-edged sword. Several of the stories in this book were obtained through such networking, but occasionally inquiries come from close, personal friends who have no history of published fiction.

Maybe I shouldn't have worried when Anya Martin asked me if I'd take a look at the story she and Steve Antczak had written. She and Steve had each done some impressive pre-professional writing, Anya as a music critic, and Steve in his cutting edge fan magazine *Science Fiction Randomly*. Then again, maybe I should have worried. The gap between professional writing and good fan writing is usually the size of the Grand Canyon.

Anya and Steve came through. Telling a new writer that they've made a professional sale is the flip side of rejecting slush. Every editor takes great pride in the people the editor has "discovered." Since then, Steve has had a story in the NAL/Roc anthology *Newer York* and Anya has become a successful freelance writer. Let's hope Anya and Steve find time soon to collaborate again.

*T*here be nothing worse than picking cotton in dee sweltering heat from dawn till dusk for dee massuh, Willie thought. All day the only things he knew were the beating of the sun on his back, the smell of his own sweat, the uncaring hardness of the ground beneath his sore feet, and the sting of hunger in his belly. Not even the smile of sweet Nell could make him forget this hell, and often he wondered how she could smile at all.

Sometimes, when they were picking close enough to each other, they could talk, and Willie would tell Nell stories about his family on another plantation. He didn't recall the name of it—he was still a little boy when he was sold off—but he often dreamed of going back there someday to see them.

"Nell, ah knows you don't believe me, but ah saws my grand-mama turn a cat into a owl. She tied dem little dolls out of straw and cotton—cotton 'cause dee cat was white. She was one of dem cats who just came, wandered in one night out of dee woods, and my grandmama seein' some fun, took her in and fed her some supper. That poor little kitty by dee end of the night, she was hoppin' around tryin' to fly, while that ol' owl, he was runnin' around on his claws, his wings leavin' a trail o' blood. He done thought dey was legs! And dee cat, she go 'whoooooooo.' And dee owl, he go 'meowrrrrr.' It was some sight to see. Oh, Nell. It was some sight to see."

"Shush, Willie," Nell said, slapping him lightly on his shoulder, but there was something in her eyes that told him that even if she didn't believe him, she wasn't really mad. "You tellin' dem tall tales again, Willie? God, he be a-watchin'."

"Ah ain't tellin' no tall tales," Willie answered, throwing her an incredulous look. "Who, me? You knows me better than to tell no tall tales."

"Yeah, Willie, ah knows you." She nodded. "Your grand-mama was a witch, and she known dem black magic from Africa. She learnt it from her mama who come on a slave ship. Ah knows you. And so what? If what you say is true, what kin you do with a spell like that? Turn a cat into a owl, owl into a cat? What use is a owl runnin' around and thinkin' he was a cat?"

"Nothing, ah reckon," Willie said, but then he paused with a tuft of cotton in his hand. He could feel an idea coming over him, flying out of the wind and into his head. He let it brew for a moment, forgetting that he wasn't picking cotton anymore. He often thought that if he just could catch enough of those ideas in his head, he could be as smart as the white man, and maybe he wouldn't have to live this wretched life no more.

"What is it, Willie?" Nell asked. "Your eyes is as big as d'moon.

"Oh," she whispered, "dee white massuh."

"That's it," Willie said. "Dee white massuh. Nell, you is real smart. You has thought of our ticket to freedom."

"Now, what you talkin' about, Willie? Dee sun's done gone to your head, boy."

"Nah, Nell, just think about it. Iffen you kin make dee cat into dee owl, den why can't you do it to people?"

"And what you gonna do, Willie, turn me into a cow? You gonna make my skin turn white with fear, boy."

"Nah, Nell, think! *Dee slave into dee massuh forever, cuz dere ain't no way to undo it once it's done.*"

Nell's eyes widened. Surely, the boy was crazy!

"Shush, Willie, shush, quick. Even if you is talkin' outta your imagination, if anyone should hear you. . . ."

"Dey won't hear, Nell. Look around. Massuh's gone for dee day, and Mistuh Brent, he's at dee other side of dee field."

Nell glanced around suspiciously. It was true that she could barely see the overseer on his brown horse floating across the top of the long stand of cotton.

"Nah, all's ah gots to do is remember dee recipe. Ah remembers dee straw, dee cotton for dee white cat, for dee white *man*. And most important of all, dee hair. Two feathers from dee owl. Two bits of fur from dee cat. Two strands of hair from me and two strands from dee massuh."

"And how you gonna git some of dee massuh's hair?"

Willie put his fingers to his chin and rubbed.

"You still do dee massuh's washing with Bessie?"

"Yeah."

"You do dee massuh's sheets?"

"Yeah."

"Den next time you do dee massuh's sheets, you look at dem real good, and ah bets you find a bit of dee massuh's hair. You brings it to me."

"Maybe." Nell still looked skeptical.

"Don't you wanna be free, to live in dee big plantation with me, to sleep in dose sheets so soft, under heaps of wool blankets, wear dresses with ruffles just like Miss Emilia?"

"It would be fine, real fine." Nell smiled. "But Willie, ah'm sorry. Ah just can't melt under dreams of your grandmama's witchcraft, no matter how pretty. Ah wish ah could, ah shore do. But ah gots to believe dis is dee only life ah will ever know, cuz if ah don't, well, Willie, if ah see some hope and den it don't come to nothing, ah don't know how ah could ever go on."

"Why, Miss Nell, I think you are going on right fine," a voice said from behind in the smoothest of Southern diction.

Willie spun around and lunged for a hunk of cotton.

"As for your friend—" Master Bishop paused long and hard, as if savoring the words. "Look into my eyes, boy. Haven't I taught you to pay the strictest of attention when your superior is talking to you?"

His eyes were steel-blue—the kind of blue that sizzled from the heat of a blaze burning deep within a man's soul. Willie had often thought that if the white men were right and there was a devil, he didn't have a black beard. He had cheekbones hollowed to the bone, a straight robust nose, a jagged chin, and lips perpetually curved in the snarl of a rabid hound dog. It was not that Willie had never seen the master smile or laugh. Willie had seen him drinking with other white men and believed for the briefest of moments that he was human. He had seen the way he doted on his daughter Emilia, and seen the man of iron collapse in tears when he talked about his sweet lost wife, "the best of all women." Maybe he was just the black man's devil. But devil, Willie thought, surely he was.

The master was dressed in a white shirt today, and the vest and pants of the black riding habit he always wore on the hunt. Willie saw his black coat draped on the back of his horse harnessed on the far side of the field. No wonder he hadn't heard the master creep up behind him. In his tall leather riding boots, he matched the stealth of the fox that he hunted.

"Nell, you're such a good girl," he said, touching a white-gloved finger to her bandana. Willie could see that she wanted to pull away.

"No matter how much this boy goes on, you keep on picking my cotton like you know you're supposed to.

"But this boy," he continued, tapping the loop of his riding crop in his free palm, "he's quite a talker, isn't he, love? And sometimes that talking takes over his good sense like a disease, and he can't stop. Now, folks don't call me a reasonable man for nothing—you know that, Nell, don't you? I don't mind him talking at night around the fire. That's your time. You can dance, sing, do whatever you niggers want to do. That's your time. But, Willie, this is the day. And what time is the day?"

He looked Willie squarely in the eyes and continued to tap his crop.

"I asked you a question, boy."

Willie opened his mouth, and for a moment he thought he was going to say "yo' time." Then suddenly it came to him that he wasn't going to say anything. He was just going to stand there, and know that no matter what the master did to him, it was going to be the last punishment he'd ever receive from him. In a day or two, it'd be *him* standing over his old body, *his* blond hair blowing back in the soft breeze, *his* hand on the black crop as it came down.

"Ow!" he yelped as the crop descended on his shoulder. He didn't want to scream, but the pain took him by surprise and yanked the cry right out of him. He'd forgotten the pain, the sharp pelts of the strap.

"On your knees, boy!"

The master grabbed him by his neck and threw him down.

"Yes, that's right, boy, support yourself with your arms, like the dog you are."

He raised the crop again.

"Now, whose time is the day, boy?"

Willie bit down on his lips to keep the words from spilling out. Between the tears welling up in his eyes, he could see Nell raise her hand to her mouth.

"What you staring at, darling?" the master yelled at her. "Keep picking that cotton."

She turned back to the cotton stalks, but Willie could see she still had one eye on him.

"Don't watch me, Nell," he whispered.

"What you say, boy? That didn't sound like the answer to my question. Come on, boy, it's real easy."

Willie felt the crop fall on him again. Again. Again. Until he had lost count of the number of blows and they started to blend together in one massive blanket of pain.

Finally, he buckled and fell facedown in a tangle of branches and scratchy clumps of cotton.

"Get up," the master yelled. "Get your ass back in the air, you filthy good-for-nothing nigger."

Willie just lay there with his cheek in the dirt and stared at its redness. Red clay so hot it crumbled. Red blood flowing from his veins into the land's heart.

"Mistuh Bishop, it ain't gonna do no good fer you to beat him no more," Willie heard the voice of Mistuh Brent say—it was the first time he had ever been relieved to hear the voice of the overseer. But then, the only thing that had saved many a nigger's life had been Brent's good business sense. "He's already gonna be out fer a day or two, and a dead nigger's no good at harvest time, especially now with war comin'."

Willie could almost quote the words as Brent said them. He imagined the gangly man in the wide-brimmed straw hat, puffing on his pipe and shaking his head. He was a man who bore no qualms about beating his niggers, but he never beat them so hard they couldn't work the next day.

"Ah, Mr. Brent, always here to temper my passions with your economics," Willie heard the master say. "Well, boy."

Willie cracked his eyes to see the master's boot tapping the ground a few inches from his nose.

"Mr. Brent has saved you again. But if I ever come into these fields and see you idling instead of working, and I feel I have to ask you again whose time the day is, well, let's just say, boy, Mr. Brent may not be able to steady my temper. You remember that, boy. *You remember that.*"

The boot moved away, and as Willie closed his eyes again, he heard two pairs of footsteps receding back towards the road. The sea of darkness then overwhelmed him.

He felt a hand touch his shoulder, gently lift his head, and offer him water in a ceramic cup. He downed it greedily, the heat peeling away from his innards with each cool sip. Finally, sighing with relief, he raised his head and saw Miss Emilia's gentle blue eyes and pale yellow hair.

"It'll be okay, Willie," she said in a voice soft as cotton. There was something about her that reminded him of lullabies, of the gentle whisper of the mother he had lost so long ago. "It'll be okay. Daddy's gone back into the house now. And I told Nell to bring you as much water as you need."

"Miss Emilia," Willie stuttered, finding he could barely talk, could barely remember what had happened—something about Master Bishop. It came back to him. He had made the master mad.

"Miss Emilia, ah don't wants you to git yourself in no trouble."

Miss Emilia simply smiled.

"No, Willie. I don't want you to get *yourself* in no more trouble."

For a moment, Willie thought he saw genuine sympathy in her eyes, as if she had herself undergone such pain. He grinned back at her, wondering. Then she stood up, and whatever he had seen disappeared from her expression. It had to be his imagination. What could the white daughter of a wealthy plantation owner know of pain?

He liked her a lot more than her father, but she came from the same stock. It wasn't her fault, like it wasn't his fault that he'd been born a slave. His only hope was that maybe, once born, he could change things.

Miss Emilia was gone now, and it was Nell who was helping him to his feet. He couldn't really walk, but he was surprised to find that despite the throbbing ache in his back he could hobble along, just barely leaning on her shoulder.

"Nell, is you pickin' up dee washing again tonight?"

"Yeah, Willie, ah picks it up every Sat'day."

"Kin you bring me dee sheets off dee massuh's bed?"

"Is it for dat magic?"

"Uh-huh."

"Willie, ah kin."

The rest of the day passed agonizingly slowly. Willy lay on his stomach on an old blanket in the shanty, waiting for Nell to bring the strands of hair. It grew dark outside the window, and he was just about sure she wasn't coming when he saw the flicker of a candle. He swallowed the pain and pulled himself up. She placed a few tangled strands in his palm and kissed him gently on the forehead.

"Good luck," she whispered, and slipped out the door.

He waited until all the other slaves were asleep, then he crept out of the shanty and went around the main house to the great oak tree that stood as the centerpiece of the plantation's yard. There, beneath the branches, he reached into his old dried leather sack and fetched out the dolls. His grandmama had told him that the magic worked best in old places, and the oak was the oldest thing he knew of. Nell said it was probably there before any black man was ever brought to America, and that it at least would still be around to see them free at last.

He laid the dolls side-by-side in the moonlight that filtered down through the branches. They didn't look anything like him or the master, and for one panicked moment he felt like a fool for what he was doing, that there was no magic and the master would find out what he had tried and laugh at him for being such a dumb nigger.

Faith, his grandmama had told him. You must *believe,* because that's how magic works.

"Ah believe," Willie whispered. He dug a small hole and buried the dolls at the base of the oak, then to the ancient tree he said, "Ah don't remember the words, Mistuh Oak, but my grandmama said dem once, and even though dat was on another plantation somewheres a long time ago, ah knows you kin still hear dem. If you could just whisper dem for me. . . ."

Then Willie started crying, and he felt ashamed by it, but he knew it was the sorrow of his people that he felt.

"Ah's just want us to be free," he told the big oak. "Dat's all I want. *Please.*"

Wind blew through the branches and the leaves rustled. Slowly, almost imperceptibly, the words floated down to him in the forgotten language he had heard his grandmother speak only once, when she used her magic.

He felt a river of soft cotton cloth beneath him—no, it was softer than cotton, smoother, more slippery. He opened his eyes and saw he was surrounded by white walls, in a bed thick with clean sheets so white they shimmered in the candlelight. For a moment he thought perhaps he had died and somehow found his way to heaven. He shifted toward the window, which was covered with lacy blinds, and winced at the expected pain. But there was none. *The pain in his back was gone.*

His heart raced. Did it work? Was he the master now? *Ah needs me a mirror,* Willie thought. *Ah gots to see!*

He sat up in the bed and looked around the room for one—when suddenly he heard the booming voice of Mr. Brent outside. He jumped up and ran over to the window to look, but it was too dark still. Was it the master in his slave's body who incurred the wrath of the overseer now? He thought of the white man awakening in that black body, and how he would scream and try to explain that it was he who was the master. Everyone would know then that the poor nigger named Willie had finally been broken.

He smiled. *Too bad,* he thought. *Too bad.*

Laughter built up inside him and he tried to keep it down, but it barreled up in his innards and burst out like torrents of rain. He laughed so hard tears streamed down his face. It was strange how soft his laugh was now; it was strange just to be able to laugh unrestrained like that, without fear. He turned to look for a handkerchief and found himself staring right into the face of Master Bishop.

He prayed it was a mirror.

"Why, my darling Emilia," the master said, his lips widening into an evil grin. "I'm so delighted to see you in such fine spirits tonight."

Willie stared down at the ruffles around his wrists, the long frilly nightgown. He became suddenly conscious of the weight that was on his chest and not hanging between his legs. In all his excitement at the spell's success, he'd failed to notice that he was not a white man, but *a white woman.*

But how could this be?

"Oh, come on, Emilia," the master said, spreading his arms. "Don't cease your merriment on my account. Won't you share the passion of your laughter with your loving father?"

Willie gazed into the master's eyes, and suddenly he knew the answer. Nell had brought him the strands of hairs from the master's sheets just as he had asked. But the master wasn't the only one who slept on those sheets, if indeed there was any time left for poor Emilia to sleep. Yes, the empathy she had held in her eyes for his suffering had been all too real.

Willie found himself backing away, overwhelmed now with the urge to kill the bastard, searching for a weapon—*anything*—and seeing nothing but the soft luxury of the bed. He threw his fist towards the master's cheek, but the master grabbed his weak wrist and held him firmly.

"My, my, I thought you had forgotten how to fight." He seemed delighted.

It was no use. Willie tried to ram his knee into the master's groin, but the stronger man parried with his own leg, thrusting the body he thought was his daughter's down upon the bed. Willie was no match for the master in this body enfeebled by shame and culture. If nothing else, his slave's body had at least been strong from a lifetime of physical labor.

For a long moment, as the master clamped his lips upon his daughter's and crammed his tongue down her throat, Willie dreamed that maybe it would be easier to escape as a white woman than as a black slave. He could pretend Nell was his personal maid, and they could flee north where the master's hand could not touch them. He had heard things were better in the North.

The master sat up and ripped the frilly nightgown in a straight line down Willie's front. Then, staring greedily at the pale white body, he unnotched his belt and began to pull down his trousers.

"You're full of so much energy tonight, my dear Emilia," he said, licking his lips. "You remind me so much of your mama."

He leaned back down on top of Willie and eased himself inside.

Nell found the body that had been Willie's sitting on a mossy slab of granite by the edge of the creek. His arms were curled around his legs, and he was rocking back and forth like a small child. Humming. The moon was sinking beneath the trees now, and she couldn't quite tell in the darkness, but it seemed like his lips were wound in the slight curve of a smile.

"It's so peaceful out here in the woods at night," said a voice too soft to be that of Willie.

"Ah reckon." Nell nodded.

"The quietest night ah've known in a long time."

Terrible Swift Saw

Gregory Nicoll

Although born in Concord, New Hampshire, Gregory Nicoll was raised in Augusta, Georgia, and now lives near Atlanta, within sight of the Confederate Memorial at Stone Mountain.

His stories have appeared in *Cold Shocks* and *When the Black Lotus Blooms,* while his novelette, "Dead Air," first appeared in *Ripper!* and was reprinted in *The Year's Best Horror* series.

His nonfiction credits are varied. He contributed to *The Penguin Encyclopedia of Horror and the Supernatural* and writes a regular column for *VW Autoist* on the virtues of diesel engines. His articles on motion pictures have appeared in *Fangoria, Cinefantastique,* and *Twilight Zone.* He was the unit publicist for the film *Blood Salvage,* which was produced in Atlanta.

You'll find Greg at many Southern conventions, often enjoying dark beer, hot chili, or a good discussion about Volkswagens.

The amputation was not going well.

It was hot as hell's own furnace in the hospital tent, its air thick with the stink of the flickering whale oil lamp, the ghostly smell of quinine, and the musky odor of sweat. The white canvas walls, which surrounded the operating table on all four sides, sealed in the heat and the smells like a poultice on a festering wound. From outside in the calm and starry night came the sounds of crickets chirping their evening song, the occasional whicker of the ambulance horses as they grazed, and the crackling of campfires. A lonely soldier blew out a slow, mournful rendition of "Lorena" on his harmonica.

But the man on the table was screaming.

Dr. Henry Lee Talmadge wiped the sweat from his forehead

and ran the back of his dirty shirtsleeve across the bristles of his bushy gray mustache, pasting down the ends against his flushed cheeks. He felt a long bead of perspiration drool from his left armpit, felt it spreading into the already dark stains in his vest. Wishing desperately he had time to pour himself a private shot of hospital alcohol, he struggled to keep his moist grip on the saw handle.

"Easy, soldier," he said to the patient. Then he turned to his assistant surgeon and ordered, "Jacob, give him more whiskey."

The tall and fair-haired Kentucky mountain boy pulled the cork from the whiskey bottle with his teeth. Jacob was a good lad, Talmadge knew, and an exceptionally dutiful medical assistant for one whose only formal training was reading Chisolm's *Manual of Military Surgery*. Jacob tilted the bottle to the screaming man's lips, struggling with one of his arms to hold down the patient as he administered the liquor with the other.

The screaming stopped as the injured soldier drank greedily from the bottle, a baby at a woman's nipple.

Dr. Talmadge was careful to wait until Jacob took the bottle away before he reapplied the saw blade. Too many times he'd seen the precious bottles dropped and spilled or shattered at the shock of the blade returning to its grisly work. The regiment's stock of these whiskey bottles was dwindling by the hour, and Talmadge shuddered at the thought of operating without benefit of the powerful Tennessee sour mash painkiller. Their supply of opium poppies had been exhausted quite suddenly two days before, though its aroma still lingered faintly in the unwashed cloth of the canvas wall tent. The recent crop of Carolina poppies had been quite good—their unripe seed capsules offered up a dark gum very similar to genuine Turkish opium in its effects.

Outside in the night, cannonfire rumbled like distant thunder. For an instant, Talmadge remembered that even as darkness fell, the mighty engines of war were still turning. He thought briefly of his fine, white two-story home in the distant city of Atlanta, wondering if the Federal Army had overrun it. Sherman's legions were on the move toward Savannah, a tide of human locusts destroying everything in their path. The proud city behind them would soon live only in memories and ashes.

The man on the table squirmed under Jacob's forceful restraint. He coughed twice, adding a faint aroma of regurgitated whiskey to the less pleasant smells in the tent. For a moment, his eyes rolled back and his head lolled drowsily to one side as the whiskey worked its power over him.

Talmadge seized the opportunity to drive the sawblade forcefully into the soldier's leg.

The thick, wet scream this produced was so loud it stirred up the horses outside the tent and cut the harmonica player short in mid-melody.

Merciful God, thought Talmadge, *this boy's bones feel as though they're forged of iron.*

A dull blaze of matchlight blossomed against the canvas tent flap. Apparently the harmonica player outside had decided to apply his lips to a pipe stem instead. A waft of fragrant tobacco smoke drifted through the seams of the tent.

Dr. Talmadge drove the blade in again, drew it back deeply, then forced it in once more. A small river of warm blood ran from the deep, narrow, quivering incision. Jacob brushed away a hovering cloud of horseflies and poured water across the incision.

Dr. Talmadge prided himself on his speed.

An amputation was a simple enough operation, of course—a carpenter could perform it as easily as a physician—but swiftness was part of its art. The terror-struck patients, already deep in shock from whatever awful misfortune made the operation necessary, were little trouble if it was all over quickly.

Over before they realized what was happening and thought about the consequences.

Before the *big* screams seized them as they realized they would never walk again. Never stroll on a summer night. Never hoist themselves gracefully into the saddle of a fine horse and set it to gallop with a kick against its flanks. Never stride into a ballroom arm in arm with a fair lady, head held high. Never wade barefoot through the shallows of a cool country stream. March no more through Georgia.

Yes, that's when the *big* scream would set in.

And ideally the patients would be recovering elsewhere, half paralyzed by fiery Confederate bourbon, when such thoughts reached them.

Talmadge estimated he'd completed the grim, bloody duty some two thousand times since this awful war began. He'd become something of a dark legend, so great was his skill. The story went that he had amputated forty-seven times in a single hour, though no man had ever actually measured him against a clock. That was at Chickamauga—the River of Death—where the soldiers were carried to him straight from the heat of battle, dozens at a time. Here in this distant field camp, many miles from the raging fires of Atlanta, the victims were nowhere near as fresh.

The soldier on the table screamed again, wrenching his leg from side to side and upsetting the even strokes of Talmadge's saw.

"Jacob," the doctor commanded, "more whiskey, quickly." He paused as the boy administered the bottle again.

At least it's only his foreleg, thought Talmadge as he watched the man suckle at the whiskey bottle. *In the fullness of time, he'll learn to manage himself quite well with a crutch.*

As soon as Jacob removed the bottle safely from the frantic soldier's reach, Talmadge drove the saw back into the deep red channel and finished the operation. The severed leg now lay on the crimson tabletop limp and motionless—in dramatic contrast to its thrashing, screaming source. The amputee wrenched like a landed catfish.

"Matthew!" Talmadge cried. "We need you!"

The tent flap was folded back, admitting a gust of cool, fresh evening air. A thin boy stepped into the opening, surrounded by a faint haze of tobacco smoke from the pipes of the men gathered outside. Matthew was younger than Jacob by at least five summers, but his perpetual weariness made him appear significantly older. The lad's face was sullen, eyes downcast, mouth set in a permanent near-frown, forehead creased and furrowed. He wore a hospital apron and carried an empty but already bloodstained cloth in his hands. Rumor had it that this boy had been a soldier but was disgraced in battle and sent back to the rear, where he'd been placed indefinitely on burial detail.

Without a word, his eyes never making contact with those of Talmadge or Jacob, young Matthew stepped to the table and wrapped the severed leg in his cloth, carefully brushing away the swarm of buzzing horseflies before making the final fold. He bore it silently from the tent. The canvas flap drifted back across the doorway behind him, a curtain closing on one of the tiny, awful dramas of war.

Dr. Talmadge worked quickly to wash and plaster the wound as Jacob struggled to hold the man still. Eventually, the frantic soldier gave up the fight and fell into a numbed daze, his breath rasping horribly. Jacob stepped outside and summoned two men with a canvas hand-stretcher, who carried the fresh amputee up toward the makeshift field hospital on the ridge.

Talmadge took the whiskey bottle, pulled out the cork, and pressed its cold glass muzzle to his lips. He took a short sip of the fiery liquor and felt its warmth spread vaporously through him. He drank again.

Jacob folded back the tent flap and fastened it open with one of the little straps.

Talmadge felt the fresh night air turn the sweatstains cool on his body. He wiped his brow with a handkerchief, daubed the moist hairs of his thick mustache, and treated himself discreetly to several more long, deep swallows of the Tennessee sour mash before placing the bottle back beside his surgical tools. Silently cursing General Bragg for banning the social use of whiskey, he resolved to buy himself an entire barrel of it when this damn fool war was over. Maybe he'd *bathe* in it.

He stepped out into the starry night, surprised at the thickness of pipe smoke from the men lounging outside. Talmadge reeled, struggling to steady himself on his feet.

Tired, he thought. *It's because I'm tired. I need a rest—maybe a little more whiskey and then a long sleep. . . .*

A match flared as one of the men relit a long-stemmed clay pipe.

Talmadge turned to look at the man, who now rose to his feet. He'd been sprawled there with the off-duty ambulance drivers. A number of those men had apparently fallen asleep, though most were still smoking lazily as they stared up at the stars. The upright man now walked toward Talmadge, pipe in one hand and harmonica in the other. He wore the uniform of the ambulance corps, his face shadowed by a downturned hat brim. Talmadge didn't remember this man, but that wasn't particularly unusual—the company had dozens of attendants and orderlies detailed from the active ranks to tend the wounded and dying.

The stranger offered his pipe. "Smoke, Doctor?"

Talmadge swayed on his feet like a windswept pine. Without a word, he placed his lips to the pipe stem and drew a sip of the sweet, soothing smoke. It tasted wonderful. It felt good.

He took another puff, savoring it in his mouth before releasing it in a long slow stream. This was no common tobacco—definitely something the blockade runners had smuggled past the Federals.

The soldier smiled, his teeth yellowed and crooked. "Your boy likes it, too," he said.

Talmadge saw young Jacob smoking a long clay pipe with the others down by a campfire. Tripods of crossed rifles encircled them like skeletons of Cherokee teepees.

"Are there more—more men requiring my services tonight?" the doctor asked. He wished desperately to rest, to sleep. The firm Georgia soil seemed to roll beneath him like the deck of a frigate on high seas.

The stranger pointed at an approaching wagon. "They come," he said grimly.

Talmadge drew again on the pipe, heady smoke swirling in his nostrils like clouds of heaven, and passed it back to the man. "Bring them," he said.

The moans of the suffering soldiers reached Talmadge's ears even before the squeak of the oak wheels and the tread of the mule team.

Jacob and the others brought in the first of the freshly wounded. The whiskey was passed between them all—patients and physicians alike—and the grisly work began again. Talmadge noticed dimly that the stranger seemed to be everywhere at once, readying men for surgery with the ceramic water pitcher and the coarse brown sponge, beckoning to the two still-waking orderlies to bear in the stretchers of wounded men, and directing the strokes of Talmadge's saw. The stranger's sweet, smoldering pipe was never far, constantly shared between all the men as the whiskey ran low. Throughout the next hour, the silent fellow dutifully refilled the pipe and relit it whenever it burned low, passing it around again and again. The harmonica protruded from his vest pocket, its end gleaming in the flickering lamplight like a bar of solid silver, but he never paused to play it—he was too occupied in assisting the surgeon with the amputations.

"Faster, Doctor," he breathed in Talmadge's ear. "There are more men waiting—more who need your skill."

Talmadge paused only for another deep draw on the clay pipe before turning back to the next patient.

"You're the one," whispered the stranger as he worked. "You're the best—forty-seven in a single hour, they say." His words were calm, reassuring, but carried a hint of fascination which Talmadge disliked. "Tonight," he continued, "tonight you will best even that remarkable record."

And so Talmadge pressed on, weary and unstable, with the stranger's words droning in his ears. The terrible swift saw did its work by the flicker of lamplight, the two orderlies struggling to restrain its drunken, helpless victims.

Talmadge's head throbbed and his nostrils burned. His throat felt clogged, dry as cotton from drinking whiskey and smoking.

Sometime in the dead of night he heard Matthew, the burial detail boy, yelling something in the distance. The words were murky, as if heard in a dream. He asked Jacob to go and see what was the matter. The boy made no move.

"Jacob," he insisted again drowsily, "go at once and see what troubles Matthew so. . . ."

Again the boy did not stir. Talmadge paused in his gory work, the saw blade rasping on bone. He heard more shouting—Matthew's voice outraged, furious—and the sounds of heavy footsteps running. The doctor slowly realized that Jacob was not in the tent. The stranger and the orderlies spoke quickly, quietly between themselves—Talmadge couldn't make out what they were saying—and then together they slipped outside. The doctor followed, struggling awkwardly with the tent flap, fighting hard

to stay on his feet. The bleeding man on the table shrieked with
outrage, his leg still hanging painfully by a fragment of bone.

In the cold night outside, the camp was in an uproar. By the
dim light of the moon and the reddish glow of the campfires he
saw men running back and forth, some with their rifles. Screams
and shouts ricocheted from all sides. An officer on horseback
thundered past, yelling out, "Where is he? Where is he?"

The oak wheels of an ambulance creaked behind Talmadge.
He turned in time to see the mule team pull the vehicle off into
the darkness at the edge of their encampment. There were several men riding on it, and though the distance was too far for
him to be sure, he felt certain that the dark stranger was among
them.

One of the men on the retreating ambulance drew a silver
harmonica from his pocket and raised it to his lips. With an air of
triumph, he began to play the "Battle Hymn of the Republic":

> *He hath loosed the fearful lightning*
> *of his terrible swift . . .*

The men vanished into the darkness.

Matthew and a group of soldiers came running up to the tent,
gasping for breath. There was shock on some of their faces,
terror on others, as they stared at him. Two of the men were
holding young Jacob, supporting his limp body as they would a
drunken man.

Now Matthew was yelling something at Talmadge, taking him
by the edges of his vest and shaking him. He slapped the doctor
hard across the face with the back of his coarse, blood-encrusted
hand. The powerful blow felt dull, almost soft, as if the boy had
merely wiped biscuit crumbs from Talmadge's mustache.

Matthew was yelling again, his face contorted with emotion.
The campfire light flickered across the scene. What was the lad
yelling? Talmadge struggled to make out the words.

"Old fool . . . know what you were doing . . . found more of
them, many more of them . . . drunk or something? *Do you hear
me?*"

Hoofbeats thundered as the officer rode up, his spurs and

saber jingling, and began to bark orders. Soldiers seized Talmadge by his shoulders. He felt the octagonal muzzle of a rifle press cool and dull against his bare neck.

He heard the men now, catching random words as they spoke.

"More of them . . . whole ward full . . . wrong legs . . . *wrong legs* . . . must've been drunk . . . captain's *leg* instead of his arm. . . ."

As they dragged him, stumbling, across the camp, Talmadge slowly became aware of the massive orange charcoal glow on the horizon and knew that the city of Atlanta was gone. Smoke filled the sky, obscuring every star.

The darkness closed around on all sides and swallowed him.

Two Yellow Pine Coffins

Robert Sampson

The silverware hidden from the Yankees on the farm of my Kelly ancestors has never been found, but in 1975 I did find treasure of a different sort at my Gilliam grandparents' home—a box of Golden Age comic books, stored in the attic and apparently undisturbed since sometime in the 1940s. I was only a novice book collector at the time, and had no experience in comics at all. Such a discovery called for serious research, and I inquired high and low for someone who could help me evaluate the find. Eventually I was referred to Robert Sampson, who lived a mere three blocks away.

Bob's true area of expertise was in pulp magazines, and on that first meeting I was treated to the glorious thrill of seeing complete runs of many of the era's rarest and most unusual periodicals. Bob had set out to write *Yesterday's Faces,* a history of the character pulps, and he was unwilling to rely on secondary sources for his information. This insistence on accuracy is both why the project has taken two decades, and why when the six-volume series was published, it received universal acclaim as the definitive viewpoint on the subject.

Born in Cleveland in 1927, Bob graduated from Ohio State and did a small amount of fiction writing, most notably landing an entry in one of the final pulp-sized issues of *Planet Stories.* He moved to Huntsville in 1960, working for NASA on many major projects. With nine nonfiction books to his credit, Bob had little time to produce short stories until his retirement in 1989. Since then, he's become a regular contributor to *Weird Tales,* and the *Spectrum* anthology series, and has had stories in *The Year's Best Science Fiction* and *Mysteries 90.* His short story

"Rain in Pinton County" was honored by the Mystery Writers of America with the 1986 Edgar Allan Poe award for Best Short Story.

Sadly, Robert Sampson died on October 30, 1992. With the *Yesterday's Faces* series, and his other historical commentaries, Bob gave us important work preserving a portion of our cultural heritage that would almost certainly been lost otherwise. Science fiction fans usually think of magazine SF as having begun in 1926 with the publication of *Amazing Stories* by Hugo Gernsback. Bob did much to dispel the darkness from the pre-Gernsback era. That he also added his own short stories to our era makes his contributions to SF all the more enormous.

Cowan flung the sow into the red dirt and threw himself on top of her. She struggled and shrieked. As the other two troopers howled encouragement, Cowan hacked at her throat with his field knife.

The sow twisted free. Thrown backward, Cowan lost his knife and sprawled heavily in the dirt. He cursed and balled himself up, hugging a kicked leg. The sow galloped away stiff-legged, splashing blood across the dust.

At that moment, three strange Union troopers rode around the corner of the barn. The sow veered wildly away from them, plunged squealing and staggering out of sight by the springhouse.

Cowan struggled up on his knees to face the riders. Red dust thickly powdered his blue regulation pants and open-necked blue shirt. Suspicion and anxiety hardened his face.

The leader of the horsemen clopped slowly toward the three dismounted men. "Two to hold and one to stab," he said in a slow, amused voice. "Or string her up and cut her throat. One man can't much do it alone."

"That's a fact," Cowan panted.

He watched the leader ease out of the saddle. He was a tall stringy man with a lot of nose and a heavy mustache scattered with white hairs. He wore a filthy captain's uniform coat and a forager cap.

He said to Cowan, "Just supposin' a man was thirsty, you suppose he might find a drink at the house?"

"We jus' got here ourselves," Cowan said. He found his knife, stuffed it back into the sheath, and began beating dust from his clothing. "We might ought to go see."

"I'm in agreement with that," the other said. "The name's Fosey."

They exchanged nods. Fosey turned to the two-mounted men and said, "Whyn't you step down, gentlemen, and see what the generous Johnnies have laid up for us in the smokehouse."

"Half-dozen hams." Cowan grinned. "A world of yams. We already been there."

"Fat Georgia," Fosey said. "A man just couldn't starve in Georgia."

"Man shouldn't, tomorrow bein' Thanksgiving Day," Cowan said. He tipped back his big head and brayed with laughter, exposing a mouthful of yellow-black teeth that must surely have given him agony at night.

They walked slowly toward the house, one of those oversized, two-story affairs, with a lot of roof and a great many chimneys, common to the larger farms of central Georgia. The whitewash badly needed freshening. Four tall pillars suspended a narrow split-shingle roof over the front entrance.

Fosey inspected it critically. "We rode around the house," he said. "Saw nobody stirring."

Cowan nodded. "So'd we."

"What corps you from?"

A careful smile bent Cowan's thick mouth. Glancing slyly at the other, he said, "This wing of Uncle Billy Sherman's army, there's the Fifteenth Corps. And there's the Seventeenth Corps. But us'ns, we sort of kinda no corps at all. We jus' marchin' through Georgia on our own."

"Kinda got lost and haven't found your way back," Fosey said.

"It's terrible hard. That's a true statement."

They crossed the porch, feet clattering on the green-painted boards. Fosey opened the dusty black holster on his left side and drew out a .44 caliber Remington revolver, long as his forearm. Clicking the hammer back to full cock, he stepped to one side of the door and bunched his fist to knock.

Before he touched the door, it swung open.

From inside the screen, a small black woman glared at them. Age had shriveled her up, bent her over, stolen her teeth, marked her face. A white-dotted blue calico dress shrouded her bony body. A dull red Madras handkerchief covered her head. Careful fingers had tied the stuff of the handkerchief into seven points that stood up around her skull like the points of a crown. Resentment drew her face, all nose and chin, to the sharpness of a blade.

She cried, high-voiced, in a lilting accent foreign to both men, "That worthless General Wheeler, first he rob us. Then them Abe Lincoln Yankees, they come an' done the same. Now here you is, grabbin' an' stealin' an' sniffin' what's left. Miss Lily and her chile gonna starve."

Fosey restored the pistol to the holster. "My compliments to Miss Lily," he said. "May we trouble you for a glass of water?"

"Water in the well," she snapped, swinging the door shut.

Cowan caught it in mid-swing and heaved the door back. They stepped into a wide, empty hall, two stories high. To the right curved an elaborate staircase, like wooden music. Directly ahead, far down the hall, double glass doors opened to a shadowy veranda. The air smelled pleasantly of floor wax and pine trees.

"Old Wheeler and them Sherman Yankees sure cleaned it out," Cowan cried pleasantly, looking around. " 'Pears like they didn't leave hardly nothin'. But maybe we best poke around, like. See if there be damage."

"Miss Lily sick. And her li'l baby, she sick, too. You take youselves off, go on."

"Poor and sick and no man around," Cowan cried. "Jus' terrible. I best look in all the drawers, maybe find medicine for that poor sick child."

"You go!" the black woman yelped. "You go!" She leaped claw-fingered at Cowan. Thrusting her carelessly away, he reached for the knob of a closed door.

Fosey said sharply, "Cowan . . ."

Feet drummed rapidly across the porch. A filthy-faced trooper wearing a ragged jacket grinned in at them. "Cowan," he yelled. "We found diggin' out back by the pines. Not even all filled in. Looks like a wagonload of specie buried there."

"Get started," Cowan said. "I'm comin' right out."

The man thundered off the porch. Cowan turned and the woman flung herself at him again, shrieking and scratching.

His eyes took on a faintly surprised expression. He slapped her casually with the back of his hand. The blow drove her back against the wall. She balanced there open-mouthed, before sagging down on one knee. She stared fixedly at her hands against the polished floor.

Fosey said in a low, hard voice, like iron become sound, "Cowan, you are under arrest."

Cowan, grinning, turned, looked down the barrel of the Remington.

"I am Captain Lewis Fosey, Third Brigade, Smith's Division, Fifteenth Corps. General Sherman's general field orders forbid entry into private homes, removal of property other than foodstuffs, and indignities to women."

Cowan, gone suddenly gray, whispered thinly, "Captain, I didn't mean nothin'."

"You're a liar and a thief," Fosey said. "A deserter and a disgrace to your unit. A damned bummer, in fact. Consider yourself under arrest and take yourself outside."

Striding past the slack-faced Cowan, Fosey leaned out the door, roared, "Hamilton! Spencer!"

The knife whispered faintly as it slipped from Cowan's sheath. The woman whimpered as he darted past her. He drove the knife twice into Fosey's back, grunting with the effort.

The Remington exploded, blasting a ragged hole in the screen, driving a hole ringed with yellow splinters into the green porch. Fosey fell against the screen. It swung open, sprawling him onto the porch.

Cowan hopped forward, clumsy in his urgency. He plunged the knife twice more in Fosey's back and snatched up the Remington.

From around the side of the house ran both of Fosey's troopers. Cowan gestured wildly at them, his eyes showing white all around the pupil.

"Woman in the house!" he screamed. "Stabbed the captain."

As they crowded past him, he shot the nearest man in the

back of the head. Bloody horror sprayed the door and began trickling down the screen. The body tumbled sideways, tangling Cowan's arm. The other trooper, young face shocked, spun around and got a thumb in Cowan's eye. Cowan triggered the Remington, heard the hard snap of a misfire. Yelling in fright, he beat the revolver against the trooper's face. The boy tumbled backward, clutching Cowan's throat and arm. They rolled across the porch, striking wildly at each other, dreamlike horror gripping their faces.

Cowan lost the revolver and could not draw his knife. His two friends pounded across the porch and tore the men apart.

Cowan struggled up, bracing his back against a pillar. Chest heaving, he gasped, "Hang onto that boy, Tucker. He's a regular. Come to hunt us down."

"Be damned," Tucker said. "Seems he found us, too."

The second man, heavy features masked by beard, looked glumly toward the dead men by the door. "You have to kill them? That's a hanging thing."

Cowan said, "Had to, Moreland. He found us out."

Moreland sighed. His eyes slipped sideways to the prisoner and slid away again. "And now we got this poor boy, here."

"I'll think of something," Cowan said, in a violent voice that suggested he had thought of nothing. He pressed one hand delicately against his mouth, feeling the scream of his bad teeth. "We gotta move these boys. Somebody ride up, first thing he sees them layin' here."

"We can use that hole around back," Moreland said.

"You find any specie yet?"

"We'd just hit wood when we heard the shootin'."

Cowan looked more cheerful at that. He said, "You take this young feller around back. Tucker and me, we'll haul these dead ones outta sight."

Tucker snorted. "I'm a better guard than a hauler."

"Best thing you do is eat," Cowan said. "Let's get a hustle on."

They hauled the bodies across the porch and around the side of the mansion, and laid them in temporary concealment behind a fat holly hedge.

"You're a sudden man," Tucker said sourly, inspecting the bodies.

"Nobody knows but us," Cowan said, buckling on the Remington.

"There's the boy."

"Well, hell, now," Cowan said, "the boy."

"These fellers just one li'l bitty patrol. Main body come down on us any time."

"Not this afternoon," Cowan said. "Tomorrow we be gone."

They crossed the unkept lawn, touched with the fitful yellow of late-blooming dandelions. Near the pines, a rough pit, nearly eight feet by five, had been hacked from the lawn. Moreland stood by it, watching the young trooper slowly shovel out lumps of red clay.

"Lookit what we found," Moreland said.

He angled one finger down at the hole. Under the red dirt showed the pale yellow of pine board.

"It's a coffin," the boy said sullenly. "I can feel it under my feet."

"Clean it off," Cowan said. "We gone this far, let's finish."

They uncovered not one coffin but two, the largest about six feet long and narrow; the smaller one obviously for a child and narrower still. Both were built of fresh yellow pine planks, neatly nailed together. The heavy plank tops contained screw holes but no screws.

Cowan and the young trooper heaved up the top of the larger coffin. Cowan knelt, his avid grin fading. The box contained only a white sheet, badly stained by mildew, and a white velvet cushion, still marked by the weight of a head.

The smaller coffin also contained a sheet and pillow. Tucked away under the sheet, Cowan found a faceless cloth doll with voluminous red and blue skirts.

He hurled the doll back into the coffin. "Sold, by God!" he growled. "But why'd they take out the bodies?"

A rill of red dust trickled into the small coffin like the fall of powdered blood.

"Let's go try our luck at the house," Moreland said. A hungry look came over his face, wiping out his expression of indolent good humor. "Nice things in big houses."

Tucker jerked his thumb toward the young trooper, sitting silent on the edge of the grave. "How about him?"

Cowan said pleasantly, "What's your name, son?"

"Hamilton. Josh Hamilton."

"Well, now, Josh, may be you might be thinkin' to jine us in our life of ease."

Hamilton's eyes drifted from them. In a low, embarrassed voice, he said, "Don't think I could."

"We might take your parole, you agreein' not to be sayin' anything about us."

Hamilton worked on some obstruction in his throat. When he got it swallowed, he whispered, "Couldn't do that. Can't promise. Not honorable. Can't do that."

"Figured not," Cowan said.

Hamilton lifted his head and set his eyes on them, a pale wondering on his face like a man finding himself lost while blackberrying. He said in a tone of remote surprise, "I got four little girls at home."

"That's terrible hard," Cowan said. Slipping the Remington from its holster, he nodded to Moreland and Tucker. "You might jus' go ahead and wander up to the house and see what's to see."

"We'll do that," Tucker said.

They strode away, feet swishing in the grass.

Cowan settled himself on the grave's edge, sitting across from Hamilton with the coffins' hollow between them.

"Now honor," he told the young man, "honor's a hard thing to get your hands on. I'm minded how we climbed Kennesaw Mountain these six months ago. Lots of us marchin' up that mountain so bold and fine. Lot fewer of us runnin' back down again. Not much honor in marchin' up and runnin' down."

"It isn't that," Hamilton said.

"When you're dead, you're dead," Cowan said. "You swell up too big for your pants and you turn black and there's a stink. Nobody says he was honorable, he wasn't honorable. They say,

my God, get him underground. No honor in bein' dead. It's jus'
a word to excuse you gettin' killed for no particular reason."

"I guess I just can't explain it to you, any way," Hamilton
said.

"Guess not," Cowan said.

The Remington, which had remained leveled at Hamilton
while they talked, gave a sharp metallic snap.

Cowan lifted the pistol and examined it with hard curiosity,
open mouth exposing his foul teeth. "Now see that," he cried.
He smacked the side of the Remington with his hand. "That's
twice she wouldn't shoot you. You're not to die by this gun,
youngster."

Hamilton said nothing. His sweating face, gone a bloodless
blue-white, bore a look of mild interest.

"I'll tie your hands," Cowan said. "Then we'll get up to the
big house. Figure what to do with you later. Them four little
girls sure got themselves a lucky daddy."

He found rope and loosely tied Hamilton's hands behind his
back. Long shadows streaked the grass. Swallows weaved through
darkened air. To the west, cold-looking gray clouds, edged rose
and orange, massed low against a lusterless sky.

"Cold day for ridin' tomorrow," Cowan said. "But long as a
man's movin', he's safe."

"You'll ride square into General Wheeler's hands one day,"
Hamilton said.

Cowan shook his head, grinning. "No, no. Nobody in these
parts but Union men and Georgia women."

He stopped abruptly to stare toward the holly hedge, then
crossed to kick among the spiny brown leaves strewing the
ground. "Now why'n hell they carry off them bodies? They
knows we got to haul them to the graves."

He turned away, setting down his feet hard, and dragged Hamilton around the house. As they stamped onto the porch, a storm
of flies whirled up around them. The blood patches by the door
crawled black with them. A shivering mat of insects clung to the
screen door, passionately feeding, emitting a heavy metallic
drone that was deeply disgusting.

From the twisting swarm, a fly nearly an inch long plunged

heavily against Cowan's forehead. Where it touched him, a dull red smudge remained.

"My God," Cowan cried, "this is terrible." He scrubbed his face violently with the sleeve of his coat, smearing a dark memory of blood along his temple. "This is worse than Atlanta, an' all them Texans dead to the front of us."

Behind the screen appeared Tucker's bearded face. He stood so close that flies seemed to creep across his features, as if he too were long dead and improbably propped against the door.

"You'd best come look at this," Tucker said.

Cowan pushed Hamilton into the great hall and followed, slashing at flies darting about his head. When the screen door slammed, a twisting uproar of insects spun around the entrance. The screen blackened as they settled again to feeding.

"Listen," Cowan growled, "what in hell's the sense you moving them dead troopers? Now we got to haul 'em all the way back."

"Didn't come a shout by them troopers," Tucker said. "Nary touched 'em. Nor did Moreland."

"I couldn't see them at the holly hedge."

"You looked wrong," Tucker said. "You looked back of the wrong bush." But fear got into his face, twisting at his shoulders, bending his body.

"By God!" Cowan growled. "So I must of. Damn if I figure how. You didn't take 'em and dead men don't wander, that's a fact."

He shook his head, not convinced. "Well, show me what you got to show me."

Tucker shuffled across the hallway to a double door at the foot of the staircase. Moreland sat on the staircase, holding his rifle vertically between two big hands.

Looking back over his shoulder at Cowan with an expression of frightened malice, Tucker turned the knob.

"This'll properly delight you," he said.

The door crept open, exposing a room thick with evening shadow. Past Tucker's shoulders, Cowan saw a pallid blur, lean and tall as a whitewashed post seen in the dark.

Before his eyes could search out details, the black woman flung herself across the entrance to bang the door shut.

She shouted furiously, "Stay away. You let them be."

Tucker twisted with a curse, grabbing at her. She shrieked and clawed.

Moreland bounced off the stairs to wrap his arms around her tiny body. She kicked at his legs, loudly furious.

"Now, ain't she totally fierce?" Moreland grinned. "Oh, my, yes."

He yelped as the black woman bit his hand.

Pushing past them, Cowan swung open the door. Beyond lay a great hollow of a room. Through draped windows filtered feeble gray light that defined no detail but only emphasized the darkness.

His eyes came suddenly to a focus. Before him stood a lean woman dressed in white, arms dangling at her sides. Dark scratches marred the bloodless pallor of her hands. Next to her, erect and still, was a small girl, also in white. They stood passive, their faces without intelligence, their eyes regarding something that hung invisible in the air between them and Cowan. They did not move or speak.

Breath whispered in Cowan's mouth. To the black woman, he said, "What's wrong with them, Auntie?"

"They's sick," she cried. "You leave them be."

He advanced a single grudging step, licking his lips. "Ma'am?" he said to the woman. "Ma'am?"

She seemed unaware of his presence. The chalk mask of her face glimmered in the vague light. Her right eye, he saw, stared upward from its deep socket; her left eye angled toward the floor. The eyes seemed filmed. He did not dare look at the child's eyes.

Their presence, so close, filled him with thin sickness. A faint, frigid wind seemed to run through him. At any moment, they might extend their arms and touch him with their limp fingers.

Fear jerked his body back. He found himself outside the door, heart violent in his chest.

He snarled at the black woman, "They're blind, Auntie."

She said, shrilly contemptuous, "My name is Lalo Hussa."

Shaking off Moreland's hands, she pattered to the door. To the blank face in the shadows, she said, "We'll have us some soup, Miss Lily. You and Little Rose jus' wait easy."

She drew the door closed upon their terrible stillness.

Tucker's voice grated in his mouth. "What sickness they got?"

Lalo Hussa said, "Jus' sick. They got the fevers. Like to burn my poor child up. They jus' like dead. The mister, he took them to the coffins, hisself. But he took them out again. Not dead. Only sick."

"They're dead," Tucker said, not moving his lips.

"I wash them," she cried. "I feed them soup. I takes care of them. They not dead."

Moreland cleared his throat and shuffled his feet. Not looking at Cowan, he said, "There's still light. Let's saddle up and ride on apiece."

"Where's the mister?" Cowan asked.

She gave him a vicious grin. In the shadowed hall, her up-turned face seemed to have no eyes. "He rode off to fight the Yankees. He come back, shoot you dead."

Cowan chuckled, said to Moreland and Tucker, "Now, we wouldn't want the mister to come back and find us gone, would we, boys?"

"Don't give a damn for him," Moreland said, and jerked his head toward the closed door. "It's them."

"Gettin' late," Tucker said. "Let's go. Uncle Billy's troopers ride by, we're catched coons."

"And leave this place without looking," Cowan cried. "That's a fool thing. By and by we'll go. But see what we find, first. Look through the drawers. Maybe silver. Maybe somethin'. Maybe Auntie, here, knows where they buried something."

"Never buried no nothin'."

"We'll need us some candles," Moreland said. "Where's your candles, Auntie?"

"My name," she said, "is Lalo Hussa."

She marched off, closely followed by the hulking Moreland, who gripped his rifle across his chest like a man walking to battle.

Tucker sighed and stepped off carefully across the hall. In the silence between his footsteps, they heard the muted humming of flies. At the door on the other side of the hall, Tucker hesitated, gingerly pushed it open as if it were hot. He glanced swiftly into the room and as swiftly withdrew. "Too dark," he said. "Let's be for ridin', Cowan."

Cowan said, "Now let me tell you somethin', Tucker." He crossed the hall to lay his hand on Tucker's shoulder. "I had a brother, once. Long time ago. Maybe I still got a brother—I ain't been back to home these many years. He come down with the fever and it burned him up. Just naturally burned him alive. You come near him, it was like comin' to the stove in winter. Now that fever burnt everything out of him, burnt his thinkin' clean away. Didn't know nothin'. Couldn't say nothin'. Sat in a chair, had to be wiped up like he was a little baby. Had to have food spooned in his mouth. My own brother, complete burnt up.

"Now you look at that woman and her chile. Now it's the same with them. Burnt up with fever. Left 'em blind. Jus' as well be dead. But they ain't dead. Jus' like my brother, all burned up."

Faint color touched Tucker's cheeks. "Think that's what happened, for a fact?"

"Look jus' like my brother."

"They do look bad, that's a natural truth."

The doors at the far end of the hall banged open and Moreland stepped in, holding a lighted candle in one hand, a bundle of candles in the other. He strode toward them, the rifle slung from his shoulder, his footsteps big and ringing in the hollow hallway.

"Here's some light," he called. "Man can see what he's doin'."

Tucker scurried to meet him. They whispered together, lighting candles and looking back toward Cowan. By this time, the hall was full of night, the air dense with shadow. Above the whispering men rose thirty feet of darkness, a towering presence peering down at them, grim and patient, examining the island of light in which they stood.

Moreland and Tucker came toward Cowan, their boots making an infernal clatter on the floor. Extending a handful of candles, Moreland said, "I heard of fever makin' 'em like that."

"I'm witness to it," Cowan said. "This young feller and me, we'll take us a ramble through these rooms downstairs. You turn out upstairs."

"Suits me," Tucker said. He glanced uneasily across the hall toward the room of the women. "You suppose they're standin' in there in the dark? Standin' listenin'?"

"Hell," Cowan said. "They can't do nothin' else."

They searched. It was a stripped house, a hollow house, an empty house. The great bare rooms rang with echoes. Nothing remained but echoes. Furniture gone, draperies gone, rugs rolled up. Rectangles of gray dust on the floors. Squares of unfaded wallpaper showed where pictures once decorated the walls and mirrors reflected the busy household.

Cowan swore low and bitterly. He swept the candle around him. Emptiness and dust, spiderwebs blurring the high corners of the room. His footsteps clattered hollowly, echoes in a dead heart.

"Took it all," Cowan said. "Loaded it in wagons and rode it off."

"The owner?" Hamilton asked.

"Looks to be. Troopers'd leave a mess. Maybe bust them some furniture, leave cabinets and such behind. But these folks didn't leave nothin'. And you can bet they for sure left nothing buried, no silver, no gold, no rings nor combs."

Slamming the door, he slouched into the hall, holding up his fragile cone of light. The candle flame reeled in the cross draught. Around him, shadows staggered like crazy things at dance. Upstairs, footsteps pounded along the halls, anger in the sound of them. Looking up, Cowan had the sudden impression that something dark and soft peered down at him from behind the railings of the upper hall.

For an instant he found himself unable to move. The footsteps from above cast sniggering echoes down the staircase. Then he recognized in himself the onset of night panic, that suffocation of terror that grips the sentry staring alone into the dark. He said savagely, thrusting away fear, "Sounds like the boys're having no better luck than us."

Doors at the far end of the hall opened. Cowan jumped, spilled candle grease across his fingers, swore with violence.

Lalo Hussa entered the hall, holding a candle in one hand,

and in the other a steaming white pot. She vanished into a room behind the great stairway. A moment later, the unsteady glow of candles spilled into the hallway.

Hamilton sniffed, and remarked, "She promised to give Miss Lily some soup."

From the hall above roared Moreland's voice: "Cowan, not a damned thing up here. She been picked to the bone."

"Same down here," Cowan yelled. "Best come down."

"Didn't I tell you?" came Tucker's sour voice. "We could've been riding this long hour. Not lookin' at bare walls."

Lalo Hussa emerged from the room behind the stairs and bore energetically down on them. "Told you," she cried triumphantly. "Said was nothin' here."

"So you said," Cowan growled.

She brushed by him and entered the room where Miss Lily and the child waited.

Hamilton said, "They've been standing there in the dark, not even a candle." His voice whispered.

"Blind people don't need no light," Cowan said.

Moreland and Tucker thumped down the staircase toward them, their faces anxious in the candle glow. Their eyes searched. The emptiness of the house rang all around them.

Lalo Hussa stepped from the dark room. In her candle's uneasy glow, they saw Miss Lily and the child following single file behind her. They moved smoothly, silently, arms at their sides, not touching each other. Their faces showed white, like those evasive patches that float, ghostly and feeble, across the night surface of a swamp.

Suddenly still on the stairs, Moreland and Tucker watched the women file by.

When they vanished into the candlelit room, Moreland eased down the stairs. He said to Cowan, "Nothin' left upstairs but the wallpaper. Let's go."

Tucker sniffed the air. "You smell that cookin'? 'Fore we go, let's get us a cup of that soup."

"I don't have no great hunger," Moreland said. "Let's saddle and go."

"Come on," Tucker said, taking Moreland's arm. "We'll fill our cups first. Then we ride. You comin', Cowan?"

"We'll follow behind," Cowan said.

He watched the two move away through the hollow whisperings of the hall. "Come on," he said to Hamilton, and pushed the young man toward the door of Miss Lily's room. "These women got to change their clothes. And where there's clothes, maybe there's rings and necklaces, too, don't you think?"

"Robbin' blind woman?" Hamilton said. "That's an evil thing."

"In here," Cowan said, shoving the door open. He lifted the candle.

The dim light touched no walls. They edged slowly into darkness that swallowed light and reflected nothing back. Gray slits marked the windows. Close around them, the black air rang hollowly. Some deep-buried sense whispered that beyond their light drifted watching things, seeking to edge behind. Their backs cringed. On the floor ahead glimmered a whitish mass. Cold ached along Cowan's nerves. He heard Hamilton's breath harsh in his mouth.

Cowan thrust out the candle. The whitish mass became a pair of mats stretched along the wall, small pillows at the heads, sheets wadded at the feet. From nails driven into the wall dangled two white dresses, long and short. An unclean odor hung in the air.

"Sleep like animals," Hamilton whispered.

"Can't be all they have," Cowan cried. "No mirrors. No shoes. Where they dress?"

He swung around, squinting into the darkness. The candle flame bobbed and shook, unstable as a frightened heart. Shadows pulsed and fled back. Near the floor gleamed eyes and pale teeth.

Cowan shouted inarticulately, lunging back, fumbling for his knife. Before he located the hilt, he recognized the staring face with its big nose and heavy mustache. The jaw sagged, exposing a gray tongue.

Hamilton said, "Captain Fosey!" in a voice not quite controlled.

Cowan, gone pale as Fosey's face, said, "They did move him, damn them."

"Moreland said not."

"Those little women sure didn't. He sure didn't walk."

Hamilton said, "There's holly leaves on his tunic. He got up on his dead legs and walked through the door and sat down to wait on us." He spoke slowly, every word shaking at the edge.

"Shut up," snarled Cowan. "Shut up, you crazy. Snivelin' like a woman. And you a soldier. Dead is dead. There sits the other one."

Candlelight fell upon a second corpse, the face shattered by Cowan's shot. The body sprawled against the wall, a few feet from Fosey.

"Dead, by God," Cowan snarled. "Brains on his face."

"They're watching us," Hamilton said.

"The dead look," Cowan said, "but damn if they see. Come on."

He jerked viciously at Hamilton's arm, pushing him toward the door. Metal-voiced, he said, "What's two dead men, Hamilton? You've seen a thousand stinking in the field. What's two more?"

"They were good to me," Hamilton said. "Fosey and Spencer. Good men." He began to cry silently in the darkness.

Once out of the room, Cowan defiantly slammed the door. A yell of echoes burst around them. Dragging at Hamilton's arm, he stamped down the hall toward the lighted room under the stairs.

In that room, Moreland and Tucker stood by a long wooden table. At each end blazed a three-piece candlestick. The backs and shoulders of the watching men seemed curiously rigid, as if they had disciplined themselves to watch some disgusting thing.

At the table, Miss Lily and the child bent over basins of soup. The liquid looked thin as pump water. Bits of orange and green vegetable floated in the pallid stuff. Not touching the basins with their hands, they sucked up the soup, bubbling and slobbering. Their strepitous mouths seemed unrelated to the staring emptiness of their faces.

Behind them stood Lalo Hussa. She glared hate at Tucker as he lifted a tin cup and self-consciously tasted its contents.

"Don't taste like nothin' at all," he said. "No meat. No salt. No nothin'."

From the pocket of his tunic, he fumbled out a small leather bag, worked it open with a thumb. He sprinkled its contents into his cup.

Lalo Hussa cried sharply, "What's that? What's that?"

"Salt," Tucker said, extending the bag. "Here."

She cried out, a single furious syllable, and slapped the bag from his hand. "Get that away!"

Polished hardness slipped into Tucker's face. His eyes became thorns. Placing the cup on the table, he caught Lalo Hussa by the shoulder, pushed her back against the wall.

"Don't you hit at me!" he said. "Don't you ever do it!"

Lalo Hussa wiggled furiously in his grip. Teeth flashed in her dark face. She squalled, "Help me, Miss Lily. Help me, Little Rose."

Tucker shook her hard, driving her head against the wall. She kicked and clawed at him.

As Miss Lily stood up, her chair banged over. She glided away from the table with easy grace, like a dancer floating through the measures of a pavanne. She did not seem to move rapidly, but before Tucker could turn, she was behind him. Her slender arms reached up.

Little Rose's chair creaked back. She came pattering toward Tucker.

Miss Lily placed pale hands at each side of Tucker's head, fingers touching his lower jaw. In the candlelight, the scratches on her skin showed as thin black lines. She pulled at his head.

Tucker's startled face twisted into the candlelight. Tucker's neck snapped with a single hard sound.

Moreland flung himself forward, clutching at Miss Lily. Tucker toppled from her hands, his legs and arms convulsing. She fell back against Moreland, and her arms reached up to encircle his neck, as if they were lovers. He stared down into her face, inches below.

Moreland began screaming.

Little Rose wrapped tiny arms around Moreland's leg. With no apparent effort, she tugged it from under him.

Moreland plunged backward across the table, Miss Lily still holding his neck. The table crashed over. Dishes clattered and spun. The candlesticks tumbled out their candles. Darkness leaped into the room, like a black thing rearing from the floor.

Two lighted candles rolled against the wall, their flames gone small and blue. Patches of white swayed around the shouting darkness that was Moreland, agony and horror in his voice.

He convulsed and heaved. The room shook as a white bundle thudded heavily against the wall. In the vague light, Cowan recognized Miss Lily's calm face. Around her body, the white dress swirled like blown mist.

She stepped forward, seeming unaware that she had struck the wall with force enough to shatter her spine. Her face held no more expression than a cake of soap. As she glided toward Moreland with her boneless flowing step, he reared erect. Grunting with effort, he heaved an indistinct blur of white above his head. In the fluttering light, the whiteness seemed somehow attached to his face.

Moreland screamed, "Get it off me!"

He crashed the blur against the floor. Shadows writhed within shadows. Cowan, struggling from behind the table, saw a confusion of movement, as if the dark mass that was Moreland stamped furiously upon an indistinct pale smudge.

"Cowan! For God's sake!"

Reaching out, Miss Lily embraced Moreland. Cowan snatched up a candle. The flame shrank to a wavering blue patch that cast no light. He could see nothing.

A heavy falling shocked the room.

From the blackness came a high, metallic squeal, thin and terrible, as if, in the darkness, an owl tore apart a large mouse.

Against the plank floor, feet beat furiously. Then not so furiously.

From the darkness, Lalo Hussa said, "That enough, Miss Lily."

Cowan's candle flame slowly lengthened to clear yellow. Across the room, he saw the shine of Lalo Hussa's eyes. He groped up a second candle.

Hamilton's voice muttered at his ear. "Cut me loose, Cowan. Cut me loose!"

On the floor, quite close to Cowan's feet, flopped a whitish mass. For one terrible moment, he thought that it would touch him. He lurched back, kicking a tin dish across the room, looking down on the flattened, wiggling thing that was Little Rose. Boot prints smudged the white dress. The shattered body attempted to rise. It could not. It crept forward in the slow, deliberate movement he had seen in soldiers disemboweled on the field. Moments before death, bodies hollow with death, they crept toward the future, limbs moving in imitation of life, as if each movement certified that they lived and what had come upon them could be denied.

From the child's distorted skull, one eye stared upward, like the eye of a flat fish.

Lalo Hussa knelt by the crawling thing.

"Baby, baby. Good li'l honey," she crooned. "You fine, honey. You go home now."

Dark fingers dipped into Tucker's salt bag. Dark fingers scattered salt into the shattered mouth.

Sudden purpose gripped the crushed body. It crept slowly past, fingers scratching on the dark floor, and butting aside the door, vanished scraping and sliding down the dark hall.

Lalo Hussa lifted her head to look up at Hamilton's rigid face. "It's the old way," she said. "Salt sends 'em to their rest."

He asked in a voice of inhuman calm, "Why did you bring them back?"

She laughed. "Had to," she said. "Had to. They gots the sickness. The mister, he laid them in their coffins hisself. Then he filled up the wagons, an' he said to me, what's left, it's yours, Lalo Hussa. Take the house, Lalo Hussa.

"But who'd leave me to keep this fine house? General Wheeler? Them white trash past the hill? So I call Miss Lily and Little Rose back the old way. The way I learn in the Caribbees, me jus' a chile, so long ago. And if people came, why here Miss Lily and her chile sick in their house and me takin' care for them. But all the time, it my house, my house only, an' nobody knowed."

Hamilton said, "Dead! My God, dead!" in a voice like scratching rocks.

"Not dead till they lay down," she said. "But now I don't need 'em no more. You jus' go stand by your friend."

"Not my friend," Hamilton said. "I'm his prisoner. Tied hands and all."

"Then go stand away, Mr. Prisoner." She swiveled toward Cowan, showing bright teeth. "You hit my face," she said.

The Remington slipped free of the holster. "Blow your damn head off," Cowan said.

Pointing the revolver into Lalo Hussa's face, he hauled back the hammer. It set with a hard click, but as it did so, he saw that the cylinder had not turned.

Understanding flared in him. Hamilton had twice escaped simply because the hammer had fallen on a discharged chamber. The linkage revolving the cylinder likely broke when he had dropped the pistol, struggling with Hamilton. But you could half cock the weapon and turn the cylinder with your fingers.

Lalo Hussa said, "Let the boy go. Kill me this man."

Miss Lily, standing passively by the door, glided forward, reaching toward Cowan, her hands palms up.

The Remington flared and bucked, spitting out hard sound. The massive ball hurled Lalo Hussa backward, slapping her off her feet, sprawling her against the overturned table.

Miss Lily's hand reached through the acrid powder haze. Her fingers at his neck felt cool and dry and hard. He felt her strength, looked past her scratched hands into her blank face. Some remote part of his mind informed him that holly had scratched her skin as she lifted dead men from the hedge.

As that picture ran behind his eyes, he clubbed the Remington hard against her head. Felt bones break. Saw her nose flatten, her skull deform.

"The salt!" Hamilton screamed.

Cowan hit her twice more, with all the despairing power of his heavy arms. The blows drove her back. Her broken face held no expression. No blood showed. She took hold of his arm, and it exploded with pain. The flesh crushed like an apple in a press.

Howling, he smashed at her hand with the Remington. Stumbling away from her, striking wildly, he tripped over a chair and, as he struggled up, saw the leather salt bag by Lalo Hussa's hand.

Miss Lily wrenched the Remington from his hand. Bone from her fractured fingers projected gray-white through the skin.

He snatched the salt bag from the floor. He dumped its contents into his palm. Wet thin sounds spilled from his open mouth. Miss Lily closed both hands around his neck and lifted him straight up from the floor. Her filmed eyes peered past him. Her broken jaw hung down. As the pressure on his neck grew intolerable, he hurled the salt into her gaping mouth.

He fell. The floor struck him a vicious blow. For a moment, she loomed over him, a dreadful figure in white, emitting a dank, musty smell, like an attic in winter.

A tremor ran through her body, shaking it the way wind shakes leaves. She turned from him. In her smoothly boneless way, she slipped through the door. Her footsteps padded away down the hall.

"God!" he cried. "God!"

He was unable to stand. He knelt by Lalo Hussa's body, feeling the floor turn under him, feeling the floor become a gulf into which he plunged, unprotected, unrestrained, falling forever.

Hamilton asked, "Is she dead?" in a slow, impersonal voice.

Cowan looked at Lalo Hussa's slitted eyes, the blood on her clothing and bubbling mouth. "She's goin'."

"You'd best cut me loose," Hamilton said.

Cowan shook his head and fumbled up the Remington. His hands could hardly grip the weapon. Bringing the hammer to half cock, he fingered the cylinder around. "I'll not be leavin' you to hang me," he said.

The hammer fell. The Remington snapped thinly. Cowan stared at it stupidly, then began to laugh. "Them's some lucky little girls," he said.

Throwing down the Remington, he drew his knife.

Hamilton pushed back the door with one toe and slipped through. Outside the door, he cried out, a single, thick syllable. His footsteps ran away through the echoing darkness.

Cowan rumbled in his throat. His mouth was one hot agony.

Heaving up on unsteady legs, he braced himself, stumbled toward the door.

"Can't outrun me with your hands tied," he yelled. "I won't hang."

He swung back the door.

Before him stood Captain Fosey and the trooper, Spencer. Their eyes did not look at him. Their mouths hung open. They stood there, quite dead, and they reached out and put their hands on him.

Cowan used the knife. But that did no good.

He did not scream long.

The Third Nation

Lee Hoffman

Although she lives in Port Charlotte, a scant hundred miles or so south of Clearwater, there are far too few times each year when I am able to renew friendship with Lee Hoffman. One such fortunate occasion came in May, 1990, when I constructed a reason to visit, with the real purpose being to ask her to contribute to this anthology. Lee doesn't drive at night, so my ostensible purpose was to transport her to Sarasota for a speaking appearance by Lee's longtime friend, Harlan Ellison. The trip went well. Harlan lauded Lee to the audience, calling her work *The Valdez Horses* "the best novel most of you will ever read." On the way back, I mentioned this project, and less than a month later received the story at hand.

Lots of people retire to Florida. The problem occurs when a writer of Lee's talents takes retirement seriously, producing no new stories for more than a decade. If you'd like to check out some of Lee's earlier work, I concur with Harlan's choice, though you'd probably be surprised to discover most of her writing has nothing to do with science fiction. With titles such as *The Legend of Blackjack Sam, Gunfight at Laramie,* and *Return to Broken Crossing,* you could probably figure that out on your own. In 1968, she received the Western Writers of America "Spur" award for *The Valdez Horses,* one of those out-of-print classics you really ought to look for.

But enough about the Westerns. Here Lee describes herself:

"Great-grandpa Ray was with Hart's South Carolina Artillery until he was wounded and captured at Spotsylvania. It was something of a disappointment to my mother's family when she married a 'Yankee' from Philadelphia. I've never decided whether

I'm a Northerner or Southerner. I was born in Chicago, Illinois, in 1932, but grew up in Savannah, Georgia. There I played on the remains of Confederate earthworks and was fascinated by stories of the Civil War, and the period of westward expansion that followed it.

"In the 1950's, I spent some time on ranches in Colorado, worked briefly for a horse trader in Kansas, then moved to New York City, where I fell in with evil companions and eventually began writing for a living. Although most of my books are Westerns, I've been a fan of science fiction, the supernatural, and horror since childhood, and have written science fiction bordering on horror, and a historical romance set during the Civil War.

"I returned to the South in 1971 and am now lazing about in Florida, devoting most of my time to attending SF conventions, dabbling in handicrafts, and watching old movies on videotape."

"If she were the two-legged kind, he'd catch 'er quick enough." Grinning, Hull poked Dayton with an elbow.

"If she were that kind, I'd be there first," Dayton said.

Hull had a wad of tobacco in one cheek. He spat, and called, "Go get 'er, Lacey! Grab 'er by the trotter!"

Lacey was a big man, and muscled like a prime bull. Despite the chill, there was sweat beading on his forehead. He pushed back his kepi and wiped at it. Like the other Bummers, his face was stained from the smoke of pine knot fires. In the long morning light his breath was faintly visible. He'd already lunged for the pig four, five times, and it had scooted away every time. Now, backed up into the angle between an old outbuilding and a piece of rail fence, it eyed him warily.

The rest of the foragers had spread out behind Lacey to urge him on and watch the fun. If it had been a full-grown hog, the lieutenant would probably have given orders to shoot it rather than waste time running the lard off it, but it was a young one and from the look of it, it had been rooting wild instead of penned to fatten. So the lieutenant stood back and let the men enjoy a little sport.

"I'll get 'er this time," Lacey said. Again, he lunged.

Again, the pig scooted away. Frantic, it charged toward the wall of men.

Shouting and laughing, the men converged to head it off.

The pig wheeled and darted toward the end of the fence.

"Flank it, boys! Flank it!" the lieutenant called.

The pig turned again, this time heading straight at Cahill.

Cahill was the youngest one in the company. He looked more like a drummer boy than a fighting man, but he'd been blooded at Resaca. Now he took pride in being one of Sherman's Bummers. As it charged past him, he grabbed for the pig. His hands connected, but the pig squirmed out of his grip. Tail up, it headed across the overgrown pasture toward the woods.

"I'll get 'er!" Cahill lit out after the high-tailing pig.

Fun was fun, but pigs were food. The lieutenant shouted, "Shoot the damn thing before it gets away!"

Nash was the sharpshooter of the company. He'd got himself a breech-loading Spencer, and claimed he could cut the middle star out of a Rebel battle flag at a thousand yards. Slinging the rifle to his shoulder, he set his sights and called, "Leave 'er be, boy! I'll get 'er!"

Maybe Cahill didn't hear him, or maybe he was just too excited and set on making the capture. He kept going. But the pig was gaining ground fast. Nash had a clean line of sight. Leading the target, he closed his finger on the trigger.

As the hammer fell, the pig swerved. Dirt and grass spattered where the pig had been. But the pig was already racing into the woods. For all it was gaining on him, Cahill was still hard after it.

"Oh, hell," the lieutenant said.

Whooping as if it were a band of Rebs they were chasing, the rest of the company lit out after Cahill.

It would have been a poor place to chase a Reb who might shoot back but, as woods went, it was a pretty good one for hunting a pig. Although the pine and live oaks held their leaves all winter, in December much of the other foliage had browned and fallen, making a crisp mat on the ground. The undergrowth was mostly a tangle of bare branches. A man could see a good ways into the woods and could hear brogans crunching the fallen leaves. The pig flashed in and out of sight among the tree trunks. Cahill, in his dark blue field jacket and light blue trousers, stayed easily visible.

Hull saw the pig scramble over a windfallen tree and Cahill spring up with a foot on the tree trunk. Suddenly Cahill disappeared behind the tree and Hull heard a high sharp scream. He thought it was the pig squealing, that Cahill'd jumped it and caught it. But the scream stopped, and a caught pig usually kept squealing.

As he reached the windfall, he saw Cahill sitting on the ground, one leg stretched out in front of him. The other was drawn up and Cahill was hugging it tight, rocking a bit. Hull had seen men hug themselves and rock that way before, on the battlefield. Wounded men.

Dayton reached Cahill first and knelt beside him. The others came up, circling around him. Hull heard Cahill saying, ". . . think my leg's broke." His voice was hoarse with pain.

The lieutenant was last to arrive. As he loped up, Dayton told him, "Sir, Cahill's broke his leg."

Hull could see what had happened. The log was half rotten. There was a hole in the top where Cahill's foot had gone in and caught. Off balance, he'd fallen, wrenching his ankle.

"Let's see," the lieutenant said, gesturing for Dayton to reveal the wound.

Dayton dropped to one knee. With his penknife, he slit the trouser on Cahill's outstretched leg. When he peeled back the cloth, there was no sign of blood and the leg looked straight. It wasn't until he took hold of Cahill's brogan that Cahill grunted with pain. Gently, he removed the brogan. Wrinkling his nose, he said to Cahill, "Don't you ever wash your feet?"

Cahill managed with a weak grin, "I didn't know you were gonna be sniffing around them."

When Dayton had bared Cahill's leg and foot, the lieutenant moved him aside and knelt for a look. He ran a hand down Cahill's shin, then touched his ankle. Cahill fought against showing pain, but he couldn't hold back a couple of whimpers.

Finally, the lieutenant stood up again and wiped his hands. "I don't think there are any bones broken," he said.

Cahill looked disappointed. "I can't stand up."

"Oh, you're hurt all right," the lieutenant agreed. "I think your ankle's dislocated. We'll have to get you back to the surgeon."

"If that's all it is, I can fix it," Heinke said.

The lieutenant gave him a questioning frown.

Heinke explained, "My pop's a horse doctor, sir."

"It's work for a surgeon," the lieutenant said.

"Sooner it's done, the better," Heinke told him.

He hesitated. "If you're sure you can do it."

"Yes, sir!" Heinke said proudly. He looked at the men gathered around. "Couple of you fellers take hold of him, hold him tight."

"I'll do it." Setting down his musket, Lacey stepped behind Cahill and wrapped his arms around the boy's chest.

"What you gonna do?" Cahill asked.

Unspeaking, Heinke grabbed the boy's foot and tugged. Cahill screamed and then went limp.

"Oh, Lord!" Lacey whispered, bracing the boy in his arms. "He's died!"

"Passed out," Heinke said. "Best thing for him." He worked at the ankle a few moments longer, then sat back on his haunches and wiped his forehead. "I expect that'll fix it. But he ain't gonna be able to walk on it for a while."

There was sweat on the lieutenant's face, too. He drew a kerchief from a pocket and wiped at it. "Lacey, can you carry him?"

"Yes, sir."

"All right, you take him back to that farmhouse."

"What about the pig, sir?" Dayton asked.

The lieutenant gave a little laugh. "That pig'll be halfway to Savannah by now."

Dayton muttered. "I had my mouth all set for fresh pork."

"Don't worry, we'll find another one." The lieutenant turned back to Lacey. "Stay with him. Soon as we forage up a horse or mule, I'll send it back for you to carry him on to camp."

"Shouldn't somebody else go along with 'em, sir? In case those Reb deserters are around here somewhere?" Hull suggested. It had been several days since a planter'd told them about being robbed by Rebs running ahead of Sherman's march, and several days before that when it had happened. The odds were against them still being in the area, but Hull had a notion to go back and explore the empty farmhouse. When the Secesh ran off in a hurry, sometimes they left valuables behind.

The lieutenant nodded. "Go ahead. Keep a sharp eye out. I'll get somebody back to you as soon as I can."

Cahill was coming out of his faint. He choked back a groan as Lacey got him up over his shoulder like a blanket-roll. Hull picked up Lacey's musket and they headed for the farmhouse.

The farm was an old one. When he got a good look at it Hull's hopes of loot sank. This place looked like it had been abandoned long before Sherman's Army left Atlanta in flames.

The house was built of rough-hewn planks that had weathered to a dreary gray. Rotting planks dangled from the walls. Patches of shakes had scabbed off from the roof as if it had an ugly disease. Both of the big brick chimneys flanking the house had lost their capping. Just a few sections of the rail fence still stood, and the smokehouse door gaped askew.

The only signs of life the foragers had seen when they first arrived were a bluejay perched on the porch roof and the pig that had been rooting around the empty corn crib. The bluejay had left when Lacey'd made his first lunge at the pig.

The jay was back when the returning men reached the house. It flew off again as Lacey set Cahill down on the edge of the porch. Cahill was keeping a diary. Once he was settled comfortably, he pulled it out and began scribbling. Lacey stretched out on his back with his hands under his head.

Hull stood a while, wondering whether he should suggest Lacey come with him. Together, they could look out for each other. But if he did find anything small enough to pocket, he didn't fancy sharing it. Finally, he gave the door a shove. It swung open.

"Uncle Billy's orders are to stay out of dwellings," Lacey called to him.

He looked back, cocking a brow at Lacey. Despite the orders, they'd gone foraging inside more than one Secesh house on this march. "It ain't hardly a *dwelling* if there's nobody dwelling in it, is it?"

Lacey's grin said he'd been joking. He added, "Remember, it's fair shares all around."

"I doubt there's anything in here but rat nests," Hull answered, hoping he was wrong. If it turned out he was, he had no intention of telling Lacey. Musket in hand, he stepped cautiously inside.

The room he entered was as damply chill as a springhouse. It was an odd kind of cold that smelled of musty decay. A graveyard cold. He tensed at a sound: a faint rustling, like the dry leaves in the woods. Rats in the walls, he told himself, that was all.

Ghosts of the dead that lurked in old houses were just tales for scaring children. If he'd ever believed in such things, he'd lost his faith on the battlefield. When a man died, what was left was cold meat, nothing more. He'd seen that for himself. If there was a spirit in a man, like the preachers claimed, it didn't linger once the body was dead. Of that, he was certain. Even so, he shivered at the feel of the place more than the chill. The house looked deserted, but somehow it just didn't feel empty.

The corners of the room were filled with shadows and cobwebs. There were old ashes in the hearth, and some shredded bits of a snakeskin rubbed off against the rough bricks. A few pieces of furniture not worth hauling off huddled in the shadows.

To his right was a half-open door. He peeked in: a battered old table and a couple of chairs, both missing splats. On the table were a stone jug, a chipped plate, and a dented tin ladle. But no cobwebs. He frowned at that. Rats didn't set out dishes. Did spooks? But there wasn't any such thing.

Warily, he peered around the room. There were plenty of cobwebs in the corners, and a pine cupboard hulked against one wall. Nothing else. He looked under the table. Nothing there. The cupboard sat flush to the floor. No room under it for anything to hide. No Rebs in here waiting to jump him.

He touched a finger to the tabletop. No dust. No dust on the jug or plate, either. How long would it take for a layer of dust to settle on the table? He wasn't sure. Maybe a few days? Whoever'd used that plate was probably halfway to Savannah by now, he told himself. Didn't even have to have been a Reb. Could have been a runaway slave or a hunter taking shelter.

He picked up the jug and sniffed hopefully at its contents. Molasses. He set down the jug and went to the cupboard. Inside he found a few pieces of battered crockery, two shriveled sweet potatoes, and several pine cones. The pine cones puzzled him.

He thought about it all for a moment, then grinned. Didn't need to have been a Reb or hunter or slave. Could have been children playing house. That would explain the pine cones.

Even so, he edged open the back door slowly and stood back as he thrust out the barrel of his musket. Nobody took a shot at it. He chanced poking his head out. Nobody shot at it, either. Relieved, he looked around.

There was a small building with a large chimney about twenty feet behind the house. That'd be the kitchen, he supposed. It seemed the Secesh had a custom of putting their kitchens a ways from their houses. Someone had told him it was to keep down the damage when the kitchen caught fire.

Holding the musket ready, he crossed the yard. He used the muzzle to push open the kitchen door. A smell of rot hit him in the face. Rats scurried wildly for cover as light spilled through the doorway. Nobody in there, he thought. At least nobody alive. Likely nothing fit to forage, either. He pulled the door shut again and returned to the house.

Not enough molasses left in that jug to make it worth carrying, and those sweet potatoes were too old and dry. He started back through the parlor.

Abruptly he halted. There'd been no sound. Nothing to grab his attention, except a feeling. A sudden sense of something wrong.

He was at the bottom of the stairs. The staircase pressed tight against one wall as it rose through an opening in the ceiling. He looked up. There was a window at the head of the stairs. Grimy shards of glass hung in the frame. The sun was high enough now to throw jagged streaks of light through the holes. Dust danced in the beams, but no cobwebs ensnared them.

Whoever'd been in the house had gone upstairs. Might still be up there, he thought. He scanned the parlor, assuring himself it was still empty, and checked to be sure his musket was still capped. Climbing the stairs, he set each foot carefully at the wall side of the tread to keep it from squeaking.

Before his head reached the level of the floor above, he pulled off his kepi and balanced it on the musket barrel, then thrust it up through the passageway.

Nothing happened.

Cautiously, he took another step, looked out onto the second-floor landing. No Rebs crouched in the shadows. Not even a small spook waving its winding sheet at him. He grinned sourly at himself for even thinking of ghosts.

There was a door to either side of the landing. Both were closed. Neither was sealed with cobwebs. He climbed onto the landing and decided to try the right-hand door first. He turned the knob slowly, then used the gun muzzle to nudge the door open. As it moved, the room breathed out the odors of decay and he could hear sounds of scurrying.

It had been a bedroom. The bedframe was gone, but an old tick lay crumpled on the floor, leaking mildewed straw through a dozen or more holes. He glimpsed a stringy gray tail disappearing into one. A litter of droppings confirmed that he'd found a rat's nest all right.

A massive clothes cupboard stood against the wall, its doors hanging open. The long-dry bones of a dead rat nestled in one corner. The skull was facing toward him, its empty sockets seeming to stare in surprise at his sudden appearance. He backstepped and closed the door.

Behind him, something squeaked.

He wheeled.

The door he faced was like the one he'd just turned away from. He stood for a moment, staring at it, listening. He could hear nothing. The noise had been another rat, he told himself. The place was full of rats.

He turned the knob, then pushed the door gently with the gun muzzle. Rusty hinges moaned as it swung open. An old clothes cupboard stood against one wall and a featherbed lay on the floor, but these furnishings did not look abandoned. The cupboard was shut and the featherbed spread out. A quilt was spread over the featherbed. And someone was under it.

The musty stink of the room was tinged with another odor, an ugly sickly odor he'd smelled often enough before.

"You there," he snapped at the quilt-covered figure on the featherbed, but he didn't really expect an answer. Not with that smell in the air. He took a step toward the body under the quilt, meaning to prod it with his musket and assure himself it was dead.

He stopped short at sight of the face. He'd recognized the outhouse stink of death, death that had been working for days, and he'd been prepared for the sight of it. Since he'd got into this war, he'd seen dead men aplenty. The sight no longer bothered him. Sometimes they'd died in horrible ways, sometimes with faces half shot off or rotted off by the time he saw them. But on the field it was always men.

This was a woman. A young woman with sorrel hair, undone and combed into a halo radiating from the splotched pallor of her face. Parchment skin molded into a taut image of the bone beneath, as if the flesh between had melted and flowed away. The mouth was open, lips drawn back in a silent mocking leer.

She hadn't died there all alone. That was damned sure. Someone had been there to close her eyes. On the lid of each was a three-dollar Federal gold piece.

He squatted to take them. As his fingers closed on one, he heard a squeak behind him. A voice struck him like a minié ball, jerking him to his feet, spinning him around. He saw the cupboard door now open and a face staring at him from inside.

"You leave my mama alone!" she screeched.

He scowled in amazement as the child lunged out of the cupboard. She was a scrawny, dirty-faced tow head. Her filthy rumpled dress was flounced with tattered lace and there were holes in stockings that looked like silk.

"You put that back!" She indicated the coin between his fingers.

Shaken, he said, "She's your ma?"

The girl nodded and repeated, "Put that back!"

He looked at the coin, then at the corpse. "Your ma's dead."

"I know that. She's gone to heaven to be with Papa, same as Grandma went to be with Grandpa," the girl said. "You give her back that there penny."

"She don't need it now."

"Does, too!"

"What for? You said she's gone to heaven."

She nodded.

"Well, the streets are paved with gold up there, ain't they? She won't miss no couple of—" he grinned slightly as he used her description "—pennies."

"Dead people gotta have pennies. They always do."

"No, they don't." He bent to scoop up the other coin. And saw the dull gleam of gold at the dead woman's throat. Nudging back the quilt, he found a lavaliere of gold set with a stone as big as his thumbnail and as red as fresh blood. His fingers clamped around it, snatching, breaking the fragile chain it hung from.

"That's my mama's do-pretty!" the girl protested.

He held up the lavaliere, letting it dangle from his fingertips. The red jewel was set into gold filigree. There was enough sunlight to set sparks flashing within the jewel. This was something worth foraging for, he thought. Hell, it was likely worth more than a foot soldier's pay for the whole war. Maybe enough to buy a partnership in a nice little saloon.

"What's the dead need with such things?" he said as much to himself as to the child.

"I don't know," she admitted, "but grandma got buried with all hers."

He looked from the jewels to the girl. "All hers?"

"She had a lot of rubies." She pointed at the stone. "That's what I'm named after. Ruby. Grandma had a whole big string of them. Mama said she wore them when she got buried."

Hull stared at the child. Was she telling the truth? A whole string of rubies would be worth a fortune. Set a man up for life. He said, "Ain't so."

"Yes it is!"

"Where would your grandma get something like that?"

"Mama said she brought them with her when she come over

from France. Mama said Grandma had to run away from the bad men who stole her plantation in France, and she brought all her do-pretties here with her so the bad men wouldn't get them, too. Grandma loved her do-pretties so much Papa put them on her when they buried her. That's what Mama said. She said she wished he hadn't done that."

Hull grinned, thinking it was a damnfool thing to do. A waste for such things to lie in a grave when the living could be making good use of them. He said, "Ruby, do you know where they buried your grandma?"

"You give Mama back her pennies."

"Here." He handed her the coins.

"And her do-pretty."

"You tell me about your grandma first. Where did they bury her?"

"In the churchyard," she said as she returned the coins to the eyelids of the corpse.

"What churchyard? Where?"

She scowled at him as if that were a foolish question. "Next to the church."

"Is it close by here? Can you show me?"

Her expression told him she thought that was another foolish question. "It's back home."

"This ain't your home?"

"Course not. We wouldn't live in no place like this. Only the Yankees was coming and we was going to Savannah only Mama took sick and we came here and the bad men came and we hid and they took our horse and cart and Mama died and I can't find nothing to eat but molasses and old dried-up sweet taters and you better give my mama back her do-pretty." As the words spilled out of her, tears trickled down her cheeks, drawing pale tracks through the dirt. Blinking, she gazed at him with a deep sadness. "You're a bad man, too, ain't you?"

"No, sugar, I ain't a bad man. I'm just a sodjer trying to get along in the world," he said, feeling sorry for the poor child. But not sorry enough to give up the lavaliere. "I don't mean you any harm, but I got a lot better use for this do-pretty than your mama—"

"Hull!" Lacey hollered from below. "Where are you? You all right?"

"Dammit," he mumbled under his breath. Over his shoulder, he shouted, "I'm all right. I'll be right down."

"I'm coming up," Lacey called back. "You found anything?"

"Who's that?" the girl asked.

"My friend," he said, but at that moment he didn't feel like Lacey was a friend at all. If Lacey saw that lavaliere, he was going to want a share, he thought as he stuffed it into a pocket. If Lacey saw the girl, he'd want to know what she was doing there. She was sure to tell him about the jewel. She was already opening her mouth like she was about to holler.

Hull wrenched her around, slamming a hand across her mouth, wildly hunting a way to keep her quiet. He could hear Lacey's brogans on the stairs. He had to keep Lacey from discovering her. He could think of only one way. Knotting a fist, he smashed it into the child's head.

The blow knocked her out all right. Hurriedly, he shoved her limp body into the cupboard and pushed the door closed. But as he let go, it started to swing open again. He pushed it back and turned the latch on it. Lacey's steps were close. As Hull snatched up the coins from the dead woman's eyes, he heard a board creak on the landing.

Then Lacey was at the doorway. He wrinkled his nose. "What the hell you found?"

"A dead woman," Hull said tautly, the coins clenched in the fist at his side. He shoved the fist into his pocket.

Lacey walked into the room and looked down at the corpse. "Poor thing. What you suppose happened?"

"She came in here and died."

"But how come?"

"How the hell should I know?"

Lacey shrugged.

Darting a look at the cupboard, Hull thought he'd better get Lacey away before the little girl woke up and began raising a racket. He said, "Least we can do is bury her decent like proper Christians."

"What about her people?"

"If she had people around here, don't you think they'd have taken care of her? Not left her lie here like this?"

"I guess so."

"We can roll her up in the featherbed. You take the bottom. I'll get the top." Hull started folding the side of the bed over the body.

A bit hesitantly, Lacey began to help. As he lifted his end, he said, "I don't much like dead people."

"Nobody does," Hull said. "That's why they bury 'em."

"Huh?"

"Come on, it stinks in here."

They carried the bundle down the stairs and through the parlor. Cahill was watching the door. As they walked out onto the porch, he asked what had happened.

"Found a dead body. Gonna bury it," Hull grunted. If the girl began to holler when she woke up, would her voice carry this far? He asked Cahill, "Can you walk yet?"

"I can't even wiggle my foot."

"Come on," he said to Lacey, and he headed for the steps.

"Set her down a minute. I got to get another grip."

"It's a woman?" Cahill asked as they put the bundle down.

"It was once," Hull snapped, impatient to be on away from the house. He turned to Lacey. "I'll carry her. You bring Cahill."

"What? Why?"

"We want to give her a proper decent Christian burying, don't we? It wouldn't be respectful if Cahill didn't come, would it?"

"I don't think—" Cahill began.

Hull cut him short. "It's the least we can do as good Christians, ain't it?"

"I guess so," Lacey allowed.

Cahill shrugged.

Hull started trying to gather the bundle up in his arms. It wasn't heavy, but the featherbed was bulky, awkward. Seeing he was having trouble with it, Lacey suggested, "I'll help you and come back for Cahill."

"No, I'll get her all right," Hull said.

Cahill asked, "Where you gonna put her?"

"Away from the house," Hull replied. "A decent distance, in case anybody wants to move in here again."

"Move into *this* place?" Lacey said doubtfully.

Hull's impatience was turning to anger. He stopped himself from snapping at Lacey. Struggling to keep his voice calm and reasonable, he said, "Somebody must own it. They might want to fix it up someday."

"I suppose so." Lacey sounded doubtful, but willing to give in rather than argue. He looked at Hull struggling to pick up the bundle. "I'd better help you."

"No!"

Cahill frowned with puzzlement at Hull's insistence. He started to speak, stopped, held up a hand. "Listen."

Hull heard the sound: the jangle and rattle of a wagon. Wheeling, he saw it on the track to the house. The team was a pair of mismatched mules. They pulled a farm wagon loaded with sacks and casks. Heinke was driving, and Yates was at his side.

"There!" Lacey said happily, "Here come the fellers. They can help us with her."

"Yeah," Hull muttered, feeling the way the cornered pig must have felt with its back to the fence and the circle of men closing in around it.

As the wagon jounced up, Yates swung himself from the seat and strode toward the porch. Toward the bundle lying on it. "What you got there? Something good?"

"A dead woman," Lacey told him.

He stopped short. "You killed a woman?"

"We found her dead. We was gonna take her and bury her proper."

Heinke halted the mules. "Load up and let's get going."

"They got a dead woman here," Yates told him before Lacey could. But then he had to leave it to someone else to explain. Lacey was eager to talk. Hull stayed silent, letting Lacey tell all he knew about it.

Heinke and Yates agreed that the woman should be given a Christian burial, but Heinke thought they ought to take the corpse on to the camp and let an officer make the final decision. Yates wanted to go on the way Hull had proposed and make a grave for her in the woods. Lacey sided with Heinke. Cahill wasn't so sure, not that he disagreed about the burial, but he didn't like the idea of riding back to camp in the wagon with the corpse. Despite its wrappings, its odor was very evident.

"Stinking or not," Heinke said, "we got to take her with us. Might be there's something on her will tell who she is so's somebody can get in touch with her kin. You want to search her here, or let a surgeon do it?"

Nobody wanted to examine the corpse. They agreed to take it back and let an officer deal with the problem.

Hull didn't care, as long as they got away from the house before somebody discovered the child in the cupboard. Really ought to let her out before he left, he thought. At least open the latch so she'd be able to get herself out.

Patting a pocket, he started for the door. "You fellers load her up. I'll be right back. I've left my tobaccer in there somewhere."

"Wait a minute," Heinke snapped. "You and Lacey found her. *You* load her up while me and Yates get Cahill on board."

"But my tobaccer—"

"Forget your damned tobaccer. I'll give you a chaw of mine. Let's get the hell going before she gets any riper."

Hull started to argue, but if he did they might begun wondering if there was something more than just a lost plug he wanted from in the house. Sucking breath between his teeth, he glanced up, as if he hoped to see through walls and floor into the bedroom, into the cupboard. There was nothing he could do about it. Not lest he wanted to risk losing the jewel, and maybe his hide.

Sighing, he turned to help Lacey gather up the bundled corpse and heft it into the wagon bed.

Despite the pain in his ankle, Cahill refused to ride in the back, so they manhandled him up into Yates' place on the seat. Heinke swung up next to him and slapped the mules into motion. The others fell in behind.

Hull fought the urge to look back. The skin felt drawn taut around his ears. He could hear a jay squawking somewhere in the trees. And something else. A faint pounding—as of small hands hammering against a cupboard door? Or was it only the blood beating in his ears?

Thrusting a hand into his pocket, he clutched the jewel. What was done was done, he told himself. Think about what he was going to do, when he'd turned that do-pretty into cold hard cash. Hell, she was only a damned Secesh whelp, anyway. What did it matter what happened to her?

For a man with coin to clink, there was always liquor to be had somewhere among the troops. Hull had the coin. He got himself thoroughly drunk that night, and again the next. The lieutenant had to know about the liquor, but he was no deacon. As long as his men did their job and didn't make trouble for him, he didn't make trouble for them. Despite the intensity of his hangovers, Hull manage to do his job. With the aid of the whiskey, he managed to wash the unwanted memories into far dark corners of his mind.

From the time they'd taken Atlanta, there'd been very little fighting, mainly brief skirmishes with militia. They found fresh earthworks near Ogeechee Church, but the Rebs had abandoned them instead of making a stand. Savannah, though, proved fortified and defended. General Sherman himself had ridden out a railroad cut for a look and almost got his head knocked off by a Rebel cannonball. So the army encamped, eating rice and tearing up railroad track, while Hazen led the 15th Corps down the Ogeechee River and captured Fort McAllister.

Union ships began bringing supplies up the river to the army, and the engineers got busy providing roads to haul them on. There was a little skirmishing and some artillery fire on both sides, but nothing serious. It began to look like Sherman was planning to settle in for the winter and starve the Rebs out of Savannah.

Then, a few days before Christmas, a buggy full of aldermen came driving out from Savannah to surrender the city. Recognizing that a stand would be futile, the Reb troops had stretched pontoon bridges across the river and evacuated up an old plank road on the South Carolina side. So Sherman's forces marched into Savannah with their muskets over their shoulders.

Off duty at last, Hull, Dayton, Lacey, and Thorne drifted together to the waterfront. Savannah sat atop a high bluff overlooking the river. Wharves and warehouses lined the street at the foot of the bluff. Where there was shipping, and much coming and going, there were always places where a man with hard money could get a decent cup of whiskey, a game of chance, and the kind of company a soldier wanted after long months of campaigning. It didn't take long to find one.

Chuck-a-luck was Hull's game and luck was with him, or maybe the dark-eyed young waiter-woman who brought drinks at his beck brought him luck as well. In no time at all, he had doubled his money.

The thrill of the winning and the whiskey burned in his veins. When the dice turned against him, he thought it was only a momentary setback, and he bet with all the more furor. It was like a fever, growing hotter and hotter. The more he lost, the more he bet.

He called for the waiter-woman to bring the bottle and stay by his side while he rolled the dice. He didn't notice when Thorne disappeared upstairs with one of the female waiters, or when Dayton disappeared with another. When Lacey tried to pull him away from the board, he only cursed, emptied his glass, and went on playing.

This time the dice paid him. With a whoop of joy, certain his luck was back, he swept his winnings to his side of the board. The waiter-woman refilled his glass and took payment from the coins piled in front of him. He didn't notice how much she took. Lacey watched another throw. Hull won again. Shaking his head sadly, Lacey left.

As the night wore on, other players left, until only three soldiers and two civilians remained at the table. Again, the dice turned against Hull. The pile of coins before him dwindled. His gold three-dollar pieces were gone. His coppers followed, one after another until every cent he'd had was gone. The hell of it was that he felt certain—absolutely certain—that his luck would come back with the next roll. But without something to bet, there would be no next roll. And no trip upstairs with the dark-eyed waiter-woman.

It wasn't until he'd awakened the next day, sad and sober, that Hull remembered the ruby lavaliere. It was rolled up in a rag, stitched inside his jacket, waiting for him to return north again, to a prosperous place where he could find someone with hard money enough to pay him what it was worth. But he still had the feeling his luck was waiting on just one more roll of the dice. He had to lay hands on some coin somehow.

There was a way. He pondered it a while. He didn't know Savannah, and he didn't trust the Secesh. Slaves, though, were grateful to the army that had freed them. Some of them were so grateful they volunteered for the Pioneer Corps. That seemed a likely place to get the information he wanted.

A broad-shouldered buck who had been a stevedore knew where to find the pawnbroker with which his former owner had done business.

The place the freedman directed him to was a ramshackle wooden cottage that looked as old as the city. There was a brick warehouse crowding it on one side without quite touching it. On the other side, weeds were overgrowing the charred timbers of a building long gone. Rats scrabbled in the weeds.

The windows of the house were shuttered. The roof sagged over the meager porch and the single chimney leaned at a precarious angle. In the long winter twilight, the place looked abandoned.

Memories Hull had pushed away stirred like waking snakes in the shadowy corners of his mind. He fought them back, refusing to recognize them, but the feeling of them squirmed coldly down his spine as he approached the house. His steps slowed. The chill within him whispered that this couldn't be the right place. Nobody with hard money would live in such a place, he thought. Nobody with any choice would. Plantation slaves had better cabins than this.

As he stood pondering, a twist of smoke rose from the chimney. Somebody was inside. Maybe somebody who could tell him where to find the pawnbroker. He stepped up onto the porch. Boards groaned under his weight. As he reached out to knock, the door opened. A man who looked as old as the house peered out at him.

Startled, he backstepped.

"Don' worry, yankee. I don' bite." The old man's words were misshapen, his voice hardly more than a rattling in his throat.

He grinned, lips drawing back from barren gums. "Wha' you want here?"

"I'm looking for a Mr. Hornbeck," Hull said. "Can you tell me where to find him?"

"Wha' you want with him?"

"Business."

"Who sent you?" He snapped the words out like an officer giving orders.

Automatically, Hull answered. "Cap'n Jarrett's Willy."

The old man gazed at him from shadowed hollows like empty eye sockets. "You know Jarrett?"

"I know Willy. He's joined the Pioneers."

"A better man than Jarrett," the old man mumbled. He stepped back, opening the door wider. "Come on inside."

Hull looked past him into a room lit only by a small hearth fire. Doubtfully, he said, "Hornbeck's here?"

"Better man than you, too," the old man added under his breath. Aloud, he said, "Who the devil do you think you're talkin' to?"

"You're Hornbeck?"

"I ain't gonna live forever. Come inside and state your business, or go 'way and leave me have my supper while I'm still spry enough to swaller it."

Hull thrust a hand into his pocket. His fingers located his Barlow knife and closed around it. Wishing he had his musket with him, he stepped inside.

Hornbeck lit a lamp and turned the flame high. That was a lot better. Hull glanced around. There seemed to be only the one room, and some kind of loft reached by a ladder. He saw a small bed behind the ladder and a comfortable-looking chair drawn up near the fire. Two side chairs faced each other across a table in front of the hearth. The walls were lined with sideboards, cupboards, chests and cabinets, no two alike. Unless somebody was hiding in one of them, Hornbeck was alone. Hull's grip on the knife eased a bit.

Hornbeck had been cooking something over the hearth. He swung the pothook out to clear the fire, then opened a sideboard and took out a bottle. He set it and a pair of glasses on the table.

Hull watched him pour. The golden brown whiskey shimmered invitingly in the lamplight. With a gesture, Hornbeck told him to help himself.

He picked up a glass and tasted the whiskey. It was the smooth, rich, sipping kind, but Hull took a long deep swallow. The heat of it in his throat thawed the chill in his spine.

"Sit down," Hornbeck said, seating himself at the table. "Show me what you've got."

Hull reached into his jacket and brought out the rag-wrapped bundle. Peeling back the rags, he sat the lavaliere on the table in front of him.

The admiration and pure greed that flashed in Hornbeck's eyes was as bright as the reflected lamplight that flashed in the ruby's heart. The old man reached out bony fingers and closed them gently on the lavaliere. He held it close to his face, studying it, turning it to catch the light. Softly, he asked, "For sale or pawn?"

"Pawn," Hull said. "How much?"

Hornbeck eyed him as intently as he'd studied the lavaliere. Setting it down on the table, he replied, "Ten dollars."

Hull snatched it. "You're crazy!"

"Gold," Hornbeck added.

"Willy told me you were fair!" Hull said as he started up from his seat. His fists clenched. He had a mind to show this old man what he thought of the offer.

Hornbeck shook his head. "I'm not fair. I'm hones'."

"Huh?"

"You take tha' to some other pawnbroker, maybe he'll offer you as much as a third of what it's worth, and when you go back for it maybe he and it will be gone the devil knows where. You wanna pawn it, you can be sure I'll keep it as long as we agree on, and I'll give it back to you for the amount we agree on. Tha's hones'. You *are* plannin' on comin' back for it, ain't you?"

"Damn right I am! I'll be back for it tomorrow."

"Then take wha' I offer. The less you take, the less it'll cost you to get it back."

Hull had never looked at it that way. It made a kind of sense. But ten dollars just didn't seem like enough, even in gold. As he thought about it, he emptied the whiskey glass.

"You know another hones' pawnbroker in Savannah?" Horn-beck asked as he refilled it.

Hull had to admit to himself that he didn't. He thought some more and drank some more. Finally, he said, "Fifty dollars."

"I thought you said you'd be comin' back for it."

"I will."

"You go spend fifty dollars now, tha's—wha'?—near four months pay for you? Where you gonna get the money to pay me back?"

"How much you gonna charge me for the pawn?"

"Quarter a month."

"Quarter-eagle?" Hull said, thinking that wasn't so bad.

"Quarter the amount," Hornbeck told him. "If I was to len' you fifty—which I ain't gonna do—you'd owe me sixty-two and a half dollars nex' month."

"You sure ain't fair!"

"If I only len' you ten, all you'll owe me nex' month is twelve and a half."

The old man was right. Still, ten dollars just didn't seem like enough. Hull said so.

Hornbeck shrugged.

Feeling put upon, Hull said, "Forty?"

Hornbeck filled his glass again and waited until he'd drunk from it before speaking. "You said you'd come back for it tomorruh?"

"Yeah."

"I'll make a deal with you, sodjer. I'll len' you twen'y-five in gold and you come back with it tomorruh, like you say, I won't charge you nothin' for the loan. But if you don't come back for it tomorra, that pretty red do-pretty is all mine."

That wasn't fair either, Hull thought. But the confidence in him was as strong and warm as the whiskey he'd drunk. He didn't doubt luck would be with him at the dice table. He said, "You'll give me a paper says all that?"

"I surely will."

They drank to the agreement. Then Hornbeck sent Hull to wait on the porch. Hull took the lavaliere with him. After a few minutes, Hornbeck came to the door and put six coins into Hull's outstretched hand. Four quarter-eagles and three half-eagles. He waited patiently while Hull tested each with his teeth.

Satisfied the coins really were gold, Hull gave over the lavaliere and Hornbeck gave him the receipt.

It was full dark and turning cold by the time Hull reached the gambling house. Half a dozen of his friends were already there, at the board. They looked surprised to see him. Even more surprised when he put a quarter-eagle on the table.

"Where you been?" Lacey asked him.

Dayton asked, "Where'd you get that?"

"Foraging," Hull said with a grin.

The others laughed.

The civilian who had the dice cup looked down at the coin, up at Hull, then off to one side. In a moment, the dark-eyed waiter-woman appeared at Hull's side with a drink.

Just as he'd anticipated, Hull won on the first toss of the dice. And the second. And again. His luck was back, just the way he'd known it would be. He was sure of it. Exuberantly, he downed his drink and called for another.

On the fourth roll, he lost, but on the fifth he won again. Well, a man couldn't expect to win *every* time, no matter how good his luck was.

The luck stayed with him until the pile of coins in front of him was glittering with gold. With such luck, he ought to buy a partnership in a gambling house instead of a saloon, he thought. The way he was raking in the money, he wouldn't have to settle for a partnership. With all this money *and* the lavaliere, he could have a whole business for himself.

When the waiter-woman brought another drink, he wrapped his arm around her waist and pulled her close, rubbing his cheek against her hip. Warm and soft and so good-smelling. He felt like running her upstairs right that minute. But the clank of money drew his attention back to the chuck-a-luck board.

The woman stayed there until he was ready for another drink. When she walked away, it was like she took his luck with her. The dice turned against him. He called her back, but that didn't help. His heap of coins was shrinking fast.

The faster it went, the harder he bet. He cursed and pushed

the woman away. He wanted no distraction. He had to win back
the gold. He had to have twenty-five dollars when he left the
table—it wasn't just a little money riding on the dice—it was a
ruby lavaliere—it was his saloon—his future.

Breathing hard, sweating, his eyes were intent on the board,
the coins, the dice. He watched the civilian's long sharp fingers
rake up the coins that should have been his—that had been his
moments before.

Again. And again.

And then there were no coins left. Nothing.

But the feeling was there, the certainty that he could win on
the next roll. That he *would* win. His luck had to come back.
His mistake had been sending the waiter-woman away, he
thought. He'd been lucky when she was at his side, hadn't he?

Desperately, he looked around for his friends he might be able
to borrow from. They were gone.

His money was gone. His glass was empty. Even the waiter-
woman was gone.

He turned to the nearest man in Federal blue. They were
comrades in arms, weren't they? A long way from home, among
strangers, among enemies. They had to stick together, didn't
they? Surely the soldier would help out a fellow with a small
loan. Just a few cents.

The soldier only laughed.

He asked another and got shoved away, called a *stinking
drunk*.

As he started toward a third, a civilian in shirtsleeves laid a
hand on his arm. "Friend, I think it's time for you to get back
to camp."

"I jus' need a few coppers," Hull whined, "jus' len' me enough
to get back in the game. I'll win nex' time. I know I will."

"You stop pesterin' the payin' customers. Go get some more
money somewheres else if you wanna get back in the game," the
civilian told him.

"But—"

"Now you go on." The man's fingers tightened on his arm,
digging in, hurting. Hull realized then that the man was as big
as Lacey, and probably as strong. Likely he could crush bone

with those fingers. Still pleading, he let himself be led to the door. The man gave him a shove and slammed the door behind him.

As he started down the steps, his foot slipped and suddenly he was tumbling, slamming face-first into the cobbled walk. He lay still, his mouth filling with the salt taste of blood, his face filled with pain.

When he finally pulled himself up, he realized he was shivering. Realized it was cold. Very cold. And very dark.

There was a lamp flickering at the corner. He staggered toward it. As he passed the protection of the corner building, a damp ugly wind hit him, cutting through his field jacket. Felt like the blood that seeped from his nose was freezing in his moustache. Wasn't supposed to get so cold in the South, was it? But there was ice skinned over the puddles in the gutters. Have to watch his step. He pressed a hand against the wall to steady himself. Had to think. Needed money. Had to get that lavaliere back.

He remembered Hornbeck's shack. The old man had been alone there. Not even a dog. Nothing there but a shriveled up old man and a ruby lavaliere. And a lot of money hid somewhere. Old bastard had no business asking a quarter a month for a loan. Damn thief. Would serve him right if he got foraged.

But where the hell was the shack? Which direction was which? He'd turned the corner and got turned around somehow. The stars were no help. A black sky was bellied down on the treetops, not blinking so much as a single star.

Wind'd be off the river, wouldn't it? Felt like it. The shack had been near the river. He headed into the wind.

As he walked, his mind drifted. On a long march a man could learn to sleep after a fashion while he was walking. Not really sleep, but an unawareness that was close to it.

Suddenly he realized he wasn't walking into the wind any longer. There was icy rain in the wind now, and he had his back to it. He had been drifting like an animal ahead of a blizzard.

Where the hell was he?

It was too dark to tell. Felt like grass under his feet. That didn't help much. Savannah was full of grassy squares. He hunkered down. Shielding it against the wind with his body, he struck a sulphur match. It flared just long enough for him to glance around, then sputtered out.

In that quick glance, he'd seen odd shapes. Low shapes. Upright slabs. Low structures. He struck another match.

Goddamn!

Tombstones. He was in a graveyard.

He felt a sudden shivering down his spine, as if snakes were squirming through it. Snakes of memory refused by the mind.

But a graveyard was no different from a field after battle, except there was dirt and markers over the dead, he told himself. He'd had truck enough with the dead in the past. He didn't fear them now. Fact was, the dead had done well by him. It was a dead woman who'd given him the lavaliere.

Remembering that, he remembered the little girl telling him her grandma had been buried wearing even finer jewels. He didn't want to remember the child. But the jewels. That was worth thinking about. He'd heard tales of grave-robbers finding gold rings on corpses. No telling what the dead of Savannah got buried wearing.

He figured this was the same graveyard he'd seen by daylight a few days before. An old place, going back to Colonial times. Not everybody in it had been buried under six feet of dirt. Some were in brick vaults.

Dead people lived good around here, he thought. The vaults were bigger than a dog tent and sure to be a lot snugger in foul weather. If anybody was to get buried wearing fancy jewelry, seemed likely it'd be the people in those vaults. If a man could get into one, no telling what he'd find.

He tried lighting another match, but the weather-damp head crumbled when he struck it. Only two matches left in the case. Best not waste them. Moving cautiously in the darkness, he groped for stone. His fingers numbed quickly in the icy wind. The rain had soaked his uniform. His whole body was going numb. But the thought of the ruby kept him going.

He found a vault by blundering into it, hitting his thigh against a corner so abruptly that it sent him sprawling. Mumbling under his breath, he got himself up and began examining the structure with his hands. It was a low brick enclosure with a slab of marble for a top. From the weathered roughness of the marble, it was old. He gripped the top and pulled. Heavy. He pulled again. It still wouldn't move. He got down on one knee and tried pushing up on it. Too damned heavy. He couldn't budge it at all.

Sitting back on his heels, he pondered the situation. Had to be some way to get the damn thing open. If he couldn't get the top off, maybe he could get in from the side.

He ran his hands over the bricks. The mortar between them crumbled into sand under his fingers. Hunting the Barlow knife from his pocket, he began to pick at the mortar.

It didn't take long. The brick he was working at began to wobble. He slammed it with the heel of his fist. It clattered into the vault, taking others with it. A dank scent of mildew gusted from the hole.

Eagerly, he clawed at the remaining bricks, pulling loose one then another, until the hole felt large enough for a man to squeeze through. Suddenly cautious, he paused. Cold rain trickled down his collar. Shivering, he struck another match. Sheltered in the hole, it kept its flame long enough for him to look in.

There was no coffin, just a heap of debris. For a miserable moment, he thought the vault had been empty. Then, even as the match was flickering out, he recognized a scattering of rotting wood and a few pieces of age-grayed bone in the debris.

The icy feeling of snakes squirmed along his spine again. But the image in his mind was a ruby bright as fire, burning away all thought, all fear. Dropping the matchstick, he wriggled through the opening he'd made.

Inside, he tried to sit up. His head hit the marble slab. Well, at least he was out of the rain, out of the wind. Propped on an elbow, he groped for the pieces of wood he'd seen. Identifying them by touch, he made a small pile of them, then struck his final match. The rotten wood was dry. It took flame readily, filling the vault with flickering light.

At last able to see what he was doing, Hull began scratching through the debris. Something round like a coin—but it was only a pewter button. He threw it on the fire. A piece of metal, evidently a coffin plate, was green with corrosion, the name eaten away. Another button. Bits of bone. A shred of rotted fabric. Broken pieces of brick. More wood.

He added the wood to his fire and continued his hunt.

Then there was no more wood and the fire was burning low. His fingers ached. He realized they were bleeding. And he'd found nothing.

The flame guttered out.

The darkness was not total. That puzzled Hull. Twisting, he turned himself within the narrow vault to face the entrance he'd made. Through it he could see a dim light. The moon had come out, he thought. That'd mean the icy rain was over. Moving closer, he peered through the hole.

The light was strange. Dim and misty, like a thin fog lying over the graveyard. There was no wind, only a silent stillness as unnatural as the light. Was it the stillness before a storm? he wondered. At least he had shelter inside the vault. Maybe he ought to stay the night there. No, he had to get hold of some money somewhere and get back the ruby.

The light was confusing. Nothing looked quite right. He thought he saw movement from the corner of an eye, but when he looked that way, there was only a tombstone.

Was it just a trick of the light? He hesitated, gazing out of the vault.

Another glimpsed motion, another tombstone.

Then he saw a furtive shape that darted from shadow to shadow.

He didn't believe in ghosts. Hell, no! It had to be something else. A grave-robber, he decided. Slowly, he grinned. The robber ought to know what grave was worth looking into. Let the robber do the work, then take his loot from him. That'd be easier than busting open vaults himself until he found the right one.

Wait! There was more than one of them.

His grin faded. More than one, more than two. It began to look as if someone was hidden in every shadow, behind every tombstone. A whole damned army of them.

Was the one he'd just glimpsed wearing a kepi? Was that a musket in the hand of the one disappearing behind a tombstone?

Oh Lord, he thought, could it be the Rebs hadn't evacuated the city? Had they just hid out? Were they massing here now to take Sherman's men by surprise? What if they found him? One lone Yankee without even his musket. What chance would he have?

His eyes seemed to be adjusting to the weird light. He could see a group of them in the shadow of a live oak. Vague shapes, shadows within a shadow. One leaning on a musket. No, not a musket. It was a crutch. Another with a bandaged head. Another with a crutch. Another in bandages.

They were coming out of the shadows, and he could see more bandages. Tattered clothes. Limping figures supported by their companions.

He sighed with relief. Not an attacking army, but walking wounded. Lame and halt, moving slowly, coming closer to where he lay hidden.

Then he saw the smallness of them. Not a man of them looked full grown. He frowned in puzzlement. A whole troop of drummer boys wounded in battle? Closer yet, and he saw more were too small even for drummers. And drummer boys didn't wear bonnets. Yes, there were girls among them, in ragged skirts, some with bandaged heads or arms or leaning on crutches like the boys. Some missing arms or legs or—God help him—was that one without a head?

They came on, and he could see their faces. White faces, and black faces, and every shade between. Round faces and gaunt faces. Hollow cheeks and hollow eyes. Eyes that gazed into the darkness, seeing into the darkness, into the vault. Staring at him where he lay. Staring at the tomb he had desecrated.

Suddenly he understood. Not from within himself. There was nothing within him capable of such understanding. It was as if they were putting it into his mind, silently, wordlessly, giving him comprehension.

They were the Third Nation—neither Union nor Confederate. The ones too young to have a say in the choosing of sides and the making of war. The ones brought into life and torn from it by acts not their own. Lives unfulfilled, bled away by shot and shell, seared away by untreated fevers and in burning buildings, shriveled by hunger and disease.

The lost children. The murdered children.

She stepped forward, a scrawny, dirty-faced towhead, her filthy rumpled dress flounced with tattered lace and holes in stockings that looked like silk.

He tried to speak, to beg, to tell her he was sorry; he'd really wanted to go back and let her out of the cupboard. But his throat was like ice and his breath a knot in his chest.

She took another step toward him.

He shrunk back into the vault. On his belly. Squirming away from her. Until he was against the wall and could go no farther.

He could no longer see her face, or anything else except the entrance hole he'd made into the vault. He could see only the light beyond the hole, the strange thin light like a luminous fog lying against the ragged opening.

Suddenly darkness bit a chunk from the rough circle of light. Then another. And another.

He realized they were replacing the bricks. Sealing the hole. And he knew, without even trying, that this time the mortar would not crumble under his knife.

Beast

George Alec Effinger

The New Orleans Science Fiction Fantasy Festival traditionally includes a panel on baseball. Some years, the panelists discuss relevant works like *Field of Dreams* and *The Natural,* but mostly we sit around and swap baseball stories. So far as I know, I'm the only person who regularly attends SF conventions to have covered a major league baseball game as a member of the working press, but even that rather substantial credential is insignificant when compared to the dedication to baseball of George Alec Effinger.

George has been a fan of the Cleveland Indians since he was seven years old, which not so coincidentally is the last time the Indians qualified for post-season play. Thirty-seven years have passed, with George's faith unshaken by the Indians' propensity for last place finishes. For the 1991 panel, George showed up wearing a Cleveland Indians uniform and recounted how, in the final days of the original Comiskey Park, he had flown to Chicago for a one-night trip—not because it was an Indians game, or because he had switched allegiances to the White Sox—but simply because he was unable to stand the thought that this was his final chance to see a game at Comiskey before the old stadium was turned into a parking lot. Although everyone on the panel had a deep love of baseball, no one could equal George's story.

The other great love of George's life is the City of New Orleans. He's lived there for more than twenty years, and much of his best writing shows the influences of the city. George resides in the French Quarter, and you can find many of the places there futuristically recreated in his much acclaimed Budayeen series.

The first of those novels, *When Gravity Fails,* was a major break-through, gaining widespread recognition in places that rarely review science fiction.

George notes that he was the first person to lose the Hugo, the Nebula, and the Campbell awards, and that his luck in winning awards hasn't been much since, either. All that notwithstanding, it was at age twenty-seven that George became the youngest person to win the South's Phoenix Award for career achievement. In 1989, he swept the Hugo, Nebula, and Theodore Sturgeon awards in short fiction for his novelette "Schrödinger's Kitten."

The effects of the brief reign of Benjamin Butler over the Crescent City can still be seen today. The story here is speculative. The history it encompasses is regrettably true.

Maj Genl B. F. Butler	Headquarters of the Army
U.S. Army	February 23d 1862

General
You are assigned to the command of the land forces destined to co-operate with the Navy in the attack upon New Orleans. You will use every means to keep your destination a profound secret, even from your staff officers, with the exception of your chief of staff, and Lt Weitzel of the Engineers . . .

Very Respectfully Your Obt Sevt
Geo B McClellan
Maj Genl Comdg USA

"Imagine a night, a soft night, a pleasant night, rather like this one but twenty-six years ago," said Thomas A. Newell, who in 1862 had been a lieutenant in the United States Army, the personal orderly of Major General Benjamin Franklin Butler. Not long after the New Orleans affair, he and Butler had parted ways, and Newell ended up a major in the Quartermaster Corps under Montgomery Meigs. Now he was a handsome man just on the far side of middle age, with black hair and mustache going gray. Newell still showed the posture that is learned only in the military.

"The temperature that night is as warm as this evening," he said, "but not oppressively hot. The humidity is high, as it almost always is in New Orleans. It's a clear and cloudless night, and the stars beam brightly, calmly. It's as if we all weren't caught up in the bloody horrors of the War of the Southern Rebellion."

"That was more than a quarter of a century ago," I said, poking at one of the late-season boiled crawfish on the plate before me. "Back then I was considerably younger, and growing up in Manchester, England. I just don't remember—"

Major Newell's gaze strayed across the street, across the square. "Mr. Pannell, everyone here who's old enough *remembers,*" he said in a soft voice. Newell stopped speaking for a moment and swallowed generously from the mug of beer at his elbow. We sat in one of the many public houses along Decatur Street, and from his perspective the retired major had an excellent view of the *Place d'Armes,* now more frequently known as Jackson Square.

"Does all this have to do with the 'Spoons' business?" I asked.

"No," he said. The wrinkles at the corners of his bright blue eyes deepened. "The nickname of 'Spoons' came along sometime early during the occupation. All the society ladies were certain that Major General Butler was making off with what was left of their silverware, and raiding the silver pieces from churches. As far as I was concerned, I never saw him steal any silverware; yet to this day if you asked anyone in town who Spoons was, the answer would be, 'Oh, yeah, Goddamn Butler, damn him to hell.' "

"It sounds as if everyone had his own strong opinion about him."

"That's a thing you have to understand about General Butler," said Major Newell. "He never seemed to grasp that New Orleans presented its own peculiar problem. The city was originally settled by well-to-do French and Spanish colonists, who became the great Creole families that rule New Orleans society to this day. Those French and Spanish chose to live on this, the downriver side of the growing city. Canal Street, for all its beauty and the excellence of its shops, was a line of demarcation between the

Creoles and the 'Americans,' who arrived in the city in great numbers during the last century.

"The Creoles will still have nothing to do with the Americans, whom they consider barbarians and who, when they first came to New Orleans from Tennessee and Kentucky and elsewhere, probably *were*. General Butler was given the task of taking the port of New Orleans for the Union, and then governing it. He had some little trouble with both."

Major Newell stopped to drink some more beer, and the bartender refilled the mug. I took the opportunity to steer him back to the main subject. "Please remember, Major Newell," I said, "I'm an Englishman residing in the States, working as a stringer for a British newspaper. My time here in New Orleans is very limited. I have a deadline from my paper, which is spending a great deal of money to learn whether or not there might be some connection between your murders in 1862 and Bloody Jack's work in London of late. Surely you've heard of the Ripper over here. There are a lot of similarities, you know."

"I've heard about him a million times," said Newell, suppressing a yawn. He would get to this matter—and others besides—but only in his own reminiscent way. I didn't care about Butler's first Negro Union troops; how his behavior affected the delicate negotiations with the European powers; how, after the war, he returned to Massachusetts a glorious hero; and how he became a Radical Republican, waving the bloody shirt and blaming the South for starting the war, an issue with little meaning compared to the dilemmas it produced.

"In any event," Newell said, refreshed, "I was speaking about one particular night. One of the things he'd done that had infuriated the local citizenry was to abandon as his headquarters the U.S. Customs House on Canal Street, and take over the entire grand and magnificent St. Charles Hotel, not far uptown from Canal Street.

"He'd done this for petty and childish reasons—he'd wanted to use parlor P, his favorite, to entertain some local military and political acquaintances. He was told the parlor was already in use by a number of other gentlemen. Butler grew irrationally angry and ordered down a rattling charge of an artillery regiment

from nearby Tivoli Circle—now Lee Circle. Butler comman-
deered the entire grand, elegant hotel, directing the artillery
pieces toward the crowd of civilians who had gathered around
the hotel to see what he'd do. He ordered the artillery to fire
on the civilians if they didn't cease their loud complaints.

"Much later that night, well after midnight, he'd unintention-
ally awakened me. He was dressing in civilian clothes; he always
did this whenever he took one of his late-night excursions. I
suppose he didn't want to be recognized so near one of the most
elegant hotels in all of America, to which he'd promptly moved
our headquarters from the unfinished Customs House. He'd
claimed the best bars, taprooms, and restaurants in the city for
the sole use of himself, his staff, and his military, political, and
commercial cronies.

" 'Restless tonight, sir?' I called from my new quarters in the
hotel, near enough to his to be available at a moment's notice,
should he require something of me during the day or night.

" 'It's all right, Newell. You'll get used to my insomniac ways.
I just need to take in some of the night air, and then I'll be fine.
You may go back to sleep.'

" 'Sir,' I said, 'if you don't mind, I'd like to walk with you.'

"General Butler only shrugged and waited for me to complete dressing in my uniform. He couldn't be said to present
an impressive figure of a man. The most frequent—and print-
able—description of him in the newspapers was 'walrus-like.'
He was bald, with very obviously crossed eyes, a droopy little
brown mustache, and the kind of sizable paunch that lets you
decide that Butler didn't spend his spare hours doing anything
more strenuous than carefully catching a kickback when it was
offered to him.

"Butler was what they then called a 'political general.' He'd
been a crafty lawyer and a politician in Massachusetts, and his
loyalties swung in precisely the same directions as the Federal
temperament. At one of the two 1860 Democratic conventions to
choose a candidate to oppose Lincoln, Butler was a pro-slavery
Democrat, and voted on fifty-seven consecutive ballots to nomi-
nate Jefferson Davis as president of the United States.

"One would expect a political general to be incompetent.

Most were. Butler, however, showed some early promise; a military historian would be forced to declare him 'at least adequate.' Not while he was in New Orleans, however, and not thereafter.''

Newell stopped to swallow some more beer, and I took advantage of the break to get back to my own agenda of questions. "There was a series of murders while Butler governed the town, wasn't there?"

Newell's eyebrows raised and he nodded. "And vicious murders they were, too. I was present at the examination of three of the bodies." He shuddered, this man who had seen so much warfare and death.

Newell and I finished our crawfish and beer, and I paid the bill. Decatur Street had in earlier times been named Clay Street and *rue de la Levée,* and there had been quite a few more changes since the old days. For instance, Jackson Square was now a pleasant place for an evening's walk; back in 1862, during the time he served with Major General Butler, Lieutenant Newell probably saw the square filled with the tents of Union soldiers sweating and suffering in the heart of the French Quarter. Not all the changes had been for the better—in those days, you could gaze across Clay Street from the square to the rolling Mississippi River. Since then, some misguided entrepreneurs had shut off what must have been a pleasant view by building unsightly and decaying warehouses and wharves.

Newell and I sat on a bench in the park and listened to a street performer render the popular tunes of the day on his cornet.

"Our troubles were twenty-six years ago," said Newell thoughtfully. "Old Butler is still alive in Massachusetts, I'm sure, but I doubt that he's guilty of much more than being a windy Northern elder statesman. The likelihood of there being any connection to the current London horrors—"

I waved a hand, knowing that Butler was a judge in the state of Massachusetts, although given to prolonged absences from the bench. He was, of course, an old man now. "It doesn't really matter if there's a connection or not, so long as the *Manchester Morning Examiner* is willing to pay my expenses for a few days to get your views and to spend some time in this most European of American cities."

"Well," said the major, "I suppose you—that is, the *Manchester Morning Examiner*—could afford to tap another keg for us. I used to have a favorite hole-in-the-wall not far this way along Chartres Street. I have great hope that it's still doing business. Wait until you see what they make the waitresses wear!"

"One of the delights I indulge in now and then when there's a bit of spare cash," I said, letting Newell take the lead, and hoping that the waitresses' outfits hadn't gone the way of so many other antique curiosities he'd pointed out to me, their former occupants now long vanished.

It was safely oyster season in some sawdust-floored places along Chartres Street, and I was going to test my new friend's mettle. I felt that I'd easily passed his crawfish test. Of course, he'd had almost a year, in 1862, to get used to both raw and baked bivalves. Oysters in all forms shouldn't present him any difficulty.

Peacefully and pleasantly, Major Newell and I walked slowly among the early-blooming crape myrtle trees and shrubs of Jackson Square. "How well I remember this place," said Newell. "One of the first times Butler walked through here, he made me stop and examine the imposing equestrian statue of Andrew Jackson. Its horse's two front legs pawed the air, Jackson himself held his cocked hat aloft and he looked fierce forever.

" 'You know, Newell,' said the major general on that first occasion, 'there's something wrong with that statue, something missing.' He gave it a few days' thought, then at last in his oratorical voice, he declared the rearing horse and its heroic rider wouldn't be perfectly suited to Butler's liking unless the words THE UNION MUST AND SHALL BE PRESERVED were carved into the granite base. He didn't bother to ask any of the local residents or merchants how this purely Yankee slogan would fit with their common attitudes, or with the seething anger that surrounded what some local Creoles still referred to as the

Place d'Armes. Butler went ahead and gave the orders for the Federal sentiment to be added immediately."

Headquarters Department of the Gulf
New Orleans, May 15, 1862

General Order Number 28.

As the officers and soldiers of the United States have been subject to repeated insults from the women calling themselves ladies of New Orleans, in return for the most scrupulous non-interference and courtesy on our part, it is ordered that hereafter when any female shall, by word, gesture, or movement, insult or show contempt for any officer or soldier of the United States, she shall be regarded and held liable to be treated as a woman of the town, plying her avocation.
By command of
Major-General Butler
Geo. C. Strong, *A. A. G., Chief of Staff.*

The oysters had gone down without resistance, just as easily as the boiled crawfish had—I'd visited the Gulf Coast states often enough that oysters were no new thing to me—and it took all my journalist's skill to keep Major Newell amused and entertained long enough for me to get the facts I needed from him.

The problem was that Newell hadn't visited the Crescent City since he'd been reassigned when Butler was removed, late in 1862, until long telegrams to him had set up this meeting. Everything was vaguely familiar to him, yet tantalizingly different. He was reliving a part of his younger days, and I didn't have time for that. I had to entrust my story to the good ship *Miss Eileen Brant,* which sailed in only four days. I had to come up with an angle for my story soon.

There is said to be an order from Butler, turning over the woman of New Orleans to his soldiers! Then is the measure of his iniquities filled.

We thought that generals always restrained by shot or sword, if need be, the brutal soldiery.

This hideous cross-eyed beast orders his men to treat the ladies of New Orleans as women of the town. To punish them, he says, for their insolence.

—The diaries of Mary Chesnut
May 21, 1862

New England's Butler, best known to us as Beast Butler, is famous or infamous now. His amazing order to his soldiers and comments on it are in everybody's mouth. We hardly expected from Massachusetts behavior to shame a Comanche.

—*Ibid.*
June 12, 1862

After New Orleans, those vain passionate impatient little Creoles were forever committing suicide, driven to it by despair and Beast Butler. As he read these things, Mr. Davis said, "If they want to die, why not kill Beast Butler—rid the world of their foe and be saved the trouble of murdering themselves?" However, that practical way of ending their intolerable burden did not seem to occur to them.

—*Ibid.*
February 16, 1865

"Hurry down here!" cried Newell in a particularly enthusiastic manner, down a dark, dank, intimidating alley that couldn't have been any more savory twenty-six years before, when the original murder occurred. I felt a shiver, but apparently Major Newell had no such qualms. He began sketching out the position and description of the corpse, and describing the crowd that had long ago assembled around him.

It was growing dark, and I was getting nervous about walking around in the maze of riverfront alleys and railyard outbuildings. I shrugged tiredly—it wasn't really important just how I felt at the moment—and I knew that I was in for a long explication from Major Newell. I paid close attention, though, because these were the details I was being paid so well to hear.

Naturally, twenty-six years later, no visible record of the horrible murder remained. Newell had thrown so many interesting facts, rumors, and anecdotes at me that I supposed it would take entire weeks to shape it all up into readable form. Unfortunately, I didn't have weeks to spare.

Newell waded through the foul-smelling trash in the alley. "Let me see: we found the first victim right here, among some broken wooden packing crates."

It didn't seem to me that the alley had improved in the slightest since the day of the first murder. "Anything remarkably unusual about the victim?" I asked.

"No," said Newell, thinking back. "A black woman, still clothed, beaten severely about the head and shoulders. My first thought, without evidence to support it, was that one or more males had dragged the victim into the alley, perhaps with robbery as a motive. Probably there were one or more forced-sex crimes committed, too, but I got very little cooperation or information from Sergeant Duffin of the City of New Orleans Police Department, who was sure that we were ruining whatever evidence remained for the local authorities to examine, as if the investigative units of the United States Army, Department of the Gulf, had no idea of what they were doing. The local Southern police and the Union forces rarely got along well. We had little cooperation from them."

"And the victim had no telltale slashes?"

"You can put that Jack the Ripper connection right out of your mind. It might make for an exciting evening's reading, but there's not much there for the serious student of true crime. Now walk with me up to the Canal Street entrance to the alley."

I didn't care if there weren't a connection, I thought. I'd make one, if need be.

There were many mazelike alleys between Conti Street and Canal Street. Most of the alleys were occupied by importers and land speculators, but one large walkway, Exchange Alley, was populated mostly by fencing masters, who gave lessons to the wealthy sons of the Creoles and the Americans. It was along Exchange Alley that Newell and I made our way.

"I'll tell you one thing that I forgot until later," said the retired officer, "and which I withheld from Sergeant Duffin. I was so astonished and appalled at finding the woman's corpse, I didn't realize that Major General Butler was no longer with me. I stopped at last and thought about our route, wondering where we'd become separated. We'd left the St. Charles Hotel and walked along Royal Street, browsing in the shop windows as the general liked to do now and then. Then we'd begun making our way back toward Canal Street, taking shortcuts through the alleys. Some of those alleys no longer exist, but Exchange Alley does, and it was along it that I realized Butler was no longer with me. It was then that I called for him, and began looking for him in some of the nearby and less pleasant alleys."

"How long was it before you found Major General Butler?" I asked.

"I heard him call me first, and he was back in Exchange Alley, standing over the body of the black woman, a look of disgust on his face. 'You see why we have to protect them,' he told me.

" 'I don't think there would have been anything we could've done to save her life.'

" 'Perhaps not,' he said. As I described, there was a look of disgust on his face, but no expression of concern or even sympathy. 'I'm going back to the hotel. You stay here and deal with the police when they come. I'm sure they'll be here soon.' Butler pressed some Union scrip into my hands. 'I'll go now,' he repeated. 'You've done an excellent job, Newell.' "

Even being a British journalist, I knew enough about American law to know that leaving the scene of a murder was a crime in itself. "You just let him go back to the St. Charles Hotel?" I asked.

"He was Major General Benjamin Butler," Newell replied. "You didn't tell him what to do, or even make suggestions to him." He took out a soft lead pencil and began sketching in the position of her body on the sidewalk. "Of course," he said in an off-hand way, "the crime was never solved."

I didn't ask why he had said "of course."

"Now come with me to Canal Street," said Newell. "It's less than two blocks from here."

Looking along Canal Street—where there wasn't a canal, by the way—to the south, we could see the Mississippi River.

"That's the scene of Butler's great triumph," said Newell, grinning. "The capture of the city of New Orleans. He'd been sent with about fifteen thousand men, and a naval detachment under the command of Captain Farragut, aided by Captain Porter, whose duty it would be to destroy by bombardment the forts that guarded the mouth of the Mississippi. Generals McClellan and Butler agreed that the city of New Orleans could not be captured unless and until those forts were destroyed.

"Well, Butler and his men waited and waited for Porter to shoot the two forts to pieces, but that never happened. Finally, fed up with trying to blast Forts Jackson and St. Philip, Farragut just slipped by them in the darkness and confusion. Later, for this exploit, Farragut was promoted to rear admiral. Anyway, when he passed the forts without a fight, he arrived at New Orleans, which promptly offered surrender to him. That wasn't the way it was supposed to happen. If you're familiar with McClellan's original orders, after Porter destroyed the forts, the way was supposed to be clear for Butler to capture the city. Instead, Farragut arrived first, and the city, knowing how things stood, took the first opportunity and surrendered to Farragut.

"A few days later, when Butler arrived, he was really angry. The great city of New Orleans, the guardian of the vastly strategic Mississippi River, was supposed to abandon itself to him, not the navy. So Butler insisted that New Orleans restage the entire surrender scene again, this time capitulating to him, the way it had been planned. So, even though New Orleans was already in Union hands, they had a whole new surrender ceremony, and Butler wrote it up and took credit for it.

"It didn't take long before 'Spoons' Butler, or 'Beast' Butler— the second was the name the citizens of New Orleans gave him after his General Order 28, the Woman Order—started getting himself deeper and deeper in trouble. In fact, Jefferson Davis, for whom Butler had campaigned so long and so hard, declared him an outlaw to be shot on sight."

The sun was coming up, and I had a lot of good information about Major General Benjamin Franklin Butler, but I still didn't have precisely what I wanted. I bid good-night to Thomas Newell and sought my bed in my small French Quarter hotel.

On the day before I got up to New Orleans a party of ruffians, headed by one Mumford, pulled down Farragut's flag, trailed it on the ground through the streets, tore it in pieces and distributed the pieces among the mob for keepsakes, their leader wearing a piece of it in the buttonhole of his coat as a boutonniere.

As we neared the city the next day the morning papers were brought to me on board the *Wissahickon* containing a description of this performance with high encomiums upon the bravery and gallantry of the man who did it. After having read the article, I handed the paper to Captain Smith and said: "I will hang that fellow whenever I catch him, and in such matters I always keep my intention."

I think a proper ending for this chapter, for the purpose of showing exactly how untruthfully and villainously Capt. David D. Porter behaved through this whole transaction of the capture and surrender of the forts, will be an extract from my official report written to the Secretary of War on the 1st day of June, the truth of no word of which for twenty-eight years was ever disputed, and then only by Porter in an interview in a newspaper, the authenticity of which he afterwards denied, and after I had put it before him as a statement of fact he never replied to it:—

—& etc.
Butler's Book
Benj. F. Butler
A. M. Thayer & Co.
Boston, 1892

"There was no more jealous, bitter man in the war than our Major General Butler," said Major Newell with a smile. We were eating breakfast in a small shop on Dauphine Street, near Canal. I was treating myself to calas—fried rice cakes—and Newel had ordered a kind of thick fried bread that was called *pain perdu,* or "lost bread." We were sharing both delicacies. I could feel the clock ticking, the calendar's pages blowing in the hot, humid air. I needed to learn more about Butler, and quickly.

"Butler hated Captain Porter until the day of Porter's death, if Porter is dead already. I don't think Butler was capable of making a true friend—just a convenient ally or an acquaintance who might someday prove useful."

"Which were you, then?" I asked, brushing the powdered sugar from the lost bread off my trousers.

"Fair to ask," said Major Newell. "I performed many vital functions for the general. I was his orderly, after all. But I was well aware that I wasn't Butler's first orderly, that he'd had a succession of them from the first day he'd organized his regiments of volunteers until the day he transferred me to the Quartermaster Corps and continued with his illustrious career."

"Do I detect some bitterness in you?" I asked, merely probing, just asking. That's a journalist's duty, you know, and it wasn't even noon yet. The *café au lait* was thick and dark and made with chicory, the way Orleanians had learned to enjoy it in the days when real coffee had been blockaded by the Union warships—except via Butler's brother, Andrew, who grew wealthy making deals across the feuding lines.

"Me, bitter, after all these years?" asked Newell with an expression as blank as the hindside of a stamp. "I was well-compensated for my duties, as I imagine all Butler's orderlies were."

I swallowed some more of the strong coffee and listened to young Negro boys tap-dancing for coins outside the breakfast shop on Dauphine Street. When I first came to New Orleans, I thought the Negro boys were "charming." Part of the local color, like the shiploads of cotton bales being wrestled on and off the wharves, or the staggering displays of azaleas in early spring. Major Newell had given me the ugly truth: most of the Negro tap dancers were put out on the street by older pimps and allowed to keep only a small portion of the money they earned. Now they all looked to me as haggard as the light-skinned kept women in their cribs in the upper part of the French Quarter.

"Do you want to talk about some of those duties?" I asked, pressing the point I'd made earlier. "Or do you now, more than two decades later, find you're permitting yourself to regret?"

Major Newell laughed, but there was no humor at all in it. "Quite the journalist, aren't you, Mr. Pannell?" he asked. "You'll trap me yet. You remember me mentioning a man called Mumford? Even his first name has been lost. What he'd done was wait for Farragut to come ashore with a Federal flag; the city tried to surrender to Farragut but he wouldn't accept. All he did was fix his flag high up on the Customs House. He warned everyone that there was a warship in the river with a howitzer trained on the flag to protect it until the blue-ribbon surrender of the city to Major General Butler, whenever he showed up.

"Well, this man Mumford—who really probably ought to be some sort of local hero, but he's been forgotten as much as a hero can be—climbed the outside of the Customs House and tore down the Federal flag. From his suite aboard ship, Butler watched and was outraged. What people tried to point out to Butler was that Mumford had committed no crime. The city hadn't truly surrendered yet. The Federal flag hadn't yet been raised over New Orleans as a token of its capitulation to Butler and the Union. Butler didn't care about such meager elements of law. He'd been outraged by what he'd seen Mumford do, and he was going to make Mumford pay."

"Does Mumford have anything to do with the second murdered victim?" I asked impatiently, checking my silver pocket timepiece. My deadline was marching nearer by the minute.

"No, not really," said Newell, surprising me. "There hadn't been a public execution in New Orleans in eighteen years. The Orleanians probably felt they were too genteel for that. Yet on the very day Butler marched into town, some old German immigrant yelled, 'Hurrah for the old flag.' I'm not even sure which flag he was hurrahing. Makes no difference. He was shot on the spot, grabbed by the ankles, and thrown into the Mississippi River. Maybe we'll have a further discussion of gentility later."

"All of this is crazy, insane," I said, scribbling furiously. This was the sort of background material I'd hoped to get from Newell, but his stories were endless and my time was not.

"It gets worse. Mumford had been captured and put on trial for his non-crime. There are technical naval reasons why Farragut's ships didn't fire on Mumford and his band of 'ruffians,' but it all amounted to the fact that it looked like rain, and the ships' guns were rendered useless because an ordnance officer had gone around and removed a vital part from each gun to keep them dry."

"I think it's time for rum punch," I said, overwhelmed by the pure lunacy of history. I signaled to our waiter. Liquor soon began arriving in heroic quantities, despite the early hour.

Major Newell was just hitting his stride. I listened and kept careful notes because he promised me that it would lead to the second murder. "The rebels never believed Butler would kill Mumford; but the rebels didn't know 'Spoons' yet. The next day, the general got a note from Mrs. Mumford saying she wished to see him. She and her children fell about Butler's feet and wept and pleaded, but he was a hard man when he had an audience. He merely told the poor woman that his sense of duty required him to see the execution through. He did express regret that Mrs. Mumford and her children would suffer a disquieting irregularity in their lives, and that if at any time in the future he could be of any help to them, they should just feel free to knock on his door."

"Kind of makes me miss England, you know, in a way," I said.

"Following the old Spanish tradition that the execution be held as close as possible to the scene of the crime, Butler ordered the terrible deed performed at the city's mint, which still had a Federal flag flying over it, companion to the one Mumford had torn down. The crowd was dangerous, filled with Mumford's low associates, all the worse for drink, as we say. Butler took no notice of the potential danger we were in. At the appointed hour, Mumford swung from the gallows; the unruly mob hushed and made away softly, and according to the general, there was never again any form of civil unrest in New Orleans as long as he was in charge."

My brows furrowed. "Was that true?"

"You're a worthless stump-jumper if you believe so," said Major Newell, downing an entire pint of milk punch in one brave draught.

"Excellent," I said, looking back over my notes. "I have the surrender of New Orleans and the execution of Mumford. Now let's hear about the second murder."

"The men of New Orleans tended to back off when they saw us coming," said Major Newell, indicating with a quick swipe of his left hand a uniform he was no longer wearing. "If one of us met two of them on the sidewalk, one of them would give way in the street, as is only natural and proper. But the women! From the most scurrilous language to the bawdiest behavior—you'd be amazed to see a group of wealthy, uptown planters' wives pass a few Federals on the sidewalk, only to kick their skirts up and over, giving the startled young Yanks the briefest and most insulting view of something they'd likely rarely seen in life."

"Yes, I see," I said, thinking of my deadline and beginning to panic. I watched Major Newell order another of what they call in New Orleans "breakfast drinks," and waited for him to continue.

"Then one day," said Newell, leaning back, his eyes drifting down decades, "a junior officer asked permission to speak to the major general. Permission was granted. The junior officer was distraught. 'I've had it!' he cried. 'And so have my men, and I don't blame them.'

"Major General Butler looked up from his desk, which was covered not with topographical maps or campaign charts, as one would imagine, but accounting ledgers. 'You've had what?' he asked. He looked to me for explanation, but I only shrugged.

"The junior officer explained. 'One of my young boys says that he was walking along Canal Street when he came upon a young woman, the wife of a prominent attorney, and a young boy about ten years old. My officer lifted his cap to them and stood aside. The boy did nothing, but the wife rushed over from the other side of the sidewalk and spat all over my lad's uniform. Now, my boys signed up to come down here and fight Rebs, and they never see any Rebs and there isn't any fighting. It's just this day-to-day harassment. It's getting to be too much.'

"The junior officer was excused and I glanced at Butler, 'Spoons Butler,' 'Beast Butler.' 'Another order?' I asked. 'Another harsh warning in the press?'

" 'You remember what happened with Order Number 28,' he said sourly. 'The local papers refused to print it. I had to go send some privates down to set the type themselves, and afterward I suspended the newspapers, just to show them who they were dealing with. Anything further along those lines would be a waste of time. No, this particular case I'll handle like a kindly old uncle, because I happen to know this prominent attorney well, and do business with him now and then. There will be no further trouble from that family.'

"Later that day, another officer appeared with another complaint. 'Now they're dumping chamberpots on us as we walk along the sidewalk!' he cried, his voice quivering with indignation.

"The major general got up from behind his desk and began to pace a little, back and forth. 'Last Sunday,' he said, 'one of my best officers dressed himself in full uniform to attend divine services. As he was entering the church, he met two young, well-dressed young women. He stepped aside to let them pass. As he did so, one of them deliberately crossed over and spat in his face. In the very entryway to a church! He asked me what he should have done against two young women. He did what I would expect any of my officers to do: he took his kerchief and cleaned his face.' "

"I don't know," I said, "I think he should've done something more."

"That's what his fellow officers said," said Newell. "But against two women? One of the other officers had the answer, though, and he said, 'I would've taken my revolver and shot the first *he*-Rebel I met.'

"Well, Butler thought that was a pretty funny idea at first, and then he thought there might be some aid in it. That's when he staged the public torture."

"Public torture!" I said, astonished.

Newell just raised a hand and waved. "We'll pass over the details," he said. "But it was that very night I heard old Butler putting on his overcoat, ready to take another stroll through the streets of the city that hated him so passionately."

"You followed him, of course," I said eagerly.

"Of course," said the retired major. "He made his way uptown from the St. Charles Hotel and toward the river, where the streets were filled with the fine houses of the Lower Garden District. I stayed about a block behind him and on the opposite side of the street. He seemed to be searching for something, rather than merely taking a midnight walk. I hurried to catch up to him, fearing that he might be recognized and harmed, or even killed in the night."

"Did he find—"

Newell's hand shook as he drank the last of his gin fizz. "I saw him leaning over the body of a young man. The unknown lad was dead, of course, as dead as any Yank or Rebel who fell at Manassas. But the horrible thing was the expression on Major General Butler's face. He showed a keen excitement, an almost obscene delight with the death-contorted corpse, and Butler's huge, avid eyes could barely take it all in. I tried pulling him away, saying 'We can't be found here like this, General.'

"He just indicated that I be quiet. His breathing came unnaturally fast, and he examined every detail of the dead young man's corpse. I saw that the boy had been strangled by strong hands, but that there were other, more horrible wounds, too, as if made by teeth and nails. Still, Butler refused to leave the grim site until reason reasserted itself.

" 'We've got to go, Newell!' he cried. 'We've got to get back to the hotel, and quickly!'

" 'Yes, sir,' I said, 'of course.'

"And then he did an odd thing: he grasped me by the collar of my uniform. 'You're the only one who understands, Newell. You're the only one who cares. Get me safely back to the hotel, and there's a hundred Federal dollars in it for you.' " Newell shoved his empty cup and saucer aside with some disgust. "I never wanted his God-be-damned money in the first place," he said.

Was a shame if you aks me the way they run Ol' Spoons out of there so fast. Everybody needs some time to prove hisself, even I had a dog I was fixin' to shoot oncet 'cause he wouldn't hunt, but when that dog saw what was in the air he hunted just fine.

I myself had very little opinion of Major General Butler, 'cause after serving in New Orleans, where I never was, the Beast went on to battle after battle, also places I never was.

—"Billy Yank" (Real name unknown)
Generals I Been Knowin'

Later in the day, Newell and I took some pleasure in riding the New Orleans Street Railway, up St. Charles past many of the great houses. Newell was eager to see how things had changed, and the entire journey to the town of Carrollton had him so astonished that it was difficult for me to keep his mind on the important questions I still had to ask. I couldn't help thinking of the stevedores and other waterfront strongarms getting the *Miss Eileen Brant* in tip-top shape, and the ship sailing without my story because Major Newell was being so slow in doling out the vital facts I needed so badly.

"It wasn't far from here," said Newell in a soft voice, as we passed the old plantation grounds that three years ago had housed a major international cotton exposition.

"What happened?" I asked.

"Oh," said Newell, leaning back against the rattling wooden seat and smiling, "this is where the general was himself accosted. We were examining something this far from the center of town— the surveyors' progress or some such—when a woman rushed up to Butler and screamed in his face. 'You're the very Devil,' she shouted. 'You're Evil Incarnate. Beast is certainly the right name for you!' "

I smiled, picturing the confrontation in my mind. "And how did the major general respond?"

Newell's expression was amused. "Old Spoons had more belly than I ever gave him credit for. He merely tipped his hat to the old harridan and said, 'I'm sorry, madam, but you've mistaken me for someone in a gray uniform riding the railway back to town. You've just missed him.' "

After that, it seemed that Newell would be content to keep his silence, which would do me no good at all. We rode up to the Carrollton terminus, paid our fares, and rode the same car back to Canal Street. Yet after a few minutes, the major's face grew grim, and it looked as if he wanted to say something. I pretended not to notice, to let Newell choose his own way of revealing what final details he recalled.

"I told you there were three victims whom I saw personally," he said at last, in a very low voice. "Let me tell you now about the third."

Still I kept my silence, but I leaned forward with eagerness and anticipation.

"The night after the woman confronted Butler," said Newell, "I heard him prepare to go out once again. Once more I followed, only this time I made no pretense of hiding myself from him. Together we walked the waterfront streets, with a thick fog coming in off the river. I suggested that we stop in some taproom for a drink or two, but he dismissed that suggestion with a curt shake of his head. Finally, he found what he was looking for. 'Her,' he said, indicating a young but unattractive woman who was loitering near a corner of Clay Street.

"I nodded and approached her. She smiled when she saw me, and she spoke a few words. I didn't even hear the sound of her voice. At first, I merely stroked her face and neck, but then I grasped her around the throat with these great, terrible hands, and in a few moments she had collapsed at my feet, just as had the others. I never wanted that. I never planned that. I don't know what came over me. I realized that I was kissing her poor, pale face, and rending the flesh of her neck and shoulders at the same time.

" 'My stick,' said Major General Butler in a hoarse voice. He was carrying, as he very often did, a heavy wooden walking stick with a grip in the shape of a lion's paw holding a ball. He pushed past me and began beating the poor, sad, dead girl. Again I saw a horrible transformation grip him, so that his face and features were barely recognizable. His mouth was drawn back in a strange grimace, his breathing was so loud that I was afraid that he'd attract attention. I could barely testify in all honor that he was still human.

" 'General,' I said, but there was no response. 'General,' I said again, grabbing his arm and attempting to stop his assault on the already lifeless young woman. It was all I could do to control him. Finally, as on the other occasions, after a little while he came to himself. He looked down at the dead woman and cried aloud in a small voice.

" 'The hotel, and quickly,' he said, as panicked as ever I'd seen him. I doubt that he ever showed such fear in the face of military combat. We found a carriage a few blocks away. Inside, he examined the blood on his walking stick and on the fur collar of his greatcoat.

" 'I'll take care of those for you, sir,' I said. 'I'll clean away every trace of blood and hair.' " I'd done that for him regularly as part of my duties.

" 'Newell,' he said simply, and then tears began to fall slowly down his cheeks. He reached into a pocket of the coat and withdrew handfuls of Union scrip and dropped it all, uncounted, in my lap. Butler was the beast they had named him, and I was but his hunting dog. I gathered the hateful money together and stuffed it into one of my own pockets."

"Why are you telling all this to me now?" I asked in breathless astonishment.

"Because," said Newell slowly and, I thought, very sadly, "I will be gone soon and forever."

I sat in Jackson Square the morning before the ship sailed, bearing my story eventually back to Manchester, and I watched the sun come up and listened to the early morning business of the town. I wondered how much of what Newell had told me had been the truth. He knew that I'd come originally seeking a connection to the Ripper horrors—had he deliberately lied and led me on? Newell had disappeared before breakfast time. Could I believe him? I asked myself again. And, for the sake of argument, if everything he told me had been literal fact, what should I write? Should I go to the authorities with my unsubstantiated accusations concerning Newell and Butler? Would the local constabulary even care after twenty-six years? And, of course, there was no longer any proof. There was no one else to interview except Butler himself. My newspaper had attempted to arrange a meeting with him, but Butler had absolutely refused.

Yet it was Newell who fascinated me, not the absurd, fatuous Major General Benjamin Franklin Butler. Newell was still of an age, I told myself. In those old days of the Southern Rebellion, he never slashed a victim; but as they liked to say in this great port city, you can always teach an old dog new tricks, if you give the dog a good enough reason to learn.

MAJ GENL. BENJAMIN F. BUTLER,
Commanding, etc., New Orleans:

General:—Your interesting despatches, announcing the brilliant success of your expedition, as well as those sent by Colonel Dem-ing and Mr. Bouligny, were duly received. No event during the war has exercised an influence upon the public mind so powerful as the capture and occupation of New Orleans. *To you and to the gallant officers and soldiers under your command, the Department tenders cordial thanks. Your vigorous and able administration of the government of that city also receives warm commendation.*

With admiration for your achievements, and the utmost confidence in your continuous success, I remain,

Truly yours,
EDWIN M. STANTON
Secretary of War

The Face

Ed Gorman

Ed Gorman is finally receiving the recognition he so richly deserves. His wonderful story "Turn Away," won the Shamus Award of the Private Eye Writers of America; his powerful "Prisoners" was on the final ballot for the Edgar Award of the Mystery Writers of America; his "Dwyer" novels of mystery and suspense have attracted an ardent following around the world; as "Daniel Ransom," he has established himself as a horror writer to watch; and if this were not enough, as editor of *Mystery Scene* magazine he has become an important force in several genres.

Dean R. Koontz has said that "Ed Gorman's work is fresh, polished, excitingly paced, thoroughly entertaining—*and* has something to say about the way we live, the way we are, and what we wish we were."

In "The Face," he shows us how we might have *been*.

The war was going badly. In the past month more than sixty men had disgraced the Confederacy by deserting, and now the order was to shoot deserters on sight. This was in other camps and other regiments. Fortunately, none of our men had deserted at all.

As a young doctor, I knew even better than our leaders just how hopeless our war had become. The public knew General Lee had been forced to cross the Potomac with ten thousand men who lacked shoes, hats, and who at night had to sleep on the ground without blankets. But I knew—in the first six months in this post—that our men suffered from influenza, diphtheria, smallpox, yellow fever, and even cholera; ravages from which they would never recover; ravages more costly than bullets and

390

the advancing armies of the Yankees. Worse, because toilet and bathing facilities were practically nil, virtually every man suffered from ticks and mites and many suffered from scurvy, their bodies on fire. Occasionally, you would see a man go mad, do crazed dances in the moonlight trying to get the bugs off him. Soon enough he would be dead.

This was the war in the spring and while I have here referred to our troops as "men," in fact they were mostly boys, some as young as thirteen. In the night, freezing and sometimes wounded, they cried out for their mothers, and it was not uncommon to hear one or two of them sob while they prayed aloud.

I tell you this so you will have some idea of how horrible things had become for our beloved Confederacy. But even given the suffering and madness and despair I'd seen for the past two years as a military doctor, nothing had prepared me for the appearance of the Virginia man in our midst.

On the day he was brought in on a buckboard, I was working with some troops, teaching them how to garden. If we did not get vegetables and fruit into our diets soon, all of us would have scurvy. I also appreciated the respite that working in the warm sun gave me from surgery. In the past week alone, I'd amputated three legs, two arms, and numerous hands and fingers. None had gone well, conditions were so filthy.

Every amputation had ended in death except one, and this man—boy; he was fourteen—pleaded with me to kill him every time I checked on him. He'd suffered a head wound and I'd had to relieve the pressure by trepanning into his skull. Beneath the blood and pus in the hole I'd dug, I could see his brain squirming. There was no anesthetic, of course, except whiskey, and that provided little comfort against the violence of my bone saw. It was one of those periods when I could not get the tart odor of blood from my nostrils, nor its feel from my skin. Sometimes, standing at the surgery table, my boots would become soaked with it, and I would squish around in them all day.

The buckboard was parked in front of the general's tent. The driver jumped down, ground-tied the horses, and went quickly inside.

He returned a few moments later with General Sullivan, the

commander. Three men in familiar gray uniforms followed the general.

The entourage walked around to the rear of the wagon. The driver, an enlisted man, pointed to something in the buckboard. The general, a fleshy, bald man of fifty-some years, leaned over the wagon and peered downward.

Quickly, the general's head snapped back and then his whole body followed. It was as if he'd been stung by something coiled and waiting for him in the buckboard.

The general shook his head and said, "I want this man's entire face covered. Especially his face."

"But, General," the driver said. "He's not dead. We shouldn't cover his face."

"You heard what I said!" General Sullivan snapped. And with that, he strutted back into his tent, his men following.

I was curious, of course, about the man in the back of the wagon. I wondered what could have made the general start the way he had. He'd looked almost frightened.

I wasn't to know till later that night.

My rounds made me late for dinner in the vast tent used for the officers' mess. I always felt badly about the inequity of officers having beef stew while the men had, at best, hardtack and salt pork. Not so bad that I refused to eat it, of course, which made me feel hypocritical on top of being sorry for the enlisted men.

Not once in my time here had I ever dined with General Sullivan. I was told on my first day here that the general, an extremely superstitious man, considered doctors bad luck. Many people feel this way. Befriend a doctor and you'll soon enough find need of his services.

So I was surprised when General Sullivan, carrying a cup of steaming coffee in a huge, battered tin cup, sat down across from the table where I ate alone, my usual companions long ago gone back to their duties.

"Good evening, Doctor."

"Good evening, General."

"A little warmer tonight."

"Yes."

He smiled dourly. "Something's got to go our way, I suppose."

I returned his smile. "I suppose." I felt like a child trying to act properly for the sake of an adult. The general frightened me.

The general took out a stogie, clipped off the end, sniffed it, licked it, then put it between his lips and fired it up. He did all this with a ritualistic satisfaction that made me think of better times in my home city of Charleston, of my father and uncles handling their smoking in just the same way.

"A man was brought into camp this afternoon," he said.

"Yes," I said. "In a buckboard."

He eyed me suspiciously. "You've seen him up close?"

"No. I just saw him delivered to your tent." I had to be careful of how I put my next statement. I did not want the general to think I was challenging his reasoning. "I'm told he was not taken to any of the hospital tents."

"No, he wasn't." The general wasn't going to help me.

"I'm told he was put under quarantine in a tent of his own."

"Yes."

"May I ask why?"

He blew two plump, white, perfect rings of smoke toward the ceiling. "Go have a look at him, then join me in my tent."

"You're afraid he may have some contagious disease?"

The general considered the length of his cigar. "Just go have a look at him, Doctor. Then we'll talk."

With that, the general stood up, his familiar brusque self once again, and was gone.

The guard set down his rifle when he saw me. "Good evenin', Doctor."

"Good evening."

He nodded to the tent behind him. "You seen him yet?"

"No, not yet."

He was young. He shook his head. "Never seen anything like it. Neither has the priest. He's in there with him now." In the chill, crimson dusk I tried to get a look at the guard's face. I couldn't. My only clue to his mood was the tone of his voice—one of great sorrow.

I lifted the tent flap and went in.

A lamp guttered in the far corner of the small tent, casting huge and playful shadows across the walls. A hospital cot took up most of the space. A man's body lay beneath the covers. A sheer cloth had been draped across his face. You could see it billowing with the man's faint breath. Next to the cot stood Father Lynott. He was silver-haired and chunky. His black cassock showed months of dust and grime. Like most of us, he was rarely able to get hot water for necessities.

At first, he didn't seem to hear me. He stood over the cot torturing black rosary beads through his fingers. He stared directly down at the cloth draped on the man's face.

Only when I stood next to him did Father Lynott look up. "Good evening, Father."

"Good evening, Doctor."

"The general wanted me to look at this man."

He stared at me. "You haven't seen him, then?"

"No."

"Nothing can prepare you."

"I'm afraid I don't understand."

He looked at me out of his tired cleric's face. "You'll see soon enough. Why don't you come over to the officers' tent afterwards? I'll be there drinking my nightly coffee."

He nodded, glanced down once more at the man on the cot, and then left, dropping the tent flap behind him.

I don't know how long I stood there before I could bring myself to remove the cloth from the man's face. By now, enough people had warned me of what I would see that I was both curious and apprehensive. There is a myth about doctors not being shocked by certain terrible wounds and injuries. Of course we are, but we must get past that shock—or, more honestly, put it aside for a time—so that we can help the patient.

Close by, I could hear the feet of the guard in the damp grass, pacing back and forth in front of the tent. A barn owl and then a distant dog joined the sounds the guard made. Even more distant, there was cannon fire, the war never ceasing. The sky would flare silver like summer lightning. Men would suffer and die.

I reached down and took the cloth from the man's face.

"What do you suppose could have done that to his face, Father?" I asked the priest twenty minutes later.

We were having coffee. I smoked a cigar. The guttering candles smelled sweet and waxy.

"I'm not sure," the priest said.

"Have you ever seen anything like it?"

"Never."

I knew what I was about to say would surprise the priest. "He has no wounds."

"What?"

"I examined him thoroughly. There are no wounds anywhere on his body."

"But his face—"

I drew on my cigar, watched the expelled smoke move like a storm cloud across the flickering candle flame. "That's why I asked you if you'd ever seen anything like it."

"My God," the priest said, as if speaking to himself. "No wounds."

In the dream I was back on the battlefield on that frosty March morning two years ago when all my medical training had deserted me. Hundreds of corpses covered the ground where the battle had gone on for two days and two nights. You could see cannons mired in mud, the horses unable to pull them out. You could see the grass littered with dishes and pans and kettles, and a blizzard of playing cards—all exploded across the battlefield when the Union Army had made its final advance. But mostly there were the bodies—so young and so many—and many of them with mutilated faces. During this time of the war, both sides had begun to commit atrocities. The Yankees favored disfiguring Confederate dead, and so they moved across the battlefield with Bowie knives that had been fashioned by sharpening with large files. They put deep gashes in the faces of the young men, tearing out eyes sometimes, even sawing off noses. In the woods that day, we'd found a group of our soldiers who'd been mortally wounded but who'd lived for a time after the Yankees had left. Each corpse held in its hand some memento of the loved ones they'd left behind—a photograph, a letter, a lock of blond hair. Their last sight had been of some homely yet profound endearment from the people they'd loved most.

This was the dream—nightmare, really—and I'd suffered it ever since I'd searched for survivors on that battlefield two years previous.

I was still in this dream-state when I heard the bugle announce the morning. I stumbled from my cot and went down to the creek to wash and shave. The day had begun.

Casualties were many that morning. I stood in the hospital tent watching as one stretcher after another bore man after man to the operating table. Most suffered from wounds inflicted by minié balls, fired from guns that could kill a man nearly a mile away.

By noon, my boots were again soaked with blood dripping from the table.

During the long day, I heard whispers of the man General Sullivan had quarantined from others. Apparently, the man had assumed the celebrity and fascination of a carnival sideshow. From the whispers, I gathered that guards were letting men in for quick looks at him, and the lookers came away shaken and frightened. These stories had the same impact as tales of specters told around midnight campfires. Except this was daylight and the men—even the youngest of them—hardened soldiers. They should not have been so afraid but they were.

I couldn't get the sight of the man out of my mind, either. It haunted me no less than the battlefield I'd seen two years earlier.

During the afternoon, I went down to the creek and washed. I then went to the officers' tent and had stew and coffee. My arms were weary from surgery but I knew I would be working long into the night.

The general surprised me once again by joining me. "You've seen the soldier from Virginia?"

"Yes, sir."

"What do you make of him?"

I shrugged. "Shock, I suppose."

"But his face—"

"This is a war, General, and a damned bloody one. Not all men are like you. Not all men have iron constitutions."

He took my words as flattery, of course, as a military man would. I hadn't necessarily meant them that way. Military men could also be grossly vain and egotistical and insensitive beyond belief.

"Meaning what, exactly, Doctor?"

"Meaning that the soldier from Virginia may have become so horrified by what he saw that his face—" I shook my head. "You can see too much, too much death, General, and it can make you go insane."

"Are you saying he's insane?"

I shook my head. "I'm trying to find some explanation for his expression, General."

"You say there's no injury?"

"None that I can find."

"Yet he's not conscious."

"That's why I think of shock."

I was about to explain how shock works on the body—and how it could feasibly effect an expression like the one on the Virginia soldier's face—when a lieutenant rushed up to the general and breathlessly said, "You'd best come, sir. The tent where the soldier's quarantined— There's trouble!"

When we reached there, we found half the camp's soldiers surrounding the tent. Three and four deep, they were, and milling around idly. Not the sort of thing you wanted to see your men doing when there was a war going on. There were duties to perform and none of them were getting done.

A young soldier—thirteen or fourteen at most—stepped from the line and hurled his rifle at the general. The young soldier had tears running down his cheeks. "I don't want to fight any-more, General."

The general slammed the butt of the rifle into the soldier's stomach. "Get hold of yourself, young man. You seem to forget we're fighting to save the Confederacy."

We went on down the line of glowering faces, to where two armed guards struggled to keep soldiers from looking into the tent. I was reminded again of a sideshow—some irresistible spectacle everybody wanted to see.

The soldiers knew enough to open an avenue for the general. He strode inside the tent. The priest sat on a stool next to the cot. He had removed the cloth from the Virginia soldier's face and was staring fixedly at it.

The general pushed the priest aside, took up the cloth used as a covering, and started to drop it across the soldier's face—then stopped abruptly. Even General Sullivan, in his rage, was moved by what he saw. He jerked back momentarily, his eyes unable to lift from the soldier's face. He handed the cloth to the priest. "You cover his face now, Father. And you keep it covered. I hereby forbid any man in this camp to look at this soldier's face ever again. Do you understand?"

Then he stormed from the tent.

The priest reluctantly obliged.

Then he angled his head up to me. "It won't be the same anymore, Doctor."

"What won't?"

"The camp. Every man in here has now seen his face." He nodded back to the soldier on the cot. "They'll never be the same again. I promise you."

In the evening, I ate stew and biscuits, and sipped at a small glass of wine. I was, as usual, in the officers' tent when the priest came and found me.

For a time, he said nothing beyond his greeting. He simply watched me at my meal, and then stared out the open flap at the camp preparing for evening, the fires in the center of the encampment, the weary men bedding down. Many of them, healed now, would be back in the battle within two days or less.

"I spent an hour with him this afternoon," the priest said.

"The quarantined man?"

"Yes." The priest nodded. "Do you know some of the men have visited him five or six times?"

The way the priest spoke, I sensed he was gloating over the fact that the men were disobeying the general's orders. "Why don't the guards stop them?"

"The guards are in visiting him, too."

"The man says nothing. How can it be a visit?"

"He says nothing with his tongue. He says a great deal with his face." He paused, eyed me levelly. "I need to tell you something. You're the only man in this camp who will believe me." He sounded frantic. I almost felt sorry for him.

"Tell me what?"

"The man—he's not what we think."

"No?"

"No; his face—" He shook his head. "It's God's face."

"I see."

The priest smiled. "I know how I must sound."

"You've seen a great deal of suffering, Father. It wears on a person."

"It's God's face. I had a dream last night. The man's face shows us God's displeasure with the war. That's why the men are so moved when they see the man." He sighed, seeing he was not convincing me. "You say yourself he hasn't been wounded."

"That's true."

"And that all his vital signs seem normal."

"True enough, Father."

"Yet he's in some kind of shock."

"That seems to be his problem, yes."

The priest shook his head. "No, his real problem is that he's become overwhelmed by the suffering he's seen in this war— what each side has done to the other. All the pain. That's why there's so much sorrow on his face—and that's what the men are responding to. The grief on his face is the same grief they feel in their hearts. God's face."

"Once we get him to a real field hospital—"

And it was then we heard the rifle shots.

As the periphery of the encampment was heavily protected, we'd never heard firing this close.

The priest and I ran outside.

General Sullivan stood next to a group of young men with weapons. Several yards ahead, near the edge of the camp, lay three bodies, shadowy in the light of the campfire. One of the fallen men moaned. All three men wore our own gray uniforms.

Sullivan glowered at me. "Deserters."

"But you shot them in the back," I said.

"Perhaps you didn't hear me, Doctor. The men were deserting. They'd packed their belongings and were heading out."

One of the young men who'd done the shooting said, "It was the man's face, sir."

Sullivan wheeled on him. "It was what?"

"The quarantined man, sir. His face. These men said it made them sad and they had to see families back in Missouri, and that they were just going to leave no matter what."

"Poppycock," Sullivan said. "They left because they were cowards."

I left to take care of the fallen man who was crying out for help.

In the middle of the night, I heard more guns being fired. I lay on my cot, knowing it wasn't Yankees being fired at. It was our own deserters.

I dressed and went over to the tent where the quarantined man lay. Two young farm boys in ill-fitting gray uniforms stood over him. They might have been mourners standing over a coffin. They said nothing. Just stared at the man.

In the dim lamplight, I knelt down next to him. His vitals still seemed good, his heartbeat especially. I stood up, next to the two boys, and looked down on him myself. There was nothing remarkable about his face. He could have been any one of thousands of men serving on either side.

Except for the grief.

This time I felt the tug of it myself, heard in my mind the cries of the dying I'd been unable to save, saw the families and farms and homes destroyed as the war moved across the countryside, heard children crying out for dead parents, and parents sobbing over the bodies of their dead children. It was all there in his face, perfectly reflected, and I thought then of what the priest had said, that this was God's face, God's sorrow and displeasure with us.

The explosion came, then.

While the two soldiers next to me didn't seem to hear it at all, I rushed from the tent to the center of camp.

Several young soldiers stood near the ammunition cache. Someone had set fire to it. Ammunition was exploding everywhere, flares of red and yellow and gas-jet blue against the night. Men everywhere ducked for cover behind wagons and trees and boulders.

Into this scene, seemingly unafraid and looking like the lead actor in a stage production of *King Lear* I'd once seen, strode General Sullivan, still tugging on his heavy uniform jacket.

He went over to two soldiers who stood, unfazed, before the ammunition cache. Between explosions I could hear him shouting, "Did you set this fire?"

And they nodded.

Sullivan, as much in bafflement as anger, shook his head. He signaled for the guards to come and arrest these men.

As the soldiers were passing by me, I heard one of them say to a guard, "After I saw his face, I knew I had to do this. I had to stop the war."

Within an hour, the flames died and the explosions ceased. The night was almost ominously quiet. There were a few hours before dawn, so I tried to sleep some more.

I dreamed of Virginia, green Virginia in the spring, and the creek where I'd fished as a boy, and how the sun had felt on my back and arms and head. There was no surgical table in my dream, nor were my shoes soaked with blood.

Around dawn somebody began shaking me. It was Sullivan's personal lieutenant. "The priest has been shot. Come quickly, Doctor."

I didn't even dress fully, just pulled on my trousers over the legs of my long underwear.

A dozen soldiers stood outside the tent looking confused and defeated and sad. I went inside.

The priest lay in his tent. His cassock had been torn away. A bloody hole made a targetlike circle on his stomach.

Above his cot stood General Sullivan, a pistol in his hand.

I knelt next to the cot and examined the priest. His vital signs were faint and growing fainter. He had at most a few minutes to live.

I looked up at the general. "What happened?"

The general nodded for the lieutenant to leave. The man saluted and then went out into the gray dawn.

"I had to shoot him," General Sullivan said.

I stood up. "You had to shoot a priest?"

"He was trying to stop me."

"From what?"

Then I noticed for the first time the knife scabbard on the general's belt. Blood streaked its sides. The hilt of the knife was sticky with blood. So were the general's hands. I thought of how Yankee troops had begun disfiguring the faces of our dead on the battlefield.

He said, "I have a war to fight, Doctor. The men—the way they were reacting to the man's face—" He paused and touched the bloody hilt of the knife. "I took care of him. And the priest came in while I was doing it and went insane. He started hitting me, trying to stop me and—" He looked down at the priest. "I didn't have any choice, Doctor. I hope you believe me."

A few minutes later, the priest died.

I started to leave the tent. General Sullivan put a hand on my shoulder. "I know you don't care very much for me, Doctor, but I hope you understand me at least a little. I can't win a war when men desert and blow up ammunition dumps and start questioning the worthiness of the war itself. I had to do what I did. I hope someday you'll understand."

I went out into the dawn. The air smelled of camp fires and coffee. Now the men were busy scurrying around, preparing for war. The way they had been before the man had been brought here in the buckboard.

I went over to the tent where he was kept and asked the guard to let me inside. "The general said nobody's allowed inside, Doctor."

I shoved the boy aside and strode into the tent.

The cloth was still over his face, only now it was soaked with blood. I raised the cloth and looked at him. Even for a doctor, the sight was horrible. The general had ripped out his eyes and sawed off his nose. His cheeks carried deep gullies where the knife had been dug in deep.

He was dead. The shock of the defacement had killed him.

Sickened, I looked away.

The flap was thrown back, then, and there stood General Sullivan. "We're going to bury him now, Doctor."

In minutes, the dead soldier was inside a pine box borne up a hill of long grass waving in a chill wind. The rains came, hard rains, before they'd turned even two shovelfuls of earth.

Then, from a distance over the hill, came the thunder of cannon and the cry of the dying.

The face that reminded us of what we were doing to each other was no more. It had been made ugly, robbed of its sorrowful beauty.

He was buried quickly and without benefit of clergy—the priest himself having been buried an hour earlier—and when the ceremony was finished, we returned to camp and war.

Colour

Michael Moorcock

Michael Moorcock produced the first magazine of his writings at the age of nine, began writing professionally for *Tarzan Adventures* at age sixteen, and was given the editorship of the publication less than a year later. He has been earning his way ever since.

He is one of the very few persons in the SF community to have an entry in *The Oxford Companion to English Literature.* (William S. Burroughs is another.) During his tenure as editor of the British magazine *New Worlds* (roughly 1964 to 1979), he fostered development of science fiction's "New Wave," a period which revolutionized the literary standards of the genre. His influence as a writer and as an editor cannot be overestimated.

Michael's notable novels, short stories, and critical writings are far too numerous to recount here in the manner they deserve. My personal favorites include his novels *The Warhound and the World's Pain* and *Gloriana,* his novella "Behold the Man," and his series characters "Elric" and "Jerry Cornelius." The former single-handedly raised the sword-and-sorcery genre to a critically respectable level, while with the latter he presaged the cyberpunk movement by almost two decades.

Born near London in 1939, his wartime childhood and rebellious teenage years are often reflected in his works. His acclaimed 1989 British bestseller, *Mother London,* draws heavily from this period. Michael has toured as a musician with England's Hawkwind, and with his own band, the Deep Fix. He has composed lyrics for Blue Öyster Cult, and written about the Sex Pistols.

When Ed brought Michael to Atlanta for 1987's inaugural

Dragon Con, it was Michael's first scheduled convention appearance in eleven years. That led to the founding of the Nomads of the Time Streams, the international Michael Moorcock appreciation society.

Having published over one hundred books, few authors have been as prolific in as many different styles at so high a level of quality. This story challenges conventional boundaries, transcending traditional narrative forms.

> The very nature of our dreams is changing. We have deconstructed the universe and are refusing to rebuild it. This is our madness and our glory.
> Now we can again begin the true course of our explorations, without preconceptions or agendas.
>
> —Lobkowitz

1. A Victim of the Game

The heat of the New Orleans night pressed against the window like an urgent lover. Jack Karaquazian stood sleepless, naked, staring out into the sweating darkness as if he might see at last some tangible horror which he could confront and even hope to conquer.

"Tomorrow," he told his friend Sam Oakenhurst, "I shall take the *Star* up to Natchez and from there make my way to McClellan by way of the Trace. Will you come?"

(The vision of a sunlit bayou; recollection of an extraordinarily rich perfume, the wealth of the earth. He remembered the yellow-billed herons standing in the shallows moving their heads to regard him with thoughtful eyes before returning their respect to the water; the grey ibises, seeming to sit in judgement of the others, the delicate egrets congregating on the old logs and branches; a cloud of monarch butterflies, black and orange, diaphanous, settling over the pale reeds and, in the dark green waters, a movement might have been copperhead or alligator, or even a pike. In that moment of silence before the invisible insects began a fresh song, her eyes were humorous, enquiring. She had worked for a while, she said, as a chanteuse at *The Fallen Angel* on Bourbon Street.)

Sam Oakenhurst understood the invitation to be a courtesy. "I think not, Jack. My luck has been running pretty badly lately and travelling ain't likely to improve it much." Wiping his fingers against his undershirt, he delicately picked an ace from the baize of his folding table.

For a moment the overhead fan, fueled by some mysterious power, stirred the cards. Pausing, Oakenhurst regarded this phenomenon with considerable satisfaction, as if his deepest faith had been confirmed. "Besides, I got me all the mung I need right now." And he patted his belt, full of hard dollars, better than muscle.

"It looked for a moment as if our energy had come back." Karaquazian got onto his bed and sat there undecided whether to try sleeping or to talk. "I'm also planning to give the game a rest. I swear it will be a while before I play at the Terminal." They both smiled.

"You still looking to California, Jack?" The black man stroked down a card. "And the Free States?"

"Well, maybe eventually." Karaquazian offered his attention back to the darkness while a small, dry, controlled cough shook his body. He cursed softly and vigorously and went to pour himself a careful drink from the whiskey on the table.

"You should do it," said Oakenhurst. "Nobody knows who you are anymore."

"I left some unfinished business between Starkville and McClellan." Quietly satisfied by this temporary victory over his disease, the gambler drew in a heavy breath. "Anywhere's better than this, Sam. I'll go in the morning. As soon as they sound the upboat siren."

Putting down the remaining cards, his partner rose to cross, through sluggish shadows, the unpolished floor and, beneath the fluttering swampcone on the wall, pry up one of the floorboards. He removed a packet of money and divided it into two without counting it. "There's your share of Texas. Brother Ignatius and I agreed, if only one of us got back, you'd have half."

Jack Karaquazian accepted the bills and slipped them into a pocket of the black silk jacket which hung over the other chair on top of his pants, his linen and brocaded vest. "It's rightfully all yours, Sam, and I'll remember that. Who knows how our luck will run? But it'll be a sad year down here, I think, win or lose." Mr. Karaquazian found it difficult to express most emotions; for too long his trade had depended on hiding them. Yet he was able to lay a pale, fraternal hand on his friend's shoulder, a gesture which meant a great deal more to both than any amount of conversation. His eyes, half-hidden behind long lashes, became gentle for a moment.

Both men blinked when, suddenly, the darkness outside was ripped by a burst of fire, of flickering arsenical greens and yellows, of vivid scarlet sparks. The *mechanish* squealed and wailed as if in torment, while other metallic lungs uttered loud, depressed groans occasionally interrupted by an aggressive bellow, a shriek of despair from xylonite vocal-cords, or a deeper, more threatening klaxon as the steel militia, their bodies identified by bubbling globules of burning, dirty orange plastic, gouting black smoke, roamed the narrow streets in search of flesh—human or otherwise—which had defied the city's intolerable curfew. Karaquazian never slept well in New Orleans. The fundamental character of the authority appalled him.

2. *Two of a Kind*

At dawn, as the last of the garishly decorated, popishly-baroque *mechanish* blundered over the cobbles of the rue Dauphine, spreading their unwholesome ichor behind them, Jack Karaquazian carried his carpetbag to the quayside, where other men and women were making haste to board *L'Etoile d'Memphes,* anxious to leave the oppressive terrors of a quarter where the colour-greedy *machinoix,* that brutal aristocracy, allowed only their engines the freedom of the streets.

Compared to the conscious barbarism of the machines, the

riverboat's cream filigree gothic was in spare good taste, and Mr. Karaquazian ascended the gangplank with his first-class ticket in his hand, briefly wishing he were going all the way to the capital, where at least some attempt was made to maintain old standards. But duty—according to Jack Karaquazian's idiosyncratic morality, and the way in which he identified an abiding obsession—had to be served. He had sworn to himself that he must perform a certain task and obtain certain information before he could permit himself any relief, any company other than Colinda Dovero's.

He followed an obsequious steward along a familiar colonnaded deck to the handsomely carved door of the stateroom he favoured when in funds. By way of thanks for a generous tip, he was offered a knowing leer and the murmured intelligence that a high-class snowfrail was travelling in the adjoining suite. Mr. Karaquazian rewarded this with a scowl and a sharp oath so that the steward left before, as he clearly feared, the tip was snatched back from his fingers. Shaking his head at the irredeemable vulgarity of the white race, Karaquazian unpacked his own luggage. The boat shuddered suddenly as she began to taste her steam, her paddle-wheel stirring the dark waters of the Mississippi. Compared to the big ocean-going schoomer on which, long ago, the gambler had crossed from Alexandria, the *Etoile* was comfortingly reliable and responsive. For him she belonged to an era when time had been measured by chronometers rather than degrees of deliquescence. He was reminded, against his guard, of the first day he had met the Creole adventuress, Colinda Dovero, who had been occupying those same adjoining quarters and following the same calling as himself.

(Dancing defiantly with her on deck in the summer night amongst the mosquito lamps to the tune of an accordion, a fiddle, a Dobro, and a bass guitar while the Second Officer, Mr. Pitre, sang "Poor Hobo" in a sweet baritone. . . . *O, pauvre hobo, mon petit pierrot, ah, foolish hope, my grief, mon coeur . . . Aiee, no longer, no longer Houston, but our passion she never resolves. Allons dansez! Allons dansez!* The old traditional elegies; the pain of inconstancy. *La musique, ma tristesse . . .* They were dancing, they were told in turn, with a sort of death. But the oracles whom the fashion favoured in those days, and who swarmed the same boats as Karaquazian and his kind, were of proven inaccuracy. Even had they not been, Karaquazian and Dovero could have done nothing else than what they did, for theirs was at that time an ungovernable chemistry. . . .)

As it happened, the white woman kept entirely to her stateroom and all Karaquazian knew of her existence was an occasional overheard word to her stewardess. Seemingly, her need for solitude matched his own. He spent the better part of the first forty-eight hours sleeping, his nightmares as troubled as his memories. When he woke up, he could never be sure whether he had been dreaming or remembering, but he was almost certain he had shouted out at least once. Horrified by the thought of what he might reveal, he dosed himself with laudanum until only his snores disturbed the darkness. Yet he continued to dream.

Her name, she had said, was West African or Irish in origin, she was not sure. They had met for the second time in the Terminal Café on the stablest edge of the Biloxi Fault. The café's sharply defined walls constantly jumped and mirrored, expanding space, contracting it, slowing time, frantically dancing in and out of a thousand minor matrixes, its neon sign (LAST HEAT ON THE BEACH), usually lavender and cerise, drawing power directly from the howling chaos a few feet away, between the white sand and the blue ocean, where all the unlikely geometries of the multiverse, all the terrible wild colours, that maelstrom of uninterpretable choices, were displayed in a smooth, perfect circle which the engineers had sliced through the core of all-time and all-space, its rim edged by a rainbow ribbon of vanilla-scented crystal. Usually, the Terminal Café occupied roughly the area of space filled by the old pier, which itself had been absorbed by the vortex during the early moments of an experiment intended to bore into the very marrow of ultra-reality and extract all the energy the planet needed.

The operation had been aborted twenty-two seconds after it began. Since then, adventurers of many persuasions and motives had made the sidestep through the oddly coloured flames of the Fault into that inferno of a billion perishing space-time continua, drawn down into a maw which sucked to nothingness the substance of whole races and civilisations, whole planetary systems, whole histories, while Earth and sun bobbed in some awkward and perhaps temporary semi-parisitical relationship between the feeding and the food: their position in this indecipherable matrix being generally considered a fluke. (Or perhaps the planet was the actual medium of this destruction, as untouched by it as the knife which cuts the throat of the Easter lamb.) Even the least fanciful of theorists agreed that they might have accelerated or at least were witnesses to a universal destruction. They believed the engineers had drilled through unguessable dimensions, damaging something which had until now regulated the rate of entropy to which human senses had, over millions of years, evolved. With that control damaged and the rate accelerating to infinity, their perceptions were no longer adequate to the psychic environment. The multiverse raced perhaps towards the creation of a new sequence of realities, perhaps towards some cold and singular conformity; perhaps towards unbridled chaos, the end of all consciousness. This last was what drew certain people to the edge of the Fault, their fascination taking them step by relentless step to the brink, there to be consumed.

On a dance floor swept by peculiar silhouettes and shifts of light, Boudreaux Ramsadeen, who had brought his café here by rail from Meridian, encouraged the zee-band to play on while he guided his tiny partners in their Cajun steps. These professional dancers travelled from all over Arcadia to join him. Their hands on their swaying hips, their delicate feet performing figures as subtly intricate as the Terminal's own dimensions, they danced to some other tune than the band's. Boudreaux's Neanderthal brows were drawn together in an expression of seraphic concentration as, keeping all his great bulk on his poised left foot, describing the steps with his right, he moved his partners with remarkable tenderness and delicacy.

(Jack Karaquazian deals seven hands of poker, fingering the sensors of his *kayplay* with deliberate slowness. Only here, on the whole planet, is there a reservoir of energy deep enough to run every machine, synthetic reasoner, or cybe in the world, but not transmittable beyond the Terminal's peculiar boundaries. Only those with an incurable addiction to the past's electronic luxuries come here, and they are all gamblers of some description. Weird light saturates the table; the light of Hell. He is waiting for his passion, his muse.)

Colinda Dovero and Jack Karaquazian had met again across the blue, flat sheen of a *mentasense* and linked into the wildest, riskiest game of Slick Image anyone had ever witnessed, let alone joined. When they came out of it, Dovero was eight guineas up out of a betting range which had made psychic bids most seasoned players never cared to imagine. It had caused Boudreaux Ramsadeen to rouse himself from his mood of ugly tolerance and insist thereafter on a stakes ceiling that would protect the metaphysical integrity of his establishment. Some of the spectators had developed peculiar psychopathic obsessions, while others had merely become subject to chronic vomiting. Dovero and Karaquazian had, however, gone into spacelessness together and did not properly emerge for nine variations, while the walls expanded and turned at odd angles and the colours saturated and amplified all subtleties of sensation. There is no keener experience, they say, than the act of love during a matrix shift at the Terminal Café. "That buzz? It's self-knowledge," she told the Egyptian holding him tight as they floated in the calm between one bizarre reality and another.

"No disrespect, Jack," she had added.

3. Il Fait Chaud

Karaquazian found her again a year later on the *Princesse du Natchez*. He recognised, through her veil, her honey-coloured almond eyes. She was, she said, now ready for him. They turned their stateroom into marvellous joint quarters. Her reason for parting had been a matter of private business. That business, she warned him, was not entirely resolved but he was grateful for even a hint of a future. The old Confederate autonomies were lucky if their matrixes were only threadbare. They were collapsing. There were constant minor reality melt-downs now and yet there was nothing to be done but continue as if continuation were possible. Soon the Mississippi might become one of the few geographical constants. "When we start to go," he said. "I want to be on the river."

"Maybe chaos is already our natural condition," she had teased. She was always terrifyingly playful in the face of annihilation, whereas he found it difficult even to confront the idea. She still had a considerable amount of hope in reserve.

They began to travel as brother and sister. A month after they had established this relationship, there was some question of her arrest for fraud when two well-uniformed cool boys had stepped aboard at New Auschwitz on the Arkansas side as the boat was casting off and suddenly they had no authority. In midstream they made threats. They insisted on entering the ballroom where she and the Egyptian were occupied. And then Karaquazian had suffered watching her raise promising eyes to the captain who saluted, asked if she had everything she needed, ordered the boys to disembark at Greenville, and said that he might stop by later to make sure she was properly comfortable. She had told him she would greatly appreciate the attention and returned to the floor, where a lanky zee-band bounced out the old favourites. With an unsisterly flirt of her hands, she had offered herself back to her pseudo-brother.

Jack Karaquazian had felt almost sour, though gentleman enough to hide it, while he took charge of the unpleasant feelings experienced by her cynical use of a sensuality he had thought, for the present at least, his preserve. Yet that sensuality was in no way diminished by its knowing employment, and his loyalty to her remained based upon the profound respect he had for her—a type of love he would cheerfully have described as feminine, and through which he believed he experienced some slight understanding of the extraordinary individual she was. He relished her lust for freedom, her optimism, her insistence on her own right to exist beyond the destruction of their universe, her willingness to achieve some form of immortality in any terms and at any cost. She thrilled him precisely because she disturbed him. He had not known such deep excitement since his last two-and-a-half weeks before leaving Egypt and his first three weeks in America; and never because of a woman. Until then, Karaquazian had experienced profound emotion only for the arts of gaming and his faith. His many liaisons, while frequently affectionate, had never been allowed to interfere with his abiding passion. At first he had been shocked by the realisation that he was more fascinated by Colinda Dovero than he had ever been by the intellectual strategies of the Terminal's ranks of Grand Turks.

The mind which had concentrated on gambling and its attendant skills, upon self-defense and physical fitness, upon self-control, now devoted itself almost wholly to her. He was obsessed with her thoughts, her motives, her background, her story, the effect which her reality had upon his own. He was no longer the self-possessed individual he had been before he met her; and, when they had made love again that first night, he had been ready to fall in with any scheme which kept them together. Eventually, after the New Auschwitz incident, he had made some attempt to rescue his old notion of himself, but after she revealed her business had to do with a potential colour-strike valuable beyond any modern hopes, he had immediately agreed to go with her to help establish the claim. In return, she promised him a percentage of the proceeds. He committed himself to her in spite of his not quite believing anything she told him. She had been working the boats for some while now, raising money to fund the expedition, ready to call it quits as soon as her luck turned bad. Since Memphis, her luck had run steadily down. This could also be why she had been so happy to seek an ally in him. The appearance of the cool boys had alarmed her: as if that evening had been the first time she had as much as been accused by anyone. Besides, she told him, with the money he had they could now easily meet the top price for the land, which was only swamp anyway. She would pay the fees and expenses. There would be no trouble raising funds once the strike was claimed.

At Chickasaw, they had left the boat and set off up the Trace together. She had laughed as she looked back at the levee and the *Princesse* outlined against the cold sky. "I have made an enemy, I think, of that captain." He was touched by what he perceived as her wish to reassure him of her constancy. But in Carthage, they had been drawn into a flat game, which had developed around a random hotspot no bigger than a penny, and played until the spot faded. When the debts were paid, they were down to a couple of guineas between them and had gambled their emergency batteries. At this point, superstition overwhelmed them and each had seen sudden bad luck in the other.

Jack Karaquazian regretted their parting almost immediately and would have returned to her, but by the time he heard of her again she was already lost to Peabody, the planter. It had been Peabody that time who had sent his cool boys after her. She wrote once to Karaquazian, in care of the Terminal. She said she was taking a rest but would be in touch.

Meanwhile Karaquazian had a run of luck at the Terminal which, had he not cheated against himself and put the winnings back into circulation, would have brought a halt to all serious gambling for a while. Karaquazian now played with his back to the Fault. The sight of that mighty appetite, that insatiable mystery, distracted him these days. He was impatient for her signal.

4. La Pointe a Pain

Sometimes Jack Karaquazian missed the ancient, exquisite colours of the Egyptian evening, where shades of yellow, red, and purple touched the warm stone of magnificent ruins, flooded the desert and brought deep shadows, as black and sharp as flint upon that richly faded landscape, one subtle tint blending into the other, one stone with the next, supernaturally married and near to their final gentle merging, in the last, sweet centuries of their material state. Here, on the old *Etoile,* he remembered the glories of his youth, before they drilled the Fault, and he found some consolation, if not satisfaction, in bringing back a time when he had not known much in the way of self-discipline, had gloried in his talents. When he had seemed free.

Once again, he strove to patch together some sort of consistent memory of when they had followed the map into the cypress swamp; of times when he had failed to reach the swamp. He had a sense of making progress up the Trace after he had disembarked, but he had probably never reached McClellan and had never seen the Stains again. How much of this repetition was actual experience? How much was dream?

Recently, the semi-mutable nature of the matrix meant that such questions had become increasingly common. Jack Karaquazian had countless memories of beginning this journey to join her and progressing so far (usually no closer than Vicksburg) before his recollections became uncertain and the images isolated, giving no clue to any particular context. Now, however, he felt as if he were being carried by some wise momentum which allowed his unconscious to steer a path through the million psychic turnings and cul-de-sacs this environment provided. His obsession with the woman, it seemed to him, his insane association of her with his luck, his Muse, was actually supplying the force needed to propel him back to the reality he longed to find. She was his goal, but she was also his reason.

5. *Les Veuves des la Coulee*

They had met for the third time while she was still with Peabody, the brute said to own half Tennessee and to possess the mortgages on the other half. Peabody's red stone fortress lay outside Memphis. He was notorious for the cruel way in which his plantation whites were treated, but his influence among the eight members of the Confederacy meant he would inevitably be next Governor General, with the power of life and death over all but the best protected *machinoix* or guild neutrals like Karaquazian and Dovero. "I am working for him," she admitted. "As a kind of ambassador. You know how squeamish people are about dealing with the North. They lose face even by looking directly at a whitey. But I find them no different, in the main. A little feckless. Social conditioning." She did not hold with genetic theories of race. She had chatted in this manner at a public occasion where, by coincidence, they were both guests.

"You are his property, I think," Karaquazian had murmured without rancor. But she had shaken her head.

Whether she had become addicted to Peabody's power or was merely deeply fascinated by it, Karaquazian never knew. For his own part, he had taken less and less pleasure in the liaison that followed while still holding profound feelings for her. Then she had come to his room one evening when he was in Memphis and she in town with Peabody, who attended some bond auction at the big hotel, and told him that she deeply desired to stay with him, but they must be so rich they would never lose their whole roll again. Karaquazian thought she was ending their affair on a graceful note. Then she produced a creased read-out which showed colour-sightings in the depths of Mississippi near the Tombigbee not far from Starkville. This was the first evidence she had ever offered him, and he believed now that she was trying to demonstrate that she trusted him, that she was telling the truth. She had intercepted the report before it reached Peabody. The airship pilot who sent it had crashed in flames a day later. "This time we go straight to it." She had pushed him back against his cot, sniffing at his neck, licking him. Then, with sudden honesty, she told him that, through her Tarot racing, she was into Peabody for almost a million guineas, and he was going to make her go North permanently to pay him back by setting up deals with the white bosses of the so-called Insurgent Republics. "Peabody's insults are getting bad enough. Imagine suffering worse from a white man. No disrespect, Jack. But that's what it means."

Within two weeks, they had repeated their journey up the Trace, got as far as McClellan, and taken a pirogue into the Streams, following, as best they could, the grey contours of the aerial map, heading towards a cypress swamp. It had been fall then, too, with the leaves turning; the tree-filled landscape of browns, golds, reds, and greens reflected in the cooling sheen of the water. The swamp still kept its heat during the day.

"We are the same," he had suggested to her, to explain their love. "We have the same sense of boredom."

"No, Jack, we have the same habits. But I arrived at mine through fear. I had to learn a courage that for you was no more than an inheritance." She had described her anxieties. "It occasionally feels like the victory of some ancient winter."

The waterways were full of birds which always betrayed their approach, but they were certain no humans came here at this time of year, though any hunters would assume them to be hunting, too. Beautiful as it was, the country was forbidding and they saw no traces of Indians, a sure sign that the area was considered dangerous, doubtless because of the snakes.

She foresaw a world rapidly passing from contention to warfare and from warfare to brute struggle, from that to insensate matter, and from that to nothingness. "This is the reality offered as our future," she said. They determined they would, if only through their mutual love, resist such a future.

They had grown comfortable with one another, and when they camped at night they would remind themselves of their story, piecing it back into some sort of whole, restoring to themselves the extraordinary intensity of their long relationship. By this means, and the warmth of their sexuality, they raised a rough barrier against encroaching chaos.

6. *Mon Coeur et Mon Amour*

It had been twilight, with the cedars turning black and silver, a cool mist forming on the water, when they reached the lagoon marked on the map, poling the dugout through the shallows, breaking dark gashes in the weedy surface, the mud sucking and sighing at the pole, and each movement tiring Karaquazian too much, threatening to leave him with no energy in reserve, so they chose a fairly open spot, where snakes might not find them, and, placing a variety of sonic and visual beacons, settled down to sleep. They would have slept longer had not the novelty and potential danger of their situation excited their lusts.

In the morning, sitting with the canvas folded back and the tree-studded water roseate from the emerging sun, the mist becoming golden, the white ibises and herons flapping softly amongst the glowing autumn foliage, Karaquazian and Colinda Dovero breakfasted on their well-planned supplies, then studied their map before continuing deeper into the beauty of that unwelcoming swamp. Then, at about noon, with a cold blue-grey sky reflected in the still surface of a broad, shallow pond, they found colour—one large Stain spread over an area almost five feet in circumference, and two smaller Stains, about a foot across, almost identical to those noted by the pilot.

From a distance, the Stains appeared to rest upon the surface of the water, but as Karaquazian poled the boat closer, they saw that they had in fact penetrated deeply into the muddy bottom of the pond. The gold Stains formed a kind of membrane over the openings, effectively sealing them, and yet it was impossible to tell if the colour were solid or a kind of dense, utterly stable gas.

"Somebody drilled here years ago and then, I don't know why, thought better of it." Colinda looked curiously at the Stains, mistaking them for capped bores. "Yet it must be of first quality. Near pure."

Karaquazian was disappointed by what he understood to be a note of greed in her voice, but he smiled. "There was a time colour had to come out perfect," he said. "This must have been drilled before Biloxi—or around the same time."

"Now they're too scared, most of them, to drill at all!" Shivering, she peered over the side of the boat, expecting to see her own image in the big Stain, and instead was surprised, almost shocked.

Watching her simply for the pleasure it gave him, Jack Karaquazian was curious and moved his own body to look down. The Stain had a strangely solid, unreflective depth, like a gigantic ingot of gold hammered by some alien deep into the reality of the planet.

Both were now aware of a striking abnormality, yet neither wanted to believe anything but some simpler truth, and they entered into an unspoken bond of silence on the matter. "We must go to Jackson and make the purchase," he said. "Then we must look for some expert engineering help. Another partner, even."

"This will get me clear of Peabody," she murmured, her eyes still upon the Stain, "and that's all I care about."

"He'll know you double-crossed him as soon as you begin to work this."

She shrugged.

She had remained, at her own insistence, with the claim while he went back to Jackson to buy the land and, when this was finalised, buy a prospecting licence, without which they would

not be able to file their claim, such were Mississippi's bureau-
cratic subtleties; but when he returned to the cypress swamp, she
and the pirogue were gone. Only the Stains remained as evidence
of their experience. Enquiring frantically in McClellan, he heard
of a woman being caught wild and naked in the swamp and
becoming the common possession of the brothers Berger and
their father, Ox, until they tired of her. It was said she could no
longer speak any human language but communicated in barks
and grunts like a hog. It was possible that the Bergers had
drowned her in the swamp before continuing on up towards Tu-
pelo where they had property.

7. *Valse de Coeur Casser*

Convinced of their kidnapping and assault upon Colinda Dovero,
of their responsibility for her insanity and possibly her death,
Jack Karaquazian was only an hour behind them on the Trace
when they stopped to rest at *The Breed Papoose*. The *mendala*
tavern just outside Belgrade in Chickasaw Territory was the last
before Mississippi jurisdiction started again. It served refresh-
ment as rough and new as its own timbers.

A ramshackle, unpainted shed set off the road in a clearing of
slender firs and birches, its only colour was its sign, the crude
representation of a baby, black on its right side, white on its left,
and wearing Indian feathers. Usually Jack Karaquazian avoided
such places, for the stakes were either too low or too high, and
a game usually ended in some predictable brutality. Dismounting
in the misty woods, Karaquazian took firm control of his fury
and slept for a little while before rising and leading his horse to
the hitching post. A cold instrument of justice, the Egyptian
entered the tavern, a mean, unclean room where even the sawdust on the floor was filthy beyond recognition. His weapon displayed in an obvious threat, he walked slowly up to the *mendala*-
sodden bar and ordered a Fröm.

The two Bergers and their huge sire were drinking at the bar with
every sign of relaxed amiability, like creatures content in the knowledge that they had no natural enemies. They were honestly sur-

prised as Karaquazian spoke coolly to them, his voice hardly raised, yet cutting through the other conversations like a Mason knife.

"Ladies are not so damned plentiful in this territory we can afford to give offence to one of them," Karaquazian had said, his eyes narrowing slightly, his body still as a hawk. "And as for hitting one or cursing one or having occasion to offer harm to one, or even murdering one, well, gentlemen, that looks pretty crazy to me. Or if it isn't craziness, then it's dumb cowardice. And there's nobody in this here tavern thinks a whole lot of a coward, I believe. And even less, I'd guess, of three damned cowards."

At this scarcely disguised challenge, the majority of *The Breed Papoose*'s customers turned like magic into discrete shadows until only Mr. Karaquazian, in his dusty silks and linen, and the Bergers, still in their travelling kaftans, their round, Ugandan faces bright with sweat, were left confronting one another along the line of the plank bar. Mr. Karaquazian made no movement until the Bergers fixed upon a variety of impulsive decisions.

The Egyptian did not draw as Japh Berger ran for the darkness of the backdoor convenience, neither did his hand begin to move as Ach Berger flung himself towards the cover of an overturned bench. It was only as Pa Ox, still mildly puzzled, pulled up the huge Vickers 9 on its swivel holster that Mr. Karaquazian's right hand moved with superhuman speed to draw and level the delicate silver stem of a pre-rip Sony, cauterizing the older Berger's gun-hand and causing his terrible weapon to crash upon stained, warped boards—to slice away the bench around the shivering Junior, who pulled back withering fingers with a yelp, and to send a slender beam of lilac carcinogens to ensure that Japh would never again take quite the same pleasure in his private pursuits. Then the gambler had replaced the Sony in its holster and signalled, with a certain embarrassment, for a drink.

From the darkness, Ach Berger said: "Can I go now, mister?"

Without turning, Karaquazian raised his voice a fraction. "I hope in future you'll pay attention to better advice than your pa's, boy." He looked directly into the face of the wounded Ox as he turned, holding the already healing stump of his wrist, to make for the door, leaving the Vickers and the four parts of his hand in the sawdust.

"I never would have thought that Sony was anything but a woman's weapon," said the barkeep admiringly.

"Oh, you can be sure of that." Jack Karaquazian had lifted a glass in cryptic salute.

8. *Les Flammes d'Enfer*

It had been perhaps a month later, still in the Territory, that Karaquazian met a man who had seen the Bergers with the mad woman in Aberdeen a week before Karaquazian had caught up with them.

The man told Karaquazian that Ox Berger had paid for the woman's board at a hotel in Aberdeen and made sure a doctor was found and a woman hired to look after her "until her folks came looking for her." The man had spoken in quiet wonder at her utter madness, the exquisite beauty of her face, the peculiar cast of her eyes. "Ox told me she had looked the same since they'd found her, wading waist-deep in the swamp." From Aberdeen he heard she had been taken back to New Auschwitz by Peabody's people. In Memphis, Karaquazian heard she had gone North. He settled in Memphis for a while, perhaps hoping she would return and seek him out.

He was in a state of profound shock.

Jack Karaquazian refused to discuss or publicly affirm any religion; his faith in God did not permit it. He believed that the moment faith turned to religion it inevitably became politics. He was firmly determined to have as little to do with politics as possible. In general conversation he was prepared to admit that both provided excellent distraction and consolation to those who needed them, but he believed they were often bought at too high a price. Privately, he held a quiet certainty in the manifest power of Good and Evil. The former he identified simply as the Deity; the latter he personified as the Old Hunter, and imagined this creature stalking the world in search of souls. Until now he had always congratulated himself on the skill with which he avoided the Old Hunter's traps and enticements, but now he had been thoroughly deceived. He had been made to betray himself through what he valued most: his honour. He was disgusted and astonished at the way in which his most treasured virtues had destroyed his self-esteem and robbed him of everything but his uncommon luck at cards.

She did not write. Eventually, he took the *Etoile* down to Baton Rouge and from there rode the omnus towards the coast, by way of McComb and Wiggins. It was easy to find Biloxi. The sky was a fury of purple and black for thirty miles around, but above the Fault was a patch of perfect pale blue. It had been there since the destruction began. Even as continua collided and became merely elemental, you could always find the Terminal Café, flickering in and out of a thousand subtly altering realities, pulsing, expanding, contracting, pushing unlikely angles through the afterimages of its own shadows, making unique each outline of each ordinary piece of furniture and equipment, and yet never fully affected by that furious vortex above which the solar system bobbed, as it were, like a cork at the centre of the maelstrom. They were not entirely invulnerable to the effects of chaos, that pit of non-consciousness. There were the hot-spots, the time-shifts, the perceptual problems, the energy drains, the odd geographies. There had been heavy snow over the Delta one winter, a general cooling, a corruscation, and the following summer, most agreed, was perfectly normal. And yet there remained always the sense of borrowed time. She had seen that winter as an omen for the future. "We have no right to survive this catastrophe," she had said. "Yet we must try, surely." He had recognised a faith as strong as his own.

Boudreaux Ramsadeen brought in a new band, electrok addicts from somewhere in Tennessee where they had found a hot-spot and brained in until it went dry. They had been famous in those half-remembered years before the Fault, and they played with extraordinary vigour and pleasure, so that Boudreaux's strange, limping dance took on still more complex figures and his partners, thrilled at the brute's exquisite grace and gentleness, threw their bodies into rapturous invention, stepping in and out of the zig-zagging afterimages, sometimes dancing with themselves, it seemed, their heads flung back and the colours of Hell reflected in their eyes. And Boudreaux cried with the joy of it all, while Jack Karaquazian, on the raised floor of the main game section where the window looked directly out into the Fault, took no notice. Here, at this favourite flat game, his fingers playing a ten-dimensional pseudo-universe like an old familiar deck, the Egyptian still presented his back to that voracious Fault, its colours swirling in a kind of glee as it swallowed galaxies, and gave himself up to old habits. Now, however, he was never unconscious.

And so Mr. Karaquazian remained in the limbo of the Terminal Café, while up in Memphis, he heard, bloody rivalries and broken treaties must inevitably end in the Confederacy's absolute collapse, unless they made some sort of alliance with the reluctant Free States. Either way, wars must begin. It seemed that Colinda Dovero's vision of the future had been more accurate than most of the oracles.

Karaquazian had left Egypt because of the civil war, but now he refused to move on or even discuss the situation. He kept his back to the Fault, which he had come to believe was the antithesis of God, nothing less than the personification of the Old Hunter. Yet, unlike most of his fellow gamblers, Jack Karaquazian still hoped for some chance at heaven, a reconciliation with his Deity. His faith was made more painful but not diminished by his constant outrage at the obscene arrogance which had led him to ruin innocent men. Yet something of that arrogance remained in him, and he believed he could not find reconciliation until he had rid himself of it. He knew of no way to confront and redeem his action. To seek out the Bergers, to offer them his remorse, had seemed to him a way of compounding his action, of attempting to shift the moral burden and, what was more, of further insulting them. He remembered the mild astonishment in Ox's eyes, and he at least understood the man's expression as he sought to defend himself against Karaquazian who, to Ox, could only be a psychopath blood looking for a coup.

Sam Oakenhurst wondered, in the words of a new song he had heard, if they were not "killing time for eternity." Maybe, one by one, they would get bored enough with the game and stroll casually down into the mouth of Hell, to suffer whatever punishment, pleasure, or annihilation was their fate. But Karaquazian became impatient with this and Sam apologised. "I'm growing sentimental, I guess."

Oakenhurst and Brother Ignatius had borrowed two of his systems for the big Texas game. They had acted out of good will, attempting to re-involve him in the things which had once pleased him. Oakenhurst had told of an illegal poker school in New Orleans where they were playing acoustic cards. Only a few people still had those old skills. "Why don't you meet me down there, Jack, when I get back from Texas?"

"But they're treacherous dudes, those *machinoix*—outlaws or otherwise."

"What's the difference, Jack? It'll make a change for you."

So, after a few more hands and a little more time on the edge of eternity, he had joined Oakenhurst in New Orleans. Ignatius was gone, taken out in some freak pi-jump on the way home, his horse with him. Karaquazian discovered the *machinoix* to be players more interested in the nostalgia and the pain than the game itself. It had been ugly money, but easy, and their fellow players, far from resenting their losses, grew steadily more friendly, courting their company between games, offering to display their most intimate scarifications.

Jack Karaquazian had wondered, chiefly because of the terror he sensed resonating between them, if the *machinoix* might provide him with a means of salvation, if only through some petty martyrdom. He had nothing but a dim notion of conventional theologies, but the *machinoix* spoke often of journeying into the shadowlands, by which he eventually realised they meant an afterlife. It was one of their fundamental beliefs. Sam Oakenhurst was able, amiably, to accept their strangeness and continue to win their guineas, but Karaquazian became nervous, not finding the sense of danger in any way stimulating.

When Sam's luck had turned Karaquazian had been secretly relieved. He had remained in the city only to honour his commitment to his partner. He felt it might be time to try the Trace again. He felt she might be calling him.

9. *Louisiana Two-step*

"The world was always a mysterious dream to me," she had told him. "But now it is an incomprehensible nightmare. Was it like this for those Jews do you think?"

"Which Jews?" He had never had much interest in history.

She had continued speaking, probably to herself, as she stood on the balcony of the hotel in Gatlinburg and watched the aftershocks of some passing skirmish billow over the horizon: "Those folk, those Anglo-Saxons, had no special comfort in dying. Not for them the zealotry of the Viking or the Moor. They paraded their iron and their horses and they made compacts with those they conquered or those who threatened them. They offered bargains, a notion of universal justice. And this gradually prevailed until chaos was driven into darkness and ancient memory. Even the Normans could not reverse what the Anglo-Saxons achieved. Their ideas gradually prevailed, but with them, Jack, also vanished a certain wild vivacity. What the Christians came to call 'pagan.' " She had sighed and kissed his hands, looking away at the flickering ginger moon. "Do you long for those times, Jack? That pagan semi-consciousness?"

Karaquazian thought it astonishing that some had managed to create a kind of order out of ungovernable chaos. And that, though he would never say so, was his reason for believing in God and, because logic would have it, the Old Hunter. "Total consciousness must, I suppose, suggest total anti-consciousness—and all that lies between."

She told him then of her own belief that if the Fault were manifest Evil, then somewhere there must be an equivalent manifestation of Good. She loved life with a positive relish which he enjoyed vicariously, and which in turn restored to him sensibilities long since atrophied.

When he left the steamboat at Greenville, Mr. Karaquazian bought himself a sturdy riding horse and made his way steadily up the Trace, determined to admire and relish the beauty of it, as if for the first time. Once again, many of the trees had already dropped their leaves. Through their skeletons, a faint pink-gold wash in the pearly sky showed the position of the sun. Against this cold, soft light, the details of the trees were emphasised, giving each twig a character of its own. Jack Karaquazian kept his mind on these wonders and pleasures, moving day by day towards McClellan and the silver cypress swamp, the gold Stains. In the sharp, new air he felt a strength that he had not known, even before his act of infamy. Perhaps it was a hint of redemption. Of his several previous attempts to return, he had no clear recollections; but this time, though he anticipated, as it were, forgetfulness, he was more confident of his momentum. In his proud heart, his sinner's heart, he saw Colinda Dovero as the means of his salvation. She alone would give him a choice which might redeem him in his eyes, if not in God's. She was still his luck. She would be back at her Stains, he thought, maybe working her claim, a rich machine-baron herself by now and unsettled by his arrival; but once united, he knew they could be parted only by an act of uncalled-for courage, perhaps something like a martyrdom. He felt she was offering him, at last, a destiny.

Karaquazian rode up on the red-gold Trace, between the tall, dense trees of the Mississippi woods, crossing the Broken and New Rivers, following the joyfully foaming Pearl for a while until he was in Chocktaw country, where he paid his toll in *piles noires* to an unsmiling Indian who had not seen, he said, a good horse in a long time. He spoke of an outrage, an automobile which had come by a few days ago, driven by a woman with auburn hair. He pointed. The deep tyre tracks were still visible. Karaquazian began to follow them, guessing that Colinda Dovero had left them for him. At what enormous cost? It seemed she must already be tapping the Stains. Such power would be worth almost anything when war eventually came. He could feel the disintegration in the air. Soon these people would be mirroring the metaphysical destruction by falling upon and devouring their fellows. Yet, through their self-betrayal, he thought, Colinda Dovero might survive and even prosper, at least for a while.

He arrived in McClellan expecting to find change, enrichment from the colour strike. But the town remained the pleasant, unaltered place he had known, her maze of old railroad tracks crossing and recrossing at dozens of intersections, from the pre-Biloxi days when the meat-plants had made her rich, her people friendly and easy, her whites respectful yet dignified.

Karaquazian spent the night at the Henry Clay Hotel and was disappointed to find no one in the tidy little main street (now a far cry from its glory) who had heard of any activity out around the streams. Only a fool, he was told, would go into that cypress swamp at any time of year, least of all during a true season. Consoling himself with the faint hope that she might have kept her workings a secret, Karaquazian rented himself a pirogue, gave an eager kiddikin a guinea to take care of his horse, and set off into the streams, needing no map, no memory—merely his will and the unreasoning certainty that she was drawing him to her.

10. Sugar Bee

"I had been dying all my life, Jack," she had said. "I decided I wanted to live. I'm giving it my best shot."

The swamp fog obscured all detail. There was the sharp sound of the water as he paddled the pirogue; the rustle of a wing, a muffled rush, a faint shadow moving amongst the trunks, so Jack Karaquazian began to wonder if he were not in limbo, moving out of one matrix to another. Would those outlines remain the outlines of trees and vines? Would they crystallise, perhaps, or become massive cliffs of basalt and obsidian? There was sometimes a clue in the nature of the echoes. He whistled a snatch of "Grand Mamou." The old dance tune helped his spirits. He believed he was still in the same reality.

"Human love, Jack, is our only weapon against chaos. And yet, consistently, we reject its responsibilities in favour of some more abstract and therefore less effective notion."

Suddenly, through the agitated grey, as if in confirmation of his instinct, a dozen ibises flapped low beneath the branches of the cypresses and cedars, as silvery as bass, so that Mr. Karaquazian in his scarlet travelling cloak felt as if he somehow intruded on all that exquisite paleness.

When eventually the sun began to wash the sky in the west

and the mist was touched with the subtle colours of tea-rose, warming and dissipating to reveal the tawny browns and dark greens it had been hiding, he grew more comfortable with his certainty that this time, inevitably, he and Colinda Dovero must soon reunite. He was half prepared to see the baroque brass and diamonds of the legendary Prosers, milking the Stains for his sweetheart's security, but only herons disturbed the covering of leaves upon the water; only ducks and perpetua geese shouted and bickered into the cold air, the rapid flutter of their wings having eerie resemblance to a *mechanish* engine. The cypress swamp was avoided perhaps because it was genuinely timeless, the only place on earth completely unaffected by the Biloxi error.

But why would such changelessness be feared?

Or had fundamental change already occurred? Something too complex and delicate for the human brain to comprehend, just as it could not really accept the experience of more than one matrix. Jack Karaquazian, contented by the swamp's familiarity, did not wish to challenge its character. Instead, he drew further strength from it so that when, close to twilight, he saw the apparently ramshackle cabin, its blackened logs and planks two storeys high, riveted together by old salt and grit cans still advertising the virtues of their ancient brands, and perched low in the fork of two great silvery cypress branches overhanging the water and the smallest of the Stains, he knew at once that she had never truly left her claim; that in some way she had always been here, always waiting for him.

For a few seconds, Jack Karaquazian allowed himself the anguish of regret and self-accusation, then he threw back his cloak, cupped his hands around his mouth, and with his white breath pouring into the air, called out:

"Colinda!"

And from within her fortress, her nest, she replied:

"Jack."

Then she was leaning out over the verandah of woven branches, her almond eyes, the colour of honey, bright with tears and hope, an understanding that this time, perhaps for the first time, he had actually made it back to her. That he was no longer a ghost. When she spoke to him, however, her language was incomprehensible; seemingly a cacophony, without melody or sense. Terrible yelps and groans came out of her perfect lips. He could scarcely bear to listen. *Is this,* he wondered, *how we first perceive the language of angels?*

The creosoted timbers lay in odd marriage to the pale branches which cradled them. Flitting with urgent joy, from verandah to branch and from branch to makeshift ladder, she was a tawny ghost, an autumn spirit.

Naked, yet unaffected by the evening chill, she reached the landing she had made. The planks, firmly moored by four oddly plaited ropes tied into the branches, rolled and bounced under her tiny bare feet.

"Jack, my *pauvre hobo!*" It was as if she could only remember the language through snatches of song, as a child does. *"Ma pauvre pierrot."* And she smiled in delight, seeming to recognise him at the same time the words came to her tongue.

Then he stepped from the pirogue to the landing and they embraced, scarlet engulfing dark gold, and it was the resolution he had so often prayed for; but without redemption. For now it was even clearer to him that the mistake he had made at *The Breed Papoose* had never been an honest one. He also knew that she need never discover this; and what was left of the hypocrite in him called to him to forget the past as irredeemable. And when she sensed his tension, a hesitation, she asked in halting speech if he had brought bad news, if he no longer loved her, if he faltered. She had waited for him a long time, she said, relinquishing all she had gained so that she might be united with him, to take him with her, to show him what she had discovered in the Stain.

She drew him up to her cabin. It looked as if it had been here for centuries. It seemed in places to have grown into or from the living tree. Inside it was full of naïve luxury—plush and brass and gold-plated candelabra, mirrors and crystals and flowing *muralos*. There was a little power from the Stains, she said, but not much. She had brought everything in the car long ago. She took him on to the veranda and, through the semi-darkness, pointed out the burgundy carcass of an antique Oldsmobile.

"I thought . . ." But he was unable either to express the emotion he felt or to comprehend the sickening temporal shifts which had almost separated them forever. It was as if dream and reality had at last resolved, but at the wrong moment. "Some men took you to Aberdeen."

"They were kind." Her speech was still thick.

"So I understand."

"But mistaken. I had returned to find you. I went into the Stain while you were gone. When I tried to seek you out, I had forgotten how to speak or wear clothes. I got back here easily. It's never hard for me."

"Very hard for me." He embraced her again, kissed her.

"This is what I longed for." She studied his dark green eyes, his smooth brown skin, the contours of his face, his muscular body. "Waiting in this place has not been easy, with the world so close. But I came back for you, Jack. I believe the Stain is not a sign of colour but a kind of counter-effect to the Fault. It leads into a cosmos of wonderful stability. Not stasis, they say, but with a slower rate of entropy. What they once called a lower chaos factor, when I studied physics. I met a woman whom I think we would call 'the Rose' in our language. She is half-human, half-flower, like all her race. And she was my mentor as she could be yours. And we could have children, Jack. It's an extraordinary adventure. So many ways of learning to see and so much time for it. Time for consideration, time to create justice. Here, Jack, all the time is going. You know that." She sensed some unexpected resistance in him. She touched his cheek. "Jack, we are on the edge of chaos here. We must eventually be consumed by what we created. But we also created a way out. What you always talked about. What you yearned for. You know."

"Yes, I know." Perhaps she was really describing Heaven. He made an awkward gesture. "Through there?" He indicated, in the gathering darkness, the pale wash of the nearest Stain.

"The big one only." She became enthusiastic, her uncertainties fading before the vividness of her remembered experience. "We have responsibilities. We have duties there. But they are performed naturally, clearly from self-interest. There's understanding and charity there, Jack. The logic is what you used to talk about. What you thought you had dreamed. Where chance no longer rules unchecked. It's a heavenly place, Jack. The Rose will accept us both. She'll guide us. We can go there now, if you like. You must want to go, *mon cheri, mon cheri.*" But now, as she looked at him, at the way he stood, at the way he stared, unblinking, down into the swamp, she hesitated. She took his hand and gripped it. "You want to go. It isn't boring, Jack. It's as real as here. But they have a future, a precedent. We have neither."

"I would like to go to such a place." He checked the spasm in his chest and was apologetic. "But I might not be ready, *ma fancy.*"

She held tight to his gambler's hand, wondering if she had misjudged its strength. "You would rather spend your last days at a table in the Terminal Café, waiting for the inevitable moment of oblivion?"

"I would rather journey with you," he said, "to Paradise or anywhere you wished, Colinda. But Paradise will accept you, *ma honey.* Perhaps I have not yet earned my place there."

She preferred to believe he joked with her. "We will leave it until the morning." She stroked his blue-black hair, believing him too tired to think. "There is no such thing as earning. It's always luck, Jack. It was luck we found the Stains. It's luck that brought us together. Brought us our love. Our love brought us back together. It is a long, valuable life they offer us, *mon papillon.* Full of hope and peace. Take your chance, Jack. As you always did."

He shook his head. "But some of us, my love, have earning natures. I made a foolish play. I am ashamed."

"No regrets, Jack. You can leave it all behind. This is luck. Our luck. What is it in you, Jack, this new misery?" She imagined another woman.

He could not tell her. He wanted the night with her. He wanted a memory. And her own passion for him conquered her curiosity, her trepidation, yet there was a desperate quality to her lovemaking which neither she nor he had ever wished to sense again. Addressing this, she was optimistic: "This will all go once we enter the Stain. Doesn't it seem like heaven, Jack?"

"Near enough," he admitted. A part of him, a bitter part of him, wished that he had never made this journey, that he had never left the game behind; for the game, even at its most dangerous, was better than this scarcely bearable pain. "Oh, my heart!"

For the rest of the night he savoured every second of his torment, and yet in the morning he knew that he was not by this means to gain release from his pride. It seemed that his self-esteem, his stern wall against the truth, crumbled in unison with the world's collapse; he saw for himself nothing but an eternity of anguished regret.

"Come." She moved towards sadness as she led him down through the branches and the timbers to his own pirogue. She still refused to believe she had waited only for this.

He let her row them out into the pastel brightness of the lagoon until they floated above the big gold Stain, peering through that purity of colour as if they might actually glimpse the paradise she had described.

"Your clothes will go away." She was gentle as a Louisiana April. "You needn't worry about that."

She slipped over the side and, with a peculiar lifting motion, moved under the membrane to hang against the density of the gold, smiling up at him to demonstrate that there was nothing to fear, as beautiful as she could ever be, as perfect as the colour. And then she had re-emerged in the shallow water, amongst the lillies and the weeds and the sodden leaves. "Come, Jack. You must not hurt me further, sweetheart. We will go now. But if you stay, I shall not return." Horrified by what she understood as his cowardice, she fell back against the Stain, staring up at the grey-silver branches of the big trees, watching the morning sun touch the rising mist, refusing to look at Jack Karaquazian while he wept for his failures, for his inability to seize this moment, for all his shame, his unforgotten dreams; at his unguessable loss.

She spoke from the water. "It wasn't anything that happened to me there that turned me crazy. It was the journey here did that. It's sane down there, Jack."

"No place for a gambler, then," he said, and laughed. "What

is this compensatory Heaven? What proof is there that it is real? The only reason for its existence appears to be a moral one!"

"It's a balance," she said. "Nature offers balances."

"That was always a human illusion. Look at Biloxi. There's the reality. I'm not ready."

"This isn't worthy of you, Jack." She was frightened now, perhaps doubting everything.

"I'm not your Jack," he told her. "Not any longer. I can't come yet. You go on, *ma cherie*. I'll join you if I can. I'll follow you. But not yet."

She put her fingers on the edge of the boat. She spoke with soft urgency. "It's hard for me, Jack. I love you. You're growing old here." She reached up one of her arms, the silver water falling upon his clothes, as if to drag him with her. She gripped his long fingers. It was his hands, she had said, that had first attracted her. "You're growing old here, Jack."

"Not old enough." He pulled away. He began to cough. He lost control of the spasm. Suddenly drops of his blood mingled with the water, fell upon the Stain. She cupped some in her hand and then, as if carrying a treasure, she slipped back into the Stain, folding herself down until she had merged entirely with the colour.

By the time he had recovered himself, she had completely vanished. There was a voice, an unintelligable shriek, a rapidly fading bellow, as if she had made one last plea for him to follow.

"And not man enough either, I guess." He had watched the rest of his blood until it had mingled entirely with the water.

11. Pourquoi M'Aimes-tu Pas?

He remained in her tree-cabin above the Stain for as long as the food she had stored lasted. She had prepared the place so that he might wait for her if she had to be absent. He forced himself to live there, praying that through this particular agony he might confront and perhaps even find a means of lifting his burden. But pain was not enough. He began to suspect that pain was not even worth pursuing.

More than once he returned to the big Stain and sat in the pirogue, looking down, trying to find some excuse, some rationale which would allow him this chance of paradise. But he could not. All he had left to him was a partial truth. He felt that if he lost that, he lost all hope of grace. Eventually he abandoned the cabin and the colour and made his way up the Trace to Nashville, where he played an endless succession of reckless games until at last, as fighting broke out in the streets between rival guilds of musician-assassins, he managed to get on a military train to Memphis before the worst of the devastation. At the Peabody Hotel in Memphis, he bathed and smoked a cigar and, through familiar luxuries, sought to evade the memories of the colour swamp. He took the *Etoile* down to Natchez, well ahead of the holocaust, and then there was nowhere to go but the Terminal Café, where he could sit and watch Boudreaux Ramsadeen perform his idiosyncratic measures on the dance floor, his women partners flocking like delicate birds about a graceful bull. As their little feet stepped in and around the uncertain outlines of an infinite number of walls, floors, ceilings, and roofs, expertly holding their metaphysical balance even as they grinned and whooped to the remorseless melodies of the fiddles, accordion, and tambourines, Jack Karaquazian would come to sense that only when he lost interest in his own damaged self-esteem would he begin to know hope of release.

Then, unexpectedly, like a visitation, Ox Berger, a prosthesis better than the original on his arm, sought him out at the main table and stood looking at him across the flat board, its dimensions roiling, shimmering, and cross-flashing within the depths of its singular machinery, and said, with calm respect, "I believe you owe me a game, sir."

Jack Karaquazian looked as if a coughing fit would take control of him, but he straightened up, his eyes and muscles sharply delineated against a paling skin, and said with courtesy, almost with warmth, "I believe I do, sir."

And they played the long forms, sign for sign, commitment to commitment, formula for formula; the great classic flat-game schemes, the logic and counter-logic of a ten-dimensional matrix, a quasi-infinity held in a metre-long box in which they dabbled minds and fingers and ordered the fate of millions, claimed responsibility for the creation, the maintenance, and the sacrifice of whole semi-real races and civilisations, not to mention individuals, some of whom formed cryptic dependencies on an actuality they would never directly enjoy. And Ox Berger played with grace, with irony and skill which, lacking the experience and recklessness of Jack Karaquazian's style, could not in the end win, but showed the mettle of the player.

As he wove his famous "Faust" web, which only Colinda had ever been able to identify and counter, Jack Karaquazian developed a dawning respect for the big farmer who had chosen never to use a talent as great as the gambler's own. And in sharing this with his opponent, Ox Berger achieved a profound act of forgiveness, for he released Karaquazian from his burden of self-disgust and let him imagine, instead, the actual character of the man he had wronged and so understand the true nature of his sin. Jack Karaquazian was able to confront and repent, in dignified humility, his lie for what it truly had been.

When the game was over (by mutual concession) the two men stood together on the edge of the Fault, watching the riotous death of universes, and Karaquazian wondered now if all he lacked was courage, if perhaps the only way back to her was by way of the chaos which seduced him with its mighty and elaborate violence. But then, as he stared into that university of dissolution, he knew that in losing his pride he had not, after all, lost his soul, and just as he knew that pride would never earn him the right to paradise, so, he judged, there was no road to Heaven by way of Hell. And he thanked Ox Berger for his game and his charity. Now he planned, when he was ready, to make a final try at the Trace, though he could not be sure that his will alone, without hers, would be sufficient to get him through a second time. Even should he succeed, he would have to find a way through the Stain without her guidance. Mr. Karaquazian shook hands with his opponent. By providing this peculiar intimacy, Ox Berger had done Karaquazian the favour not only of forgiving him, but of helping him to forgive himself.

The gambler wished the map of the Stain were his to pass on, but he knew that it had to be sought for and that only then would the lucky ones find it. As for Ox Berger, he had satisfied his own conscience and required nothing else of Jack Karaquazian. "When you take your journey, sir, I hope you find the strength to sustain yourself."

"Thanks to you, sir," says Jack Karaquazian.

The olive intensity of his features framed by the threatening madness of the Biloxi Fault, its vast walls of seething colour rising and falling, the Egyptian plays with anyone, black, white, red or yellow, who wants his kind of game. And the wilder he plays, the more he wins. Clever as a jackal, he lets his slender hands, his woman's hands, weave and flow within the ten dimensions of his favourite flat game, and he is always happy to raise the psychic stakes. Yet there is no despair in him.

Only his familiar agony remains, the old pain of frustrated love, sharper than ever, for now he understands how he failed Colinda Dovero and how he wounded her. And he knows that she will never again seek him out at the Terminal Café.

"You're looking better, Jack." Sam Oakenhurst has recovered from the *machinoix's* torments. "Your old self."

Jack Karaquazian deals seven hands of poker. In his skin is the reflection of a million dying cultures given up to the pit long before their time; in his green eyes is a new kind of courtesy. Coolly amiable in his silk and linen, his raven-black hair straight to his shoulders, his back firmly set against that howling triumph of Satan, he is content in the speculation that, for a few of his fellow souls at least, there may be some chance of paradise.

"I'm feeling it, Sam," he says.

Thanks to Garth Brooks, Doug Kershaw, all the artists on Swallow Records, Ville Platte, LA, and friends in Atlanta, New Orleans, Houston, West Point, MS, Hattiesburg, MS, Oxford MS and Oxford UK, where this was written. Special thanks to Ed Kramer and Brother Willie Love . . .

Caroline and Caleb

Richard Gilliam

Among my favorite childhood vacations were our frequent family trips to Tennessee's Great Smoky Mountains. I was maybe seven when we made the first of the visits. What I remember most was my grandparents complaining how Gatlinburg had changed. Too many tourists, and there was a new motel on the road leading into the national park. You should have seen it back in the old days, they said.

I remember looking out from the porch at our motel. There were maybe four other motels in view, and off to the side was a shaded creek where my sister waded in her brand-new bathing suit. I was much thrilled with the Smokies. We had a small mountain on the back of our farm, but nothing to compare with Clingman's Dome. Best of all, Tennessee had pinball machines, a devil's tool not found in Alabama. We visited there often, but somehow once I went off to college, it was nearly twenty years before I again got closer than Knoxville.

When I returned in the mid-eighties, I was the one shocked at the change. Huge hotel complexes dominated the skyline, and the downtown traffic resembled any urban city at rush hour. Worst of all, the pleasant creek had become a concrete water culvert, void of trees and other foliage. The park was still preserved, but the city had been irreversibly altered. It was all I could do to keep from telling my friends that they should have seen it back in the old days. Must have been the pinball machines. My grandparents said that once you let the motels put them in, the rest of the town goes to seed.

I am well mindful that future generations will visit Gatlinburg and look back on this era as the old days. It is the nature of change to do so. Commercial development is often beneficial—more people enjoy the Smoky Mountains today than ever before, and hotels are needed outside the park to house them. Even so, I cannot help grieving for some of the cultural flavor that has been lost. You really should have seen it back in the old days.

Caleb was thankful that the snow was light. To the east, the top of Jefferson Mountain glowed red as the sun began to climb. Caleb could just make out Buckman's Pass, maybe a quarter of the way around the north side.

"Snow's just starting, boy." Henderson's voice boomed across the stillness of the covered air. "We best be on our way."

"Yes, Paw," Caleb replied respectfully, though he thought his father wrong. The clouds were forming from behind and were not a threat to the journey. They'd be out of this snow in an hour, probably less, and given Henderson's surehandedness with the ox-cart, certainly by the time they reached the pass. Caleb didn't know why the wind never blew toward Jefferson Mountain, but he knew it never did, at least not across their valley.

Caleb tightened the cinch. "Sampson's ready," he said quietly as he climbed into the cart.

Henderson handed his satchel to Caleb and took the reins. "Let's go," he said, not to Caleb and not to the ox. "We'll reach the church with an hour to spare."

Travel by cart was slow, much slower than if they had horses, but like Henderson the horses had gone to fight the war, and unlike Henderson, the horses hadn't returned. There wasn't a finer ox in east Tennessee than Sampson, everyone said so. He could tote a load so heavy up either side of the pass it'd break an axle if a person was so foolish as to try it. Unfortunately three hundred pounds of man and boy traveled no faster than a ton of corn when it came to taking the cart into Drake's Crossing.

Caleb was mostly as big as Henderson now, and probably a touch taller. He thought the war had shrunk his paw, at least last July when Henderson had finally gotten home from Appomattox. Paw's face looked harder, more tired, and he was a head shorter than Caleb had remembered.

Rebecca said Caleb was just silly. A boy who'd become sixteen as the war ended should know he'd be as tall as the father he hadn't seen for four years. And a good thing the war had ended too, just as Caleb had become of an age to fight. No family anyone knew of sent two of its men to the war and had them both return.

Rebecca was gone, taken to Chattanooga by Walker, her bridegroom, who'd been given a foreman's job at the textile warehouses by the colonel for whom he'd fought at Manassas.

In peacetime, even a recent peacetime, being nearly eighteen was fearfully long for a woman to wait and find a husband. That'd been the happy part. Telling Paw that Rebecca had a beau. Telling him that Maw had died of consumption that February was hard. The venison Caleb had killed had nearly gotten her through the winter, though not quite. Caleb was glad he didn't have to face Henderson. Rebecca had done it for him, not saying a word, simply leading her father to the spring where the stone marked Elizabeth's rest.

This cold had been new, disturbing the momentum of the spring, which had already seen crops begin to sprout. Henderson seemed both indifferent and immune to the weather, wearing only the lightest of concessions.

Snugly wrapped in a woolen shirt, fur-lined coat, and beaver cap which didn't quite cover his bright blond hair, Caleb was more thirsty than cold. "All right if I take a drink, Paw?" he asked. Henderson reached for the leather satchel and handed the skin jug to the boy.

"Likely to freeze today," he said tersely. "Maybe the snow will keep the cold air away until we get home."

Caleb drank. The water was sweet and warm.

His father smiled. "Nothing better than water from a mountain spring." Caleb smiled back. It was good to see his father relaxed.

"Nothing at all, Paw," replied the boy.

"I want you to walk the pass in front of Sampson. Make sure the rocks aren't going to fall and hit the cart. Mind you to have no sharp noises. The cold has a way of making sharp noises rile the mountain. Lost Old Jim Stowe that way, maybe around '59. Back before the war, anyhow."

"Sure, Paw. I remember Jim Stowe. We all went to his services. Just after the church were built."

"That's right, boy. Just after they built that church. Disgrace first service held in that church were for a piece of trash like Jim Stowe. Took him a squaw and lived near to the top of Jefferson Mountain. She got kilt too, in the avalanche. Couldn't bury her with the white folks, of course, even if Jim's brother Henry tried to make it so. Don't really know what they did with her body. Cherokees must have came and got her. Cherokees take care of their own."

Caleb had liked Jim Stowe and Little Bird, but knew it would be disrespectful to say so. They had settled near the cave where Caleb had played since the earliest days he could walk the mountain. He saw them often, and Little Bird had taught him passages in the caverns Caleb had not suspected.

Henderson was much shamed when Caleb had cried at Jim Stowe's funeral, though Elizabeth had thought her husband too harsh. Only girls and weak children cry in public, Henderson had said, as he ordered Caleb to return to the cart until the services were over. Only very weak children cry.

Caleb had cried only once since, not at his mother's death, when Rebecca needed him to be strong, but when his father had looked for the first time on Elizabeth's grave. Caleb had kept his tears a secret, staying to the hickory trees behind the spring. Henderson waited until Rebecca left, and then cried alone at the grave—so many deaths, so many battles, so little to have come home to, so little to have fought for. Caleb's tears fell for his father.

Occasionally the wagon's wheels would slip as the soft dirt of the valley gave way to the hard, ice-crusted mountain mud. Sampson's cinch would jerk, but the draft animal missed not a step, trudging the ever-steeper path.

The sun was full up now as they entered the pass. Sampson had known when to stop. Caleb climbed warily from the cart, testing both feet on the frozen surface.

Huge icicles hung like the sword of Damocles from rocky outcroppings on either side of the narrow route. There was less than half a wagon's width to spare. Caleb knew to check the downward side for other traffic. He saw no tracks in the surface to indicate others were going in the same direction and, on the other hand, couldn't imagine why anyone would be traveling away from Drake's Crossing on the Sunday when the circuit preacher would be arriving.

Snow almost never made it to the pass, though a white cap stayed across the top of Jefferson Mountain throughout the winter. Satisfied it was safe to proceed, Caleb walked softly to within sight of the cart and signaled his father forward.

Caleb cared little for the fire and brimstone sermons of the Reverend Josiah Haggerty. The reverend was said to have a voice so powerful even the Prince of Darkness cringed to hear it, though Caleb thought it edged and unpleasant. Certainly it was more of a voice than Hoyle Thompson, who, with his wife Emma Mae, led the services on the three Sundays between the Reverend Haggerty's visits.

God's calendar occurs each year, but turmoil the magnitude of the recent unpleasantness won out over the traditional messages of the season, it being the first anniversary of Lee's proud surrender. The black-clad reverend was in fine form, filling the pulpit far more than his five-foot frame had a right to.

Satan was everywhere, all the more so now that evil flowed unchecked from the North. Only Jesus Christ could save the good folks of Drake's Crossing from the perfidiousness of carpetbaggers and scalawags. Despite the booming of the reverend's voice, Caleb's thoughts wandered as they had on most previous Sundays. He'd overheard Hoyle tell Henderson that the property taxes were going up for the farmers, and worst of all, they were to be due come August, well before any money could be earned from the crops. No one had any money nowadays, not that there'd been that much before the war, either. Caleb mused that Jesus would be of little use when Burke Walters, the tax collector, made his rounds, then suppressed the idea, fearful that even an unspoken blasphemy could damn his soul.

The church was filled as he had rarely seen it. Folks from near to far as Knoxville had been arriving since Thursday for the swap meet which preceded each of the reverend's monthly visits.

Many of the veterans of the Army of Northern Virginia wore

their gray and tattered uniforms, a few just arrived home and with no better clothes. Several Union veterans were to be seen, and a prayer was said for James McPherson, commander of the Army of Tennessee, at whose death outside Atlanta Sherman had cried, and at whose side these Union veterans had fought.

Some of the Union veterans wore medals, mostly from the Georgia campaign. The Confederates wore none, a condition declared by Robert E. Lee, who said all who took up the cause to be heroes. Three of the Confederates carried copies of dispatches in which they were mentioned, this being the highest individual recognition to which a Confederate soldier had been allowed to aspire.

The other Army of Tennessee, the one under the command of Joseph Johnston, had remained at large well past Lee's surrender, pursued by that portion of Sherman's army who had not also quit. Tennessee folk had known all along their men to be the most dedicated, and much pride rested in the fact that theirs had been the last Confederate Army to yield the quest. And in the finest of ironies, it was a Tennesseean, Andrew Johnson, and not the South's wartime adversary, Abraham Lincoln, who held the Union presidency.

After Appomattox, no person truly entertained thoughts that the war was anything but over. Perhaps if Jefferson Davis had reached Texas, a new base could have been consolidated, but alas, Davis had gotten no farther than Georgia. Even yet came occasionally the rumors of new armies being formed near the Rio Grande. To a farmer in east Tennessee, Texas was only slightly less mysterious than China, and Mexico was the other side of the moon.

There was not a person Caleb knew who was not in Drake's Crossing that Sunday, save his sister and her husband, who were most certainly worshipping in Chattanooga, and save Henry Stowe, whose faith had been taken from him by the Cherokee heathens. Even Real Pappy was said to have left the deep hills and have come to the area.

The Reverend Haggerty felt duty bound to offer a prayer for the souls of all those who died in the conflict, including the assassinated Lincoln, and did so despite only a grudging murmur of participation from those in gray. A separate prayer for the beleaguered President Johnson met with a far more spirited approval.

Henderson, as the highest ranking officer present, was asked to lead the prayer for the sixty-seven young men of the county that had headed off to war and not returned. Caleb swelled with pride as Henderson took his place to the right of the pulpit. In the Confederate armies, all officers below the rank of brigadier were elected by the troops. Most of the veterans present had served with Henderson and still looked on him as their leader, despite Henderson's refusal to dress in his uniform, even for such a hallowed occasion.

His father prayed for peace, and for forgiveness of enemies, quoting not the scripture but speaking directly from the heart. Caleb thought this was the better message from God, to be good to one another, and to be thankful for all blessings, rather than the you'll-go-to-Hell-if-you-sin sermons specialized in by the ordained.

The prayer over, Henderson took his seat. Caleb felt a lifting in the spirit of the gathered, though to be truthful, this had been caused possibly as much by the anticipation of the soon-to-follow church picnic as it had by Henderson's words of hope.

As the reverend began the closing benediction, Caleb noticed the brown-haired girl sitting in the far left of the church. The yellow ribbon holding her ponytail stood in pleasant contrast to the somber bonnets of the matrons of the congregation.

She was, to Caleb's eyes, more pretty than Rebecca. Her skin was clear but not pale, and the green of her eyes sparkled from a face that smiled even when it was serious, as it most appropriately was now in this place of God. "Caroline," the reverend had later said as he introduced the community's newest family. "Caroline." Daughter of Ezekiel and Nora, sister to Erasmus, former resident of Nashville, a town which had grown too large for the simple tastes of those born to a love of the land. Wearing his Confederate gray, Ezekiel sat with perfect uprightness as the reverend proclaimed his heroism and wounding in defense of the bridge at Antietam Creek.

Caleb marveled at the intentness with which Caroline studied the sermon. The reverend's message had grown old to him the seven years he had heard it. Even the blessing cautioned against the paths to perdition.

Whatever the reverend might think eternity to be, Caleb knew it to be that time between now and the afternoon lunch. There he might have a chance to hear Caroline's voice and take the memory of it back to his valley.

The wheeze of the organ startled Caleb. He watched as Henderson placed a small envelope in the collection plate. Caleb knew this to mean his father had parted with one of the last of his few gold coins. It would have been poor taste to have flashed the coin, most of the congregation having nothing more valuable to give than Confederate currency. A hymn was sung and the service concluded. As the double doors at the back of the church were opened, the sun streamed in and the worshippers streamed out.

Caleb reached the exit before Caroline, the Colton family having been honored with the front pew for this their welcome. He shook hands with Hoyle Thompson, as did Henderson, who paused under the overhanging roof to chat. Caleb did not join them, positioning himself by the oak tree between the door and the tables where the communal lunch awaited. Each new moment was a disappointment as the church emptied without the Coltons emerging.

The crowd around the door had thinned to where he could see into the sanctuary, but Caroline and her family were not there. He scanned the grounds, finding the family leaving by a small door to the rear of the one-room building. The Reverend Haggerty held the carriage as first Nora, then her husband and children climbed aboard. Caroline was last, and Caleb could swear there was an expectancy in her smile as she boarded.

Nothing, not the most succulent chicken, nor the best-cooked possum, tastes good to a young man who has had his hopes of courting raised and ended in so short a period of time. Pies covered with meringue and confections of various delights failed to lighten Caleb's heart.

Hoyle's daughter Becka passed around a tray of pralines and taffy. She was grown to fourteen now, and with the departed-to-

Chattanooga Rebecca having relinquished her seniority to their commonly shared name, told all who would listen that she was forever disdaining her diminutive appellation for that more womanly sounding designation she had been given at birth. She took special time to pass by Caleb, hoping the broad-shouldered youth might pay her some fancy, but he did not.

"Cold stayed to the other side of the mountain, but you know'd it would, didn't you?" a male voice said softly.

It took Caleb a moment to recognize the words had been directed at him. It was not a large man who spoke them, but his weather-beaten face and buckskin clothes told Caleb at once who the stranger was.

"Lots you know about that mountain, young Caleb." The man spoke again.

"You know my name?" said Caleb. He could not recall having heard of Real Pappy inside Drake's Crossing before, and certainly not on the grounds of the church.

"It's not time now, but there's much we will speak. The answer to your more urgent question is that Ezekiel Colton is first cousin to the Reverend Haggerty. They've gone to the old Denton place to have the reverend bless the land. Right good idea, blessing the land, though I ain't so sure the Reverend Haggerty's the best person to do it. You knew that too, didn't you— about the reverend, I mean. Not much power behind his piety."

"Why have you come here?" Caleb asked.

"Lots of people come here today, young Caleb. I'm nothing special," said the mountain man.

"I thought you were a legend. . . ."

"I'm no more legend than you are." The man spoke slowly. "The girl, she's a good one. Her heart's about as fluttered as yours right now. Don't worry. They'll be back in an hour or so. Have your father talk to hers. Tell him to hold for a good dowry. Ezekiel will be glad to trade a daughter for a son-in-law, especially one like you."

"I'm to marry, just like that?"

"The reverend leaves Tuesday, so I wouldn't waste any time asking him to set a date. Lots of marriages take place quickly after a war ends. No one will mind yours."

"I'm to leave my father, so soon after everything?"

"Your father has his own journey to make, just as you have yours," said Real Pappy.

How do you know these things? Caleb thought, but did not speak aloud.

"The same way that you do. Now get. We'll talk more when it's time. 'Nother fella I want you to meet, but I can't rightly bring him amongst these fine folks." And with that the mountain man walked into the woods, disappearing quickly, without so much as having stirred a notice from those gathered.

Ezekiel had feared his daughter might not welcome being arranged to so unfamiliar a family, but Caroline's eyes told her father not to be concerned. Henderson's corn mash had eased the negotiations considerably, though Ezekiel deemed himself to be of moderate temperance and accepted the offering in the name of hospitality only, lest Nora's displeasure fall upon him. The bride price was set at two cows, a steer, and Verda, Caroline's horse, the latter of which she had raised from a foal. The date was set as the next visit of the Reverend Haggerty, four weeks hence.

The Denton farm had lain fallow for three years, and its fields were clogged with briars and weeds. The clearing had to be done quickly, lest the planting time be missed. Caleb agreed to organize the preparing of the land, such work to be completed before the marriage. Both families were well pleased.

It was, to be spoken more accurately, the Colton farm now, but folks' minds change slowly, the Dentons having cropped the place since before the states were first united. No Denton men returned from the war, and the three Denton women had all died of the same consumption that had taken Caleb's mother. With taxes unpaid, and an unjust government to which to pay them, a small consideration to the Denton cousins in North Carolina had legitimized the sale.

Henderson went away for ten days, returned, saw all was proceeding well, and left again. When he returned a second time he brought with him a surprise, a widow and her three children, announcing this to be a double wedding.

*   *   *

Caroline regretted she and her beau saw so little of each other. Not that he wasn't around—the half-day ride between the farms made it impractical for Caleb to return home until the Colton fields were prepared for planting—but he slept each night in the barn, it being improper for two young people to stay under the same roof during betrothal.

It was at evening meals that Caroline shared time with Caleb, and she grew to love him more with each passing day. There was much, so much, she wanted to talk to him about, but with both parents and her brother nearby, she felt constrained, lest her giddiness make her appear to be an infatuated child rather than a mature woman of fifteen, ready to marry.

Nora did such as she could to give her daughter the privacy she wanted, but there was little that could be done to distract Ezekiel, who was determined that Caroline remain his daughter while she was within his household. The men left each dawn and returned after dark, with only the smoke from the quenching of the clearing fires telling Nora when to have the supper ready.

Game was plentiful in the untilled fields, and a steady stream of quail, rabbit, duck, and deer passed across Nora's table. Erasmus, who while in Nashville had never hunted anything more than an excuse to miss school, grew quickly to the art, a most willing pupil at Caleb's hands. It was well too, for Ezekiel, although a good farmer, proved to be a clumsy hunter.

The fields were finished seven days before the wedding, mostly thanks to Caleb's desire to have a few days to prepare his own home for Caroline.

Henderson's bride, the widow Marston, had 300 acres of tillable land on the Virginia side of Bristol. Accordingly, Henderson's wedding present to Caleb and Caroline was the land and the house where Caleb had lived since birth.

Caroline wanted to visit Caleb's house, but deferred to her father's wishes that she not. No matter, she thought, she and Caleb would live there long enough after the marriage.

The Reverend Haggerty's wedding gift came by way of an itinerant merchant—a bolt of white cotton cloth, more than enough for a dress for Caroline. The dressmaking skills were mostly Nora's, due not to any lack of effort or aptitude on Caroline's part, but rather to a wartime lack of cloth.

When Ezekiel took the dowry to Henderson, Caroline felt sad at seeing Verda leave, knowing the sacrifice her father had made giving away the family's only horse. Verda had avoided service in the Confederacy through the good offices of cousin Josiah, who, as a circuit preacher, had convinced the conscripting quartermaster that the animal was necessary were he to continue spreading God's Holy Word to the troops throughout Tennessee.

Weddings at Drake's Crossing were performed at the end of the regular service. Both families, including the groom, were seated and participated in the usual Sunday observances. Only the brides and their fathers waited outside, this being a tradition based in superstition rather than scripture.

Betty Marston proved to be delightful company, as did her father, Walter, a sprightly gray-haired gentleman just short of sixty. He had driven his covered carriage—more of a coach, actually—down from Virginia, pulled by a team of four horses, which he had recently won from a carpetbagger in a poker game.

Caroline had not heard the word carpetbagger previously, but knew the meaning from its use—a person from the North come to profit from the misery of the South.

The presence of the coach was fortunate, the late cold having given way to strong rain, with thunderous clouds providing an unbroken pall.

Despite the noise of the store, Ezekiel and Walter made mentalk, mostly of war and politics, while the women—Caroline believed a maiden in her wedding dress had a right to be considered a woman—spoke of plans for life with their newly chosen men. All four considered themselves fortunate to be in such good company, rather than listening to yet another sincere but laborious sermon from the Reverend Josiah Haggerty.

Hoyle Thompson appeared at the door, and Caroline knew the moment of her marriage had arrived.

"My, such wind!" exclaimed Betty as the quartet transferred from the carriage to the porchlike entrance of the church.

"Oh! My dress!" squealed Caroline excitedly, the rain blowing at her back. Ezekiel, noticing Walter had taken a position between the wind and Betty, likewise protected Caroline.

"Can't enter just yet. Not till Emma Mae plays the music," asserted Hoyle, pulling his coat collar up over his neck.

Boom! Ezekiel thought himself back at Antietam, then saw the broken tree limb which attested to the power of the lightning that had just struck.

The organ, as if having been given its cue, began the wedding march. Hoyle opened the doors, and the party entered, first Betty, then Caroline, and then the men.

The lack of sunshine gave a gloomy cast to the sanctuary. Oil lanterns illuminated the side walls, and candles were positioned behind the altar. Caroline simply decided to ignore the dreariness.

Hoyle brought the doors together, and Caroline thought she heard an extra thud as they closed.

Caleb saw Caroline to be beautiful, even in a damp wedding dress. As she took her place next to him, he felt a warmth within him, from the fire that can only be fueled by love.

The moments passed in a daze. With only Caleb's presence registering, Caroline heard herself say, "I do," and assumed Caleb, as well as Henderson and Betty, to have said the same.

They were all pronounced, the brides were kissed, and the procession left the altar. Hoyle waited at the back of the church as the happy couples walked proudly down the center aisle.

He opened the doors, and everyone saw the horrified look on his face. Sticking from the right half of the door was an Indian arrow, adorned with feathers of a ceremonial significance.

In the rain stood Henry Stowe, his mouth open as if to shout. Only a gurgling whisper came forth, obscured by the wind. A strong gust bellowed from behind the church, rocking the estranged Christian backwards. And with that Henry fell dead, blood pouring from a gaping hole where his heart had been.

Only Caleb looked toward the woods and saw the two watchers who stood dryly under a tarp which had been sharply strung between two pecan trees. Caleb paused, bowed his head, and said a silent prayer for Henry Stowe. When he looked again the two had vanished.

*   *   *

Caroline's first view of the valley came as Sampson took the crest of Buckman's Pass. Bright flowers adorned the way, and Caroline could only imagine the ice that had covered the road a scant month earlier. It was, to her way of thinking, the most beautiful valley she had ever seen, maybe God's most beautiful gift since the Garden of Eden. She saw the spring, its meandering creek separating the mountain from the valley, and their cabin nestled against the forest. Her heart knew she had found home.

Caleb stood some hundred paces forward, his hair adding yellow to the reddish tint of the evening sun. His trim shadow ran long, almost to the crest, the length shortened as he and the cart approached each other.

Sampson didn't slow as Caleb climbed back aboard. Caroline smiled brightly as her husband pointed out the house and the fields. She cuddled her arm under his, so as not to interfere with his hold on the reins. Caleb held back slightly on the brake, there always being the risk the sharp downgrade would give the cart too much momentum. Caroline didn't mind the deliberate pace; she was torn between her eagerness to be carried across the doorway of her new home and her desire to make this splendid journey last forever.

Caleb gazed with wonderment into Caroline's eyes, basking in their emerald richness. The pathway was not so steep now, and Caleb allowed Sampson to gain a little speed, though not so much that he looked away from his beloved.

Neither lover gave current thought to Henry Stowe, nor the unpleasantness at the church. When she had thought of it, Caroline considered it in the context of the war. So many men had come back dead or maimed. She had known Henry Stowe not at all and could think of several potential beaus her family might have suggested to her, had the young men not fallen in distant fields. She thought of the war's dead as returning home, though their headstones marked graves that did not contain their bodies.

Town consensus held that a wild animal had killed Henry Stowe, though a few thought him to have been burst by lightning. None could explain the arrow. No white man of Drake's Crossing had been killed by the Cherokee since the great removal some seventeen years prior. Maybe a thousand or so Indians remained, mostly on the North Carolina side of the mountains.

Henderson had offered the most commonly accepted explanation, that the arrow came from a hunter chasing the animal that had clawed the life from Henry Stowe. Caleb believed his father to be mostly right, and had no better accounting, the ceremonial feathers notwithstanding.

The unexpected storm made their plans to spend their wedding night in the cabin in the valley impractical. Emma Mae had offered the hospitality of the Thompson household, much to Becka's glowering displeasure. The latter was mollified somewhat when Erasmus paid her a smile as he unloaded his sister's trunk.

The wedding social had to be canceled. There were only two buildings in Drake's Crossing large enough to hold the congregation—the church being too sanctified to host such frivolity, and the livery stable being far too unclean.

Caroline was pleased they had chosen to delay their consummation for one night, though Emma Mae had been most tactful in keeping Becka and Hoyle out late as they made their usual Sunday evening visits ministering to the sick. She wanted to know Caleb first in their own home, and he had felt the same way of her.

The next noon had seen the skies cleared and Henry Stowe set to rest at the side of his brother. Caleb had insisted they attend the service, assuring Caroline they would reach their home no later than dusk. It would be a late dusk Caroline observed, but the precise time didn't matter. She and Caleb held onto each other as they entered the new world that lay before them.

It was in late August, just after Caroline had told her husband she was with child, that Caleb next saw Real Pappy. With him was a Cherokee brave who stood more than a head taller than Caleb.

Caleb was tracking a small red wolf, a rarity in the Smokies, when he noticed the mountain man and his black-haired companion. They were some twenty paces east, directly in the path of the animal's spoor.

"Cherokees believe it's a sin to kill a wolf." Real Pappy spoke quietly. The wind was still, and only the distant voices of birds caressed the air. "You can kill all the foxes you can find, for they are a troublesome pack of mischievous knaves, but it is a sin to kill a wolf."

Caleb paused. He had never killed a wolf, and only twice had seen the catch of hunters who had.

"Not many wolves left in these parts. White folks got rid of the wolves before they got rid of the Cherokee," Real Pappy continued.

"You said we'd talk." Caleb struggled for a reply.

"Talkin' now we are, Young Caleb, or have your ears failed you today?"

"My ears are well. What is it you would talk about?" said the youth.

"Not so fast. Ain't you gonna ask me how've I been, or 'bout the weather? Might actually be something you need to learn about the weather."

"Are we to talk of weather?" Caleb asked.

"Later, if you get that far. Right now we're going to talk about wolves. This feller would appreciate it if you wouldn't run off all the game," he said, gesturing to the Cherokee.

"Run off the game? It's the wolf who eats the game," Caleb said.

"One small wolf is going to eat a whole mountain of game? Do you need so much that there is none left for him?" asked Real Pappy.

Caleb was taken aback. He had never considered the chase from the wolf's viewpoint.

"Cherokees believe that killing a wolf causes the animal spirits to leave an area. And they ought to know. They been watchin' these parts more years than you can think of. Ruin your gun, too, if you used it to kill a wolf. A thing just don't never work right if it's taken blood from a wolf."

Caleb started to speak, then decided he had nothing worth saying.

"Wolves are right special to my friend here, in particular since this one has been visited by the Great Raven himself," Real Pappy continued.

"The Great Raven?" Caleb asked, not having heard the term before.

"A special animal spirit. Some tribes believe he created these mountains. Tried to steal fire for his people and beat his wings too close to this earth. Others say it was a buzzard, or maybe an owl. Can't rightly say myself. Ravens lead wolves to where there is game. The wolf makes the kill and then there is food for the raven."

Caleb looked at the brave. He stood shirtless, wearing only a deerskin breechcloth and moccasins. Though the knife strapped to his belt looked more utensil than weapon, the notched bow and painted quiver spoke of his prowess as a hunter. "That's quite a bow," Caleb commented, not really expecting a response and altogether surprised when the Indian handed him the item of interest.

"He understands us?" asked Caleb. The astonishment was evident as he examined the bow.

"Makes his letters too, he does, both in Cherokee and in white man talk," the mountain man replied.

"Then why doesn't he answer for himself?" Caleb inquired.

"Oh, he answers," Real Pappy said, pausing for effect. "He just doesn't speak. Took a vow to the Great Raven he wouldn't until his sister was avenged."

"His sister?"

"You knew her. Took herself a white husband and lived near up to the top of this mountain. Mighty angry her family was too when she took herself a white husband."

"She died in an avalanche," Caleb said. "How do you get revenge against a mountain?"

"She was killed by the Raven Mocker. Had her heart cut from her body and hid in a sack. So did her husband. Same thing happened to his brother, but you saw that at your weddin'."

"Tell me about the Raven Mocker," said Caleb with uncertainty.

"Now you're catchin' on. Asking about the stuff that matters. Might make a person worth knowin' out of you yet," cackled the old man.

"Little Bird was killed back before the war. It was seven years more until Jim Stowe died. What happened in between?" asked Caleb.

"The war, you young fool! The war! Why would a hungry Raven Mocker hang around here when there was a war full of battlefields to cut hearts from?" said Real Pappy. "Came back changed. More nasty. Stronger evil. Got that from hangin' around Christians."

"How's that?" Caleb asked.

"A thing changes dependin' upon what kind of company it's keepin'. You seen it. You hang around people what got love in their hearts, you get more love, too. Christians believe in a special kind of evil. Damns souls to an eternal hell. The Raven Mocker just picked up some worse habits to go with his already bad ones."

"What was he like before—the Raven Mocker?" said Caleb.

"Hard to say. Cherokee had no way to write stuff down before Sequoyah figured one out, and that wasn't until 1819. Cherokee spent more than two hundred years being changed by the white man at that point. Got real civilized, did the Cherokee. Built themselves houses, bought fine China, kept black slaves. Just like the white man. Some say it was because they took the white man's ways that their gods allowed them to be driven from their land."

"To Oklahoma?" said Caleb.

"That's right. To Oklahoma. Cherokees helped Andrew Jackson get rid of the Creeks, then Jackson got rid of the Cherokees when he had no more use for them."

"Andrew Jackson was a great President," said Caleb assertively. This was one fact everyone in Tennessee knew.

"Great President if you were a white man. Not great at all if you were Indian or Negro. It's all a matter of from what side you look at a thing," said Real Pappy.

"And the Raven Mocker?"

"He's a night creature, mostly, has to disguise himself during the day. Used to be he kept the hearts to add to his own life. If he took one from somebody that was supposed to live another twenty years, it was twenty years before he needed another heart. Took a few for sport, of course. But not like during the war. More than twenty thousand men dead or near dead in one battle at Antietam. Before the white man, it took hundreds of years for the Raven Mocker to see that many die."

"With so many hearts, he must be immortal," Caleb said.

"Not so. Not so. As inconvenient as it was having your heart taken by the Raven Mocker, it didn't really used to do you no longtime harm. When your heart stopped beating, after twenty years or so your spirit floated on up to the great western sky, just like it'd done if you'd died natural. The war changed that. The war and the Christians," said Real Pappy.

"How did it change?" asked Caleb.

"The hearts started to rot away before they stopped beating. Soon as they were black, they stopped beating at all. Most of them crumbled before they were removed. The more good in a person, the longer it took—but even the strongest of hearts can't withstand evil forever. Damned to hell, I suppose. The great western sky seemed a much nicer choice, but Christians don't believe in it, and there are too many Christians around for them not to get their way."

"What about Heaven?" Caleb inquired.

"Good question. 'Cept I reckon it to be real hard to get forgiven up to Heaven when you die tryin' to kill somebody else. Christians say you'll be forgiven if you love Jesus. Hard to love Jesus or anyone else for that matter while you're out there killin'—particularly when you're killin' so you can keep some other people as slaves. Not that the North was any more noble. Most of them was killin' for money, or maybe out of being mean. Hard to find much goodness in a war."

"But President Lincoln freed the slaves!" cried Caleb defiantly.

"Like shit he did! The proclamation of his didn't say it was wrong to own slaves. Just that it was wrong to own them while you was rebelling against the United States. Lincoln was cold dead in his grave eight months before the slaves here in Tennessee were freed. Same for Kentucky, Delaware, and a bunch of other places you ain't been. Like I said before, it depends on how you look at things."

Caleb paused. This was an awful much for him to consider, and he still had doubts about the Raven Mocker. "Something you want me to do?" he asked.

"You're free to go kill that wolf. It's your choice to do or not.

Doesn't hurt to know a little more before you go to do something. Might even want to try that bow you're holdin'."

Caleb flexed the weapon, drawing the bow string back to his ear. He noticed the Indian smile as he did.

"You've held a bow before," said Real Pappy.

"Little Bird's. Only hers was much smaller," replied Caleb. "I think I won't—kill the wolf, that is. Does your friend have a name?"

"He's called Night Raven. That's his white name, of course. Your tongue would get all knotted up if you tried to pronounce his true name."

"I am pleased to meet you, Night Raven," said Caleb, turning toward the brave. The Indian widened his smile, nodding his head forward in acknowledgement.

"He is pleased by your greeting, but he has known you for seven years now. Who do you think it was what flushed that deer into your path last winter when your mother was so sick? His sister's spirit asked him to protect you, and now she asks your help in freeing her heart from the Raven Mocker."

"Yes, of course, but why me and why now?"

"Our enemy isn't purely a white man's demon, nor is he the Cherokee spirit witch he began as. It's going to take all of us to free his catch. And he's got friends, too, the Raven Mocker does. But they're not your concern right now."

"What can I do?" asked Caleb.

"You'll have choices to make. Just try to remember the other view as you make them," said Real Pappy.

"Just that simple?"

"Nothing's simple, my young friend." The old man slowed, looking deeply into Caleb's eyes. "Now let Night Raven show you how to use that bow he's going to give you. Your gun has a boom that runs game off clear to the next county. Right useful skill, being able to hunt game without scaring everything off the mountain with your first shot. 'Bout time you learned. . . ."

Caroline's condition hampered her not at all as she wandered along the creekbank. Honeysuckle filled the air and the soft coo of doves rolled along with the water.

She never tired of visiting the spring, nor walking alongside the brook that supplied water to the fields of corn in the valley. Her true joy came from the plants, so varied and so fragrant in the early morning air. Caleb had left before the dawn, excited over the tracks of a large dog he had spotted late the previous afternoon. The animal's howl had awoken them in the night. Caleb thought it to be a wolf, and thought it best to tend to the matter immediately, lest the creature feed on the chickens, or perhaps on the cattle or on Verda.

He had left the horse behind, not that Verda wasn't adept at the mountain. It was Caleb that was less adept at Verda, a result of being a young man who learned much of his hunting after the horses had gone off to war.

Occasionally an upturned tree left its roots in Caroline's way, the trunk forming a natural bridge to the higher and steeper mountainside. With water so abundant, the tree hardly seemed to mind growing on its side, the green growth of the branches winding their way among the neighboring foliage.

The sun was up now, and Caroline hurried to sip the dew, lest it be lost till the next morning. Only the spring gave water as fresh as the dew.

As she idled in her thoughts of her husband and their forthcoming child, Caroline began to sense that she was being watched. It wasn't Caleb, of that she was sure, for his presence never failed to send a warmth into her spirit. This was a softer and more troubled essence, though she felt it not to be a threat.

Caroline rested on a mound of moss, its green velvet supple with luxury. A nearby cedar shaded her, the scent traveling on the soft breeze following the creek across the valley.

As she lay her head to rest, a muted cry drifted across the water. Caroline dismissed it at first, so peaceful was her rest, but it grew louder, as did the harsh rhythmic thud of wood being struck by a heavy object.

She stirred, only a little at first, then enough to stand and peer toward the sound. Caroline could see no farther than the higher opposing bank and the trees growing there. She climbed atop the roots of a nearby tree-bridge and tentatively began to cross the water.

The creek was wide though shallow—maybe five feet at the deepest. Caroline decided there was little chance a fall would hurt her or her unborn child. The difficulty would be ascending the steep bank were she to lose her footing on the trunk. She estimated it to be seven paces across the tree to the safety of the branches where she could obtain a handhold.

Letting go of the root, she stuck her arms out for balance and committed to covering the distance without pause. The leather soles of her shoes gripped not at all, but her balance stayed true. It was no more than a moment before she had hold of the far branches and stepped once again to the ground. The cry and the thudding seemed much louder. Caroline wasted no time entering the woods, pursuing the sounds.

She did not recognize the glade she came to a few moments later, nor did she expect to, so seldom did she venture onto even the lower reaches of the mountain. There, not more than forty paces ahead, was an Indian woman beating the side of a walnut tree with a rock. The woman's other hand was held firmly against the bark, and it unnerved Caroline to realize that it was her hand and not the tree which was being hit by the rock.

"No! Don't!" Caroline shouted in horror at what she saw. The Indian, however, proceeded with her efforts. The hand was quite bloodied, more so than Caroline thought possible. A steady red stream poured quickly toward the tree's roots and the woman's black hair was soaked with a crimson mud from the wound.

Caroline was relieved when the woman stopped, though she felt her heart beating strongly. They faced each other now, close enough to touch. The woman dropped the rock and raised her hands. Caroline could see the injury was limited to the index finger, which dangled freely against the palm and was nearly severed from its socket.

"Spear-finger! Spear-finger!" screamed the strange woman. A bloody gush splashed forward. Caroline felt herself involuntarily retch, a deep heave rising from her stomach. She had eaten only lightly this morning, and the bile burned her throat as it came.

Her stomach lurched thrice, emptying, then twice more in a dry retch. Caroline coughed as she regained her composure.

The woman was gone, though her dismembered finger lay on

the bloodied soil. Thoughts did not come clearly to Caroline, and she wondered to herself why she picked up the finger and placed it in her pocket.

The way back to the creek was much longer than she remembered, but as long as the ground extended downhill, she reasoned she was heading toward the valley. The feeling of being watched returned, though this time the presence was malevolent and cruel. Caroline looked back, scanning the upward reaches of the mountain.

When she turned to continue, Caroline found herself plunged into a deep pool of water. Swiftly the current drew her from the shore. She felt reassured by the water, having grown up on the banks of the Cumberland River, and having first swum its width before her eighth birthday.

She could make out the far bank clearly and the narrow shoal leading to it. Determinedly, Caroline set off toward the closest landing.

On shore there waited a woman, and as Caroline lifted her head from the water she was surprised to see it was Nora.

"Mama! Oh, Mama!" Caroline cried as she reached the slender beach. "How did you know I needed you now? I'm so happy to see you!"

The woman stretched her arms, and Caroline ran to her embrace. *Strange,* Caroline thought, when her mother did not speak. Stranger yet when she noticed her mother's forefinger was twice the length it should be. "You're not my mother!" Caroline shouted as she looked about for anything usable as a weapon.

The woman, now resembling an old hag, held herself between Caroline and the forest. No rocks graced the shore, nor did any plant reach the water. Caroline backed toward the basin, then edged to the right in an effort to flank her adversary.

The beach continued as far as she could see, and the forest lay dozens of yards away. Caroline was astonished at the quickness with which the old woman matched her every move. A drooling grin was set upon her face, and the yellowing of her teeth did not disguise their sharpness. The elongated finger probed toward Caroline, closing the gap between them. It looked to be as hard as rock—the tip a jagged point where the nail should have been.

Caroline paused and gathered her thoughts. She was taller than her adversary, though not as bulky. Outrunning her opponent was unlikely, and returning to the water served no purpose, as Caroline could now see the beach formed a perfect circle around the lake. Perhaps a blow to the head would work, but it was unlikely Caroline could get that close before being skewered.

Suddenly, the Indian woman with the maimed hand appeared. The old woman hissed. It was the first sound she had made. The woman's presence sparked the memory of the finger in Caroline's pocket. Intuitively, Caroline reached into the pocket to feel the odd prize. She was surprised to find it hard and long, much like the finger of her adversary.

As the Indian woman approached, the hag turned toward her and increased her hissing. Caroline seized the chance and lunged with the weapon, piercing the old woman's chest. An acrid steam spewed forth, but the hag seemed unfazed, shifting her attentions to Caroline.

Their bodies pressed against each other as the hag used her superior weight to unfoot Caroline. Neither foe could angle for a blow at the other as they rolled to the sand, the Indian woman watching quietly from a short distance away. Caroline was first to her feet, and stomped at the old woman's bony hand as the other pushed upward from the beach.

A pain-drenched growl filled the air, the hag clearly injured. Caroline kicked again, but this time struck the crone's arm to little effect. The old woman seemed stronger and had nearly righted herself.

Caroline had but one chance to retain her advantage, and that was to lunge at the hand in an attempt to pierce it with her weapon. Quickly she dove—her aim true, pinning her target into the damp shore.

Black blood spurted across Caroline's face, stinging slightly as she rolled into the water to rinse her eyes. As they cleared, she saw the Indian woman bend and take Caroline's weapon. The hag lay surrounded by her own blood—her life force spilled beyond recovery.

The Indian woman returned her finger to its socket and pointed to a break in the trees. Caroline rose. She moved toward the woman, opening her arms in a gesture of friendship, but the Indian shook her head no and again pointed at the opening. Reluctantly Caroline followed the command.

When she reached the trees, Caroline turned to wave at her strange friend. The Indian smiled and waved in return. Caroline backed into the grove, trying to keep sight of her companion. The earth beneath her feet gave way, and she stumbled down a steep embankment. Again she felt the splash of water, but this time she recognized her creek and the tree-bridge across it. Unhurt, she waded to the valley shore, washing the dirt from her body. Satisfied to be in familiar surroundings, she set off at once toward the house to await Caleb's return.

Caleb cared little for the swap meet, but for Caroline, who perhaps missed the conveniences of Nashville, it was the two days each month when she might obtain items for their home. Caleb most looked forward to spending Saturday evening with Erasmus and Ezekiel, while Caroline and her mother busily worked to knit for the forthcoming child.

Were these better times, there might have been a debate over whether blue or pink was the appropriate color for the bunting under preparation. As it was, the only yarn available was a utilitarian gray-white that would at least serve to keep the child warm.

The name of the child had been settled easily—Andrew John after Caleb's maternal grandfather if a boy, Jennifer Susan after Caroline's great aunt if a girl. The family had taken to referring to the child as "Andy or Jenny," as though it was one name, and sometimes as "Jenny or Andy," so as not to improperly influence the child toward one sex or the other.

There had been a tax sale that afternoon, Burke Walters auctioning off three tracts of land confiscated by the state. No local person had been able to raise the money to bid, and the new buyers were said to be land speculators operating out of Chattanooga.

Burke had scowled as he handed Caleb a receipt for this year's taxes, paid by Henderson from a trust account he had established at the Bank of Bristol. Caleb knew there were at least five other farms in the county likely to fall under from unpaid taxes. Rumors held that the land speculators paid a finders' fee to people such as Burke for letting them know when distressed property could be acquired for a fraction of its worth.

Caroline had smiled and, as a matter of manners, forced herself to make pleasant talk with Burke as they shared a pitcher of sun-sweetened lemonade on the porch of the Thompson home. When his eyes dwelled on her perhaps a bit too long, Caroline shifted her posture so that her high-necked blouse no longer drew tightly across her bosom.

The tax collector had proposed the child be named Adrian, a name he considered suitable for either sex. Caroline politely thanked him for the suggestion, though she thought his attention inappropriately given to a married woman.

Through the window in the Colton guest room, Caroline and Caleb could see the barn where Caleb had lived during the betrothal. Caroline teased her husband that perhaps it would have been romantic if he even just once had tried to scale the two-story house to her window during their courtship. Not that she would have allowed him entry—but the attempt would have been sweet.

Caleb reminded her that windows permitted egress as well as ingress, and besides, had he sneaked into the house, there would have been Nora and Ezekiel and Erasmus listening to their activities. No, he countered, if Caroline had been really romantic, she would have realized that joining Caleb in the barn was the only sensible choice.

Neither reminded each other of the extraordinary encounters four days prior. The odd sight of Caleb approaching the house with a bow and quiver strapped to his back had told Caroline that Caleb's day had been perhaps as remarkable as hers.

She had suggested only that her encounter was a dream, one she had awoken from as she carelessly rolled into the stream. Caleb accepted it as real, and most certainly it was, whether or not it was dreamed.

The tangibility of Night Raven's gift verified the reality of

Caleb's encounter. With the corn yet a good six weeks from harvest, Caleb had taken to spending much of each day practicing his aim, and had seen his distance accuracy increase greatly.

It was not a good stand of corn, Caleb regretted. The lingering cold had delayed planting, as had the three weeks spent clearing the Colton's farm. Of late, a smut had stunted the ears, few of which grew with uncrooked rows. Caleb had looked forward to the cash the corn might bring, though there would be very little money left over after Caleb had stocked provisions for the winter.

Caroline, too, had been troubled by the blight, not for the money lost, but for the ill comfort it caused the corn. How disagreeable, she considered, to have a black fungus growing on your skin.

Her view on the weeds clogging the fields differed from that of her husband's. To Caleb, weeds were an enemy that stole growing space from the corn. To Caroline, weeds were simply plants that grew where you didn't want them. That they grew in the cornfield didn't make them bad plants; after all, they had grown in the valley for much longer than had the corn.

Caleb teased her about the weeds, asking her if she replanted them in the forest after pulling them from the field. Caroline laughed, but never answered.

The morning came late when you slept near a town. Caleb just couldn't get used to a house full of people who chose to stay in bed until after the sun was up. Fortunately it was only one morning a month.

No trading was allowed on the Lord's day, which suited Caleb just fine. The quicker to be over the church services and on to the picnic. As was her custom, Nora fixed the family a huge breakfast—a skillet full of fresh-laid eggs scrambled light, small ham steaks with bacon, and a bowl of grits laden with newly churned butter. Caroline fixed the biscuits and set the table, then called the menfolk inside from their early chores.

Caleb wondered why everyone ate so much food on this one day of the month. A bite of hardtack and a ladle of water sufficed for breakfast most mornings. Silliest of all, the whole town would do it again by early afternoon, with every cook in Drake's Crossing bringing their finest dish to the post-services social. Afterwards, another month with not much to distinguish one day's meal from the next, unless you shot it yourself or pulled it from a stream. If he was lucky, Nora would have a pie left after the social. Caroline's pies were passable, but she had not yet acquired the full range of her mother's skills in the kitchen.

Caroline sat intently during the services, but Caleb paid little attention to the Reverend Haggerty. The reverend was condemning all unbelievers to the fiery pits of Hell, or to be more accurate, it was God who had promised to do the condemning, though there was no doubt the reverend wanted to be right alongside helping.

Caleb missed his father, though they each took pains to write each other on a regular basis. Walter had continued his good fortune at the expense of the carpetbaggers and now owned a racing horse, which he had acquired on a trip to Kentucky. Things were good between Henderson and Betty, and, also importantly, between Henderson and Betty's children. Caleb planned to visit his father as soon after the birth as Caroline and the child were able to travel.

Caroline nudged her husband occasionally lest he miss standing for a hymn or be late on a responsive reading. She was hardly more interested in the sermon than was Caleb, but out of respect for her cousin she sat attentively, as though she were hearing the message for the first time. Both husband and wife smiled as they sang the final hymn, and joined the Thompsons and the Coltons outside.

The bright August sun brought with it a clear, high sky. Two central tables held the foods, a third the beverages. Caroline offered to help Emma Mae and Becka with the servings, but Emma Mae told Caroline in a stern and certain tone that there were ample women in the community available to help without resorting to inconveniencing the pregnant ones.

Ezekiel and Hoyle laid claim to the largest of the picnic tables, and were joined by Caleb, Caroline, Erasmus, and the Reverend Haggerty. Erasmus gave a particularly polite thank-you to Becka as she served him his plate, on which she had piled the choicest portions from each dish.

At the next table, not more than ten feet to the left, sat the tax collector with the land speculators.

"Didn't see you at church this morning, Burke Walters," said Emma Mae as she brought a plate of food to the reverend. "Can't say as I saw any of your friends, either. Mighty poor of you to show up on the church grounds for the food but not the message. Which of these dishes is yours, anyway?"

"Watch your tongue, madam. I had intended to join you, but lost track of the time while discussing business with these gentlemen—business vital to the prosperity of our town," replied Burke.

"Vital to your prosperity, not to mine. Heard you sold out the widow Radford yesterday. Her husband was killed alongside McPherson fighting for the Union, but you never felt much loyalty for one side or the other, did you?" replied Emma Mae.

"How uncivil of you to say so. May I remind you I merely performed the duties of my office, or would you have the paying of taxes be an optional matter, something a person does if they feel like it?" said Burke.

"Even the tax office should show compassion," said Emma Mae. "There's a difference between a person who don't pay their taxes because they're going through difficult times, and a person who just plain tries to cheat. But I guess that's obvious; you wouldn't know the difference."

"How rude of you to cause this unpleasantness in front of these gentlemen. I apologize to them for your remarks. Would you have the folks in Chattanooga think Drake's Crossing a home for ignorant rubes? This man here represents the Pennsylvania Textile corporation. We could have a factory in this town if we play our cards right. Wouldn't that be wonderful? The prosperity of a factory while the rest of the South starves," said Burke.

"No one's starving here, Burke Walters. We grow more than enough food for ourselves. What do we need with a factory, except to increase the value of the land your crooked friends just bought?"

"Now see here, woman. That is slander, and we've all heard

you say it. These men are all lawyers and their word will be believed in any court in this land! Just because your taxes are paid doesn't mean you have a right to spread lies about the tax collector. There are courts to punish loose tongues such as yours," said Walters.

"Enough!" shouted the reverend angrily. "You've both profaned the Sabbath. God will see to the punishment of the wicked, not you Emma Mae. Besides, Mr. Walters has been generous in his support of the church, even if he seldom attends. Now enough. Let us enjoy the Lord's bounty without this bothersome bickering."

"Thank you, Reverend," said Walters, smiling with satisfaction.

"As you will have it," said Emma Mae. "I've invited Louise Radford to stay with us until her relatives in Roanoke can be located. Doesn't look to be much of her family left."

"That's fine, Emma Mae," said Hoyle. "Now let's do as the reverend says and enjoy this fine meal the Lord has provided for us." And with that, Hoyle bowed his head and began a prayer of thanks, certain that he would add several extra blessings to this message, allowing the solemnness of the prayer to lessen the ill feelings.

Caleb never knew when he would see Real Pappy or Night Raven. Sometimes they appeared shortly after the visit of the Reverend Haggerty. Sometimes they didn't visit for weeks on end.

Real Pappy had been pleased to hear of Caroline's success against Stone Finger, but that was months ago and Caroline had not been troubled since. The mountain man thought it likely the Raven Mocker lived in the caves near the ruins of Jim Stowe's house, cautioning Caleb not to go too close, lest he encounter their foe before proper preparations were made.

The Raven Mocker had struck twice more among the Cherokee, and a white traveler was said to be missing on the road to Knoxville.

Burke Walters had struck four times. Hoyle Thompson successfully arranged a charity event raising the tax money for the fifth family, who had had two sons killed in the war.

The winter ice made tracking harder in some ways, easier in others. Night Raven had been much help, showing Caleb how to use the weather to his advantage. There was little to hunt, the time of year making game scarce.

Caleb had made no money on his corn. The blight had worsened before the harvest, and he had spent his last cash on two sacks of meal at the January swap meet. No game had graced his table for more than three weeks. What vegetables that were stored were all given to Caroline, whose belly had swollen out of proportion to her increasingly gaunt frame.

"I think I feel two different kicks," she had told her husband, much to his surprise and to his happiness.

"What if it is two boys or two girls?" Caleb had thought aloud. "More names to think of."

"I wouldn't worry," came Caroline's smiling reply. "One of them kicks like a girl. The other like a boy."

Emma Mae had recommended a midwife who was willing to stay with Caroline at Nora's during the week of confinement preceding the birth. Caleb was eager to have Caroline join her mother, but when the appointed time came, so had a foot of new snow, and there was little Caleb could do but help Caroline be comfortable in their cabin.

He could probably perform the delivery, thought Caleb. He had delivered several calves and a foal once, and was in much demand by his neighbors at Drake's Crossing when they needed help with their livestock. He toyed with the idea of taking Verda into town for help, but how could the help come? Even if Caleb could negotiate the mountain on horseback, it was doubtful the midwife could.

Some days the weather would clear, but never did it warm above freezing. The heavy drifts of snow hardened but did not leave. Fresh snow fell some days, though on most it did not. Caroline thought the birthing would occur on Saturday, two days hence. Her spirits were high, her confidence strong. She had a warm home, clean linen, a fire by which to boil water, and a husband who was known for his hand in veterinary matters. Many women had successfully given birth under much worse conditions with no help at all.

Caleb awoke before each dawn and saw to the feeding of Sampson, Verda, and the two cows. The steer had been sold to buy winter provisions, and for a dress for Caroline's birthday. The chickens, of which there had been but few to start with, had all been consumed before Christmas, a decision made easier by the ever-decreasing volume of eggs they had produced.

The milk from the cows was the only new food Caleb could depend upon, and though Caroline would feed the infants at her breasts, their milk was needed to replenish Caroline's vitality. Chickens were easy to replace, but a milk cow slaughtered for beef was a waste of a valuable animal.

Caroline did not complain. There were still potatoes and dried carrots in the cellar, of which Caleb ate little even during the harvest times when they were plentiful. The cornmeal was palatable, though tedious on an everyday basis.

It was Friday morning, and Caroline had assured her husband the night before it was all right if he used much of the day for hunting. "I think the birthing will come Saturday, probably near midday. A rabbit would be nice for stew, if one can be coaxed from his lair," she had told him. "A good stew would help me build my strength." Nonetheless Caleb had awoken early, some hours before the dawn, eager to return before midday Friday.

She lay sleeping as he left, the down comforter softly covering her from her neck to the base of the bed. Caleb leaned over and kissed her, brushing her hair back from her cheek as he did. He closed the door quietly but firmly, careful not to disturb her rest.

Caleb hunted with both the bow and the rifle now, adeptly switching between the two. Night Raven had shown him how to adjust the quiver harness to hold the carbine, its short barrel an advantage when carried with a bow. Fortune was with him, Caleb thought, when a large cottontail crossed his path soon after he began to climb the mountain. He gave chase, readying his bow as he ran.

The rabbit was heading uphill, toward a cluster of boulders and the safety of his warren. Caleb stopped and drew his bow— not the shot he had hoped for, but a later firing was unlikely. The cold air added a sharpness to the whistle of the arrow and a crack to the thud as the rabbit fell. In the moonlight, Caleb could see a crimson stain blotting into the snow. His hit had been solid, the animal lying only a few paces from the point of impact.

Caleb drew the arrow from the game, being careful to clean the blood from the point before returning it to his quiver. He took his knife and slit the rabbit's throat, prying back the head to allow the blood to drain. The hardest of the labors ahead were Caroline's, but Caleb nonetheless felt pride at being able to lay this fine cottontail on the table before his family. When the blood had drained, he wrapped the animal in a deerskin, and stored it in his pack.

Caleb had taken no more than a step toward the valley, when a magnificent buck came dashing past, racing higher into the mountains. Caleb drew his rifle. No sense worrying about scaring game when he had a rabbit in his pouch and a deer in his sights. He fired, but his shot glanced off a hickory tree as the buck ran farther up the mountain.

Hunting before dawn was Caleb's favorite challenge. The animals were fresher and stronger at that time of day—most of them having arisen for the same reason as Caleb, to get an early jump on the day. This buck was unusually fine, at least ten points on the antlers.

The buck drove deeper into rocky woods. Caleb followed at a deliberate pace, not trying to match the animal for speed, unconcerned about losing the tracks in the snow and ice.

Suddenly Caleb felt a sting across his forehead, just below his hairline. A large black crow, probably a raven, had pecked at him; it did so again as he headed up the mountain.

"Shoo!" he cried, swinging his fist at the bird. His forehead bled slightly as the bird retreated to the shelter of a tree limb. Caleb knew he could not get a clear shot at it with either the bow or the rifle. He had no need to kill the bird—crow's meat was so tough and stringy as to be uneatable—he merely wanted to proceed with his hunt of the deer.

The buck had paused atop an outcropping of rock, and Caleb hurried a second shot, which went even wider than the first. The deer dashed away, and Caleb followed, noting the cresting of the sun in the distance.

Caleb forgot about the raven, so intent was his concentration on his prey. The buck too was intent on the chase, leading Caleb in a zigzag pathway toward the mountaintop. After maybe two hours Caleb paused, resting on one of the many boulders he had climbed.

The buck was tiring, too, and stopped when he saw his pursuer stop. Caleb readied a third shot. The deer jumped as Caleb pulled the trigger. The bullet flew through the spot vacated by the buck, striking the small red wolf which unbeknownst to Caleb had spooked the animal back down the mountain.

Caleb felt bad as he rushed toward the wolf. The wolf ran also, in the opposite direction from the buck. Caleb could see the animal limp, and assumed it to be struck in the foot or leg. The blood trickle was slight, and Caleb was relieved to know the wolf was not seriously hurt.

Returning his attention to the buck, Caleb loaded a fourth shot, taking position on the forward edge of the rocks from which he had last fired. For the first time he was above the deer, with a clear, unobstructed shot. He took aim and squeezed the trigger, happily anticipating the problem of dragging so large a creature down the mountain.

When Caleb regained consciousness, his first thought was that the sun was unusually pale, even for winter. So pale, in fact, that he could see the stars around it. He stared at the sky in disbelief, up toward the ledge from which he had fallen, realizing finally that night had returned.

His gun lay next to him, its barrel split open as though it had been unable to contain the power of the shot. Weak metal, thought Caleb. He had heard of such accidents but never seen one.

The slight powder burn on Caleb's face hurt little compared to his concussion from the fall and the throbbing pain in his left foot. He was unable to move his leg from the knee down, his ankle tightly wedged between two rocks. The more he pulled, the more his foot hurt. He tried shifting the heavy boulders but lacked the strength and the leverage.

The cold bit at him. His jacket had preserved some of his body heat, but the fall had knocked his cap from his head, contributing

to the chill Caleb felt. Despite having just regained consciousness, Caleb wanted to sleep, the cold inviting him toward its
oblivion.

As his head cleared, Caleb thought of Caroline. No, the children would not be born yet. It was still Friday night, perhaps
very early Saturday morning. Of this Caleb was confident. He
knew he could not have survived had he remained unconscious
into Saturday evening.

He wanted to sleep, so badly he wanted to sleep. He hoped
he would dream of Caroline, that if he was to die here his last
thoughts would be of her.

There was an excellent chance she could bear the children
without his help, though he might still perhaps reach her in time
if he could free his foot. Reach her, Caleb thought. Not much
chance. He was as good as dead.

He reached for his pack and removed the rabbit. It was frozen
solid, though Caleb tore off a small piece of flesh with his teeth
and thawed it in his mouth until it could be swallowed. The snow
and ice would provide ample moisture. Caleb figured he could
give up quickly, or he could take another day to die.

He rested his head on the stony pillow beneath him. He could
see his blood on it, though the worst external injury he had
suffered was a scraped scalp. His foot was badly bruised and
sprained, perhaps even broken, though he could still wiggle his
toes.

His eyes were open, and he decided to last it out as long as
he could. Dying was no problem. He could open his shirt and
jacket, exposing his chest to the cold. Probably would take less
than an hour that way. Were he to prolong the process, he could
surely last until daybreak, probably throughout the day, and
maybe a little past the next nightfall. No longer, he thought. And
maybe not that long.

The raven was back, making more noise than Caleb thought
he would ever hear again. Now that he remembered, it had been
the raven's cawing that had brought Caleb back to consciousness.
Caleb tried to think of some way the raven could help free him,
but could not. He was thankful for the companionship. It was
not quite so lonely as dying alone.

The raven rested just out of reach. No matter. The frozen rabbit provided better nourishment than the bird would have. Occasionally the creature would peck at Caleb's head, sometimes hitting a point on Caleb's already tender scalp. The pain was excruciating. With each peck, Caleb's body convulsed uncontrollably, his foot throbbing with more intensity at each strike.

As the raven played tag with an increasing frequency, Caleb resolved to be rid of it, loneliness or not. If he could never again fire the rifle, at least its stock might make a useful cudgel. He gripped the damaged barrel near its end.

Caleb did not stir, so as to deceive the bird of his intention. His arms rested at length, the barrel in his hands, the stock across his legs. He saw the bird take flight, circle, and take a bead on his head.

With all his might he lunged at the bird, stretching his arms and his body to their limit. He felt the wooden stock strike flush against the bird's wing, knocking the barrel from his hands. Pain streamed through Caleb's body. The bird struck the snow in front of Caleb, then struggled along the ground away from him.

To his surprise, Caleb found that his foot had come free. Despite the cold, the ankle was swollen to the point that Caleb tried neither to move it nor to put weight on it. The initial fall had ruined his bow. Too bad—it might have made a good crutch. The rifle was likewise useless, the stock having splintered against a boulder.

Caleb resolved to use the ice to his advantage, sliding down it in small increments. The boulders proved to be the biggest problem, though his arm strength allowed him to lower himself past the obstacles.

As the sun rose, Caleb reckoned himself to be only a little ways closer to the cabin than when he had started. To avoid the difficult rocks, he had traveled more sideways than down. If not injured, he could have reached the cabin in three hours or less, but, with his foot unable to sustain weight, Caleb doubted he could make it before nightfall.

His exertions had rekindled his body heat, and he had regained his cap, which he had discovered some twenty feet from where he had landed. He could reach his home, of that he was certain, but one slip as he descended the several small intervening cliffs, and he was dead.

He saw the wolf he had shot, not much worse for the experience except for a slight limp. The wolf came close to Caleb—he could feel its hot breath—but never allowed himself to be touched. The wolf charged to a specific point downhill, then ran back to Caleb, repeating the measure four times. Caleb resolved to follow the animal. He had no better route to take.

By late afternoon Caleb could see real progress. He was within two miles of the creek and could see the smoke from the chimney fire at his house. The sight of the smoke warmed Caleb nearby as much as would the fire itself. Caleb wondered how Caroline had fared. Possibly her labor had been delayed, but Caleb thought the deliveries to have occurred as foreseen.

The wolf had invariably found the easiest path down the mountain. What few rock formations Caleb had encountered had been easily traversed. He acquired a broken tree limb, healthy and firm, but severed from its trunk by the weight of ice and broken into pieces. He tested several, selecting one to help him walk.

The sun set as Caleb crossed the creek. Two hours, maybe three, and he would be home.

While still at least four hundred yards from the house, Caleb knew something was seriously wrong. He had just rounded the final turn in the road when he noticed that the door to the house stood open. Every bit as alarming, the chimney was empty of smoke.

"Caroline! Caroline!" he called, probably too far away to be heard. He cursed his carelessness on the mountain.

Caleb hobbled toward the door. A heavy flapping distracted him as a dark-winged silhouette cast its shadow across the house. Caleb paused to look. The moon set high, and he could see that the creature flying away from him had the size of a full-grown man. He could clearly make out a cloth sack tightly held in the creature's talons.

The cabin's furniture lay strewn about in utter disarray. On the upturned bed Caroline's naked body sprawled across a bloody pool, the corpses of the two infants mockingly cradled in her arms. Her face was blue—the umbilical cords of her progeny tightly wrapped around her neck. Her eyes, no longer green, bulged as though searching for help. Against the empty socket where her heart had been rested the children, their tiny hearts likewise torn from their torsos. Their mouths were open, their first breaths having been their last.

Caleb fell to the floor and cried until the sun rose. The pain in his foot was noticeably less as he dug Caroline's grave next to Elizabeth's, then the children's next to Caroline's. He wrapped the bodies in linen, then placed them in their graves. Caleb wasn't sure whether you said the prayer before you put the dirt back, or afterwards, so he prayed at each point.

That task completed, Caleb took two jugs of kerosene from the store closet, and placed one in his knapsack. The other he emptied onto the bloodied blankets on the bed. Though the fireplace burned no longer, the reading lamp in the window remained lit. Caleb removed the glass chimney and touched the wick to the bed. The fire spread instantly.

The heat from the flames warmed Caleb's back as he walked out the door.

About halfway to the mountain caves, Caleb had been joined by Real Pappy and Night Raven. The latter had his right arm bound to his chest, and his elbow rested in a sling. The rocks on which they sat faced northward, giving them a view both of Caleb's valley and the cluster of buildings named Drake's Crossing.

From his pouch, Real Pappy had drawn a white creamy salve, which he applied to Caleb's ankle and scalp. The relief came quickly, though some soreness remained. Sundown neared, and Real Pappy invited Caleb to share the lean-to he had prepared among the trees.

The Cherokee brave remained outside, standing watch. Caleb nestled into the bearskin blankets. Bears could kill a man with the swat of a paw, but no animal provided a skin as large or as thick as a black bear. He had not slept a proper sleep since Thursday night, and neither the cold nor Real Pappy's snore disturbed his rest.

When he arose, it was midmorning. The smell of chicory wafted in the air, and he could hear bacon sizzling on the fire.

"Have a little," said Real Pappy, offering the tin cup to Caleb. "It's not coffee, but it'll do on a cold day." Caleb took the beverage.

"Just what was you planning on doing?" asked the mountain man. "Gonna charge up this mountain and set things right? Don't you think if it was that simple we'd have done it before now?"

"No more waiting," said Caleb.

"Yes. That's obvious. I've been wrong twice now about when our foe would strike. I take the blame for what happened to your wife," said real Pappy.

"No. It was my fault. I had food. I did not need to chase more. You warned me not to use a weapon that had injured a wolf. I was thoughtless, and I was not there to protect Caroline at a time when she was unable to protect herself."

"We all could have done something more. Can't change any of it, except what lies ahead. Like I asked before. You got a plan?"

"No." Caleb looked at the ground. "I guess I was going to get myself killed."

"Worse than killed. Your heart would have ended up rotting away with the others in that sack. You can't see Jesus or go to the great western sky when your heart's been rotted away. Besides, you just gonna let her horse starve in its corral? The cows and the ox might survive the winter, but not a penned-up horse."

"The horse will be okay. Eventually the Coltons will come to check on us."

"That they will," said Real Pappy. "Do you think they deserve to find three new graves and a burned-out house—with no word from you? You still ain't learned much, and there's not time now for you to take a day to go set it straight with them. Maybe afterwards."

"After what?" asked Caleb.

"After we steal the sack, the one where he keeps the hearts! Don't you think of nothin' for yourself? We'll do it during the day, when the Raven Mocker can't take his natural form—then set a trap and lure him there at night."

"Can we do it? I mean kill him?" Caleb asked.

"Maybe. Not much left if we don't try," said the mountain man.

"Today?"

Real Pappy smiled. "Not a better day available. Old Raven Mocker might still be a little tired after the fight Caroline gave him the other night."

The torches Caleb had made proved unnecessary. Most of the kerosene remained, but Night Raven had given his sling to the cause. Caleb had found the heart sack near the cavern's entrance, hidden behind a large rock and covered with a shallow layer of dirt.

"Good thing to know that the Raven Mocker can't see in the dark," said Real Pappy.

"How's that?" asked Caleb.

"He can probably see at night better than we can, but if he could see in total darkness, he'd have buried his sack deeper into the cave."

"What now?" asked Caleb.

"He's probably resting. Takes himself an animal form when he does that. Probably a bear or an elk. Something large, so he can rest all of himself at once. Maybe a human—particularly with him spendin' so much time around humans the past few years."

"What kind of trap do we set?"

"Gotta be a natural force. Guns won't hurt him. Not even arrows. Maybe a fire or a bolt of lightnin'. I ain't no good at controlling lightnin' myself, though I knew a colored woman once who was taken with the way. No, gotta be something natural like a rock what kills him."

"Or a cord of ice," said Caleb.

"Now you're thinkin'," said Real Pappy. "A long, sharp cord of ice. And I'll bet you're thinking of just the place, too."

It was when Nora hitched the steer to the buckboard that Ezekiel realized she was serious about trying to cross the mountain and see Caroline. She had not seen her daughter since three Sundays prior, and Nora was taken with an uncontrollable fear.

Her efforts awoke the Reverend Haggerty from his slumber in their guest room. Slowly he arose and pushed open the shutters to the window. "Wait! I'll be the one to go," he shouted, temporarily stalling the argument.

When he joined them downstairs, still clad in his dressing robe, he could see it was not anger but worry which had caused the voices to be raised.

Ezekiel stood firm. "I'm her father. It's my duty to go, if the trip be made."

"How many days will you wait?" asked Nora. "There's no sign this snow will lessen before April."

"Not to praise my own name, of course, but I've not missed a Sunday yet in fifteen years of service to the Lord," interjected the reverend. "Lots of snow and some pretty mean shooting in those years. I'm not due in Mooresville till Thursday. I'd say I'm the better choice to try the mountain than either of you. Besides, I've got the only horse amongst us."

"You'll return tomorrow?" asked Nora plaintively.

"Yes, of course. I can easily ride by moonlight if the need be. Done it many a time."

"Bless you, Josiah," said Ezekiel, much relieved. "There's ham hock remaining from yesterday. Allow us to ask you to carry it to Caleb and our daughter. After you've had your fill of Nora's breakfast, of course."

It was Real Pappy's idea to burn the hearts one by one, starting with the blackest ones first. "Might burn some of the evil out of them," he said.

Only a few of the hearts held the redness of blood as Caleb removed them from the sack. He had feared to plunge his hand into the darkness, so he had opened the mouth of the sack and shaken the hearts out, then rolled them across the ground with a stick. Caleb had removed maybe a hundred now, and the sack was no less full than before.

"That's enough," said Real Pappy. "Start your fire."

Even left-handed, Night Raven had proven adept at digging a hole in the road through Buckman's Pass. Caleb's fire had softened the ice, more than a foot thick in spots. They had cleared nearly a ten-foot ground area—more than enough to set the trap.

Caleb had seen hoofprints heading toward the valley, and wondered if perhaps Erasmus or Ezekiel were on their way to the cabin.

The hole had to be deep enough that the Raven Mocker would be trapped sufficiently long to allow their attack to succeed. Just short of seven feet down, they struck rock, and spent the remaining hour before sundown tossing the dirt around the cliffs so as not to reveal the pit.

Night Raven covered the hole with one of Real Pappy's bearskins, then covered the skins with crushed ice indistinguishable from the more solidly packed road surrounding it.

The trap laid, Night Raven and Real Pappy climbed the rocks, taking positions above the disguised hole. Selecting an icicle that was longer than he was tall, Real Pappy began chipping away, weakening the frozen water's grip on the mountain. Night Raven climbed higher, finding a spot that gave him a vantage over the tops of the surrounding trees. He could see the sky clearly in every direction and would know when their foe approached.

Caleb waited for the dark to come. He had set his fire on a flat rock, some ten feet up the craggy cliff, directly above the trap. The slow constant thumps of the many beating hearts he had stored distracted Caleb, and he tried to put them from his mind. His hiding place was slightly recessed. He was satisfied the Raven Mocker could not reach him by air. To ensure his foe stepping onto the proper place, Caleb had positioned the sack in the roadway.

As the last glow of red set in the west, Caleb shoved a particularly blackened heart toward the fire. A foul odor arose, and Caleb coughed when its bitter fragrance touched his nostrils. The other hearts beat faster now, and Caleb could see the sack alive and pulsing. A loathsome cry issued from deep within the fire, and a gust of white smoke shot skyward.

Caleb pushed a second heart into the flame. A fresh odor arose, no less malevolent than the first, but altogether different. The cry was different too, and a chill shuddered through Caleb as he realized, for the first time, both the nature and the power of his foe.

*   *   *

Josiah Haggerty had been much troubled at finding the ruined house and the three graves. Caleb, Caroline, and their newborn, he had thought—but who had done the burying? He had no doubt the Cherokee savages had committed the massacre, but what Christian person would have left a cross at the head of each burial and then kept it a secret at yesterday's church meeting? And if the Cherokees had killed them, why did they leave the animals, the only things worth stealing on the entire farm?

He wasted little time in leaving the accursed site. Verda took her bridle easily, her reins tethered to his saddle. Probably would be well after midnight before he reached the nearest shelter at Drake's Crossing, he decided. Fortunately the road had both a hard crusting of ice and a light covering of powder. Nora would never have made it in that silly buckboard, the reverend thought. The powder that helps a horse's footing would just have made the wheels slip.

His confidence in his mounts notwithstanding, Josiah kept the reins tight as the horses trudged along the upward path. An unpleasant smell was on the air, and as he climbed the odor grew stronger.

He disembarked as he neared the pass, the reflections of night adding treachery to the road. The caw of a crow drifted toward Josiah. Above the shadows, he saw the black bird hovering most strangely, as though favoring one wing.

He could clearly make out a fire ahead, its flickers shooting intermittent streaks of light into the pass. In one of the flickers, he thought he saw a monster, but it disappeared, as if it had descended into the road.

A low-pitched growl began to fill the air, a sound the reverend was certain could come only from Satan. Josiah Haggerty froze. He had not yet been seen, and if he remained still, maybe he wouldn't be.

Caleb's heart was lifted as he saw the Raven Mocker trapped in the pit. The raven with the hurt wing circled above, as if to taunt it. Caleb shouted to Real Pappy, "Now! Do it now!"

The old man didn't answer, and Caleb could see him across

the way striking vainly at a column of ice. Caleb left his perch to attempt to join him, then realized the Raven Mocker had almost climbed from the hole.

Drawing his knife, Caleb leapt toward his enemy. He landed on its back, striking at its neck. The thick covering of feathers protected the bird, and Caleb dropped the weapon. With his hands, he groped for the creature's eyes.

A talon seized his wrist, and in a moment he was on the ice, the Raven Mocker looming over him. Caleb felt the claws pierce his chest, still conscious as his heart was torn from his body.

Even in the dim light, the reverend recognized Caleb. In anger he rushed forward, only to see the bloody mass lifted tauntingly toward the sky.

"Oh no!" the reverend shouted. "Please God, not us all!" His shrill voice filled the night air, covering both the wails of the burning hearts and the self-satisfied grunts of the monster. Even the cracking of the ice could not compete with the voice of Josiah Haggerty.

Real Pappy felt the cord giving way. Small rocks bounced downward. He thrust all his weight onto the ice, gratified to feel it freed. He was falling with the spike, and a good thing too, or else he would have missed the Raven Mocker. Real Pappy tilted the enormous icicle just a little, driving the end into the top of the creature's head.

More ice and rocks followed. A boulder struck first the circling bird, then careened into the circuit preacher, crushing his chest. The horses skittered and ran, barely escaping the avalanche. Buckman's Pass lay desolated. Not a trace lay visible of any who had struggled there.

Caleb was the first to recover from the transition. He was acutely aware of a pleasant warming light from above. The souls were stirring now, and even the Raven Mocker began to rise. They were all whole, the bodies restored to the hearts, and Caleb struggled for a glimpse of Caroline among the thousands of blues and grays before him.

Slowly, some began to go upward toward the warming light, while a few, a very few, searched for a way into the earth. A sulfurous odor arose, and Caleb could see a stairway leading deep into the bowels of darkness from which a cordon of red-robed acolytes emerged. Seven of them grabbed the Raven Mocker, dragging him toward the stairs.

Futilely, the human part of the creature struggled to free himself from the hold. The feathers mutated into skin, the eyes and beak into the face of Burke Walters. "I did my job!" he screamed to his captors. "Just doing what I was appointed to do! Have mercy, oh Master! I did my job well. I deserve better than this." Sobbing uncontrollably, he was led into the earth, never turning his head toward the light that glowed above.

The most amazed person at this all was the Reverend Haggerty. He was fascinated by the stairs, and wandered closer so that he might peer down them. Caleb saw Night Raven approach the preacher, Little Bird and her husband at his side. "Don't you want to go up there?" asked the Indian, pointing toward the warmth in the sky.

Yes, thought the reverend. When a heathen brave comes up and points out heaven to you while speaking in perfect English, it is indeed time to leave for glory.

The dead flowed to their chosen reward at an astounding pace. A few headed into the great western sky, and Caleb was reminded it was Colonel Eli Parker, a Seneca brave, who had inscribed the articles of surrender signed by Lee and Grant at Appomattox.

"You're welcome to come with us if you've a mind to." It was Real Pappy.

"No. I've got business here," said Caleb.

"You'll be welcome, whenever you're done, in any of these fine places. Lookin' forward to sittin' around the lodge with Night Raven, myself. Tells me he's got another sister even prettier than Little Bird," said the old man.

The mountain was almost empty. A few souls were still deciding what to do, but mostly the uncommitted drifted back toward town, toward the life they had known.

"Not everyone goes right away," said Real Pappy. "Peace be with you, young Caleb. I suspect we'll meet again. By the way, my name's Clarence. Might need to know that if you ever look me up."

"Thanks. I plan to do that someday. Now, you've got a journey to make and I have someone to find," said Caleb.

"She'll be where you know her to be," said Night Raven, turning toward Real Pappy. "Now come, old friend. We have brothers to join."

Caleb watched as his companions made their way into the great western sky. They waved to those heading into the warmth, a few of the soldiers signaling back. The sun was rising now, and it was time for all souls to be in their place.

"Husband." The sound came softly from the valley. "Husband, I am here, and so are our children."

"I am with you," came the reply. "I am with you always."

Caroline looked up from the valley and saw the yellow of Caleb's hair reflected in the sun as it rose behind the mountain. Caleb looked below and saw the green of Caroline's eyes in the cedar trees, set against the rapidly melting snow. Andrew and Jennifer played in the spring and along the creek, and their laughter was so loving, even the doves marveled to hear it, as did all who came the way of the mountain and the valley.

Grabow and Collicker and I

Algis Budrys

By my tenth birthday, I had outgrown the Huntsville Public Library's rather limited collection of science fiction. There is only so long you can read Verne, Poe, and Wells before realizing almost nothing post-1940 was available on the shelves. My most prized Christmas present that year was ten dollars and a trip to the local newsstand. This was an era when nearly all paperbacks cost 35 cents or less, and I took an entire afternoon agonizing over the selections. It was a watershed moment in my young reading experience.

Among the twenty-five or so books I bought, most were standard space opera or similar light reading, but one novel, *Rogue Moon* by Algis Budrys, stood out above all the others. Rather than dealing with invincible heroes on alien planets, it centered on real-life people trying to solve a believable scientific problem. The depth of the characterization and the contemporary setting was unlike anything I had read at the time.

It wasn't until Chicago's World Science Fiction Convention in 1982 that I met "A.J." As I recall, I was much at a loss for words on the occasion. Three years later, A.J. was the toastmaster for the Deep South Science Fiction Convention in Huntsville, the first convention for which I was involved in the selection of the guests.

There are lots of interesting facets to A.J.'s career. He served as an assistant to his father, the Consul General of Lithuania in New York City, holding a captain's commission in the Lithuanian army. His editorial career includes work at Gnome Press, Regency Books, and Playboy Press. His highly regarded short story "Master of the Hounds" became the 1972 motion picture *To Kill a Clown,* with Alan Alda and Blythe Danner, while his novel *Who?* was adapted into a 1974 feature film starring Elliott Gould and Trevor Howard.

So preeminent is A.J.'s position as a critic, *Benchmarks: Galaxy Bookshelf,* his collected reviews from 1965–1971, is considered a definitive statement on modern science fiction's most fertile period. Among his many awards is the Medal of Honor from the Society of Writers at The United Nations. There is much, much more, and I haven't even gotten to A.J.'s Rand McNally book on bicycle repair. Someone someone will write a great book about Algis Budrys.

Very few people have excelled so well as a writer, editor, and critic, or have held such a strong influence for so long. In a very real sense, this anthology is a direct descendant of *Rogue Moon* and the impression it made on me. A.J. calls the effort at hand his first "intentional" horror story. We are pleased to be able to offer it to you.

"I dream, Johnnie . . . I dream all the time," Cash said, a haunted look in his remaining eye. "I dream of home, I dream of Clara, I dream of the baby. All the time." He laughed, partway . . . a hollow sound, with the loneliness baying in it. "It wouldn't be so bad if I didn't dream."

"I don't dream," I replied.

We were in the trenches at Cold Harbor, piled up, waiting for our next use. Two hundred men, or what was left of manhood, of Pedrick's Special Corps, Attached USA. No one had ever seen Pedrick; I doubted if he still existed. Dr. Karl Grabow existed, bending over us in the night, seeing which ones still retained essential function, sending the ones who were too shot up to a place no one dared to think of. Grabow was an old man; older than us, anyway, in an old clawhammer coat and a shirt that was white under the soil and things that clung to it, and carrying what seemed like an endless supply of fluid in big, clumsy hypodermics.

Grabow had a counterpart who introduced new bodies into our group, to replace the ones Grabow sent away. Harlow Collicker was amazingly pale, amazingly young, amazing in that he had a peg leg and a claw for a hand but was otherwise dressed identically to Grabow, though his shirt was a little cleaner, lurching and fuming over the ground, leading his daily troop of replacements, who lurched and did not fume after him, because they were past fuming. Nobody ever saw Grabow and Collicker together; Grabow came at night, Collicker at dawn. No one came in full daylight. There was no need, and there was copious revulsion.

"Aw, gee," Cash said, "I wish this were over. I wish I could lie down somewhere and forget about Clara."

"Well, step in front of a shell."

Cash gestured awkwardly. "You know I wouldn't do that. I wouldn't let you fellows down like that."

Well, that may have been a load of manure. The fact was, it was almost as hard to get yourself hurt, if you were trying, as it was to not get hurt if you weren't. And considering that it took a lot more to stop us. . . . I mean, Cash had taken one in face yesterday, and he was never going to do more than turn your stomach ever since, but basically he was still functional. What startled me, some, was that he was still talking, considering that part of his brain was gone, but perhaps it wasn't an important part. Or perhaps something had removed the part of mine that formed these judgments, but in running my hands over my head as soon as I thought of this, I found an unbroken surface. No, I decided, Cash meant it, more or less.

But it was no good, dreaming of the Claras, or the babies . . . no good at all, anymore, and I wished Cash didn't do it, though in fact it did no harm; it was just excess baggage, and Cash should get rid of it.

My own dreams, now—I had lied to Cash—my own dreams were martial, and mostly glorious.

God! Banners and bugles, cavalry charges and musket smoke, . . . ah, well! Oddly enough, the dreams of a young recruit signing up, on a frosty Connecticut morning, to carry a musket that weighed startlingly, and wear a blue cap that sat oddly on one's head . . . the dreams of a young recruit, as I said, sometimes did play out, in rough semblance at least; at least, when translated

down from an Olympian view of the battlefield to the reality of
one man, dashing in terror through the bushes but dashing forward, eyes focused down to the point where everything beyond
a narrow tube of vision was just a blur, just a blue blur or a
gray. But more often, truth to tell, it was Secesh bayonets at
dawn, and minié balls for luncheon and supper. God!

And the war went on. Men came and went. Came and went.
But I, although Johnny had pinked me now and then, neverthe-
less stayed, and officers came to depend on me. And gradually
I came to an understanding that all that was involved was continuing to go forward; that all the rest was illusion and fustian,
signifying only the unbelievable good spirits of new recruits and
the folderol of officers. I came to realize, as my well-learned
lesson from the war, that I would live or I would die, and that
I would continue to go forward until I died or the war ended,
and all else was illusion and fustian.

And so, when one day they asked for volunteers—unmarried
men only, with no living relatives—I wondered what that might
be. And found myself, much to my bemusement, standing in the
short line outside Grabow's tent.

Grabow was younger then, last year, and much cleaner. Much
cleaner, though not necessarily more sensible. He saw us one at
a time; and in time my turn came and I stood before him inside
the tent, with him seated at a deal table on a folding chair, and
an endless supply of hypodermics on another table behind him.
A fresh supply of hypodermics bubbled and boiled in a kettle to
one side. "I want to try an experiment," he said, staring at me
walleyed. "An experiment."

I shifted my feet in the mud. "What are you talking about?"

"Assume you died," he said.

Well, that was not much of an assumption. You do not believe
you'll die, of course, but your mind simply figures the odds and
knows that it is the more daring assumption that you'll live. War
. . . war is stupid, and often utterly without point, and young
men die so that old men can make what point there is. But we
go to war so often. So often. And we die.

I looked at Grabow from under the bill of my cap, and said:
"And . . . ?"

Grabow waved at the rows of hypodermics. "I offer you a second chance."

Well, the short of it is, you cannot see how it could do any harm. So you—if you're me—come out of the tent rubbing your arm, and not much changed, really. It's a different matter when Cash comes out of the tent rubbing his arm, and you round on him and you demand: "What have you done? What have you done, Merton Cash! You have a wife . . . a baby!"

"Well," he shuffled and stammered, "I—ah, I couldn't have you think that I—I couldn't let you have me a coward."

"Coward! You blamed fool, all you've done is ensure that if you die, Clara won't even have the comfort of your bones! You'll be shot and shelled until your own mother wouldn't recognize you, and do you think Grabow could ship you back, if he were so minded, which he's obviously not?"

"Ah . . ."

Ah. Ah. My dreams became more vivid with Dr. Grabow's fluid boiling in my veins, ready to take over if the blood should run out. Dreams . . .

I was in a tent with Grant, and Grant had his jaw clamped around a cigar, which I recall was half-smoked and badly bitten, and he was saying to a man whose features I could not make out, "I can succeed without them!"

"Well, I have no doubt. No doubt at all," the featureless man said. "I merely point to this as a method for keeping the casualty figures down."

Grant shuddered. Grant! Shuddered. He turned to me. "What do you think?"

And I dreamed ahead . . . at men struggling through luxuriant and fecund growth in someplace called the Philippines, while silent death found them at every turn; at men in long lines of trenches for years at a time, while strange machines smashed at them on the ground and from the air; at men engaged in over half the world, and machines ever more curious, until finally they . . . God, no, whole cities at a blow! And the people melting. . . .

"It is the only means," I seemed to say. "The only means to keep war from spreading to the civilians."

And Grant stared into the future with me.

The featureless man turned into the lamplight, and I saw that it was Mr. Lincoln, with a terrible visage and a terrible nod. "So be it," he said, and buried his face in his hands, which let me see the wound behind his ear.

It was in the early days of '64 that a Johnny bayonetted me through the heart. I recall a surgeon bending over me, and then the look on his face, and the outraged way in which he said: "Get it off my table! It's another one of Grabow's litches!" and I knew then that it was all over for me; that I had crossed over a divide over which there was no going back. No going back ever.

And Collicker came for me, amazingly gentle, and led me away from the places of men, and put me with the others of my kind, to await the need for a particular assignment or another that the living would only do with great reluctance. I remember that although there was no ostensible reason for it, I avoiding looking into the faces of the men around me as Collicker led me away, and they drew back as though from something unclean. Something unclean. Yes. Well. I did not look much into the faces of those of my own new kind, either; for one thing, they were many of them not whole, but I think largely it was something else: of what use was it, really, to look at each other?

And in course of time, here came Merton Cash, whom I did look at because he came with a crooked grin and puppydog enthusiasm, and only a little missing at the time—they had shot him in the stomach—and he greeted me like a fond relation. I would have wept.

"Ah, ah," he flurried, "it's so good to see you again!" And even Collicker took note, staring incredulously, then limping away a little more hastily than usual. "You know, it's not so bad," Cash said. "I knew it was over when the pain in my belly went away at last. There's advantages."

But now was later, and Cash dreamt of Clara and the baby, whom he would never, never see again, and I dreamt my dreams.

I dreamt my dreams. And the summons came, and we went up against the redoubt at Cold Harbor. And it was terrible.

I lay in a windrow of the dead, all feeling gone from hips, down, trying to turn my body so I could keep firing, but a dead Irishman lay across my chest, and if I had needed to breathe, I don't think I would have lasted until Grabow came for me just at dusk. And he looked at me, and pulled the Irishman off me, and without saying a word, pulled me off the dead Irishman, so that I understood, at last, that I was all gone below the hips; below the hips, I had been struck by the same cannonball that had struck the Irishman, and below the hips I was all gone.

And Grabow loaded me on to a cart, with others, and took me away.

And in due course, when my turn came, he fretted and picked through his stock of parts, and he sewed on a pair of legs only slightly mismatched, and in the morning Collicker came and took me back to the waiting survivors of Pedrick's Special Corps, Attached USA, along with many other men who were patchwork, and still we did not come up to two hundred, so brutal had Cold Harbor been.

Cash was there. He had been shot through the throat, so he could not tell me what he dreamt of; his face, what was left of it, looked haunted so sore it made my heart ache so that it would have burst, had it not been burst already.

And I thought of the bodies that had used these legs before me, and the bodies gone to wherever Grabow took the remains which were minced too fine to be useful any longer, and I understood that every fragment yet lived, in a sense, and dreamed, though I suppose some pieces dreamed more in the mumbling sense than in real dreams, and, oh, God, how did Grabow bury them?

The Unknown Soldier

Kristine Kathryn Rusch

When I received my guest packet for the 1991 New Orleans Science Fiction and Fantasy Festival, I was pleased to see the programming schedule included an appearance with Kristine Kathryn Rusch, whose work I greatly admired but whom I had not yet met. The panel, which was on writing criticism, went well, with Kris charming both the audience and the panel members. It was a high point for me of what was an outstanding convention, and besides, even if the convention hadn't been good, New Orleans is one of my favorite cities.

The Cajuns have a word, *lagniappé,* which in its origin was the small gift tradesmen gave to their customers, and which in its modern usage denotes an unexpected benefit. This story is that unexpected benefit, the fortunate surprise I received at the convention when Kris inquired if there was still time to submit a story to the Civil War anthology she had heard about.

In her first two years as a professional writer, Kris managed three Nebula nominations, two Hugo nominations, a Bram Stoker nomination, and a World Fantasy Award. She received the 1990 John W. Campbell Award as the outstanding new SF writer. Kris has published more than forty stories, and along with her partner, Dean Wesley Smith, founded Pulphouse Publishing, where she served as book editor. In 1991 she was named editor of the venerable *Magazine of Fantasy and Science Fiction.* If you haven't been keeping count, that's two major awards, six other nominations, the founding of her own publishing company, and the editorship of SF's most literate magazine—all in two years. You would be hard-pressed to find anyone who has accumulated such impressive credentials in so short a period of time.

Kris has a strong sense of both traditional values and suitable iconoclasm. Assigned to create a Christmas story at a writers' workshop, she bucked the grisly slasher trend favored by her co-participants, composing a gentle fable of how Santa's son missed his father on the holiday. Kris' story was the first to sell, appearing in the scouting magazine, *Boy's Life.*

She has continued to develop cross-genre popularity. Her Nebula nominated story "A Time for Every Purpose" was anthologized in *The Year's Best Crime and Suspense Stories.* Kris' anthology, *The Best of Pulphouse,* showcases those stories published in the hardback magazine she and Dean founded. She has five novels awaiting publication, plus her much acclaimed, *The Mists of Power,* published by NAL/Roc in 1992.

Kris has had a consistent interest in the Civil War. It was her major area of concentration for her B.A. in History from the University of Wisconsin–Madison, and her much acclaimed novella "The Gallery of His Dreams" deals with battlefield photographer Mathew Brady. Here is the extra benefit from our panel in New Orleans—appropriately brief but potent—as good *lagniappé* should be.

He finds himself in his own nightmare. Cold deeper than any he has ever felt, wind whistling through the makeshift barracks, hunger eating away at his stomach. His feet are wrapped in ripped cloth—his shoes long worn down by marching, marching, marching. He doesn't remember throwing them away, even though the soles were gone. Perhaps someone stole them on the long train ride to this prison camp on the outskirts of a Wisconsin town.

Other men huddle around him, some clinging to threadbare blankets, others clustered together for warmth. The fire in the stove is not as bright as before, now only a little more than glowing coals—the guards will not build another until morning. He sits as close to the stove as he can, a prime position won because he can still fight. The warmth coats his left side, making the right even colder. He stares through one of the chinks in the wood, seeing the large white flakes drift down to the earth. He has heard of snow, has seen it now, day after day, week after week, but he still does not understand it. How can anything so cold be so fragile?

He asked one of the guards once, but the guard just laughed at him. *I'm assigned here same as you,* the guard said. *Only I didn't turn traitor from my country.*

Traitor. He doesn't consider himself a traitor. He is a soldier, a man called to serve, not by Jeff Davis, not by the Confederate States of America, but by his family, people who lived in New Orleans through one regime after another, who fought to protect bayous and cypress trees and warm sunlight falling on the backs of their necks. People who believed not in a cause, but in a place. A place he might never see again.

He slides closer to the stove, so close that a slight movement would cause him to burn his left arm. He doesn't know what he believes in. Used to be he believed in himself, in his future, in his own powers as a human being. But his powers disappeared along with his shoes, and his future disappeared when he took his father's horse and rode off to enlist. He has no dreams left. Only nightmares. One particular nightmare that may or may not come true.

He first had the nightmare as a young boy. It was a hot July night. The shutters were closed, letting in only a slight breeze to disturb the oppressive air. His overstuffed mattress felt damp, and sweat ran off his small body. He wished himself cold, wished for cold, and dozed . . .

. . . *seeing the rags on his feet, the torn gray pants made so lovingly by his mother. The heat from a fire touched his left side, but the rest of him was cold—so cold he never thought he would be warm again. He wrapped his body into a ball, shivering. Then the wooden door opened to a world of white—and slashed across it, blood . . .*

He woke up, a scream buried in his throat. Then sat, realizing that no one was coming to him. He was in his room, safe and alone. Only when he touched his skin for reassurance, the left side was too hot, and the rest too cold.

No one speaks in this godforsaken place. They all stare straight ahead, as if they are looking backwards at their lives. He can see forward for some of them—a sometimes-gift his mother denied. His grandmother never did. She called it "the sight," and she used it. Only after he enlisted, she would never again use it on him.

He glances around the room, sees things that are going to be: the too-thin man in the corner, dead, placed in the icehouse with the other bodies to be buried come thaw; the man asleep on the only bunk, walking home to a magnificent plantation in Georgia, finding nothing but ash-covered Doric columns; the man beside him, face hidden behind a white hood, whipping his horse near-death chasing a black man across a field.

Sometimes he spends hours with these future visions, but they all end the same. Used to be when he turned the sight on himself, he saw a myriad of things: sitting, as an old man, in front of a tumble-down shack, children playing around him; a book about the "old South," held in a woman's gnarled hand, his name in gold leaf on the spine; standing beside his mother in the house of his birth as blue-clad soldiers clatter in, leaving muddy tracks on the polished wood floor.

The last time he saw any of those dreams, he still lived in the New Orleans house. His father's near-lame horse remained in the barn. He called on the sight the day his grandmother introduced him to a red-haired girl, and saw even more futures: a burned Great House; their bodies, naked and entwined; a red, squalling infant; another woman, long black hair trailing to her waist. He tried to call up those images after he enlisted, but could not. When he took his father's horse and rode toward war, all those dreams disappeared. Now, when he turns the sight to himself, he sees nothing. Nothing at all.

Except his past:

"Your grandmother wants you to marry." His mother took her lemonade into the garden and sat on the wrought iron chair, her skirts falling across her legs like a fan. A carriage rumbled past the gate, then there was silence. He always thought of the garden as a green sanctuary in the middle of the city. "I do not."

"But, Mama." He protested more out of duty than desire. He was not in love, but he wanted to do what his grandmother bade him. He gazed at the shuttered windows of the house, willing her to come outside and defend him. Since his father's death in Mexico, his mother had wielded too much power. His grandmother appeared on the porch as if she had heard his summons. She nodded once and started down the stairs.

"You don't care for this girl, and you're much too young. You have plenty of time—"

"He doesn't have time." His grandmother stopped just short of the bench. She stood on the path, the sculptured hedges behind her. "A man is remembered by doing great deeds, creating beautiful things, or having a family that lives beyond him. He has no time to do great deeds nor to create beauty. He only has time for a family."

His grandmother's words chilled him—and with the cold came the memory of the nightmare, the rags on his feet. He had that dream every night since his father's death.

"The war will end soon," his mother said.

"Wars never end," his grandmother replied.

He can't even remember the girl's name, nor her face, only the softness of her bosom against his chest as they danced. He hasn't married, hasn't had a family. Before the occupation, his mother left New Orleans to live with friends in Atlanta, and his grandmother—his grandmother died the night he left. He has heard rumors of the burning of Atlanta, and his dreams lead him to believe his mother is dead. He is the last, the keeper of his family's lives, guardian of the future. And he has created nothing of beauty, done no great deeds.

This morning, he woke up believing today is the last day of his strength. The last day of conscious choice, before he becomes as vacant as the men around him, surviving only by sheer luck or fortitude.

Perhaps the vision he has left is not a nightmare. Perhaps it is his great deed, the thing that will make him remembered.

He has been thinking of this for some time. If he can get the others to rebel, they might be able to escape, to find their own ways home. The barrack guards are strong, but the rest are mere German bumpkins, pulled in from the fields. The train station is a short ride away, and the trains are still running regularly. He can hear the whistle at the usual intervals, speaking to him of safety, of freedom, of warmth. Of home.

Great deeds. All a man needs is one. One will last him his lifetime, give him the home and family, and make him remembered. One act. . . .

The door does not open until the barracks are nearly dark, the stove almost cooled. As soon as the cold air drifts in, he launches himself toward it, hitting the guard full across the chest, butting his head against the guard's chin. Blood gushes out the guard's nose and spatters the snow. A small feeling of victory rises in him, followed almost as rapidly by a sense of disquiet. There is more to the nightmare than he can remember.

The other men watch with disinterest from the door. He yells to them: "Come *on!*" and begins to run before he notices whether they respond. He imagines them rising on stiff legs to follow him toward freedom.

His own legs are stiff, but they move well enough. The air is cold, colder than any he has ever breathed, so cold it freezes his lungs. The snow has finished, but he can feel its remnants, wet and soggy against the rags on his feet. He will worry about that later, when he is free, when he is on the train.

He runs down a well-worn trail, past other barracks, some with light in the window and thin curls of smoke rising from the chimneys. Not cells, surely, not anything more than guard quarters for the Northerners who keep the Southerners imprisoned.

As he passes them, another shiver of victory captures his chest. All he has is the poorly guarded gate to cross, and then he's in the open. He can hear no footsteps behind him—no guards or other prisoners tracking him. Only his own harsh breathing. The breath plumes before him like the steam from a locomotive. Free. Free. He is free.

Too late he sees one of the bumpkins beside a building. The lump isn't even wearing a uniform, just the wide homemade pants and heavy jacket of a farmer. The bumpkin raises his rifle—and he leaps to avoid the shot. In that split second, the sight comes to him, and he sees his mother recoiling as a soldier slams a rifle butt into her face. The soldier sets the house on fire, and as it burns, his mother lies unconscious on the floor.

"No!" he cries, and then a burning pain scrapes into his chest. He is still airborne. On the snow beneath him, the familiar blood-stain pattern blooms, the one that has haunted his dreams, and he remembers the part of the nightmare he has always forgotten upon wakening:

The pattern ends against a man's body twisted and half-buried in snow. The eyes are open, lifeless, and the skin almost blue with cold. This man is cold, as cold as a man ever gets. The body gets moved to the icehouse, to wait for the thaw, when it will be buried in a mass grave with a hundred others, all unknown.

"No!" he cries again, and lands so hard that the breath escapes his body. His arms cross, his legs bend at odd angles, and pain like he has never felt shoots through him before numbing into nearly nothing.

Soldiers, his grandmother said once about his father's death fighting Santa Anna in Mexico, *fools who die for another man's folly.*

He now knows why she wouldn't touch him, why she only used the sight on him once. He was given vision so that he could make choices. He didn't look; he didn't see. The choice he made was the one he was supposed to avoid.

Cold. He is so cold.

And alone. He wants the bumpkin to come over, anything to give him one last chance at making an impression. But no one comes. He tries to close his eyes, but his strength is gone. The last thing he sees is something he has seen before, but never understood—the zigzag pattern of his own blood on freshly fallen snow.

Cold.

He will never be warm again.